THE BOY
with the
SUITCASE

Cathy loves writing because it gives pleasure to others. She finds writing an extension of herself and it gives her great satisfaction. Cathy says, 'There is nothing like seeing your book in print, because so much loving care has been given to bringing that book into being.' Cathy lives in Cambridgeshire.

Also by Cathy Sharp

Halfpenny Street Orphans
The Orphans of Halfpenny Street
The Little Runaways
Christmas for the Halfpenny Orphans
The Boy with the Latch Key
An Orphan's Courage

Children of the Workhouse
The Girl in the Ragged Shawl
The Barefoot Child
The Winter Orphan

East End Daughters
A Daughter's Sorrow
A Daughter's Choice
A Daughter's Dream

Button Street Orphans
An Orphan's Promise
An Orphan's Sorrow
An Orphan's Dream
The Lonely Orphan

CATHY SHARP

THE BOY
with the
SUITCASE

HarperCollins*Publishers*

HarperCollins*Publishers*
1 London Bridge Street
London SE1 9GF

www.harpercollins.co.uk

HarperCollinsPublishers
1st Floor, Watermarque Building, Ringsend Road
Dublin 4, Ireland

Published by HarperCollins*Publishers* 2022
1

A catalogue record for this book
is available from the British Library

ISBN (PB): 978-0-00-853120-1
ISBN (TPB): 978-0-00-853121-8

Typeset in Sabon LT Std by Palimpsest Book Production Ltd,
Falkirk, Stirlingshire

Printed and Bound in the UK using 100% Renewable Electricity
at CPI Group (UK) Ltd

CHAPTER 1

'And that's for being late wiv me tea!' Reg Parker made a half-hearted swipe at his wife's head with the palm of his hand. She jerked out of the way; having learned to know what was coming, he seldom managed to hit her these days. All bluster and growl, that was Reg now, Rose thought without bitterness.

'I was on late shift at the factory,' Rose replied. 'You knew that, Reg. No good you moaning about it, either. You're away at sea more than you're here, and I have to work or I'd go mad sitting here twiddling my thumbs now the lads have gone.'

Both her sons had left home in search of work; the eldest, Terry, had followed his father into the Merchant Navy but her younger son, Peter, was an engineer and working on the ships up north at the moment. The onset of war had brought more work to the shipyards, which was a good thing, but it meant her son had left home at seventeen, emptying the house that was now so lonely at night when Reg was away. He wasn't much of a husband, but she hated living alone and she seldom saw her sons. Terry had married a few months back and his wife, Shirl, was expecting their first child, but they lived down in Portsmouth so it was unlikely Rose would see them more than once in a blue moon.

Thank God she had her friend Dora Blake and her kids to keep her company, Rose thought, as she busied herself getting tea for Reg, whose first action after yelling at her had been to open a bottle of bitter and drink it straight from the bottle. She sighed inwardly, hoping he wouldn't get drunk. It was his last night of shore leave, possibly for months, and though she sometimes found it hard to live with him, especially when he drank heavily, when he was away, she missed him. She supposed she still felt something for him despite his rough ways and his readiness to slap her when he was in a mood.

Why didn't I marry someone more like Dave Blake? Rose wondered. Dave was a few years younger than her and had still been at school when she'd left to work in the factory; by the time he'd finished his apprenticeship in the docks, she'd met and married Reg. Truth to tell, she'd really fancied Dave then, perhaps even loved him. But once Dave saw Dora Collier there was no one else in the world for him. He instantly fell for her good looks and brilliant smile and, as far as Rose knew, he was still head over heels for her, even though they were married with two children. Dave had started out repairing ships before discovering that he could get more work and have a better life working on the cruise ships as a steward. He liked the feel of the sea under him, he'd told Rose one night when they were all having a drink in the local during one of his frequent shore leaves. The ships he worked on did trips of no longer than two weeks and he got a couple days leave at the end of each one, much better than Reg who was away for months at a time.

'What I'd really like is to work on the fishing boats, some place like Yarmouth or down in Cornwall, where the kids could enjoy good clean air and the smell of the sea,' he'd said then.

'Sounds wonderful, Dave. Why don't you do it?' Rose asked.

'Dora won't leave London. Says she's a London girl and she wouldn't know anyone down there. She knows everyone where we live.'

Dave hadn't been born in London. His parents were from Norfolk originally but had moved to London to find work in the 1920s and he still had family there – a cousin he mentioned sometimes and seemed fond of, though he seldom saw her. Rose thought she was a few years older than Dave.

'Fair enough,' Rose agreed, 'but I reckon if you were my man, Dave Blake, I'd go wherever you wanted!' She'd laughed when she'd said it to diffuse any tension, but the truth was, she still fancied him. He'd always been special, Dave Blake, and she'd seen him battling the bullies at school even though he was small for his age. Once, she'd used her status as monitor to stop him getting thrashed. He'd smiled at her shyly and she'd never forgotten that smile – and when she'd seen him again, three years after she left school, she hadn't been able to believe the change in him, because Dave had grown and grown. He was a six-footer now, with wide shoulders, and woe betide anyone who bothered him these days. Not that he used his fists without cause; he didn't, but he hated injustice and any bully would get short shrift.

Rose gave herself a mental kick up the rear. No sense – or decency – in mooning over her best friend's husband. Instead, she lavished her affection on his two lovely kids who called her Aunt Rose: Davey, who was every inch his father's boy down to the dark hair and chocolate-brown eyes, and sweet little Alice, fair and delicate with blue orbs that lit with excitement each time she was given a sweet or a cake Rose had specially baked for her. She took after her mother and there was no doubt that Dora was lovely to look at.

Rose chuckled to herself. She stood no chance of getting Dave Blake's attention and didn't expect it, but a girl could dream, couldn't she? Even if she had only a few years to go to forty! She wouldn't have taken the chance if it had come, if she were truthful. Dora had been her best mate since she'd come to work at the factory after Dave volunteered for the Royal Navy. Much to Dora's disgust, he'd signed up as soon as the war was declared.

'No choice,' he'd told Rose. 'What kind of a bloke would I be if I took a shore job when they need strong men like me?'

Rose's smile vanished like morning mist. This bloomin' war! Dave didn't come home so regular now, none of the men did since that rotten old Hitler went bonkers and started a war. Stood to reason, didn't it? The German leader must be mad to start

4

another big war. Rose still remembered the last one, all the pain, grief, suffering and want it had produced, even if she had been a youngster then. No wonder Dora moaned all the time. The whole nation would be grumbling soon enough. The last conflict went on for more than four years – this one would probably be the same, despite all the jingoistic songs about hanging out their washing on the Siegfried Line . . .

'Are you goin' ter be all night at that bloody sink?' Reg's truculent tones broke Rose's reverie. 'I'm goin' down the pub. You know where to find me if yer need me.'

Rose didn't answer. She didn't fancy a trip to the pub. Besides, she had a load of ironing to do. Reg would expect all his stuff to be ready and packed into his kitbag for him in the morning when he got up – undoubtedly with a headache – to catch the early train. Oh, she would be glad when he'd gone and she could get off to work and her mates, even if it meant she'd be alone again.

Dora Blake sighed deeply. This work was boring enough at the best of times, but when there was nothing much to look forward to when she got home, it became even more tedious and she felt the weight of her responsibilities like a heavy blanket. Two kids forever hanging on her skirts. Not that Davey did that much these days, but Alice was a clinger and Davey's eyes reminded her of his father. When she broke a promise or forgot to get home on time, his eyes seemed to accuse her – just the way his father's did when she didn't live up to his high standards.

'I'll bet you miss your Dave being around,' her friend Rose Parker said as Dora glanced yet again at the clock on the factory wall. 'I know I miss having a man about – even though Reg is a mean old so-and-so, he's better than nothin'.' She gave a cackle of laughter and received a suspicious look from Mrs Winter, their bossy line supervisor. But there was nothing to see: Rose's hands, assembling the delicate parts that were coming down the line, hadn't stopped for a second. She clicked, twisted and sealed automatically, putting the finished item into a trolley behind her at the same time as Dora, leaving the supervisor nothing to say, except, 'Watch what you're doing, Mrs Parker. That stuff you're handling is dangerous, you know.'

'Yeah, I know.' Rose pulled a face and rolled her eyes at Dora. As if they didn't know that it was dangerous work, that the products they handled could cause an explosion if not treated with care. It was a munition factory, after all. 'Don't fret, I shan't blow you to kingdom come.'

'She's on the warpath again,' Dora whispered. 'I heard Mr Smith telling her that we'd got to up our work rate again to keep up with the government's demands.'

'What the bleeding heck do they think we are, machines?' Rose said, then yelped as she faltered and stubbed her finger on a sharp piece of metal as she made a grab for it before it passed her by. 'We already do more than they do in their precious little offices.'

Dora agreed, her face alight with amusement. Rose always had something to say, and she made the tedium of their working day easier to bear. None of the women on the assembly line had much time for the Government. If they'd handled the crisis in Europe a bit better, maybe they would have avoided getting the country embroiled in another war. Dora was always miserable because Dave was away for long periods now, and Rose never stopped moaning about the war.

'My Reg had a good job on the short-haul shipping working out of the London Docks,' she'd told Dora when the pair of them answered the call for women workers at the factory that had once made machinery for plant hire. 'Three to four weeks away at most. Four months he says he'll be afore he gets leave this time. Why did the silly devil want to go and join up for the Atlantic run – answer me that?' It was one of the most dangerous sea lanes these days, constantly under bombardment from above and beneath the waves. And even if he had a few hours on shore leave, his ship might dock anywhere from Portsmouth to way up north, so he'd told Rose not to expect him home unless he sent word.

'To get away from your tongue, Rose Parker,' her neighbour in the line on the right side quipped. 'Poor bugger only wanted a bit of peace.'

'I wasn't talkin' to you,' Rose replied, giving Jill Relland a slaying look. 'When I want your opinion, I'll ask for it.'

'Hoity-toity, ain't we?' Jill Relland grinned, used to Rose's sharp remarks. 'Think yourself lucky he didn't run off and leave yer years ago. He was a looker when you caught 'im.'

'What are you hintin' at, you miserable scrawny bitch?' Rose's eyes flashed with temper.

'Ignore her, Rose,' Dora warned. 'Old Icy Drawers is watchin' you . . .' Mrs Winters was looking at Rose again, eyes narrowed.

Rose nodded and subsided, but Dora knew that Jill Relland was in for a mouthful if Rose caught her alone in one of the back streets they passed through on their way home.

Home for both Dora and Rose was a place called Silver Terrace where the back-to-back houses had all seen better days, and the landlord didn't want to know about repairs. If your husband was any good with a hammer and nails, you were lucky. He needn't bother asking for someone to come and fix a broken window hinge or a cracked tile, he just got on and did it himself. Should he be a bad handyman – which was unusual in the lanes and terraces so close to the East India Docks – he asked a mate to do it and bought him a couple of pints in the pub. But that was before the men all went off to the war. Now it was down to their hard-pressed wives to fend for themselves.

Dora smothered another sigh, glancing at the high windows. It was overcast outside, and drizzling. She shivered at the thought of the walk home. Would the working day never be done? As usual, Sally Collier, Dora's mother, was fetching the children from school and she always fed her grandchildren – just a bit of bread and jam or dripping, and some cake when she had the ingredients to make one. Davey relished the dripping when he got it, but Alice wouldn't touch it. She preferred strawberry jam.

Dora helped her widowed mother to eke out her

8

slender funds, but the fact was that no one in the terrace had much money to spare, which was why both Dora and Rose had jumped at the chance to earn a couple of quid a week extra. Rose had worked elsewhere before the war, but this job paid more, because of the danger. Still, as Rose said, it wasn't dangerous if they all stuck to the rules and did their work properly.

Dora hadn't worked since her marriage until now, because Dave hadn't wanted her to, telling her that he would and could support his family because when he'd been working the cruise ships he'd made more than half his wage again in tips from grateful passengers, particularly the American ones. He told Dora they always gave too much, because they hated to look mean or cheap.

Dave had spent long hours at sea even then and she'd missed him when he was away. He loved the work, said it was good to look after folk who appreciated it. She'd known he'd be home every two to three weeks, so it hadn't seemed too bad, because when the ship was being cleaned and reprovisioned, he had two or three days at home and he always took her out and made a fuss of the kids. While he was away, she sometimes left the kids and went off for a quick drink with her mates at the pub. Young Davey could look after his sister and he did; he would soon fetch help if needed, but he was a capable lad and did as he was told. Mind you, the look he gave her sometimes when Alice was crying and she ignored it made her uncomfortable – far too like his dad! She supposed he would be off to sea when he was older.

Dave had filled his son's head with tales of the sea.

'The cruise ships are regular income and you like living near your mother,' he'd told her a few months before the war became unavoidable, 'but one day I want to move on to deep-sea fishing. That wouldn't be in London but on the coast somewhere, and the income isn't so regular. But I could have my own boat, Dora, and it would be a better life for us all.'

Dora wasn't so sure. London suited her. There was always something going on and a pub where she could meet people she knew. If they moved, she would be a stranger, alone even more – no, she couldn't leave her mother and the familiar streets where she could always find company for an hour or so. Dave just didn't understand. He loved his family, she knew that, but Dora wanted more than a nice home; she needed a bit of life and a little fun now and then – and she wouldn't get much of that stuck in a cottage miles from anywhere.

'Mum helps me with the kids,' she'd told him. 'I'd be hard put to it to manage without her help, Dave, so we can't move away. When they're older and I can work full-time, it might not seem so bad you being away all the time and me not knowing when you'll be back.'

Dave hadn't liked her answer, but she'd refused to give in. After all, he'd known she was a London girl through and through when he married her. She wasn't at all sure she would want to move away to the coast, even when the kids were old enough to look after themselves most of the time, but she didn't need to tell him that until a decision had to be made . . .

Lost in her thoughts, Dora forgot to clock watch. Then the buzzer went and she heard the machinery slow down as the night shift came in to take over – the work never stopped because it was vital to the war effort. Rose muttered a hallelujah under her breath and Dora laughed. Neither of them much liked the work they did, but it kept shoes on the children's feet, as the saying went, and a good many kids in London didn't have any shoes.

Both Dora and Rose's husbands had arranged for them to get half of their pay, but his Royal Navy pay wasn't as much as Dave had earned before the war. And even with the little coming her way, for some unknown reason it didn't come regularly and Dora hadn't received a penny for the last three months. At least she had the meagre income from her work to get them through. With no young children, Rose was a little better off but spent most of her money sending her daughter-in-law lots of presents.

Dora was several years younger than Rose. She'd married Dave when she was seventeen and he was twenty-six so there was quite an age gap between them. Perhaps that was why their children hadn't arrived for some years, or it might have been because Dave wasn't always around. They'd almost given up hope of having children when Davey was suddenly on the way – after a trip to Clacton, where they'd spent a wonderful week together, on the beach every day, dancing every night. Alice had come along almost two years later and that had been enough. Dora then tried to make sure there were no more, though she'd never told Dave. She knew he wouldn't

11

have minded a few more but two were plenty to look after and clothe in Dora's opinion. Any more and she'd be no better than a skivvy.

Davey was very much his father's son in every way and he'd taken it upon himself to protect his sister as soon as he was able to fight; that had been by the time he was seven and a half. He'd come home with a torn jacket and several cuts and bruises on his face, refusing to tell them what had happened. His headmaster was more forthcoming. Another boy had been bullying some of the little girls – including Alice – so Davey had waded in and given the ringleader a good clout.

'Of course, I had to punish him for fighting,' Mr Meadows had told her and Dave. 'However, I have to say you have a son to be proud of, Mr Blake – even if he did break school rules. I also punished the boy he battered for bullying and I've told Davey he must report what he sees from now on, not take punishment into his own hands.'

'He might as well have saved his breath as tell my son not to fight,' Dave had said afterwards, looking proud. 'I was the same as a lad – and I still need to use my fists sometimes. There's a certain class of bully doesn't respect anything but a fist in the face.'

Dora had known her husband had a bit of a reputation for fighting before she married him, but he'd told her he only resorted to fists when there was no other way. She asked him to talk to Davey and he did – and after that they had no more visits from the headmaster.

Curious, she'd asked her husband what he'd said to their son.

'I told him to wait and corner the bully outside school hours,' Dave told her. 'That way he wouldn't get punished for it – and I told him to fight fair and only when he has to. It's no use forbidding him, Dora. He'll only hide it from us.'

Dora knew how independent and strong-willed her young son was, although he'd only be ten years old in July. He was as stubborn as a mule and would do as she asked him, but only if she was fair and just in her decisions. If she tried to make him do something he considered unfair, Davey argued his corner and nine times out of ten she gave in in the end.

Approaching her mother's house, Dora saw that the children were playing in the street. Davey and some other boys were kicking a football and Alice was playing hopscotch by herself. She frowned, because they should both be doing homework. Davey usually had sums and Alice needed to be reading one of the books her father had insisted on buying for her. Dave wanted her to train as a typist or something worthwhile when she got older.

'I don't want my daughter in the jam factory,' he'd told Dora. 'I don't know what the lad will do – probably follow me to the sea, but the girl needs to get herself out of these streets, Dora.'

'What's wrong with them? I grew up here and we've done all right.' Dora had felt Dave was attacking her. He'd had a better education than she had and she often wondered why he'd picked her.

'Aye, we do all right,' Dave agreed with a little frown of disapproval. 'But I'd like to move on one day, Dora. You know that. There's a better life some-where.'

Dora hadn't answered him then. She knew what he was hinting at – the fresh air of the sea and a boat of his own. Maybe it would be all right, but she wasn't ready yet – especially while her mother was still going strong. The truth was she wouldn't know what to do away from the streets she'd known all her life.

'Where's your gran?' she asked Davey now. 'Have you had your tea?'

Davey shook his head. 'Gran wasn't feeling well, so she said you'd get our tea when you came home and sent us out to play.'

'Gran's ill?' Dora felt a spiral of fear go through her. Her mother had worked all her life until the last year or so and was as tough as old boots – or she'd thought she was. 'What's wrong?'

Davey shrugged. 'Dunno, somethin',' he offered. 'I asked if she wanted me to get her a cup of tea and she just said to get outside out of her way.'

'That doesn't sound like Gran,' Dora said, worried now. 'Fetch your sister and come in. I'll see if she'll let me help her and then we'll go home. I've got some sausage meat in my basket. I'll make supper with that tonight.'

'Cor! Smashing!' Davey said happily and ran off to fetch his sister.

Dora had been going to save the sausage meat for the next day – Saturday – but she'd buy a bit of cheese and make a macaroni cheese instead. Or make toast and Welsh rarebit. She'd planned a casserole for Sunday, because it would last for several days and she could just warm it up when she got home at nights, adding fresh vegetables and potatoes. By midweek they'd all have had enough of it, she was sure, and it would become more of a vegetable soup, but it was cheap and filling and all she could afford. Davey would sooner have bread and butter, he'd told her that more than once, but she thought the casserole had more goodness in it.

As soon as she got into her mother's kitchen and saw the state of it, Dora knew something was really wrong. Sally Collier always kept her kitchen immaculate and had taught her daughter to do the same. The washing-up was piled in the sink and a basket filled with dirty clothes was in the doorway to the scullery, spilled on its side; the clothes had fallen out and next-door's cat lay sleeping on them. On closer inspection, she could see the floor hadn't been washed in a while. Why hadn't she noticed before? Perhaps because she'd been tired and full of her own woes.

'Mum, what's the matter?' she asked, her heart jolting with fear. Dora might be a bit of a selfish cow at times, but she cared about her mother. 'Are you really ill?'

'I'm all right,' Sally began but then gasped and clutched at her chest. 'Well, tell the truth I ain't. I've 'ad a pain here for a few weeks now. Didn't take much notice fer a while, but it's got worse . . .' She sat back in her chair and closed her eyes.

'Have you been to the doctor?' Dora asked, knowing the probable answer. Her mother never went to the doctor and like many of the people round here

15

she really couldn't afford to. Dave had always insisted that they pay four shillings a week to join the doctor's panel.

'It might seem a waste when you don't need him,' he'd told her. 'But if one of the kids – or us – gets ill, you'll be glad of it.'

'Please, Mum, you must see him,' Dora said now. 'I'll pay for the visit . . . No, don't refuse. I rely on you for the kids. You know that, so don't get all prickly.'

'Wasn't goin' to,' Sally said. 'I already asked him what's wrong and he says I'm wearing out, Dora – says it's wear and tear on me 'eart. I've worked too 'ard all me life and now I'm payin' the price.'

Sally had given birth to six children and had five miscarriages. All but two of her children had died in childhood of various illnesses and Dora's brother Jeb had run away to sea at the age of sixteen. Sally's husband had wanted him to train as an engineer and made him stop on at school to take his higher exams, administering a beating when he played truant, so he'd run away to hire out on the ships. In a letter he'd sent his mother, he'd said he wanted to be free but would come back and see her once the old man was dead and gone.

Sally's husband had been a strict, religious man who believed in the strap as a means of teaching right from wrong and both Dora and Jeb had suffered it during their childhood, though Dora less often than her rebellious brother.

Their father had been dead ten years – he'd passed on a year after Jeb ran off – but Jeb had never

16

returned to visit his family, though Dora had once had a letter from America with a banker's draft for ten pounds to give to his mother. He'd told her he was doing fine, promised he would return one day, but since then they'd heard nothing.

'Can he give you anything to help?' Dora asked now, looking anxiously at her mother.

'He gave me a bottle of medicine for the pain,' Sally said. 'I took a spoonful but it didn't touch it so I ain't took no more.'

'Mum, you should. It might help.'

'Nah,' Sally replied with a twist of her mouth. 'Me time is almost up, gal. I'll be leavin' yer soon enough, but I'll be 'ere fer the kids fer as long as I can.'

'Oh, Mum!' Dora swallowed a sob. She knew she'd relied on her mother too much since Dave left for the Royal Navy, but she hadn't known who else to turn to. Obviously, she would need to find an alternative soon. 'Surely it's worth trying your medicine to see if it helps?' What would she do without her mother to fall back on when the kids needed minding?

'Why? I've lived long enough. You don't want to worry about me, Dora – but you'll need to sort out someone for the kids when I've gone.'

'I can look after you, Gran,' Davey said, sidling up to them. He'd obviously been listening. 'I can make you a cup of tea, and get me and Alice something to eat. I'm old enough and I can do it if you let me. Can't I, Mum?'

'Yes, you're a good boy.' Dora looked at her mother uncertainly. 'I need to go to work, Mum, but I'll do what I can when I get here at night. Maybe first thing as well.'

'Don't put yourself out on my account,' Sally said. 'You've got more than you can do now. Let the boy try if he wants. He can have his grandfather's silver watch and chain. Sell them for a few bob, if he likes. They're no good to me where I'm goin'.'

'Mum, don't! We don't need to sell Dad's watch.' Dora could hardly hold back her tears. 'I really love you, even if I do take you for granted.'

'I know that, girl,' Sally said and laughed. 'Don't look so miserable, I'll last a bit longer – and when I've gone, you'll manage. You'll 'ave to, won't yer?'

Dora shook her head. The thought of losing her mother made her feel so alone. 'I need you,' she whispered. It was selfish of her. She should be thinking of her mother's suffering but she couldn't face the thought that someone she'd always relied on wouldn't be there.

'Yer need that man of yours back,' Sally told her. 'Yer can't have him while there's a war on, but when it's over, you let him take yer away from London. It will be a better life for you and the kids, Dora.'

Dora sniffed and dabbed at her eyes with a handkerchief. 'Maybe,' she agreed. 'If you ain't here I might as well.'

'He's a good man, your Dave,' her mother told her. 'Hang on to that one, gal, and don't let your foolish fancies ruin what you have together. London's only a place. Yer can't keep your feet warm on a place. Yer need a man fer that.'

'I know. You don't have to tell me,' Dora said.

'I love Dave and I want him back. I wish the bloomin' war had never started.'

'It will be over one day,' Sally said. 'Just keep out of trouble until then – no other men, Dora. If you slip, you'll be sorry.' She fixed Dora with a hard stare, making her blush. 'I know you like a bit of a lark, but be careful.'

'I don't – I haven't,' she protested.

'Do you think I don't know that Mick George is sweet on you, Dora? He's a crook and got a bit of money – but remember he's only after one thing. Let 'im 'ave 'is way and you'll lose everythin'.'

'I've no intention of—' Dora glared at her mother. 'I don't know why you even suggested it.' Maybe she flirted a bit now and then but she'd done nothing wrong – a little kiss in the pub yard didn't count, did it? He'd just grabbed her as she was on her way back from the toilets; it wasn't her fault and she'd pushed him away.

'Just givin' yer a piece of friendly advice,' Sally said. 'I was a looker in me young days, just like you, and I 'ad the men after me. I knew your da would've killed me if I'd dared to even give them the time of day. Dave ain't violent – leastways, not to you and the kids – but don't push him too far, love. I'm just warnin' yer.'

'Yeah, I know.' Dora knew her mum was telling her this partly to warn her and partly to get away from the subject of her illness. 'You needn't have bothered, because I'm not interested in Mick George.'

'Good. An' make sure yer ain't interested in anyone else either.'

19

Dora turned away from her mother's eyes. Sally saw too much. And she did like Mick – despite loving her husband – but she knew he was dangerous and had long ago made up her mind to have nothing to do with him. Still, she couldn't resist smiling when he teased her . . .

CHAPTER 2

Davey lay awake a long time after Mum came to see that he and Alice were in their beds. They had single beds separated by a big mahogany chest of drawers that they had to lean forward to see round. Their mother often said that one day they would need their own rooms, but their terraced house had just the two up and two down, with a lean-to at the back. Dad said she was dreaming – unless she let him take her down to the coast where he could get them a nice cottage and have his own boat to go fishing.

'It would be a better life for the kids,' Davey had heard his father say before he went off to enlist to fight for King and country. Mum hadn't liked that either and they'd had a screaming row – at least, Mum screamed and Dad answered in his slow, deep voice that had always made Davey feel safe.

He no longer felt safe. Gran had said something very disturbing that afternoon – well, two things really. She'd spoken of her time coming – of a time when she was no longer there in her little house, and that worried and upset Davey, because Gran was always there for them with her warm jam tarts and seed cake at the weekends. Gran was solid and reliable, and his mum – well, she wasn't always. She didn't always keep her word when she said she'd do something. It wasn't just now that it had started either. Even before she'd gone to work at the factory, she would tell little lies, like telling Dad she'd been late at Gran's when really, she'd been flirting with someone she'd met on her way home. She often did that, giggling and twirling her hair with a finger, her eyes bright with mischief.

Davey didn't think Mum did anything truly wrong. She just liked to talk and laugh and the men liked her, calling out to her and talking to her with their eyes. His dad called it flirting and got cross over it sometimes. They'd had one of their quarrels when they got back from the pub a few nights before he left to go to the war back in August. It was April now and they hadn't seen any sign of war in London except for all the men and women in uniform though he knew there was fighting in France.

'Why do you do it, Dora?' Dad had asked Mum. 'Why do you encourage that sort? You know what Mick George is – and, if you're not careful, he'll do something you won't like one of these days. You can't lead a man like that on and not expect to get burned.'

'Oh, don't be so stuffy!' Dora replied, flying into a temper. 'He bought me a gin and orange and I thanked him, that's all.'

'I had already bought you a shandy, Dora. You should have refused. What do you think he and his mates say about you behind your back?'

22

'Mick knows I'm just being friendly,' she'd answered sulkily. 'I'd never do anything wrong, Dave. You know I love you.'

'Yes, I know,' Davey's father had said, his voice softening. 'But Mick and his friends think you're an easy target. They're a bad lot, Dora, and you know it. They're all involved in crime, one way and another, even though they've not been caught yet. The only reason he doesn't try anything on is because I'm around and he knows I'd thrash him if he laid a finger on you. I've always been able to put him down in a fair fight and he respects me for it, but he'd love to best me some way.' Mick George was a small-time gangster who ran a betting shop and handled a few stolen items. As a consequence, he always had money in his pockets, money he flashed about when it suited him – and he liked doing it when Dora was around.

'Don't be cross.' Davey remembered that Mum's voice had taken on a coaxing note. 'I was only being friendly, Dave, I promise you. I can't help it if men look at me – you knew how it was before you married me . . .'

Davey's father had shaken his head and sighed. 'I knew how it was then, Dora, but you should stop flirting now for the sake of the kids – and for me. Please, love. I'm asking you not to flirt.'

'I don't mean to do it,' she replied and now there was a placating tone in her voice. 'It just happens and I can't stop myself smiling and chatting. There's no harm in it, Dave. You must know I wouldn't do anything to ruin what we have.'

'Not as long as I'm around to keep you safe,' he'd

growled. 'I know how to take care of my own, Dora, but if I'm away, just be careful. That's all I'm sayin'.'

Gran had told Dad he had the patience of a saint. 'You should give her a smack and make her mind you, Dave,' Davey had heard Gran tell him once. 'She's not a bad girl but she was always a bit flighty. Her father gave her a hiding once or twice when she was young for talking to strangers.'

'And what good did that do?' Davey's father had replied calmly. 'No, I won't hit her, Sally. But if she ever betrayed me that would be the finish. I wouldn't have her back and she knows it. Besides, I don't own her, if she'd rather be with someone else that's her choice.' Gran thought Dad should be harder on Davey's mother, but it wasn't his way. He got angry sometimes, but believed that it was wrong to dictate. If she went too far, he would turn his back on her and take his kids away, and she knew it – but he gave her enough rope. Thus far Dora hadn't tried pulling too far.

'She would be a fool to lose you,' Gran had told him. 'You should get her away from London, lad. She'd likely settle down then. That Mick George has always been after her.'

'Aye, I know it – but she chose me, Sally. She could've had him, she told me he'd hinted at it a few times. He would've wed her. He may care for her in his way – but he can't lie straight in bed that one, and she knows that it is only a matter of time before the law gets him and he'll be in and out of prison all his life.'

'Then why does she flirt the way she does?' Gran had demanded and Davey's dad had shaken his head.

'It's just the way she is.' He'd run fingers through his thick wavy hair. 'I love her and I shall until I'm in my grave, Sally. I took her knowing who she is, and I'll put up with it for as long as she keeps this side of the line.'

'Why can't she be more reliable and think of you and the kids?'

Dad hadn't answered her then and Davey knew why. Mum got carried away sometimes. She'd be chatting with friends and forget to go to the shops for their tea, or she'd put a cake in the oven and then start making a new dress or something for Alice and remember it when she started to smell burning. She'd laugh and cut the burned bits off and then she would smother it in lovely coffee-flavoured buttercream and no one knew it had almost been ruined. No, Mum wasn't always reliable, but she was a lovely mother and he loved her, just as Dad did despite her faults.

Davey smiled as he thought of the stories she told them and the cuddles and kisses she gave Alice and him. He loved his mother, but he couldn't always be certain she would be there for him and his sister on time. She never turned up at school fetes and she'd promised to watch Davey run for the school, but she had forgotten all about it. She'd forgotten when Alice had to go to the dentist with toothache and Davey had had to ask Rose to take her instead. Davey made excuses for his mother, because he loved her and sometimes she could be wonderful – but he was never quite sure of her.

Dad had told him to look after his mum and Alice before he left.

'I know you're only ten and it's a tall order,' Davey's dad had said, smiling and ruffling his hair with his big, gentle hand. 'But you're a good lad. You're like me, Davey, reliable and trustworthy. I have to go to war, see. The country needs men like me, men who are used to the sea and willing to fight. I don't like leaving you all, and I promise I'll come back – but I know I don't need to worry, because you'll look after your mum and sister.'

Davey had glowed with pride when his dad spoke to him that way. He felt ten foot tall and as brave as a lion. 'I'll look after them,' he'd promised. 'Leastways, I'll look after Alice. Mum might not let me look after her.'

'You be a good boy for her and do your best,' his dad said, and Davey nodded. They understood each other. They were men of the world together and it was an unspoken bond between them. Dad was great. Whenever, he was home he took Davey to the docks with him and showed him the magnificent ships that carried food and essentials to and from the port. 'That's what keeps the world going,' he'd remarked once. 'The sea can be a cruel mistress, Davey lad, but she gets into your soul and you can't resist her. It's our ships and our navies that make us great as a country, Davey. We'll always be strong while we have those. I've always had a love of the sea. I gave up the idea of long voyages for your mum's sake, but she calls to me sometimes, the sea. In my heart I'm a fisherman and that's what I'll be one day.'

When they weren't visiting the docks, they played football in the street, and visited travelling fairs – and once the circus – but Dad didn't like the way they caged animals and made them do tricks, so he told Davey the circus wasn't for him. Now and then he took Davey to the cinema to see a cowboy film, or a Disney cartoon if Alice was with them. Those treats were reserved for birthdays. There were plenty of other things to take up the precious time they had together when Dad was home. He'd never been away more than a couple of weeks at a time before, but since he'd joined the Royal Navy it had been nearly ten months and all they'd had from him was some postcards showing views of the sea. Mum said they'd been posted in Gibraltar.

'Davey, are you awake?' His sister's voice out of the darkness brought Davey's thoughts back abruptly. 'I'm scared. Can I get in with you?'

'Yeah, all right,' he said and heard her scramble out of her bed, getting in with him a second or two later. She smelled of soap and water because Mum washed her every night. Davey was allowed to wash himself now and he usually had a lick and a promise if he could get away with it, though Mum would have him in the tin bath in the kitchen on Saturday afternoon without fail. She said she couldn't have dirty kids letting her down. 'What are you scared about?' he asked his sister as she snuggled up to him. Her slight body was a little thin, but she was warm and her presence was comforting.

'Where's Dad?' she asked in a small voice. 'Why doesn't he come home?'

'Cos he's away fighting the war – or training to,' Davey replied. 'I 'spect he'll be fighting soon, cos he

27

knows the sea and it's just the fighting bit he has to learn, shooting at enemy ships and planes.'

'What does that mean?'

Davey considered before answering. Alice was a bit timid and if she understood that the fighting meant Dad's ship could be sunk by enemy fire, she would cry. *He* felt like crying when he thought about it, but of course he would never do that. He had to look after his sister and his mother, for Dad. Mainly Alice. She was so small and vulnerable and she needed her brother to take care of her.

'It means we're goin' to teach Hitler a lesson,' he told her after a moment in language that wouldn't frighten her. 'He's a bad man and he's hurtin' folk, so Dad and other brave men are going to give him a good smackin' so he stops.'

'Ah, that's all right then,' Alice said and snuggled in closer. 'It's just I heard someone say that Dad might be killed.'

'Who?' Davey demanded instantly, his nerves tingling. 'It's a lie. You tell me who said it and I'll give 'em a smack.' Her next words shocked and frightened him.

'That man Mick,' Alice said innocently. 'He asked Mum what she was going to do if that fool of a husband of hers went and got himself killed. It was when we went down to the corner shop on Saturday.'

Davey replied with deep scorn, 'Take no notice of him, Alice. He tells lies.' Like his father, Davey had no time for the good-looking spiv in his smart suits who smelled of scent – well, it was hair oil, he knew that. Real men smelled of grease, sweat and salt like his dad, or Imperial Leather soap when he'd had a bath.

'He gives me sweets,' Alice informed him. 'Mum says we mustn't take sweets from strangers but she lets me have sweets from Mick. He tells me it's a secret, but Mum knows so how can it be?'

A secret from their father! Mick was sly and a bad one, just like Gran said. If he offered Davey sweets, he would throw them back in his face.

'You shouldn't take his sweets,' he told her gruffly. 'He's no good.'

'He gives me Tom Thumb drops – they're my favourite,' Alice said as if that was explanation enough for why she took them. 'Will it take Dad long to give Hitler a thrashing?'

'Nah, I shouldn't think so,' Davey said, though he frowned and shivered in the darkness. He'd heard someone say in the street that things didn't look too good in France so far and that worried him, but there was no point in upsetting Alice. 'Go to sleep now, Alice. If Mum hears us talkin', she'll come in and make you get back in your own bed.'

'You won't go away and leave me, will you?' Alice said in a small voice and he put his arm about her thin body and felt her snuggle into him.

'Nah, I shan't leave yer,' he said gruffly. Then, not knowing why he said it, added, 'If we were ever separated, I'd come back and find you as soon as I could, Alice. I promise.'

Alice gave a little sigh of content. 'Really, truly, cross your heart and hope to die?' she asked.

'Yeah,' Davey said. He'd promised his father and

now he'd promised Alice. He would not forget or break his word if he could help it. 'Go to sleep. Nothing is going to happen to us while we're together.'

Rose baked some cakes and took them round to Dora's on Sunday morning. She'd heard about Sally being sick. News spread fast in the lanes and she liked Dora's mother, who was a hard worker.

'I made these for the kids to save you,' she said and smiled as little Alice sidled up to her and slid on her lap. She took a packet of sherbet dip from her pocket and gave it to her, placing another for Davey on the kitchen table. 'I can help a bit at weekends – at least until they put me on extra shifts. I said I'd do it cos I had nothin' to do on a Saturday morning but if I'd known I'd have refused, Dora, love.'

'Mum's no trouble – or not much yet,' Dora said truthfully. 'She thinks it's just her heart wearing out but she's got so thin. I reckon it's something more, but she won't have the doctor, says if her time is up, she's ready.'

'That's a pity,' Rose said. 'I'll call in and see her later – ask if there's anything I can do.'

'Oh, don't bother,' Dora said. 'We'll manage, Rose, and she'll hate it if she thinks folk are talking about her.'

Rose felt a bit hurt at having her offer rejected but Dora could be prickly and she knew Sally was the same way – private, they were. Daft really, because the whole street was willing to help anyone, but you couldn't barge in if you weren't wanted.

Rose spent an hour sitting with Dora, talking and

playing with Alice and Davey. They were lovely kids, just like their dad who'd made sure they had manners. Rose thought of her own lonely kitchen. She wasn't looking forward to going back and wouldn't have minded a chat with Sally but if it would upset Dora . . . sighing she took her leave. She couldn't risk upsetting her friend, because she still wanted to see the kids. Rose thought the world of them, Alice because she was so sweet and loving, and Davey because he reminded her of his father.

Rose scrubbed her already spotless kitchen from top to bottom, making it smell as fresh as a daisy. Then she looked round for something to do. A sherry bottle stood on the sideboard but she refused to look at it. A drink down the pub with friends was one thing, but once you started to drink alone – no, she wouldn't go down that road, even if she was lonely.

She drew the curtains, shutting out the darkness of the night and then put the kettle on. She'd bought some pink wool the other day and she had a pattern that would make a lovely little cardigan for Alice. Smiling, Rose got her needles out. It was something to do. Perhaps one day she would have grandchildren to make a fuss of, but until then she would do what she could to help Dora and her kids.

Rose hadn't needed that extra shift at work, but the money could be put by for a rainy day. Mind you, she might even buy a treat of some kind for Sally and call in. Maybe she would like it, no matter what Dora thought.

Just as she was about to settle down with her knitting, her back door opened and her neighbour from two doors down walked in. She had a cracked cup in her hand and looked at Rose sheepishly.

'Couldn't lend me half a cup of sugar, could yer, Rose?'

'Yeah, why not?' Rose said and got up to fill the old cup from her blue bag on the shelf. She filled it almost to the top and handed it to her neighbour. 'Ran out sudden then, Beattie?'

'You know what I am, Rose. Never make ends meet wiv all them kids round me – five of me own still and six grandchildren and they all expect cakes and sandwiches on a Sunday. How can I manage it?' Beattie Goodger was eagerly eyeing the rock cakes Rose had kept for herself.

'Go on, then.' Rose took two from the plate and handed them to her. 'Fresh this morning.'

'Yeah, I smelled 'em when yer had yer back door open,' she said and grinned. 'Yer a good friend, Rose. One day I'll repay yer.'

Rose smiled ironically as the woman went off clutching her treasures. Beattie Goodger would never manage to repay her, but Rose knew that she had a hard struggle. Her husband was a lazy so-and-so and never did a day's work if he could get out of it. He was in and out of work all the time, and he had flat feet so the army wouldn't have him even though there was a war on.

It reminded Rose that she wasn't that badly off after all. Her husband had always worked, and he didn't always drink. She loved him once and she thought he appreciated her, even if there wasn't a lot of love about these days. She chuckled and told herself that she could always go to bed and dream about the day Dave Blake told her he'd always loved her – a dream she allowed herself to indulge in now and then.

'Fat chance of that, Rose Parker!' she said aloud and smiled as she settled down with her knitting. Daft bugger she was, but not daft enough for that.

CHAPTER 3

'You're never goin' ter send them kids to the country?'
Rose said in an astonished voice. 'You'll be lost
without that pair. Don't do it, Dora. You'll only regret
it. You didn't send them when they were tellin' yer
to last year an' most of the kids who did go were
back 'ome by Christmas cos there were no bombs
like they said there were goin' to be. Same thing'll
'appen this time. I know Dunkirk were terrible, but
it was also a miracle, gettin' all those men off the
beaches, hundreds of thousands of them. Don't you
send 'em away, whatever the Government says.'

'They'll be safer and better off there,' Dora replied
a little guiltily as Rose continued to stare at her in
dismay. 'Dave is always sayin' how they'd do better
at the seaside.'

'That's if you were with them,' Rose countered.
'He means if you and he lived there and you know
it. To send them kids away to strangers ain't fair.
They'll feel abandoned and, knowin' that lad of yours,
he'll run away and come home.'

'What else can I do then?' Dora demanded, guilt

turning to annoyance in her face. 'You don't know how hard it was looking after two children with Dave away on the cruise ships. And now Ma is fadin' day by day. She kept it from me for weeks and it's only two months since she told me but now I can see she's goin' downhill fast. It's changin' her, destroyin' her.' She gave a little sob of desperation. 'What am I goin' ter do without her, Rose? I can't manage on me own!' Having her mother there had given Dora a little freedom when she needed it; now she would be tied to the kids the whole time. She loved them, of course she did, and Rose knew that, but she needed a little bit of fun now and then.

''Ave you seen the doctor, then?' Rose asked at her most practical. 'Asked him what's wrong?'

'Yes . . .' Dora sniffed and dabbed at her face. Their tea break was almost over and she couldn't show signs of grief when she was working on the line. The women who worked beside her would sneer and tell her to toughen up. Rose was the only one she could tell her troubles to. 'He confirmed that she was dyin', says it's her heart and there's nothin' they can do. I asked him about the pain in her guts, but he said it was just bellyache. She's just worn out, so he says.'

'Well, Sally's had a hard life,' Rose said. 'Your father used to knock her about, Dora. She had all them miscarriages cos of 'im, I reckon, though she never told a soul. Always preachin' about religion and livin' right, and behind closed doors he was a right bully. And then she went out ter work when he died of the drink. My old man swears it was his liver

35

that got him, though Sally always said he suffered from his guts at the end.'

'I hardly remember him,' Dora said. 'If he drank, she hid it from me. Mum was always there for me, Rose – and since I had the kids, she's been wonderful. It's up to me to look after her now and I intend to.' She took a deep breath. 'So Davey and Alice will be evacuated to the country for a while and I'll take Mum to live with me and give her house up. I'm going to ask Mr Smith if I can go on shorter hours, otherwise I'll give up work for a while.' Blinking back her tears, she turned her head as the whistle went for the end of tea break. 'It won't be for long, so Dr Martin says.'

'I'd help yer wiv money if I could,' Rose said. 'But me daughter-in-law is havin' that baby and she's relyin' on me to look out for her, says she can't manage on what Terry sends her.' She pulled a face. 'I never knew a girl who let money slip through her fingers the way our Shirl does.'

'You spoil her, Rose,' Dora accused. 'I reckon you give her half your wages.'

'I give her what I can,' Rose agreed. 'But Terry's a good lad and he asked me to look out for her while he's away.'

'You'll look after Shirl for me, won't you, Mum?' Terry had asked on his last brief visit. 'If anything should happen . . .'

Rose had promised she would and she did her best by sending her daughter-in-law a postal order most weeks. She could have done more if they'd lived in London but it was their choice to live where Shirl could be on hand if her husband's ship put into its home port.

Although her eldest boy was at sea just like Dora's husband, her younger son was still in a protected job, though the last brief letter she'd had from him had said that he was thinking of joining the army. She'd shown it to Dora.

I don't want to join the Merchant Navy like Dad and Terry. I think I'd rather fight on land than at sea, Ma, but they say they need me here. I might come home and visit for a day or so and then decide . . .

'I could help with yer ma now and then on a Saturday if yer like?' Rose offered as they walked back to the assembly line. Inside, the stink of hot metal assailed their nostrils and the clatter of machinery drowned out Dora's reply but she smiled and nodded.

Dora was reluctant but knew she might need help now and then. She wanted to keep doing a few hours each week, because otherwise she wouldn't be able to afford to send the kids a few treats now and then. And whatever Rose said, her mind was made up. She would feel miserable when the kids left on that train, but all the arrangements were made and it was the only way. Once they were safe in their temporary homes – it was only for a short time and their own good – she would be able to look after her mother properly.

'Oh, Dave,' she sighed as she thought about what her husband would say. 'Don't make me feel guilty –

your son will do that well enough and I know Rose thinks I'm a terrible mother. But I don't have a choice. What do you want me to do – let Mum go to that dreadful place to die? You know the workhouse is her worst fear . . . all right, it isn't called the workhouse these days but it's not much different.'

Dora often talked to her absent husband when she was anxious or unsure, mostly in her head but sometimes she said the words aloud. She knew instinctively that he would approve of her caring for her mother, who he liked, but not her decision to evacuate Davey and Alice.

'I can't manage it all alone,' she murmured as she approached her mother's house. 'I would if I could—'

'That's the first sign,' a cheeky voice said behind her. 'What's up, Dora? You look down in the mouth – and talkin' to yourself ain't good, love.'

'Mick George!' Dora said crossly as she turned to look at him. 'I ain't got time for your nonsense. Mum's real bad and I need to get 'ome and see to her.'

His smile vanished instantly. 'I'm sorry about that, Dora, love. Anythin' I can do to help you?' He looked concerned and her irritation melted. A little smile came to her lips. He was good-looking and his flirting made her feel young and pretty. Surely there was nothing wrong with a little flirting – even a swift kiss on the cheek now and then? 'Money – or someone to look after Sally while you're at work?'

'Thanks, Mick,' she said. 'You know I won't let you give me money, don't you? Dave would beat the life out of me if I did that.'

'He shouldn't go off and leave you to manage alone

then, should he?' Mick looked at her with what Dora believed was real affection. 'You know I've always had a soft spot for you, love. You only have to ask and you needn't work another day.'

'I do it for company as well as a bit of extra money,' Dora said. 'I've asked down the factory today and they'll let me do just afternoons for a while. I can get someone to sit with Ma for a few hours then. I'll manage, Mick – but thanks for the offer.'

He hesitated and it seemed as if he wanted to push things further. 'The offer still stands and it always will,' he said. 'No strings attached. I want you, Dora – but I don't want to buy you. It was a genuine offer of help.' He walked away without waiting for her answer and she sensed he'd been hurt by her refusal.

Dora felt a bit sorry for him, but she knew she mustn't step over that line. If she took anything more than a drink from Mick, he would push her a little further and then a bit more and it would be the end of her marriage because she didn't trust herself to be alone with him. She *did* love Dave and in a straight choice between the two, her husband was the winner hands down, but he wasn't here and she was lonely. Lonely and afraid. Supposing Dave was killed? How would she live then? Without her mother and without Dave she would be lost. And she'd always liked Mick – fancied him a bit, truth be told. Dave was a good husband and father – but well, Mick was fun.

Rose thought she should keep the kids at all costs, but Dora knew that she would find it much too diffi-cult to cope with them as well as her sick mother. If that made her a bad person then she must be, because she'd made up her mind to let them go – just until things were easier again. Somehow, she would find time to talk with her friends and especially Mick.

'What has your mother decided, Davey?' Miss Bristow asked at the end of school the next day as Davey collected his sister from the girls' playground. 'Is she going to do the sensible thing and send you to the country for the duration?'

Davey shook his head determinedly and clutched Alice's hand. 'We ain't goin' nowhere, miss,' he said boldly, quaking inside because Miss Bristow was the head teacher and he was in awe of her. 'Dad wouldn't let her if he was here.'

'Your father is a brave man and has gone to fight for his country,' Miss Bristow replied. 'Your mother came to ask my advice the other day and I told her I thought she should send you, at least for a while. You know that your grandmother is very ill, don't you?'

'Yes, miss.' Davey didn't much like the stern head-mistress and he knew instinctively that he wouldn't like to be sent away to the country – wherever that was – and nor would Alice. 'But I help Gran; and Mum – she can't manage without me.'

'I see.' Miss Bristow looked down her thin nose at him. 'Well, tell your mother I need to know by the weekend. We have to supply names and numbers by then. Most of the children in your class are going, Davey, and we shall be closing much of the school for the duration. Only the older boys and girls will still be attending. They have important exams coming up and then they will be leaving.'

On their way home, Davey thought about what Miss Bristow had said. He held tightly to Alice's hand. It was common knowledge that most of the younger children were leaving London to stay in the country and if the schools closed down then he could stay at home and help his mother out, Davey reckoned. He didn't mind getting Gran something to eat or making her a pot of tea. He could bring in coal and coke and have a go at chopping wood for the range, and he could make the beds and tidy up. The rest of it was women's work and didn't matter anyway. Who cared about a bit of dust or clean clothes?

'You ain't sayin' much.' Alice's eyes were questioning as she looked up at him, skipping at his side on their journey to Gran's. There was less than two years between them but he was a lot taller and stronger than his little sister. 'Are yer upset wiv me?'

'Nah, course not,' Davey replied and squeezed her hand. 'Just thinkin' over what Miss Bristow said about goin' to the country. I don't want to and nor do you, Alice. Remember that, no matter what anyone says. We don't want to go.'

Alice nodded happily. She always did whatever Davey said, unless her mother had expressly forbidden it, but her brother hardly ever told her to do anything naughty and she trusted him implicitly.

'Do you think Gran will have baked us a cake today?'

'Nah, shouldn't think so,' Davey said. 'She's too ill, Alice. Mum might bring us one from the shop.' Their mother only baked cakes and jam tarts at the weekend, but they'd eaten the last tart the previous evening. On very rare occasions their mother might bring home a shop cake as a special treat, but Davey didn't hold out much hope of that in his heart. So, when they entered the kitchen and he saw four madeleines sitting on a plate waiting, suspicion entered his mind. What were they for?

'Is Gran better?' he asked in case it was a celebration.

'Your gran isn't going to get better,' his mother told him with a little frown. 'You're old enough to understand now, Davey. Gran is very ill and one day she won't be with us anymore.'

'I know,' he admitted. 'I wondered why you'd bought the cakes, they're my favourites.'

'I know that, Davey,' his mother said and smiled uneasily. 'I've got something I need to tell you.'

'It isn't Dad?' he asked, fear jumping into his heart.

'No, it isn't Dad,' she replied, looking distinctly uncomfortable now. 'Eat your cakes, Davey, Alice. I'll tell you after tea.'

And then of course he knew. Mum was going to try and send them away . . .

'You can't mean it?' Davey stared at his mother in dismay when she finished explaining what she intended. 'You're sendin' us away to live with strangers?'

'I think it's best for you, Davey,' she said. 'Really, it's for your own good, love. They say the Germans might start dropping bombs on us soon, so you and Alice will be safer in the country. They'll bomb London, because of the factories and the docks, and they'll bomb other cities and ports too but the countryside will be less of a target so you'll both be all right there.'

'No, we don't want to go!' Davey set his face

stubbornly, his feet astride. 'Miss Bristow says you need to let her know by Saturday if we're goin' and I told her we weren't.'

'You had no right to say that, Davey. *I* make the decisions, not you.'

'We're not goin', Mum,' he repeated stubbornly. 'We want to stay here. You can get Gran round here and I can look after her while you're at work. The schools will be closed so I can be here and do things, save you the trouble.' Davey saw the hesitation in his mother's face. 'I can do most things. You know I can.'

She shook her head. 'No, Davey, you can't keep her clean or change her bed and her clothes, and she needs that now. If I don't look after her, they'll put her in the infirmary and that's a horrible place. I'll just be working part-time, and I'll write to you and send you cards and treats when I can, Davey. It will only be until your dad returns and it will be safer.'

His mother had promised to get his boots mended but she'd forgotten so he'd taken them to the menders himself; he'd paid for the repair with the money Rose had given him for cleaning her windows. He'd been saving to buy Alice a doll he'd seen in the second-hand shop and would have to start saving again. So he didn't hold much hope of his mother sending them treats once they were away. Davey felt chilled all over. If his mother did this, something bad would happen, he just knew it.

'We'll run away and come back,' he said, angry with her now. 'Dad wouldn't let you do it and you know it!'

*

43

Davey was right. Even as she filled out the form and signed it, Dora knew Dave would hate what she'd done.

'If you want them to be safe in the country, go with them . . .' Dora could almost hear him saying the words in her ear, but she refused to listen. She couldn't work and look after her mother while still caring for the kids. The only way they would let her work just afternoons was if she stopped until five. Which meant there would be no one there when the kids came home from school for more than an hour and a half. It just wouldn't work. She would be looking after her mother in the mornings when they needed their breakfast and again in the evening when she got home and took over from her neighbour. Besides, it was a constant struggle to feed and clothe two kids. Sometimes she just felt she couldn't cope with it all.

'It's no good, they have to go,' she said aloud. 'Don't blame me, Dave. You should be here when we need you.'

Dora knew it wasn't fair to blame her husband. Perhaps Rose and he were right – perhaps the children *should* come first, but she couldn't bear to send her mother to what had once been the workhouse and was a grim dark place, even though it had doctors and nurses now rather than wardens. It was the rotten hand life dealt sometimes and she felt close to despair as she contemplated her situation. She needed help she knew wasn't coming and it made her shed a few tears of self-pity before she lifted her head defiantly.

She'd made her decision and that was that. Davey

and Alice were joining the other children due to be evacuated and she wouldn't give it another thought. It was for the best, after all.

Rose was very thoughtful that evening. Should she offer to take the children in until Sally passed and give Dora the break she obviously needed? It was what she wanted to do, what her instincts were telling her she ought to do, but it would mean a sacrifice on her part. She'd have to cut her working hours and that meant Shirl would get less in her postal order, but surely it was the right thing?

There was no time like the present. Rose put on her coat because it was strangely cool these June evenings and walked the short distance to Dora's house. Through the window, Rose could see her friend sitting in her kitchen, drinking tea and looking downright miserable. Rose tapped the door and then walked in. Dora's head came up in surprise.

'Something wrong?' she asked anxiously. 'I've only just left Ma – she isn't worse, is she?'

'Nah, not that I know of at any rate,' Rose said. 'I've had an idea, Dora, and don't be annoyed with me. I ain't pokin' my nose in and it's just a suggestion – but what if I took the kids in for a while, just until you're ready ter have 'em back?'

As soon as the words left her mouth, she could see Dora didn't like it. 'Just thought it might make it easier for you,' she added lamely. Rose wasn't sure why Dora was so annoyed by the offer, unless it touched her pride. A lot of women were sending their kids to the country so that was all right – but to let a friend take them was admitting she couldn't cope. It was the only reason Rose could think of. 'Sorry if I put my foot in it.'

Dora hesitated, then, 'They'd be round here all the time, under my feet, wantin' to see me and their gran. No, thanks all the same, Rose. It was good of you to ask but a bomb could fall on your house, same as mine. They'll be safer in the country. That's what their teacher thinks and I reckon she's right.'

Rose knew she'd lost the argument. Dora had convinced herself that she was doing it for the kids and there was no changing her mind.

'Right, I'll be off then,' she said. 'I'll be seein' yer, Dora.'

'Yeah,' Dora answered in an off-hand manner and Rose knew she wouldn't be forgiven for her blunder for a while.

Her eyes stung with tears as she walked home. She was going to miss seeing those kids.

'Well, if it isn't Rose Parker.' The masculine voice made her look up and she saw it was the manager from the munition factory. 'You look as though you've found a penny and lost sixpence.' He was grinning at her. 'Something wrong, Rose?'

'Nah, just been to see Dora,' Rose replied. 'Her ma's sick.'

'Yeah, she asked for extra time off so I might have to let her go. We need workers, not slackers.'

'You wouldn't do that, Harry!' Rose forgot her rule never to call him by his first name, though they'd been good friends at school, even though he'd been a few years ahead. 'She needs a bit extra when she can earn it.'

'We have to fill our quota, Rose, you know that,' he said and then grinned. 'But because you asked nicely, I'll wait a bit longer, see how she shapes up.'

'Thanks . . .' Rose hesitated and then started to walk on but he caught her arm. 'Harry, if you're goin' to ask me to 'ave a drink down the pub the answer is no – like always.'

'How about a cup of cocoa at yours, then?' he persisted. 'Just for old times' sake, Rose.'

'We're friends, Harry,' she said, 'and that's all we ever were.'

'I know, but I get lonely on my own. Just a cup of cocoa, please?'

'What will my neighbours think?' Rose stared at him hard and saw that he was telling the truth. He was lonely, just like her. 'Come on, then. We'll sit in the kitchen and I'll make cocoa – but that's all. Reggie will kill me if he hears I've had a man in the house.'

'You can tell him I came round to see you about a promotion at work.'

'Have yer?' Rose demanded instantly but he shook his head.

'No, but you're my best worker and the one I wouldn't want to lose.'

'Get in, then.' Rose jerked her head at her kitchen door, which she hadn't locked. No one in the street locked their door. Most had nothing much to steal and it just didn't happen round here. Locals wouldn't take from their own and there were better homes to rob elsewhere. 'But remember – one cup and you go!'

CHAPTER 4

His mother was really going to do it! She was sending them away and Davey could hardly believe it was happening. Alice was snivelling and clinging to their mum's hand. She'd begged to be allowed to stay with her, but their mother had shaken her head, simply repeating over and over again that she was doing it to save them from getting blown up in their beds. 'If that Hitler's planes come over in the night and bomb us, you'd die,' she'd told Alice, who had promptly burst into tears. 'You don't want that to happen and nor do I. Cheer up, love. You'll enjoy the country. There's lots of things to do and see, and good food too.'

'Then why aren't you coming?' Davey asked, his tone and look accusing. 'We wouldn't mind goin' if you were coming too.'

'I'm not allowed and I've got to look after Gran,' she answered so quickly that he knew she'd rehearsed it. 'She couldn't come either. This is a privilege just for children like you – the lucky ones, who will be staying in good homes and be given good food.'

Davey looked around the crowded railway platform with sullen eyes. There were hundreds of children gathered with their mothers. And it looked as though some of the mothers were going with them because they were getting on the train with their children, though to be fair most weren't. A lot of them were sniffing into their handkerchiefs and one woman was sobbing as another led her two children away. Miss Bristow was with the children from their school. At first it looked as if she was boarding the train because she was carrying a case, but then Davey saw a boy a bit younger than him standing behind her.

Miss Bristow came up to them and smiled her saccharine smile, the one she used when you knew you were in trouble. 'Ah, Davey, there you are. I'm so glad I saw you. This is my nephew, Peter. Will you please look after him for me?'

Davey wanted to refuse but he was still in awe of his headmistress. 'Yes, if you wish, Miss Bristow,' he said.

'Thank you so much,' she said and handed him a ten-shilling note. 'That is in case you need anything on the journey, any of you, and if you don't spend it all, you may keep it for taking care of my nephew until you get to the hall where you will be chosen.'

'What do you mean, chosen?' Davey asked suspiciously.

'The kind people who have volunteered to take you in will choose who they want to live with them,' Miss Bristow said. 'Be sure to stick together and go to the front of the group. That way you'll be seen first by those most eager to take you in.'

Davey placed the ten-shilling note in his trouser pocket for safety but didn't thank her. He reckoned it was a bribe, because she went off straight away and didn't look back at Peter once. He stared miserably at the ground and looked scared to death. Davey was feeling much the same, but he wouldn't let it show.

'It's all right, mate,' he said after a few seconds. 'I reckon it'll be all right once we get to the country.'

'What do *you* know about it?' Peter answered and stuck his tongue out at him. 'You've never been, have you?'

The difference in his speech from theirs was apparent from the first word. Looking at his smart school blazer and grey trousers, Davey worked out that he was one of the private school kids. He'd seen a smattering of them in the crowd, their maroon blazers distinctive. He wondered why Miss Bristow hadn't placed him in the care of one of those boys – a few of them looked to be a year or two older than he was. It was a mystery until Peter glared at him.

'My father was killed last week,' he announced. 'Mummy said there's no money for private school now and she was going to send me to my aunt's school, but Aunt Liz said I should go to the country until Mummy feels strong enough to look after me.' To Davey's horror, he saw that Peter was crying silent tears that ran down his cheeks but made no noise.

His hostility vanished just like that and he felt sorry for the younger boy. How dreadful would he feel if his dad had been killed? His smashing, wonderful dad who he loved and loved him. It didn't bear thinking about and Davey's mood lightened. Suddenly, he realised that his situation was no worse than most of the other kids waiting to board the steam train that had just drawn into the station. He turned to his mother.

'Will you be all right on your own, Mum? Are you sure you can manage?'

She looked at him for a moment and then he saw she had tears in her eyes, tears she was struggling to hold back. 'Yes, thank you, Davey,' she said and bent to kiss him and Alice, hugging them both for a moment. 'Oh, I shall miss you – and you can come home as soon as the danger is over, I promise.'

'We'll be all right,' Davey said. 'And if we don't like it, we'll come home anyway.'

'Then come along, you two,' she replied and moved determinedly towards the train. 'You too, Peter – your aunt didn't tell us your second name?'

'It's Saunders,' Peter said in a small, polite voice. He stayed close to Davey's side as Mum checked them on board with the lady in charge. She was very efficient and she asked them if they had their lunch boxes and a case. Mum looked at Peter, who had a small case, but there was no sign of the food parcel he was supposed to bring for the journey.

'I don't think Peter has anything,' she said. 'My two have sandwiches, cake and biscuits.'

'Peter can share ours,' Davey volunteered. 'I saw what you packed, Mum. You gave Alice twice as much as she'll need, and I can spare some of mine.'

'I wanted to be sure you weren't hungry . . .' Again, his mother looked on the verge of tears. Davey suspected she might be regretting her decision to send them away.

'We needn't go,' he said hopefully but she shook her head.

'Don't make it harder, Davey. I'll get down to see you as soon as they let me know where you are, as long as I can find someone to look after Gran or . . .'

Davey nodded solemnly. He knew just what she meant, but he wasn't going to ask her again if they could stay. He was glad his mum seemed upset before they boarded the train, because she jolly well should, but after waving a couple of times, she turned and walked away. Alice was sobbing and Davey put his arm round her shoulders but she kept crying. She wasn't the only one. A lady on the train was trying to comfort several weeping children and another was making sure they found a seat and their luggage was in the rack above. Davey stood on the seat and put his case and Alice's haversack together on the rack. He knew that some of her things were in with his, but Mum only had the one case. If they split them up, he would have to say – but surely they wouldn't? Mum had promised she'd arranged for them to go together. Davey felt a moment's panic, because it was suddenly all so real and so frightening.

He squared his shoulders. 'It's all right,' he told his sister. 'We'll stay for a bit if it suits us, but if it isn't nice we'll run away and come home.'

Peter had taken a book from the case that contained his gas mask and sat in the corner seat near the window, his head bent over it, though Davey suspected he wasn't actually reading it. All the children had the gas masks they'd been issued with the previous year. Alice had refused to put hers on when Mum tried to remind her how, but Davey had practiced and knew he could help her if she needed it.

'Do yer know how to use your gas mask?' he asked Peter, feeling the weight of his responsibility.

Peter looked up, faintly superior. 'Yes, of course. Do you?' he asked.

Davey felt like smacking his ear but restrained his feelings. His father should have taught Peter some manners. 'Of course I know what to do. I wanted to be sure you did if we needed them in a hurry.'

'It won't happen,' Peter replied. 'My father told me it is very unlikely. They used gas in the trenches in the last war where it was effective. But it is much harder to kill a civilian population that way – they'll simply bomb our cities and ports when they're ready. My father told me that before he went off to fight.'

Suddenly, Peter seemed older than he was and Davey looked at him with new eyes. 'Your father was regular army, was he?'

'Yes, Captain Peter Saunders,' he said. 'My aunt says he's won a medal for bravery . . .' Peter's mouth wobbled then and his air of superiority left him. 'I wish he hadn't. I wish he was still alive and back with us.' He sniffed hard, obviously trying not to cry.

'Yeah, I wish my dad was home too,' Davey replied. In normal life Davey would probably never have met or talked to a boy like Peter. They came from very different backgrounds and he wasn't sure he liked him much, but he shared a bond with him. Their fathers had gone off to fight and they were being sent away from their homes.

'Are you hungry?' he asked. 'Mum packed us some egg sandwiches and some chicken paste.'

'Could I have an egg sandwich – or do you want them?' Peter replied, obviously remembering his manners belatedly.

Davey opened his parcel. He knew that he had two egg sandwiches and so did Alice. He offered an egg one to Peter.

'You can have one of mine, and a paste sandwich later if you'd like.'

Peter nodded. They both took a sandwich and started to munch. Davey asked Alice if she wanted to open her food but she shook her head. She was playing with a bit of wool on her fingers, doing cat's cradle, and apart from an occasional sniff seemed to have settled down. Davey left her to get on with it. She'd had toast and jam for breakfast and wouldn't be hungry for a while. He'd eaten three slices of bread and dripping but was still hungry. He was always hungry and Mum had packed them plenty of sandwiches. Davey knew he'd probably eat some of Alice's so there should be more than enough for Peter too.

When the train finally disembarked and after all the frantic searches for children who had somehow got mislaid on the journey but were eventually found, either in the toilets, and carriages other than the ones they started out in, or in one case the guard's van, they were ushered into a large hall not far from the station they disembarked at. They had to walk in single file, shivering in the cool wind blowing flat over the countryside. Davey had caught sight of a river just before the train reached their destination, a town they'd been told was called Ely.

Everyone was clutching their personal belongings, gas masks, cases, a few toys that were being held on to for dear life, and soggy greaseproof paper bags from leftover food. Peter, Davey and even Alice had eaten all theirs on the journey, which had seemed to the children to go on forever; most had screamed and fought after the first air of subdued misery had worn off and the excitement of being on a train took over. A few fierce fights had broken out between the private school boys and the others but that had been further along the corridor and their carriage had been fairly peaceful, perhaps because they shared it with a male teacher and an anxious mother who was taking her daughter to live with friends in the country.

Some of the children had already been allotted and when their names were called out people came forward to claim them. Davey had pushed through to the front, as Miss Bristow had told him, taking Alice and Peter with him, but it was a while before some of the other folk came to look, walking up and down the line as if inspecting them.

Eventually, a man with a thin face and gold spectacles that lodged on his nose precariously stopped in front of them. He nodded to himself and pointed to Davey. 'You'll do.'

'What about Alice?' Davey said and set his feet firmly apart, refusing to budge. 'You have to take my sister too – or you can't have me!' No way was he going to let them be split up. He'd take Alice home first, even if Mum was angry and he got a smack across his ear!

'Do I, indeed?' the man said and frowned.

'Yes, that's right, Mr Greenhough,' a female voice said from behind him. 'Davey and Alice go together – look, it says so on their identification cards.'

'Right, then I suppose it will have to be the pair of them – my wife fancied a girl anyway but I need a boy to help me in the shop.'

The woman in charge hesitated and then nodded as she looked round the hall, which was emptying fast. There were more children left than people to take them and she was clearly worried that they would not all find homes.

'Very well,' she said and crossed their names off her list. 'Go along, Davey, and take your sister with you.'

Still Davey hesitated. 'What about—' He started to ask about Peter, but at that moment a pleasant-looking woman turned up and put a hand on the other boy's shoulder. She smiled at him. 'Would you like to come and live with me?' she asked.

'Yes, please,' Peter answered and went off without a backward glance.

Davey remembered the ten-shilling note in his pocket. He hadn't spent a penny because the drinks of squash had been supplied free. Watching them leave and seeing the way they were talking animatedly to each other, Davey wished the nice lady had chosen them but the man with the glasses was looking at them impatiently.

'Come on, then,' he muttered. 'I haven't got all day. I've had to wait until all the best went and my wife can't cope with the shop in the evening rush.'

Davey felt a trickle of ice at the nape of his neck. He knew instinctively that he'd been picked because he was big and strong for his age. This man hadn't taken him on from the goodness of his heart, he was looking for a worker he didn't have to pay more than the food on his plate and a bed to sleep in. Davey's only hope as they were taken outside was that the man's wife would be kinder than her husband.

It was a forlorn hope, Davey realised, as Mary Greenhough looked them up and down. She was a scrawny woman with thin lips and dark hair streaked with grey drawn back tightly into a bun at the back of her head. Gran always said that a woman with thin lips had a grudging nature. Davey didn't know if that was generally true or not, but it certainly was in this case.

'Two of them, Sidney?' she questioned in a strident tone. 'The boy looks as if he'll work, but the girl is too young to do much. If I set her to scrubbing the floor, she'd take all day over it and then it won't be done properly.'

At this prospect, Alice started to wail, clinging on to Davey's hand in a way that told him she was terrified. 'It's all right, Alice,' he told her and raised his head defiantly. 'I'll help Mr Greenhough,' he said boldly. 'I'm used to work, but leave my sister alone. She didn't come here to work and if you ill-treat her – or me – we're off home.' Davey jutted his chin.

No one was going to harm his Alice if he could stop them!

Mary Greenhough gave a harsh laugh. 'Will you listen to that, Sidney? You got yourself a pig in a poke all right. You should've let me go. I'd have sorted a good one out.' Her eyes flashing with temper, she turned on Davey. 'While you're under my roof, you will do as you're told – or you'll feel the back of my hand.'

Davey wanted to tell her that he wasn't afraid of her, but Alice was – and besides, he'd already made up his mind they weren't stopping here. They hadn't come far from the railway station and he'd be taking Alice back as soon as they could slip away. When Mum heard how they'd been treated, she would be up in arms and if she didn't come storming down here to seek retribution, she would at least see they were better off at home with her.

Seeing the woman was waiting, Davey decided to be diplomatic. 'Sorry, missus,' he said in a low voice. 'I don't mind working – but Alice is too little.'

'How old is she?'

Davey decided to knock a year off his sister's age to protect her. 'She's not seven yet, missus.' In fact, she was almost eight but small for her age.

Mary Greenhough's eyes narrowed but she accepted what he'd said. 'You'd best take him out to the shop,' she said to her husband. 'They'll be in soon for their papers and their fags. The floor is filthy again where the mud has been tramped in. These farmers and their boots! Get the boy to sweep the floor.'

Davey grinned to himself. He could sweep a floor

and do most things if he wanted. The shop itself was warm and dry and smelled of all kinds of things like carbolic soap and tobacco, and he thought it was a pity the owners were so mean. He wouldn't have minded working here for a while if they'd been welcoming like the woman who had taken Peter. He cursed his luck. Why couldn't he and Alice have been picked by someone like that?

CHAPTER 5

Fortunately for Davey's plans, they were given a little room behind the shop to sleep in. A mattress had been placed on the floor and a couple of blankets thrown over, with one long pillow between them.

'I don't like it here, do you?' Alice asked when they'd been shut in for the night. 'I want to go home.'

Davey placed a finger to his lips, hushing her. He crept to the door in his socks having removed his boots and listened. Once he was certain that no one was listening, he went back to her.

'We're not stopping,' he said and put a hand to her mouth to prevent her joyful reply escaping. 'They won't let us leave if they know what we're planning so we have to be very quiet, Alice. I know where he put the key to the shop door so when it's quiet upstairs, we'll let ourselves out and go back to the station.'

'How will we get home?' Alice asked, puzzled. 'It costs money to go to London, doesn't it?'

'I've got ten shillings Miss Bristow gave me,' Davey said confidently. 'I think it will be enough – but if it isn't we'll hide in the toilets when the inspector comes round.'

Alice nodded solemnly. Her eyes were round and scared, but she trusted her brother. 'They took your case and my satchel away with our spare clothes,' she whispered.

'We'll just have to go without them,' Davey said. He knew his mother would be angry at the loss of their extra clothes, but he also knew he couldn't risk looking for them. They had to go now, because he'd overheard Mary Greenhough saying they could send Alice to someone Mary knew and just keep him. Sidney Greenhough had been pleased with the way he'd worked and given him two wrapped toffees. Davey had them in his pocket now for the journey. All they'd been given for supper was a slice of bread and dripping. Alice couldn't eat hers, it was too greasy, so Davey had finished it. He regretted the sandwiches he'd shared with Peter – he'd bet the other boy had had a better tea than they'd been given by the mean old skinflints. Davey couldn't wait to get away.

They crept out about an hour or so later. Davey almost left the door unlocked but thought he might be blamed if the shop was robbed so he relocked the door and let the key drop to the floor inside. It made a bit of a noise but, as they hurried away into the darkness, there was no shout of discovery or pursuit and so they stopped running when they reached the end of the street. Davey knew that the railway station was down the hill and then turn to the right and just keep going until you got there. It had seemed only a couple of minutes away in the old delivery van that had brought them to the shop, but it was much further to walk when it was cold and dark and the wind was blowing. Being alone in the dark in a strange town was scary, too, and he held tightly to Alice's hand so she didn't get lost.

'I'm cold and 'ungry,' Alice wailed after they'd been walking for several minutes.

'I know, so am I,' Davey replied, gritting his teeth. 'But we can't get back into the shop, so we have to keep going – and you'd hate it there, Alice, even if they kept you. But they talked about sendin' you somewhere else and you'd be on your own then. We'll be at the station soon and we can catch a train. If there isn't one for London there, we'll wait in the special room I saw when we got off the train. It will be warmer in there.'

'I want Mum,' Alice moaned miserably.

'I want to be 'ome too,' Davey agreed. 'Mum should never have sent us away.' He was cross with his mother. How could she let them be sent to a place like that?

'She said it would be like a holiday but it was horrid.'

'It was what I expected,' Davey replied flatly. 'Stands ter reason, they ain't gonna give yer a home fer nuthin'.'

Alice shuffled her feet. 'I wouldn't 'ave minded 'elpin' wiv the cookin' if she'd been nice. I 'elped Gran wiv her cookin' sometimes.' She sniffed audibly. 'I miss bein' wiv Gran . . .'

'Yeah, that used ter be all right,' Davey agreed. He'd loved Gran's home and the smell of fresh baking and her sleepy old cat that seemed to spend its life between the hearth rug and Gran's lap. 'But we can't go there no more, Alice. Ma let the house go because she was takin' Gran back to live wiv us yesterday.'

'I know – Gran's goin' ter 'eaven soon, ain't she?'

'Who told you that?'

Alice shrugged. 'Gran did. She said I shouldn't cry or be sad, because it was a lovely place and she would be glad ter go. She said one day, if I was kind and good, I might go there too. If Gran's there it would be nice . . .' She sounded wistful and Davey put his arm about her shoulders protectively. He loved his sister and knew it was his job to take care of her, just the way he'd promised Dad.

'We shan't go to Heaven for years – not until we're old.' He stopped and pointed ahead. 'Look, Alice, there's the station!'

There was a big round clock on the wall with a white dial and thick black numbers. It was ten thirty but there was nothing to say when a train would arrive or where it was going. But Davey thought that if they went on to the platform opposite the one they'd got off at, that would be where the train for London would come in.

Davey approached the ticket office cautiously. An elderly man sat there reading a book. As Davey cautiously asked about the price of fares to London, he peered over the top of his gold-rimmed glasses at him.

'Single or return?' he barked out sharply.

'Single,' Davey replied and was told it would be five shillings if he was travelling with a fare-paying adult. He paused for a moment and then asked how much it was if he was travelling alone.

'You ain't allowed on the train alone, young 'un – where's yer ma?'

'She sent me ter ask,' Davey said, improvising swiftly as the man's eyes narrowed in suspicion.

'Here, you ain't one of them evacuees, are yer?'

Davey ran out of the station. Alice was shivering outside in the bus shelter. 'What's wrong?' she asked, looking frightened.'

'The ticket seller says we can't travel without an adult,' Davey said and frowned. 'We'll wait until he's reading his book again and then we'll sneak past and find the waiting room.'

'I want Mum!' Alice's tears spilled over and ran down her grubby cheeks. They hadn't been told to wash before going to bed and she'd got dirty on the train coming down.

'No good crying,' Davey said. 'We'll go in in a minute – but don't make a sound.'

He peeped round the corner to see if the man in the kiosk was reading, but just as he did, two soldiers in uniform arrived and went to the counter. They asked for tickets to London, sounding loud and boisterous, as if they'd been drinking. Davey, taking advantage of the distraction, seized Alice's hand and quickly tugged her through the office and onto the platform. He propelled her down it and into the waiting room.

Alice sat down and Davey did the same, smiling at her. She snuggled up to him. 'Will Mum be cross when we get 'ome?'

'Nah, shouldn't think so,' Davey lied. Mum would be furious with him. She wouldn't blame Alice. She would know it was his fault. 'She'll be cross with them people when she hears what they were plannin' to do.' He crossed his fingers and hoped she wouldn't send them straight back.

The soldiers arrived a minute or two later. They were drinking, holding a bottle of whisky they were sharing between them. Perhaps because they were inebriated, they ignored the children and talked about where they were going.

'Now we've been kicked out of bleedin' France, I reckon they're sendin' us off to bleedin' Egypt. Now Italy's come into the war on 'itler's side they could attack us there from Libya to get a hold of the Suez Canal what we're protectin' cos it's our link to India,' one of them told the other and grabbed the whisky, taking a deep drink. 'Make the most of yer leave, mate. I doubt either of us will get back again.'

'Don't be such a miserable so-and-so,' the second soldier said. 'I told my Kate I'd be back, and I shall.'

A whistle from outside alerted them all to the arrival of the train. Alice grabbed Davey's hand and he took her out in the wake of the soldiers. Several men and women disembarked and in the general hubbub, no one noticed the children. They entered the second-class carriage at the same time as the soldiers and no one challenged them. They settled down in a corner and the soldiers lounged over the rest of the seats, still drinking and muttering as the doors were slammed shut and then the train moved off.

After a while, as the soldiers appeared to fall asleep,

Davey motioned to Alice and took her out into the corridor. They walked through the almost empty train until they found an empty compartment near the toilets.

'If we hear the ticket inspector coming, we'll go in there until he's past,' Davey said.

'Why?' Alice asked, sucking her thumb.

'Cos we ain't bought tickets,' Davey said. 'I could've paid but he wouldn't let us travel alone.'

Alice nodded, her eyes wide and scared. 'I want Mum,' she said for the third time since leaving the shop. Davey sighed but didn't answer. He wanted to be home too, and he knew they'd be in trouble if they were caught, but he would keep a sharp ear out and if he heard the ticket inspector's voice, he'd be off to the toilets in a flash.

As it happened, the only time the inspector boarded the train was shortly before morning, an hour or so before the train reached London station after an interminable journey when it would stop in the middle of nowhere for ages for no apparently good reason. Luckily, Alice had wanted to go to the toilet, so they were already inside when the inspector went past. To be safe, Davey waited until the next stop before leaving the toilet.

No one else got on the train and they returned to their carriage and tried to sleep for a while. When they pulled into Liverpool Street Station, Davey woke Alice and they left the train. He felt pleased with the way things had gone and was grinning with triumph until he saw the barrier and the man collecting tickets at the end of the platform. So that's why they hadn't checked the tickets as often as he'd thought they might. He halted, panicking as to what to do – there was no other way out. Suddenly the two soldiers they'd avoided earlier came falling out of the carriage, drunkenly shouting and swearing, then they started throwing punches at each other.

Davey saw the ticket collector start towards the soldiers and, in the confusion, he and Alice slipped through the barrier unnoticed. Then, grinning in triumph, he saw that there was a café open and had a great idea. He would use some of Miss Bristow's ten shillings to buy breakfast for himself and Alice. It was too early to get Mum and Gran up and he was hungry.

Inside the café it was warm and smelled of grease and stale sweat. An old tramp was sitting in one corner drinking tea. It was him Davey could smell.

He told Alice to stay close beside him and went up to the counter. A bored-looking woman asked him what he wanted. He ordered a cup of cocoa and a bacon roll, which cost him one shilling and threepence.

When he'd been served, he carried the cocoa and the roll back to a table as far as he could from the dirty tramp and divided the roll between him and Alice. 'We'll share the cocoa,' he told her. 'Drink some of it but leave me a little.'

Alice ate her share of the roll with evident delight and licked the grease from her fingers. She drank nearly three quarters of the cocoa but there was enough left for Davey to wash his share of the food down. He considered buying more but decided he might need the money for other things. They still had some distance to travel to get home and the bus ticket collectors wouldn't let him get away with travelling for free.

Davey knew exactly which bus he would need to get home and he searched until he found the right stop. There was a surprising amount of traffic, despite the early hour, and they found a shelter where they could wait until the right number came along. Davey found seats at the back of the bus and handed over sixpence to pay their fares. He was given a penny change, which he put in his pocket with the other lucky pennies and the silver he had over from their breakfast. Miss Bristow's ten shillings had been very useful. Davey might have managed without it, but it would have been harder.

As the bus slowed down at their stop, Davey's feeling of contentment faded. He'd got them home, but Mum was going to be very cross with him . . .

CHAPTER 6

Dora was making a cup of tea in the kitchen when the pair of them burst in. They'd seen the light and couldn't contain their joy at finding her up so early.

'Mum, she was so nasty – we ran away!' Alice told her before Davey had time to give his carefully prepared speech. 'She was goin' ter make me scrub floors and they didn't feed us and—'

'What the hell are you two doing back in London?' Dora burst out. 'And where are your things?'

'She took them away,' Davey said. 'We couldn't look for them because they would've caught us – and he said we'd get the stick if I disobeyed him or cheeked him.'

'Had you been rude, Davey?' Dora's eyes narrowed.

'No, Mum. I didn't mind sweepin' his shop and clearing up, but she was nasty about Alice. I heard her say they would give her to someone else because she wasn't old enough to be much use.'

Dora felt a flash of anger but not with the children. 'They weren't supposed to make you work like that – a few small chores, perhaps, that wouldn't hurt

69

you, but not treat you like slaves. I'll go round later and complain at the council office.'

'Thanks, Mum.'

'I love you, Mum.'

'And I love you, Alice – both of you. I sent you to the country for safety, not because I don't care.' At that moment she meant every word. They were her kids and no one else had the right to hit them, though she might give Davey a tap now and then if he needed it.

Davey smiled up at her in approval and Dora's heart caught because he looked so much like his father at that moment. She steeled herself to resist the joy creeping into her heart. 'Just be quiet, you two. Your gran is sleeping at last. I've been up with her half the night and I want her to get some rest.'

'Can we have a cup of tea, please?'

Dora nodded. 'Are you hungry? I've only got toast and dripping – or a scraping of jam for you, Alice. There's only one egg and that's for Gran.'

'Is she any better?' Davey asked, feeling sad as he thought about the old lady he'd always loved.

'No, she's not and she won't be,' Dora said tonelessly. 'If you want the truth, she probably won't be around much longer so I need all my energy for looking after her and the few hours' work that I can manage now.'

Dora put the food on the table, nodding as her children ate it hungrily, even Alice. 'So those people didn't feed you,' she said. 'Well, I can't blame you for running away, then – and I'll be after your stuff. If they think they can sell that and get away with it, they've got another thing comin'!'

'Does that mean we can stay and help look after Gran?' Davey asked hopefully.

'No, it doesn't.' Dora knew she had to nip such hopes in the bud. 'It means I'm goin' ter get yer stuff and then arrange for you to go elsewhere.'

Alice pushed her unfinished bread and dripping away and started to weep noisily. Davey gave Dora his unflinching stare.

'We shan't stay there if we don't like it,' he said, jutting his lip. 'We'll go and we'll try it – but if they're horrid again, we shan't stay.'

'While you're here, you can make yourself useful,' Dora told him, refusing to give in. She gave him a tap round his ear to warn him. A little part of her wanted to put her arms around them both and tell them she would never let them go anywhere without her again – and that children's officer was going to get hell for letting them go to bad folk – but she was so very tired. It was proving almost impossible to look after her sick mother and work at the same time – and yet she needed those few hours and the little extra money they brought in. Food was expensive these days. Everything seemed to have risen in price since the start of the war and Gran couldn't eat a lot of things. She needed milk puddings, eggs, fruit and treats like a bit of tinned salmon in a little sandwich with the crusts cut off. It was no good serving her a stew made of scrag-end lamb, because she couldn't keep it down.

Dora was angry with her husband even though she knew it wasn't his fault, though yet again his promised wages hadn't arrived. And without Dave's money, Dora had no choice but to work at the same time as she cared for her sick mother. At this rate, she soon wouldn't be able to feed either of them properly – and she had no chance of giving the children the lives they deserved. Sending them away really was her only choice – or so it seemed to Dora that morning.

Rose had been giving her some funny looks recently, but Rose didn't have a sick mother to care for. She smothered the thought that her friend had offered to have the kids. Dora had no idea why she'd refused, perhaps pride or even jealousy? Dave always said what a decent woman Rose was and hard-working, but that had grated with Dora, as if he were comparing her and finding her wanting. A couple of times she'd thought Rose was after her Dave. But of course that was daft; he would never look at her when he could have Dora – so why not let her take them?

'I doubt we'll get things arranged for a few weeks,' she said and saw Davey's face light up. Alice was playing cat's cradle with a bit of wool and hadn't heard, but her intelligent son had and she could see the light of triumph in his eyes.

'Here.' Dora shoved a florin into Davey's hand. 'Go to the corner shop for me while I take Gran's breakfast up. I want a loaf of bread – and if they've got a couple of eggs to spare, you can bring them. I'll make a fatless sponge with jam filling for yer tea.'

Davey took the money and went out quickly. Dora knew that he would bring her shopping back safely and if he couldn't buy the eggs she needed, he would return with the change. He was a good boy and perhaps she could manage after all. She'd saved a little money to buy good food for her mother so perhaps she could find enough for the children too.

Rose was just leaving the corner shop when she saw him. She stared in surprise and then a big grin spread over her face.

'Decided to come 'ome, 'ave yer?'

'Yeah – they were awful,' Davey said. 'Alice was scared – they were goin' ter make her scrub floors or give her away, so I got us home.'

'And how did you do that?' Rose chuckled. 'No, perhaps it is best if you don't tell me, at least not now. Come round later and I'll have something for the pair of you.'

Davey grinned. He knew she liked him, Rose realised. She couldn't push Dora into letting her have the kids, because if something should happen to them, if a bomb should fall and kill them, she would blame herself. She hoped Dora wouldn't send the children away again and that meant Rose would be seeing them as much as she could.

Smiling to herself, Rose took her shopping home and then got ready for work. She was never late and she did her work well, even if she sometimes talked too much for old Icy Drawers, Mrs Winters, the supervisor, who considered herself above the line workers. If she was ever made a supervisor, Rose thought, she'd know better than to put on airs the way that one did.

Her thoughts went to Harry Smith. He'd reluctantly gone after his one cup of cocoa. Rose had felt sorry for him. She knew only too well how it felt to be lonely and for two pins she'd have asked him to stay the night, but it would have been all over the lanes in no time and Reg would go mad when he got back, and she didn't truly fancy Harry Smith, not enough to live with him.

Now, if it had been Dave Blake asking to stay the night . . . A naughty smile touched Rose's lips. She wouldn't have had to think twice about that one. She was laughing inside as she walked into the factory twenty minutes later. None so daft as a woman mooning over a younger man, she thought, mocking herself, but there was only three years' difference between them, after all . . . She shook her head scornfully. It was never going to happen.

Rose had had her chances with other men over the years. She wasn't bad looking with her glossy dark hair that waved naturally and her hazel eyes – a bit on the plump side compared to Dora, who had kept her willowy figure despite two kids, but she wasn't fat. She could have left Reg and found herself a new man, but she was too mindful of what was right to do that, which was the only reason she'd kicked a reluctant Harry out into the night. If she wanted to leave her husband, she'd do it the right way and tell Reg. He might let her go but he'd likely give her a black eye first. Worth it if she truly wanted someone else, Rose thought, but she didn't – at least, not anyone she could have . . .

Davey saw the man standing outside their house looking up at the windows as he returned with his mother's shopping. He recognised him at once because he'd seen his mother greet him with a smile many times.

'Are you waitin' fer Mum?' he asked. 'She's busy lookin' after Gran – me gran's real sick.'

'I thought you'd gone to the country?' Mick George said, looking at him uncertainly. Davey didn't like him, because he was always trying to send him off somewhere when he wanted to get Mum alone.

'I didn't like the people they put us with,' Davey said, 'so I came home.'

'Enterprising lad, aren't you?' Mick said and grinned suddenly. 'Want to earn a shillin' fer yourself?'

'Maybe . . . depends what yer want me to do,' Davey said carefully. Dad said this one couldn't lie straight in bed and Davey wasn't going to risk his father's disapproval by doing something against the law.

Mick took a handful of change from his pocket. 'Slip this into your mum's purse or her pot on the mantel when she isn't looking. I know she's short of money, but she won't take anything from me.'

Davey held out his hand. He looked at the half-crowns and florins and knew there must be at least thirty shillings. If Mick had given him notes Mum would know something was wrong, but Davey knew how to make sure she didn't catch on.

'I'll spread it around, in her pockets and the drawers and so on so she finds it a bit at a time,' he said and slipped it into his own coat pocket. 'Why are yer doin' it, mister – are yer sweet on her?' He gave Mick a hard look, daring him to admit it.

Mick considered for a moment, then inclined his head. 'You're a bright lad, Davey. I've always cared about Dora, ever since we were kids – but she fell for yer dad and wouldn't look at me. I don't mean her any 'arm, nor yer dad – just want ter make sure she's all right.'

'Yeah, I believe yer,' Davey said, because he thought Mick was genuine in this anyway. 'Thanks, fer the money. Me dad's pay ain't turned up again, must have got lost somehow.'

'It's the bloody Government department,' Mick said. 'They've mislaid somethin'. Dora needs to complain down the post office, fill out a form, but your mum was never one for fillin' forms.'

'Can you get it for her?' Davey asked. 'I'll see she does it, if you give it to me.'

'I'll see what I can do,' Mick replied and winked. 'You and me will make a good team.' He handed Davey another shilling, but Davey shook his head.

'Nah, you've given me money for Mum,' he said. 'I don't need payin' ter 'elp her.'

'All right,' Mick said. 'I'll be seein' yer then.' He sauntered off down the lane and Davey went into the house.

The money he'd accepted would help his mother a lot, but he knew his father wouldn't like it and nor would his mother if she knew but Davey reckoned that what she didn't know wouldn't hurt her.

He deposited the eggs and bread on the kitchen table. Alice had found a doll she'd left behind and was playing with it. Davey decided to follow his mother upstairs and see how Gran was getting on. As he reached the top of the stairs, he caught the stink of vomit and urine and hesitated. He knew Gran was ill, but she'd always put on a brave face with him and he hadn't quite understood what Mum had to do, but, as he stood in the hall and watched his mother struggle to lift Gran to change the soaked sheet beneath her, he realised just what caring for her meant. Running forward, he pulled the wet sheet out and saw the old newspapers Mum had put beneath it to save the mattress. There was a fresh pile on the chair beside the bed.

'Thanks, Davey,' she said and he could hear the relief in her voice. 'Are the papers soaked?'

'Yeah – shall I take 'em away and put them fresh ones there?' he asked and did so as she nodded. Gran's face was white with strain and he saw how old she suddenly was and how ill and it made him want to cry. Instead, he helped his mother straighten the bed and then took the wet papers and sheet down to the scullery.

He left them there and went into the kitchen, putting some of Mick's money into Mum's house-keeping pot and some into her purse. He shoved one half-crown down the side of Dad's chair and put another under the mat.

Mum came in before he had time to hide any more. 'What are you doin', Davey?' she asked and he produced the coin he'd been hiding under the mat.

'I just saw this,' he said and held it out to her. 'It must have rolled under the mat.'

'That's good,' she said, looking pleased. 'You've got sharp eyes. I've swept up a dozen times and never spotted it.' She looked at the things on the table and her few pennies change. 'Here's tuppence – you can buy some sweets and share them with Alice.'

Davey would have refused but she'd said he was to share with Alice so he couldn't. Anyway, he had more coins in his pocket to hide for her and they would keep her going for a while.

Davey visited Rose with Alice at tea-time. Davey had helped his mother as much as he could in the house, and after she'd gone off to work, he had taken his sister for a long walk down by the river, ending at Rose's house after the factory hooter sounded just after four. She'd had time to prepare a plate of sandwiches and had cakes on the table.

'There you are, my loves,' she said, and Alice ran to her, holding tightly to her hand. 'Sit you down and tuck in – there's jam and paste sandwiches and a nice Madeira cake for afters and rock buns too. I made them last night.'

'You must have known we were comin' home,' Davey said and grinned at her. 'If you've got any jobs, Aunt Rose, I can do them for you.'

'Well, you can sweep the yard and the path outside, and if you have time wash my downstairs windows.'

Rose smiled at him. She always gave him the same jobs, which he performed very well. It was a way he could earn a few pennies and she liked having him around on a Saturday morning, though at the moment she was working an early shift on Saturdays as well as her full-time job all week. The factory was working all hours and still they couldn't get the orders out quickly enough. Rose shuddered to imagine what was happening to all the stuff they churned out. The lives lost on both sides just didn't bear thinking about.

Rose didn't hate the enemy the way some folk did, because she blamed Hitler. The German who had kept the second-hand clothes shop in Commercial Road had been from that country and Rose had got on well with him, but he'd been forced to close his little shop and disappear as soon as the hostilities began, poor man. Rose often wondered where he was and how he was managing when she passed his empty premises. He'd done no one any harm but his windows had been smashed and the walls smeared with red paint, so he'd done the wise thing and disappeared. Rose hoped he was all right . . . perhaps he'd managed to leave the country and go home, though she seemed to recall that he was also Jewish, which meant he probably wasn't welcome there either.

Rose didn't understand why men seemed so keen on wars, rushing to join up and singing about it, as though it was something wonderful. All she wanted was a bit of peace and quiet now and then, and someone to love. There was a lot of love inside her and she'd long ago decided that it was a waste of time offering her affection to Reg. He didn't know the meaning of the word. At least for a little while she could lavish some of that love on Dave Blake's kids.

Davey was telling her something about Mick George, but she'd been lost in her thoughts and missed the first bit. She frowned at him. 'The less you have to do wiv his sort the better, Davey. You know yer dad wouldn't like yer hanging around 'im, love.'

'Yeah, I know,' Davey agreed. 'I know what I'm doin', Aunt Rose. I shan't let him get me into bad ways.'

'That's right, Davey,' Rose said and smiled. He wasn't a bad lad. He was his father's son through and through. She decided she didn't need to worry about him. His mother was another matter. She saw her struggling, and Rose worried about her a lot.

CHAPTER 7

Davey saw Mick George again three days later. He met Davey as he and Alice returned from going to the church playgroup, which had been set up to amuse the few children still resident in the lanes.

When Davey saw Mick, he was holding a brown paper carrier bag. He handed it to Davey. 'Tell your mum I sent these for Sally,' he said. 'She'll take them, but don't tell her about this . . .' He handed Davey a lot of silver coins. 'I've given you a few extra because I may not be around fer a while.'

'Where are yer goin'?' Davey asked and Mick hesitated.

'I've got ter make meself scarce,' he said and grinned. 'The coppers are lookin' fer me, been tipped the wink, see. Got a friend in the nick – heard it on the grapevine, see – and he told me they're comin' so I'm orf fer a while. Take care of yer mum, Davey.'

Davey thanked him and he was gone, whistling as if he hadn't a care in the world. Davey watched him go, wondering what it must be like to live the way Mick George did. He had money to spare – which most folk round here didn't – but he could be arrested and go to prison if the coppers got him.

Davey didn't think prison would suit him – and his dad would kill him if he did anything wrong, but Dad wasn't here and Mum would never know.

He decided he would tell her the things in the bag came from the church. She would never suspect any different and she might not accept them if he told the truth, despite what Mick said.

He unpacked the bag on the kitchen table. There were six eggs, a half a pound of butter, a packet of tea, a packet of chocolate digestives, some boiled sweets and a bag of sugar.

When his mother came in, she looked at the things in surprise. 'Where did this lot come from?' she asked.

'From the church,' Davey said with his fingers crossed behind his back. It was a lie but it was told for her good so that made it all right, didn't it? Davey felt a bit guilty, but he didn't think he could give it all back, especially when Alice had already grabbed the sweets and was investigating them with evident pleasure.

'Really?' His mother smiled with surprise, not suspecting a thing. 'That's wonderful, Davey. I must thank the vicar when I see him.'

Davey felt a cold shiver at his nape. Mum didn't go to church regularly, but the vicar hadn't given up on her and he called on all his parishioners in time. If Mum remembered to thank him, he would deny it and Davey would be in trouble . . .

The news of Mick George's arrest was followed by a visit from the vicar two days later. Rose had told

Mum about Mick's arrest when she called round to see her for a cup of tea, bringing a bit of fruit cake with her, eager to share it and her news with them.

'You could have knocked me down with a feather when I heard,' she said. 'I thought you'd want to know. They've got him this time, Dora. Everyone says he'll go to prison for five to ten years for burglary and receiving stolen goods.'

'Mick is a fool sometimes,' Dora replied crossly. 'It was the reason I turned him down when he asked me to be his girl years ago, and I would have even if I hadn't met Dave. Why must he steal when he could do anything? What did he steal?'

'Food, that's why they'll throw the book at him,' Rose told her triumphantly. 'He and some others robbed a van transporting tea, biscuits and stuff like that.'

'Food!' Dora was stunned. 'That's not his usual style – what made him do it?'

'Folk don't like it because the shopkeepers are charging more than they should,' Rose said. 'Mick must be a daft bugger, just like you said, cos he's been givin' the pinched stuff to all his friends and neighbours. Well, you know things like that get out.'

'What kind of things?' Dora asked, frowning.

'Tea, chocolate biscuits, sweets, cakes, all that kind of stuff.'

Mum looked thoughtfully at Davey but didn't say anything. However, when the vicar visited an hour or so later that same morning, she thanked him for the things the church had given them.

'Oh, it was nothing, Mrs Blake,' the vicar said, thinking she'd been one of the lucky ones to receive a packet of tea and a few biscuits by the ladies of the Mother's Union because of her own mother's illness. 'We'd have liked it to be more but times are hard.'

'It was still kind.'

'We do our best,' he said. 'Well, I wanted to speak to you. I know Mick George was a childhood friend of yours and I'm sorry there is such sad news. It was most unfortunate.'

'Unfortunate?' Dora frowned. 'Mick stole that stuff, vicar. He knew what could happen.'

'Yes – but he did it more for others than himself, at least this time,' the vicar sounded apologetic. 'I know one shouldn't condone theft, but he gave it all away to folk in the lanes. When they arrested him, he said he was giving back what had been taken by unscrupulous shop keepers.'

'Silly idiot,' Dora said crossly. 'He always was soft that way, that's why I can't help liking him, even though he's wrong to do what he does. Now he'll pay the price.'

'Yes, I'm afraid he will. They are getting very strict about food theft now – and you can understand why with all those merchant ships being sunk.' The vicar shook his head. If the Food Ministry didn't put the lid on these things, it would get out of hand and there might not be enough to go round, because most thieves sold their stolen food at inflated prices, which ordinary folk couldn't afford. It was only Mick who had given it away. 'Well, I must get on, but don't think too badly of him, Mrs Blake. It was a Robin Hood gesture, and I was quite touched by it myself.' The vicar stood up, preparing to leave.

Dora saw him to the door, but she shook her head as she shut it behind him. The vicar was a soft fool but even though it had been a rather nice gesture of Mick's it was plain daft. Mick might have known someone would blab.

She saw Davey sitting on the mat with his sister and her smile vanished.

'Davey, come here,' she said in a stern voice. 'I want the truth – and no lies. If you lie to me, I'll take your father's belt to you. Where did that food come from? It wasn't the church, was it?'

'No.' Davey hung his head. 'He said to tell you it was from him for Gran but I thought you might not accept it if you knew it was—'

'From Mick,' Dora said with resignation. She looked at him and then sighed. 'Don't you realise that stuff was stolen? What do you think your dad would say to that?'

'He would have refused it,' Davey said. He lifted his head. 'Mick knew you weren't gettin' Dad's money, so he wanted to help.'

Dora looked at him in suspicion. 'What else did you take, Davey?' Her gaze narrowed. 'He gave you money as well – that half-crown and a bit more. I knew I didn't have that much in my purse. I thought perhaps you'd earned a bit and not told me, but it was from him.'

Davey hung his head as the enormity of his crime came home. 'Yes. Sorry, Mum, but I knew you were worried.'

'I've been worried and tired and unhappy,' she told him. 'But not as unhappy as you've just made me,

Davey. You've lied to me and that means I can't trust you. You've let me take money from him – from Mick. I can't be beholden to him. You don't know what you've done.'

'He's been arrested . . .'

'That doesn't make it better,' Dora said. 'Well, I was thinkin' of lettin' you stay, but they've sent your stuff back and I've been told you can go somewhere else next week and that's just what you'll do.'

'Mum, please don't send us away! I'll earn the money and pay him back,' Davey said but Dora shook her head.

'No. I've made up my mind. You're goin' and that's that.'

Rose didn't like Mick George much. He was too sure of himself and she didn't hold with pinched stuff, but she had to smile when she heard the story. He'd been giving all that food away to friends and neighbours and despite doing something halfway generous, someone had reported him to the police. Well, that would teach him not to do daft things, though she wouldn't mind betting he would wriggle out of it somehow – Mick was the kind who would fall into a cesspit and come up smelling of roses!

At work everyone was talking about it and having a good laugh. Rose had a bit of a giggle with Harry Smith over it on their break. Harry often took his break at the same time as hers and they would chat. She knew he smoked, but never in the factory, where it would be dangerous, or around Rose, because she'd told him she didn't like the smell.

'It clings to your clothes and smells on your breath,' she'd told him the night he came for cocoa and since then she'd noticed the smoke smell had gone.

She asked him about it that morning at work. 'Given up the smoking then, Harry?'

'Yeah, I reckoned it was a mug's game – and me chest has been better since I stopped. I shan't start again.'

Rose smiled to herself. It took willpower to give up and you needed a good reason to drive you. Rose thought she might know Harry's and wondered if his resolution would last. She was pretty sure that he'd given up smoking because of her and she liked that. Some of the women she worked with were always trying to quit, but she knew most of them still had a crafty fag before they passed through the factory gates, though anyone bringing cigarettes into the factory would be instantly dismissed. It was far too dangerous. They handled inflammatory materials and one slip could make the whole place go up in flames.

'I wondered if you'd like to go to the flicks with me one night?' Harry asked that morning and Rose laughed.

'You're a trier, Harry Smith, I'll give yer that, but you know my answer.'

'You're a hard woman, Rose Parker,' Harry said but he was smiling. 'One of these days you'll say yes, you wait and see.'

Rose hid her laugh. She suspected that one of these days she might give in to temptation.

CHAPTER 8

'What do you mean you can't send Davey with Alice?' Dora asked the woman behind the desk. 'Last week the girl in your seat told me there was a family willing to take the pair of them. I told you, it's too hard to look after them and my mother – and my husband's navy pay hasn't arrived for more than three months.'

The woman looked bored but consulted her notes. 'It says here that you've already sent off your form asking where the money is, so it's sure to turn up sooner or later and the back pay with it.' She yawned, clearly uninterested in Dora's problems. 'We can split the kids up, but that's all there is on offer.'

'Where will you send Alice?' Dora asked. It wasn't what she'd wanted or been promised, but she couldn't cope with them both at home just now.

'The girl will be sent to a farm somewhere called Littleport – that's in Cambridgeshire. Not many miles from where she was before, in fact. They already have five other evacuees.'

'Five?' Dora was astonished. 'Are they made to work?'

'The boys might help on the farm sometimes, just small things, but we haven't had one complaint and no one has run away so it must be all right.'

'Well, I suppose that would be acceptable,' Dora said and sighed. 'What about Davey?'

'He's different; we've been told he was difficult to manage and we think he was behind the return home last time so he'll be given the chance of a new life in Canada. It's a wonderful country and the kids who get sent there are lucky. You'll either have to keep him or let him go – he can come home after the war if he wants to.'

'Are you sure it's safe?' Dora asked uneasily. This wasn't what she'd expected or hoped for – it was one thing to send him to the countryside, another to a completely different country where she mightn't hear hide nor hair of him. 'Supposing the enemy sinks the ship.'

'That isn't likely to happen. The U-boats are after merchant ships, not kids,' the bored woman said. 'Now, do you want the place or not?'

Dora hesitated a moment longer and the woman started to close her book. 'Do I 'ave to pay anythin'?'

'No, it's free,' the woman said and wrote something down. 'Have him here on Monday morning at nine sharp. They won't wait, so if you don't show you've lost your chance and you won't get another. He's lucky to be offered it after what he did.'

'He only came home,' Dora said, instinctively defending her son. 'He's not a bad boy.'

'Let him stop home and help you, then.'

Dora turned and walked out. For two pins she

would have told the woman what she could do with her passage to Canada. Her doubts gnawed at her all the way home but when she got there, Gran had been sick and there was blood in the vomit. Davey had gone next door to fetch the neighbour and for the next hour or so she completely forgot what she'd done in the turmoil of getting her mother cleared up and settled. She would have to ask the doctor to call again. This wasn't just her heart wearing out and Dora needed to know what was happening.

It was only that evening when she put Alice to bed that she told the children they were to be parted. 'I'm sorry but they wouldn't take you together,' she said. 'They think Davey would run away again and so they're splitting you up. It's a lovely farm with animals and things where you're goin', Alice.' Dora didn't know if that was true but the words checked the tears welling in Alice's eyes. She didn't say anything to Davey but as she'd expected, he asked.

'Where are they sending me, then, the coal mines?' His tone was harsh and angry.

'If they were, some would say you deserved it after all the trouble you caused. I had to pay good money to get your stuff back – cost of the postage and their trouble sending it. Besides, you've let me down, Davey.'

Davey's eyes were sullen as he looked at her. 'Where are you sendin' me then?'

'The only place for you is a new life in Canada,' Dora said not looking at him, because she would see accusation in his eyes. 'It's a wonderful chance for you, Davey – and after the war you can come home if you want.'

'I'm not goin',' he said, and she heard the stubborn note in his voice. 'Alice can't manage without me.'

'Yes, she can. She's nine now and you're eleven in July, Davey. You're both old enough to look after yourselves. I'll visit Alice when I can and I'll write to you, Davey. You can let me know where you are, and I'll send you cards and presents on your birthday.'

'I'll run away again.'

'If you do, I'll have to ask the orphanage to take you on,' Dora told him, feeling angry that he was making it so hard for her. Life was just too difficult and she needed a rest from having to look after her children. 'You know I have enough to worry about with Gran, Davey. Why can't you think of me for once?'

'Dad will hate you if you do this to us!' Davey said. 'Please, Mum, let us stay and I'll find work on the docks to 'elp yer. Alice will be miserable on her own. She might die of it!'

'Don't be foolish,' Dora snapped, her patience at an end. He made her feel guilty, just like Dave did when she didn't come up to his standards. 'You're goin' on that ship if I have to get someone to carry yer on board.'

Davey looked at her hard for a few minutes and then bowed his head. 'I'll never forgive you – never,' he said, 'and Dad won't neither.'

He was right. Dave wouldn't like it. Dora had a sinking feeling inside. 'I know, but it isn't my fault,' she said, resenting him for telling the truth. 'But you let me down, Davey. Remember that. You lied to me and shamed me.'

Davey got up and ran downstairs and out into the street. Dora had seen the tears in his eyes and her heart told her to go after him and tell him she loved him, promise she wouldn't send him away, but something stopped her. She didn't know what it was – some stubbornness inside or just plain worry. In the spare room, she could hear Gran being sick again and closed her eyes. It was too much. She couldn't manage. Besides, the children would be better off somewhere else. Davey was bright and he'd make something of himself in Canada; there was more chance for kids over there than here in London's East End. Some people who emigrated became rich and she'd heard it was a beautiful country. It might have been better to send Alice too, only the woman had said there was only one place left.

Davey ran and ran until he was out of breath and then bent over as the pain hurt his chest and he had to lean against the wall to recover. He'd been crying when he'd bolted but now his tears had dried and he just felt angry and bitter – against his mother, but also life. It wasn't fair that he and Alice were being split up just because they'd run away from that dreadful place. If they hadn't frightened Alice and had given them both a decent meal, they would have stayed – for a while, anyway. Surely it wasn't a crime to come home? Besides, despite what his mum said, Alice would be miserable without him to look after her like always. She would cry and be unhappy – and he'd promised his dad to look after her and now he couldn't. His throat felt tight with tears and his chest hurt but he held his emotions inside, because men didn't cry, did they?

'What's up then, lad?'

Davey looked round and saw a face he knew. 'I thought they put you in the locker?' he said and Mick grinned.

'They couldn't make the charge stick. Only one person's word and no evidence,' he laughed, 'it had all been eaten. I've got friends and a smart lawyer – he got me out. They'll need to catch me red-handed before I go down.'

'It's your fault,' Davey said bitterly. 'It's cos you gave me that stuff that she's sendin' me away!'

'You goin' back to the country then? It's best you do, lad. Once that Hitler's lot start bombing us, you could be killed.'

'I'm bein' sent to bloody Canada,' Davey said resentfully. 'Cos they say I'm too much trouble.'

Mick looked at him. 'How about I have a word with your mum? I might be able to get her to change her mind.'

'She'd likely give me a hidin' fer tellin',' Davey said. ''Sides, it is all your fault. We don't want nuthin' from you.'

'Well, if you change yer mind . . .' Mick sauntered off whistling and Davey watched him go, feeling angry. No one cared what happened to him. He might as well be dead.

He lingered in the pitch-black streets for as long as he could bear and then made his way home, half afraid that his mother would have locked the kitchen door. But it was open and there was a rock bun left on the kitchen table with a cold cup of cocoa. He could hear Mum upstairs moving about; she was looking after Gran again. It was a full-time job for her and she herself had only the sofa to sleep on now with Gran in her bed.

Davey sat down and ate his bun and drank the cocoa, even though it was cold and there was skin on the top. He was still sitting there when Mum came down carrying dirty sheets and he could see that she looked tired to death, her face grey and stained with tears.

'Is Gran dead?' he asked fearfully.

'No, but I sometimes think it would be better if she was,' his mother said. 'I hope to God I never see this much pain and mess again.'

Davey was smitten with guilt. 'I'm sorry, Mum,' he said. 'I'm just upset to be parted from Alice.'

'I know,' she replied with a sigh. 'I do love you both, Davey, honest I do – but it's too much for me. I'm goin' to have to pack my job in altogether and I may not get it back when she's gone . . . but I can't be up all night and work too.'

'I know. I wish I was older so I could help more.'

'So do I. I know you try . . .' she said and then she started crying.

Davey felt awful. He went to put his arms around her and she hugged him. 'Don't cry, Mum. It will come right when Dad comes home.'

'If he does,' she said. 'I haven't heard from him for weeks. I don't know if he's hurt or dead and I feel so alone . . .'

Davey wanted to tell her she wasn't alone and beg

94

her to let Alice and him stay, but he kept silent. Instinctively, he knew she was at breaking point. She'd never been as steady as Gran or Dad and he understood he couldn't push her any more.

'I'll go to Canada, Mum – but I'm comin' back one day. I don't want to stay there forever.' He'd promised Alice he would and somehow he would keep his word to her, though at that moment he wasn't sure how or when.

'You may love it out there,' Dora said half-heartedly.

'Perhaps I shall,' he agreed. 'But England is my home and I want to be with you, and Alice and Dad – when he comes back after the war.'

'That woman said you could come home after the war if you want, but she didn't say who would pay.'

'Dad will, cos he'll want me back,' Davey said, pretending to be cheerful. He wanted to cry and beg to be allowed to stay but pride had taken over and he couldn't say the words. 'I'll be all right,' he said stoutly for his mum's sake. She was so tired she couldn't take any more hassle and his dad would tell him to be strong for her. He would prefer to stay here and look after her, but it seemed she would be better off without him.

As if understanding what was in his mind, his mum smiled at him. 'I know you will, because you're strong and independent like your dad.'

The next couple of days went by in a flash. Gran was a bit better, and Davey's mother did some cooking, biscuits and cakes that the children liked.

She said they could each take some with them and for a while it was like it had been in the days before Gran got ill and Dad went off to war.

Mum had arranged for someone to look after Gran for an hour while she took Davey to the office. He wasn't the only one there that morning. Six other boys, most of them a few years older than Davey, and one little girl who was about the same age as Alice. Davey felt sorry for her because her grandmother had brought her and she was crying.

'I want Mummy,' she whimpered as her grandmother pushed her towards the others.

'Your mother is dead, girl, and I can't look after you,' the woman said, looking weary. 'God knows I've tried, but it's too much for me and you'll have a better life where you're goin'.'

The girl stood alone, tears rolling down her cheeks. Davey looked up at his mother. 'You'd better get home to Alice and Gran,' he said. 'Make sure you keep in touch with Alice, Mum. She'll be lost and lonely without me to take care of her.'

His mother's face was very pale and she looked as if she might burst into tears. 'You'll be all right, Davey, won't you?'

'Course I will,' he said stoutly, and she nodded, bent down and gave him a fierce hug and a kiss on the cheek, then turned and walked off without looking back once. Davey fought down the urge to scream and yell to her to come back. He waited until she'd gone and then he turned to the small girl, who was now sobbing. 'What yer,' he said with fake cheer. 'My name's Davey, what's yours?'

She hesitated a moment and then said tearfully, 'I'm Beth and I want ter go 'ome.'

'Nah, yer don't,' he said, still in the same upbeat tone that hid his fear. 'We're goin' on a ship to a new life in Canada. It will be fun!'

Beth stuck her thumb in her mouth, then, 'Where is Canada?'

'It's near America,' Davey said, remembering the atlas on the wall at school. 'It's a big country but it's nice there and we'll be together for a while.'

'Thank you, young man,' Beth's grandmother said looking relieved. 'Will you look after her for me?' She bent down and gave the girl a twist of sweets. 'I'm sorry, Beth. I'd keep yer if I could, but I can barely keep goin' meself these days. One day yer dad may come back and I'll let him know where yer are and he can fetch yer home.'

Beth's grandmother turned to Davey. 'Look after her,' she said and held out a shilling. 'Take it, I can't give yer any more than that, but take care of her, lad.'

'I'll try but I don't want the money,' Davey said. 'I don't think we can spend it where we're goin'.'

Two young men and a woman had entered the office. One of the men blew his whistle. 'Will mothers and relatives please go now?' he said. 'We want to talk to the children and we're leaving in five minutes.'

There was a general hubbub as children clung to the mothers who had been brave enough to deliver their children. Davey saw the group had grown by another three. Two more boys and a girl a little older than him. The girl gravitated towards them as the parents departed, giving Davey a nervous smile.

'Are you looking after your sister?' she asked. 'My name is Julie.'

'I'm Davey and this is Beth – but she isn't my sister.'

Julie nodded. 'My father was killed in France,' she said in a flat voice that hid her emotion. 'My mother is ill and my grandparents are dead. The council decided this was best for me. Is your mother dead, too?'

'Beth's is, but mine is looking after Gran. She hasn't got enough money or time for me or my sister. Alice is being sent to a farm but they said I should go to Canada, because I ran away last time.'

Julie nodded. 'I tried to run away from the orphanage. It was horrid there and I was afraid of . . . someone. It will be better in Canada. Matron told me so.'

'Yeah, Mum told me the same – do yer believe them?'

'I don't know,' Julie admitted. 'We'd better listen now – they're telling us something.'

They were being told to line up in pairs. Beth put her hand in Davey's and Julie tagged on behind them, another young lad coming to stand beside her. He heard the boy tell Julie his name was Arthur.

They were told they were going on a bus with other children to Dover, where they would go on board a ship.

'Many of you will be wondering what Canada is like,' one of the young men said. 'I was sent there when I was your age and I lived on a farm. The people that took me on were kind and I learned to love them. I've had a wonderful life out there and that's why I decided to come back and help transport more of you out there to the kind of life I've had, away from the dirt and fogs of London.'

None of the children said anything but Davey heard whispers and giggles. The man's kind words had helped many of them to get over their fear of the future and they all went quietly out to the bus and took the seats that were available to them. Davey, Beth, Julie and Arthur kept together in their pairs and once they were all on board it began to move off.

The woman came round and distributed a food parcel to each of them and a bottle of drink. 'You have to share the drink,' she said. 'One between two and they have to last until we're on board the ship.' She handed them paper cups. 'There will be a toilet break every hour or so but please try to wait and don't wet yourselves.'

Davey looked at her scornfully, but Beth squirmed in her seat. 'I want to go now,' she whispered to Davey.

'Please, miss,' Davey said and got a sharp look. 'Beth wants to wee now.'

'She should have gone before she left home.' The woman looked annoyed. 'Can you wait?'

Beth shook her head. 'I'll wet my knickers . . .' she whispered.

'Wait while I fetch the pot then.' The woman went off and returned with a china chamberpot, which she handed to Beth. 'Put it on the floor and squat down,' she ordered, looking at the curious faces around them. 'Avert your eyes, children.' She stood in front of their seat to shield Beth and Davey looked studiously ahead as Beth relieved herself near his feet. Once she'd finished, she pulled up her knickers and handed the pot to the woman, who looked at it crossly and then took it away, pouring it carefully into a bucket with a cover over it, although she spilled a few drops due to the motion of the bus.

'No one else wants to go, I hope?' she said. 'There will be a toilet break after we leave London.'

Beth was weeping silently. 'Don't cry,' Davey said. 'It's not your fault if you wanted to go. They should have let us go at the office – they must have a toilet there.'

'I wet my dress,' Beth explained. 'It feels horrid on my legs.'

'Here.' Davey took a large handkerchief out of his pocket. 'Dry yourself on this. It belongs to me dad. I found it in his drawer and I wanted something to remember him by.'

Beth accepted it gratefully. 'I'll give it back when it's clean,' she whispered and proceeded to wipe her legs and rub at her dress.

'It's all right,' Davey said and she smiled, offering him the packet of sweets her grandmother had given her. They were Tom Thumb drops and he took two of the tiny fruit sweets to suck. They were Alice's favourites too, though he preferred lemon sherbets or peppermint bullseyes.

As the time passed, more than an hour, Davey was sure, he began to look out of the window at the countryside. Except for his trip to Ely, he'd never been out of London in his life, so it was different and exciting and he began to think that perhaps Canada would be too. Maybe it wouldn't be as horrid as he suspected, and he would come home if he hated it.

CHAPTER 9

'I'd hoped the news would get better after Dunkirk,' Rose told Dora when she called round to see her that weekend. 'But it's gettin' bloomin' worse by the day – we ain't doin' very well, Dora, love. My cousin George's wife reckons them Nazis really are planning to invade us – she reckons come next Christmas we'll all be saluting and chanting like them Brownshirts . . .'

'You can't take notice of the papers,' Dora told her. 'I 'ad a letter from Dave yesterday and he reckons where he is things are fine.'

No wonder Dora was looking a bit more cheerful, Rose thought. She'd been distinctly down in the mouth since she packed young Davey off to Canada. Rose had been shocked when she'd told her what she'd done, angry too, but there was nothing she could do or say and she reckoned Dora was paying for it without her putting her oar in.

'He would say that so you wouldn't worry,' Rose replied with a shrug. 'Anyway, how is Sally now? I was wondering if I could pop up and see her?'

'If you don't mind the stink of vomit and piss,' Dora said, sighing. 'It gets me down sometimes, Rose. I miss the factory and the banter on the line.'

'Give me the chance to stop and I'd take it like a shot,' Rose told her. 'I thought you were gettin' yer money from Dave's wage now?'

'Yeah, thank God, and I got the back pay as well so I paid me overdue rent and bought Gran some soft cheese. I sent some sweets down to Alice, too.'

'How is she doin' then?' Rose asked with a murmur of sympathy for the little girl. 'Has she settled down there?' Knowing Alice, she suspected there had been a lot of tears when she was sent away without her brother to look out for her.

'She sent me a postcard sayin' she was fine and the farm animals were nice,' Dora said, 'but she had help with writing it so you never know if it's true. They may have told her to write it. I worry after the last place.'

'How do you know she 'ad 'elp?'

'Because farm and animals were spelled right – and while Alice is a great reader, she can't spell for toffee.'

Rose nodded. 'My old man can't neither. *I* know what he means, though he reckons it's code so no one knows what he's sayin' on them cards. That's all he's allowed to send, just a brief message.' Rose gave a cackle of laughter. 'Not that he'd send hearts and roses if they let 'im, but the daft so-and-so would probably say where he was and get himself in trouble.' Rose stood up. 'I'll just pop up and see your ma, Dora, so if you want ter nip to the corner shop or anything I'll be here until you get back.'

'I'll just go down the road then to the market. They're cheaper than the corner shop. Thank you.'

'You do what yer like. I've got time to stay for a while.'

The opportunity for a few minutes to herself was too good to miss. Rose always cheered her up and she'd been feeling down ever since she'd left Davey in that office – guilty, too, in a vague, uneasy way. Ought she to have let him go all that distance? Dora had begun to have doubts about the wisdom of it ever since Dave's letter arrived asking after the kids. Would he be furious with her for letting Davey be sent to Canada? He might not mind Alice going to the country so much – he could fetch her back from there, but Canada was a long way away and it would cost a lot of money to get there and back when the time came. Maybe there would be a scheme to fetch the kids back if you applied. After all, she'd got her back pay after she'd filled in that form thanks to Davey and Mick George who had told Davey what to do. So maybe there was a way of getting Davey back once she'd seen Gran through to the end.

Dora's mind wandered as she walked to the small market two streets away. It was just a few stalls that set up on Saturdays, but they had nice fruit and vegetables and were cheaper than the shops. She thought about Mick George. She'd seen him outside the house a few times and she'd found small gifts on her back doorstep – a bunch of flowers and some sugar and tea. No note accompanied the gifts, but she knew where they'd come from all right. She had no idea how he'd avoided the slammer and she'd been going to give the gifts back, but then she'd run out of tea when Gran wanted a cuppa, so she'd opened it and then it seemed daft not to use the sugar too. She wouldn't have taken money, but these gifts could easily be stolen as last time, and that made her uneasy. Mick was a thief and Dora hated that about him – yet his smile cheered her, and she'd waved to him when he'd stood underneath Gran's window and blown her a kiss the other night.

She had no intention of getting involved with him. She would be a fool to do something like that when she had a good husband. Dora pushed all thoughts of Mick George away. She was married to Dave and she loved him, though she wasn't sure when she might see him again. Remembering the question on his card about how the kids were doing, Dora felt that sense of unease. What was she going to tell him about his son?

She'd been told the children would have a chance to write once they were settled, but supposing Davey didn't? Supposing he just disappeared off the face of the Earth?

Dora suddenly shivered. If anything happened to Davey, her husband would half kill her! And things did happen. Ships were being sunk all the time. What if Davey and the other kids never reached Canada?

Davey was sharing a cabin with his friends, the two boys in the top bunk and the girls in the bottom. They should have been segregated but the girls had hung back when cabins were being allocated and by the time it got to their turn there was only one left. When asked if they minded sharing, Julie said she was used to sharing with her brothers at home and the slightly hot and bothered steward said that in that case it was all right. It was a lie, Julie didn't have any brothers, and when the steward left, she'd laughed.

'I sometimes make up stories to get my own way. Do you?' she asked Davey, looking triumphant.

Davey shook his head. 'Dad would take his belt to me. He says tell the truth and shame the Devil no matter what. You have to take your punishment like a man.'

'Daddy never knew I told lies,' Julie said. 'He thought I was his little angel . . .' Her face crumpled, her air of bravado slipping away. 'I wish he wasn't dead. I want to be back home with him.'

'Yeah, I know,' Davey said. 'We all want to be home but we're on this ship headin' for Canada and there ain't much we can do about it.'

'How long before we get there?' Arthur piped up. 'I don't like being on a ship. It makes me feel sick!' He followed this up by promptly bringing up his breakfast on the cabin floor.

'Ugh!' Julie wrinkled her nose. 'That's awful!'

'I'll clear it up, it ain't as bad as Gran's,' Davey said. He saw the rolls of toilet paper on the side table and seized one, pulling lots off so that he could wipe up all the vomit. The smell lingered and he wondered what to do with the paper. The funny little windows didn't open – or he couldn't see how to open them if they did, so he took his unpleasant tissue up the steps they'd come down earlier and made his way on to the deck. It was the first time he'd been up here since they boarded and were hurried away below decks. Crossing to the open rails, he threw the smelly mess as far as he could but the wind blew it straight back into his face and he heard laughter behind him.

'You need to check which way the wind is blowing, son,' a man with a beard and smiling eyes told him. 'Especially if you're emptying slop buckets.'

'My friend was sick,' Davey said, rubbing at his face in disgust.

'You cleared it up, did you?' the sailor asked and approached him. He was holding a wet cloth and he wiped it over Davey's face. 'It ain't dirty – only been cleaning a bit of paintwork. Captain's fussy about things like that.'

'Thanks.' Davey could still smell the vomit a bit but he liked the sailor so didn't let on. 'How long will it take us to get there, mate?'

'Depends on whether we have good weather. Mebbe a couple of weeks if we're lucky or three if we're not.' He grinned. 'If the captain feels like it, we can get there pretty fast, but we have to keep an eye out for squalls and mebbe a bit of ice sometimes.'

'From them icebergs what are at the North Pole?' Davey said and the sailor laughed.

'Know a bit don't you, lad? Are you a good scholar?'

'I like learning when it comes to things like that. Dad said I should be an engineer or somethin' – learn a good trade that was always needed.'

'Yeah, sensible that is. Where is your dad, then?'

'In the Royal Navy. He went to fight the Nazis.'

'Good man, then. I'm Albert,' the sailor said. 'I'm on deck early in the mornings, so if you need anything you just come and ask me, right?'

'Yeah, all right,' Davey said. 'When do we get fed?'

Albert threw back his head and laughed heartily. 'A man after me own heart,' he said. 'The steward will tell you, and I'll give you some good advice: you get as much down as you can, lad, because a lot of it may come back up.'

'Nah,' Davey said. 'Me dad's a good seaman. He worked on the cruise ships before the war and I'm like him.'

'Cruise ships, was it? Lucky him. I was in the Merchant Navy for years. I always fancied getting a trip in one of those fancy liners but never got round to it – and this job is just temporary. I like to stick to coastal work these days, don't like to be away from home too long at a time, see. Got me reasons.' He tapped the side of his nose and grinned. 'Well, I'd best get back to work but remember I'm here early mornings if you want to talk.'

Davey nodded and ran back the way he'd come. The cabin still smelled a bit of vomit, but the others were sitting on the bottom bunk, just waiting for him to return.

'Has anyone been to tell us where to eat?' he asked and they shook their heads.

'I'm 'ungry,' Arthur muttered. 'I feel bad.' He wretched again but nothing much came up.

Julie fetched a bit of paper. 'There's a sort of toilet in there,' she said, pointing to a small door. 'I couldn't find a chain. I think there's a bucket underneath.'

107

Davey looked inside the cubbyhole where a wooden seat had been set up over a bucket for them to use. He knew there were bathrooms, he'd seen them, but this was obviously meant to ease the pressure. With two to three hundred children on board and crammed into the cabins on all decks, the toilets would be busy places. It would be easier to use this makeshift toilet in the night and then empty it in the morning – in the bathroom rather than over the side, though. Davey didn't want to risk it all coming back into his face, though he didn't mind taking it down the corridor to the bathroom.

His thoughts were interrupted at that moment as a steward came to tell them that a meal was being served in the dining room for this deck.

'There are three decks,' he told them, 'in case you hadn't noticed. You're on the middle deck so don't get lost and don't go to the deck above or below. Remember your cabin number so you can tell a member of staff if you do get lost.'

Davey kept his mouth shut. He fully intended to explore as much of the ship as he could during the voyage and he knew the number of their cabin. By the time they reached Halifax, which was where they would be docking, he would know all he needed to know about this ship.

For a moment his thoughts went to Alice. He wondered how she was getting on in her new home without him to look after her. Davey had always protected her from other children, making sure she didn't get bullied, but now she would have to stand up for herself and he wasn't sure she could. The thought made his throat tight with emotion, because he could imagine her tears, and the memory of her clinging to him the night before he'd been sent away was sharp. He'd hugged her and comforted her, telling her that the war would soon be over and he would come back, but his heart ached for her. Could he ever redeem his promise to Alice and return for her? He'd think of a way. Somehow he would return to England and find her. He would, even if it took him years.

Much as the children might wish otherwise, the ship continued to steam ahead, night and day carrying them to a new life. As the days passed they got used to life on board. They were summoned for meals and were allowed on deck, shepherded like sheep here and there. Most of them were too scared to deviate from the orders they were given, but Davey had no fear either of the ship's officers or the sea. Whenever he got the chance, he went up onto the deck and met his new friend Albert quite often in the early morning and the sailor talked to him, telling him stories and things about the ship.

Standing on deck on the night of a storm, Davey watched the sailors battling the elements and thought that the storm would be frightening if you let yourself be scared. The sky was almost black, rent now and then by jagged spears of white light. Davey wanted to go to the rails and watch the sea boiling and thrashing around them as the waves hit the sides of the ship with tremendous force, but he understood there would be danger and the sailors would be distracted by him.

They were used to him coming up now and talking to Albert. He knew several by name now – Sam and Jack and Phil and Sid – and they were all friendly, giving him a pat on the head and sometimes a square of chocolate.

So as not to get in their way that night, he kept close to the stairwell, just watching, enjoying the excitement of his first storm at sea.

'What are you doing up here then, Davey?' Albert asked. He hadn't noticed his approach in all the noise of the wind. 'Be careful, lad – we don't want you going overboard.'

'I won't,' Davey said. 'It's great up here – I love it!'

'Ah, you're a proper seaman.' Albert nodded approvingly. 'Got your sea legs straight away. This is only a little squall, we'll be out of it soon.'

'I think I want to be a sailor one day,' Davey said. 'Maybe a fisherman.'

'Aye that's a good life but a hard one,' Albert said. 'I'm glad you're enjoying your first voyage, Davey.'

'I wish it would go on forever,' Davey said wistfully. 'I might not like what happens at the other end.'

'Why is that then?'

'The last place I went to, they were mean and only took us in so they had someone to work for them.'

'That won't happen in Canada,' Albert said but he looked thoughtful. 'We'll have to make sure you go to good people, lad.'

Davey grinned at him. 'Can I live with you and your wife, Albert?'

'I don't have a wife.' Albert's smile dimmed. 'I had

110

one once, but she couldn't stand me being away at sea so she ran off with a shopkeeper. She said he had more time and money than I could give her.'

'I'm sorry, Albert. I shouldn't 'ave asked.'

'Nay, lad. I was well rid of her.' Albert winked. 'Plenty more fish in the sea, eh?'

Davey nodded, but he suspected Albert cared more than he was letting on, because he looked a bit sad, though he was trying to pretend he wasn't – just the way Davey's dad did sometimes. Davey didn't know why his dad should be sad – unless it was something his mum did. Might be her flirting upset him. Davey felt a wave of loneliness suddenly and it made him say, 'I could live with you and then you wouldn't be alone when you got back from a trip.'

Albert didn't seem to notice. 'Off with you then, lad,' he said gruffly. 'Some of us have work to do.'

Davey nodded and went back to his cabin. It was daft to start missing his mother and father and Alice, because he knew he had no choice but to go on with the life he'd been given. He wasn't sure what would happen when he reached Canada, but in the meantime, he had friends to look after. He just hoped Alice was all right.

Alice glanced round the bedroom she was sharing with another small girl. It was pretty and there were two of everything; two beds, two white-painted chests, one holding her few things, and two chairs, also two washstands with jug and basin sets covered with pink roses. It was a very big, spacious room and Alice had never seen anything like it before in her life – and it was so clean. It smelled of lavender and polish and scrubbing and she liked that smell; it was a relief from the vomit and urine that had pervaded her own home before she left.

She sat on the edge of the bed and sucked her thumb, almost afraid to move in case she made a mess or did something wrong. Tears brimmed in her eyes but she dashed them away, because she'd learned crying never helped anything. Once upon a time her mummy and daddy had picked her up if she cried and kissed her better, but that didn't happen any more. Alice was old enough to understand that it was something to do with Gran being ill. She'd heard Mum say Gran was dying, but wasn't quite sure what that meant, though she thought it might mean Gran would be in Heaven.

One of her school friends had told her they put dead people in the ground and that had frightened Alice. She didn't want Gran to be put in the ground, but Davey had told her that when she died Gran would go to Heaven, and that must be right. Davey always told her the truth and she missed him terribly. If only he hadn't been sent away from her!

'Sure to be in Heaven,' her brother had said confidently when they'd spoken of where Gran would go. 'That's where all the good people go – to be with Jesus, so Gran will be there. You know who Jesus is, Alice. We celebrate His birthday at Christmas and He died to save us all, so there's nothing to be frightened of. Gran's spirit will be with Him and she will be happy. Remember how she used to say, "Sweet Jesus save us!" when we were playing her up?'

That had made Alice feel better but then they'd sent Davey off to somewhere called Canada and she'd been left at home with Mum and Gran for three days – and that had been difficult, because Mum was busy and tired and cross. Alice had cried most of the time until she was brought here.

It was nothing like when she'd been sent away before. She'd come down in a car and had lots of stops on the way for drinks and visits to the toilets. She'd come straight here, where she was expected and welcomed by Mrs Greene who had given her a glass of milk and a rock bun, then brought her up here and told her to rest for a while.

Alice hadn't tried to sleep. It was all lovely but overwhelming and she just sat timidly, waiting. When the door opened, she tensed, anticipating some sort of reprimand, but Mrs Greene was smiling as she entered.

'We've got a surprise for you downstairs,' she said. 'You'll have to share it with Mary – she's our other evacuee and she came from London too – but the boys have the dogs to take for walks and I know girls like to cuddle . . .'

Alice took her big, work-worn hand and held it tentatively as Mrs Green led her back down the stairs to the large airy kitchen. All the rooms in this house were so much bigger than Alice was used to.

A little girl with short blonde hair that curled all over her head was sitting on the mat, waiting. She was very pretty and smiled and held out her hands to Alice.

'Come and sit with me. Auntie Annie has something for us, but we have to share.'

Alice nodded and went to squat on the mat with her. 'I'm Alice.'

'I know. I'm Mary and we call Mrs Greene Auntie Annie.'

Mrs Greene had fetched a big basket into the kitchen. It was covered with a white cloth and Alice thought it must be a cake, but when the cloth was removed, a little head peeped out. She gave a cry of surprise and pleasure as she saw the black kitten with a tiny white spot on its chest.

Alice had wanted a kitten for ages but Mum always refused, saying it wasn't suitable where they lived, but now here it was – a real live kitten. She had to share it with Mary, but she decided that was all right.

'What's its name?' Mary asked as the basket was placed on the rug so that they could pet the kitten.

'That's for you two to decide,' Annie Greene said. 'And Mary is right. You may call me Auntie Annie if you choose, Alice.'

'Is it a little girl or a boy?' Alice ventured a question, her hand touching Mary's as they stroked the kitten's soft fur.

'A boy,' Annie told them. 'Ernie brought him in from the farm. The farm cat had another litter and we keep at least one out of every litter and give the others away. They control the pests on the farm.' Alice wasn't sure what pests were but didn't like to ask.

'I think we should call him Sooty,' Mary said, 'because he's mostly black – like the stuff in the chimney.' Her china-blue eyes fixed on Alice's face. 'Do you like the name?'

Alice decided that she did. 'You can take it out of the basket,' Annie said with a smile. 'I have to get on with dinner. The men will be in soon and there'll be no peace then, so you'll need to take Sooty up to your room. We'll put a tray of cat litter there and you can teach the kitten to use it.'

Mary nodded. 'We had a tray for our cat at home. We got it when my mother discovered mice in the pantry so she let me have a cat to scare them off, but when my dad went to war and she became ill she had to give it away and send me here – but it's only until she's better.'

'My daddy is in the Royal Navy,' Alice told her tremulously. 'Gran is ill – that's why I'm here, but Mum says she'll visit when she can and I can go home when it is safe.'

'Well, this is your home for now,' Annie said, looking up from the board where she was chopping onions and carrots. 'You'll go to school with Mary and you'll be fine here until the war is over.'

Alice didn't look up. She was absorbed by the kitten, its warmth and softness, and she wasn't sure what she wanted. If Daddy was home, she would gladly go but it was nice here in this big kitchen with Auntie Annie, Mary and the kitten.

CHAPTER 10

Dora looked at the most recent money order she'd received for Dave's pay and back pay. Perhaps if this had come more regularly, she wouldn't have let the kids go. She could have afforded to stay home and look after them all. Her thoughts had begun to dwell on the children more and more in the days that had followed Davey's departure for Canada. The time had flown by and dragged at the same time. She didn't want to admit it even to herself but she missed his cheery smile and independent manner more than she had expected. She'd had a letter from Dave that week and he wrote that he hoped he would be seeing her soon. As the days passed, she began to feel anxious about what he might say to her.

Hearing her mum's bell ring, Dora got up from the kitchen table and answered the summons. As luck would have it, her mother seemed to be in remission at the moment. She wasn't in as much pain – or she said she wasn't, at least – and she hadn't been sick as much recently.

As she paused outside the sickroom, Dora caught

the acrid smell. The brief period of remission was clearly over and it looked as though it would be another busy day looking after her patient. At least it would stop her thinking about the kids and feeling sorry for herself.

It was an hour before she was able to return downstairs. She put the dirty linen in the copper in the scullery to soak and went to the kitchen to make a cup of tea. Just as the kettle boiled, she heard something outside the door and looked up, wondering which of her neighbours was about to walk in. Most of them didn't bother to knock round here and sometimes that could be inconvenient. She braced herself as the door opened and then Dave walked in. Dora felt a surge of delight and moved towards him eagerly.

'I've just made a pot of tea,' she said, smiling at him, but her smile faded as she saw his cold look and knew he'd heard about the kids.

'Where's my son?' he demanded. 'Tell me, Dora – is it true? Have you sent him off to Canada on his own?' Her face must have reflected the truth, because his became tight with disgust. 'A boy who's not even eleven yet, a boy you were supposed to love, and you sent him away.'

'Dave, my mother is very ill. I couldn't cope and your wages weren't paid for a long time. Someone mislaid a form and I had no money to buy food for them. Besides, everyone said it wasn't safe here . . .' Dora's excuses tumbled out but she could see they fell on deaf ears.

'Have you had one bomb drop yet?' His anger cut like a knife.

'N-no . . .' she said and her heart stopped as she saw the ice in his eyes. Dave had never looked at her so coldly. 'I told him you'd fetch him back after the war.'

'You damned bitch!' Dave loomed over her and lifted his hand. For a moment Dora thought he was about to batter her but his hand froze in mid-air and then he lowered it again. 'No, that's too easy. Where's Alice? I've been told she's gone too.'

'She is in the country, on a farm. I had a letter from Mrs Greene, the farmer's wife, telling me she has a kitten and is settling in well.'

'You can count yourself lucky she is, because if anything bad happens to either of my kids resulting from what you've done, I'll swing for you, Dora. You'll wish you'd never been born by the time I've finished with you.' He dumped his kitbag on the floor and turned towards the door again.

'Where are you going? Don't you want a drink or something to eat?'

'Not with you,' he said bitterly. 'I'm going round the council office and I'm going to tell them to get my boy back, and I'll go down to see Alice wherever she is.'

'B-but what about me?' Dora asked.

Dave turned his cold eyes on her. 'You can go to hell, where you belong, Dora. Any woman who deserts her kids for her fancy man isn't worth the spit.'

'It wasn't for a man – my mother is sick!'

'Aye, and that Mick George has been seen hanging around, bringing you things. Don't expect me to believe you haven't been seeing him. Sally sleeps sometimes. I'm not a fool, Dora. I know you fancy him.'

'No, Dave, please, it isn't like that!' Dora cried but he'd gone.

Her eyes filled with tears because she did love him. She always had – and she did wish she hadn't sent Davey away. It wouldn't have been so bad if he'd gone to the country, but Dave would never forgive her for letting his son go all the way to Canada. Dora knew he never spoke idly. If something bad happened to either of the children, he would kill her . . .

Alice was in the school playground at break when the teacher beckoned her. She looked at Miss Robinson uncertainly but the teacher was smiling.

'You've got a visitor,' she said, 'who is waiting over there?'

Alice looked in the direction the teacher indicated and gave a little scream of delight. 'Daddy!' she cried and rushed at him. He caught her and swung her high in the air. 'Are you home for ever?'

'No, just for a short visit,' her father said and gave her a big hug. 'I wanted to make sure you were all right, Alice.' Setting her down, he took her hand. 'Your teacher says I can take you back to the farm so we can talk to Mrs Greene.'

Alice looked up at him in wonder. 'I thought I'd never see you again,' she confessed, clinging tightly to his big hand.

'I'm fighting to keep you and everyone safe,' her father said, 'but I'll always come back, Alice – that's a promise.'

Alice didn't know that it was a promise no man fighting for his country could be sure of keeping. She simply looked up at him with adoration, skipping along at his side.

Once they got to the farm, Auntie Annie was pleased to see him. She put her big kettle on to boil and made a pot of tea, and she got the cake and biscuit tin out. Her cakes and biscuits were always homemade and her father remarked on how good the oatcakes were.

'I can see Alice is settled and happy here,' he told her. 'Are you prepared to keep her until I can return to collect her, after the hostilities are over? I can't pay much but I will pay something towards her board and lodging.'

'Bless you, Mr Blake,' she said with a smile. 'We're only too pleased to look after your Alice. She's been as good as gold and I love having her with me. She's learning to cook, aren't you, Alice?'

'I like cooking with Auntie Annie,' she said and looked at her father. 'Have you seen Davey?'

'No, but I'm going to find out where he's been sent.'

Auntie Annie looked at him. 'If I'd known before Alice arrived, I'd have had him here. We've got several boys and they're always into mischief but one more wouldn't have made much difference.'

'Unfortunately, the council decided Davey would be better off in Canada and I think my wife got pushed into the decision. Once I know where he's been sent, I'll be doing whatever I can to get him home.'

'Well, I suppose he might be better off over there,' Auntie Annie replied. 'They have plenty of food and resources and it's safer there than Europe.'

'Aye, if he were with folk he knew,' Dave agreed. 'But I'd rather he'd come here.' He smiled at her. 'At least I can rest easy in my mind knowing she's safe here.' He looked at Alice with love. 'I know you'll take care of her.' He took out his wallet and extracted two pounds. 'I know it isn't much, but I'll send more when I can.'

'I'll keep it for treats for her,' Auntie Annie said. 'You don't need to do it, Mr Blake, but if you want to that's up to you. We're lucky here on the farm and we wanted to do our bit.'

'We've been lucky she landed with you,' he said, nodding at Alice and then he stood up, shaking hands with Auntie Annie. 'I'll be on my way. I've still got things to do, but thank you for caring for her.'

'Who could help it? She's such a lovely child.'

He bent down and kissed Alice. 'I shan't take you back to school because you would be coming back home again shortly, but you be a good girl for this nice lady and I'll come and see you when I can.'

'Is Mummy coming to see me too?' Alice asked. 'She said she would, but she hasn't yet. She sent me some sweets once . . .'

'Your gran is ill and she has her hands full,' he replied, looking a bit strange. 'Just you remember we love you and that I'll be back.'

Alice and Auntie Annie went out to the gate with him. He was just in time to catch the bus he needed to take him to the railway station in Ely and he waved before he got in and the driver moved off. The bus stop was right outside the farm gate and Alice knew that Auntie Annie used it on Thursdays to go to the market. Alice also knew that the village near the farm was called Littleport and that it was just a few miles

121

from the market town she'd been sent to the first time she'd left home. Davey had taken her home then but he wasn't here now and she wished he was, because it was really nice here and it would have been even better if they could be together.

'I didn't show Daddy the animals or my kitten,' she said, feeling disappointed, after he'd gone. 'He didn't stop very long.'

'No, he won't have a very long leave and he has to go back to London before he returns to his ship.'

Alice nodded. Even before the war, Daddy's visits had often been short. They were always fun and happy times, but this had been extra short and it made her feel a bit tearful.

'Come along, Alice,' Auntie Annie said and held tightly to her hand. 'You can help me start to get tea ready. All the boys and Mary will be back soon.'

Alice went with her, smiles restored. Daddy had given her a little packet of sweets, which were in her pocket. She would share them with Mary but not with the boys, who were boisterous and sometimes pulled her or Mary's hair. They got into lots of trouble, scaring the chickens and the ducks, sending them scattering through the farmyard – and she'd heard Auntie Annie's husband scolding one of them for teasing the pigs. It was Josh who was mostly in the midst of the trouble. He wasn't much older than Davey but he was cheeky and caused a lot of chaos in the farmyard at times. Alice didn't like him much.

She wished that Davey had been here to protect her from Josh and stop him pulling her hair. Alice still had no real idea where Canada was; her teacher had showed her on a globe but that didn't mean much to her. She knew it was a long way, though, so she didn't think Daddy would have time to visit Davey and she felt sad for her brother wherever he was. Alice wasn't sure whether he would still be on the ship or in Canada, but she hoped he was all right.

Dora looked at her husband as he stood in the kitchen, her heart in her mouth as he just stood there without speaking. 'How is Alice then?' she ventured at last.

'Alice is lucky. She is being well looked after and I've asked if she can stay there until I get home for good.'

Dora hardly dared speak, he was so angry. 'I thought she could come home after Mum's gone, it can't be long . . .'

'No!' Dave gave her a hard look. 'I don't trust you, Dora. She's better off where she is. I just wish I could say the same for Davey.'

'What do yer mean, better off where she is – and what about Davey?' Dora's heart sank. Something must have happened for him to look so bleak. 'They told me all the kids go to good homes out there.'

'Well, they've lost their records of where Davey went,' her husband said and she gave a little start of distress. 'Don't make out you care. You don't or you wouldn't have let him go.'

'But how could they lose the record of where the children went?' Dora said. 'It was all written down in a book – he was going on a ship to Canada.'

'That much they know – but they don't know what happened to him when the ship docked in

123

Halifax,' Dave said gruffly. 'The woman in the office said when the children disembarked he wasn't anywhere to be seen. The children he shared a cabin with denied all knowledge of his whereabouts.' He glared at his wife. 'I'm not leaving it there, Dora. I'll be doing all I can to find out what happened. I've been told he was on the ship a few hours before it docked but then he wasn't; they say a thorough search was made but they couldn't find him. He'd simply vanished.'

Dora sat down, feeling sick and faint. 'He's drowned,' she moaned and put her head in her hands, the tears coming noisily. 'My Davey's dead and it's all my fault.'

'You shouldn't 'ave let him go,' Dave said heavily. 'But it ain't your fault, Dora. Someone should've been looking out for him.' She glanced up at him and saw the grief in his face but his anger had gone, at least for the moment. 'We don't know if he's alive or dead yet – and I can't think he's gone. Davey was too sharp to have fallen overboard, leastways, he wouldn't unless there was a nasty accident. The woman swore to me that she knew nothing more and that it may just be a slip-up, that someone probably neglected to tick his name off the list. She says it hasn't happened before to her knowledge and she's goin' to look into it for me.'

Dora looked up at him, hope in her eyes. 'So, there's a chance he's all right? He could still be alive?'

'Knowing my son, I'd say so. I want you round that office every week, Dora. I have to return to sea but you've got to plague the life out of them until they tell you what happened to him. Promise me you will?'

Dora took a deep breath and then nodded. 'Yes, I'll

go every day until they tell me what happened to Davey,' she said. Hesitating for a second, she went on, 'I'm sorry I let him go. I was tired and worried and I didn't think it through properly. I thought he'd be all right.' She really had thought he would manage fine. How could he simply have disappeared?

'They told me you might not have got a choice anyway,' Dave said. 'Davey was on a list as being at risk, because of running away from that shop. Apparently, those shopkeepers said he'd been very sullen and uncooperative. A lot of kids are being sent overseas even if their parents don't want them to go. Most are orphans or victims of abuse, but it's policy to send the kids if they're livin' in poverty – and with you not gettin' my money regularly . . .'

Dora held her breath. Was he forgiving her? Her hopes faded as he picked up his kitbag. 'I have to get back to the ship. I'm not sure what happens next, Dora. You've let me down – but if you make sure you do what you can to find him, maybe we can sort things out next time I'm home.'

'I'll do me best,' she promised and then he was gone, without kissing her goodbye – the first time ever. Upstairs, she could hear her mother being sick and she turned wearily to go up to her. It wasn't fair! She'd done the best she could. It was all the fault of this rotten war. If Dave had been home, none of this need have happened. And yet, she knew deep down that it was her fault. She could have refused to let Davey go, could have insisted he went to the countryside or kept the kids at home with her . . .

CHAPTER 11

'Where are we goin', then?' Davey asked, looking up at Albert as they got on to the coastal bus. He'd been staying with Albert in a boarding house near the docks since leaving the ship nearly a week earlier. 'I thought you had to report to your new ship in a couple of days?'

'I do,' Albert said and frowned at him. 'But I have to settle you first. That trick you pulled when we docked, that was what decided me. I'd had it in my mind to see if the captain would let me take you on, but I wasn't certain he would, then when no one could find you, the folk who wanted you to live with them gave up and went home. They live a fair distance away and weren't best pleased – moaning about the cost of the fares and hinting they wanted compensation. I didn't much like the look of them, so I never let on I knew where you were.'

'How did you know where I was?'

'Because you asked questions about the best places to hide on a ship and I told you that the lifeboats were always the first place we look for stowaways and that if I was hiding I'd go into the food store and get behind the empty boxes because they're unloaded after we dock but not for some hours, by which time it would be safe to come out and get in one of the lifeboats.'

'That's what I did. Someone looked in the store-room but only a quick glance round.' Davey nodded, feeling pleased with himself. 'I didn't want to be found when the others were being taken off. Those people who came for me run a hardware store – and I didn't fancy it,' he said as if that explained his actions. Two days before they'd docked, the purser told them who they had been assigned to and Davey decided to hide. There was no way he was going back to another family who wanted him to work in a store. His dad had always told him not to go off with strangers, but Albert was his friend now. 'I was thinking if I could stay hidden until the ship went back to England, I could remain on board and sneak off when we got back home, but then you found me.'

'You'd have had a long wait. The ship is going to load a new cargo here and then they're bound for Malta,' Albert said. 'They won't be back home in England for many weeks yet – you would have starved unless you managed to steal from the kitchens.'

'But you're not going to Malta with the ship?' Davey was puzzled.

'No,' Albert said. 'I only signed on for that last run because I wanted to see a friend of mine in England. I prefer the shorter runs between here and the United States if I can get them. And safer by far than the Atlantic run with America not being in the war; that apart, it suits me better.'

127

'Why?' Davey asked curiously.

'I've got a particular reason and you'll find out soon enough. If he'll take you on, we're home and dry, but if he refuses, I'm blessed if I know what to do with you, lad.'

'Put me on a ship goin' home,' Davey replied. 'I thought I could mebbe live with yer for a bit? I could work and earn my fare.' He gave Albert a pleading look. 'I'll work hard – whatever you want.'

'Will you take care of someone for me while I'm away on my voyages?' Albert asked him. 'My father was a sailor. Merchant ships like me for years and then a deep-sea fisherman for a while. Now he lives alone in a little shack in a very isolated spot. There are woods, a lake and a long sandy beach along the inlet. The Mi'kmaq people have homes in the area but they're pretty spread out so it's a pretty solitary way of life.'

'Who are the Mi'kmaq?' Davey asked, his interest caught. 'I don't know the word.'

'It's the name of some of the indigenous people – folk who lived here long before people like us came, Davey. They lived by fishing and hunting and made everything else they needed themselves and they signed treaties with Britain in the eighteenth century which allowed them to go on living the way they did, unlike tribes in other areas when the European settlers moved into their traditional lands. These other tribes lost some of their proud heritage and now they live as best they can. Some move near the towns and take modern work but others try to carry on in the old way.'

'That's sad, and it's not right.'

'I agree with you, Davey. It wasn't right they should lose what was theirs and my father says it goes against the grain with him, but the powers that be ignore the likes of us.'

Davey nodded. He hadn't wanted to be put on a ship for Canada, but it had happened. 'And where does your father live?'

'It's where we're going now, lad. He's getting on in years, and though he manages to trap or fish much of his food, I worry about him, especially at night. He's so independent he won't move nearer to the only friends he still has, where I could get him a woman in to clean and cook now and then and a doctor to call. He's too stubborn and independent. He resists all attempts to help him. My plan is to tell him I want him to look after you.'

Davey looked at him for a long moment. 'Yeah, I'll do that – and will you send me back to England one day in return?'

Albert reached out his arm and offered his hand and they shook solemnly. 'That's a bargain, Davey. The old man doesn't have more than a couple of years in him, but I want him to be comfortable in his last days. You care for him and I'll make sure you get home – I'll take you myself.'

'Right. I'll do my best, but if he's anythin' like my gran, he will insist on doin' most things himself.'

'I just can't bear the thought of him lying ill, perhaps too feeble to get up and make himself a cup of hot coffee.'

'I ain't never made coffee, but if you show me,

I can do it,' Davey said. 'I can make tea. It ain't that much different.'

'Pa will show you how he likes things . . .' Albert hesitated. 'He's got a rough tongue on him, but you won't mind that?'

'Nah. A lot of the blokes round where we live curse and go on somethin' awful,' Davey said. 'Mum didn't like it much, but Dad said to ignore it.'

Albert nodded and grinned. 'You'll do, lad. I reckon the pair of you will get on fine.'

Davey nodded. They'd stayed in port for a day or so, because Albert had been looking for work of the kind he preferred and needed. Davey understood why he didn't want to make the longer voyages. He wanted to be able to visit his father and take him food supplies.

They left the coastal bus at a small town and Albert hired a truck and then went into the only food store in sight. He came back from the store loaded with a big heavy sack filled with tinned foods, flour, coffee beans and sugar. As he got into the driving seat of the hired truck, he grinned at Davey.

'Pa likes sugar; it's one of his few luxuries. He fishes from the beach and snares small mammals for his food mostly, but I bring him this food each time I come back so if his snares are empty for a few days, he has something to eat.'

Davey grinned. 'Is it all gone when you come back?'

'Mostly,' Albert said. 'He asked me for tinned peaches this time and some strawberry jam.'

'I like jam,' Davey said. 'Ma usually kept it for Alice and I had the dripping she bought from the butcher. It was all right, although I prefer jam, but there wasn't enough for both of us all the time.'

'Good thing I bought four large jars then,' Albert said, smiling. 'You won't get many luxuries here, Davey. You might have got more if you'd gone with the folks that came for you. I dare say they were decent people, though a bit on the tight side the way they were moaning about the expense.'

'I don't want to work in a shop even if they are nice folks,' Davey said. 'I'm going to be a seaman one day – like my dad and yours. Like you too.'

'Yeah, I reckon it is in your blood, just like it was in mine. My first memories are of Pa taking me out on his fishing boat – not the one that went deep-sea fishing, he never owned one of those, but a rowing boat. Sometimes the sea was calm and smooth and other times Ma used to fear we'd both be drowned it was so rough – but we always got back safe. Pa said if you treat the sea with respect, she does the same for you. I ain't sure that's true any more.'

'I thought we might sink the night of the storm,' Davey said. 'But I wasn't afraid. It was exciting.'

'Aye, that's the way she gets you,' Albert replied with a thoughtful look and then nodded. 'I think you'll get on well here, Davey. Pa will resist at first, but he'll like you.'

'I hope so,' Davey said. 'What will you do with me if he won't have me?'

'Mebbe you'll have to go to the hardware store after all.'

Davey shook his head. Some of the children had been taken miles across Canada, far away from the sea to all kinds of locations; farms, shops and industrial towns, according to the information the purser had given them.

'We're trying to give you a similar background to the one you came from only better,' he'd explained when the children were gathered. 'In some cases, you may not be able to stay in a similar environment, but mostly we've sent you to towns, because most of you came from London.'

Some of the children had looked pleased and chattered excitedly, others looked scared or miserable. The girls who had travelled with Davey were going inland to a farm together and they seemed happy enough, because they liked animals. Arthur had been assigned to a tailor who had two little girls of his own. It sounded a good match for him, because he'd tended to cling to the girls on the voyage out. Davey wasn't sure where he was to have been sent, but Albert told him it was a small town a bit further down the coast, though some miles inland.

The scenery was changing now and they had left all sign of civilisation behind; farms, houses, even proper roads were no longer to be seen. Here it was wilder, with lush growth and huge trees that Albert said were Douglas firs, and he caught sight of water sparkling here and there through the trees.

'There are lots of small lakes and inlets hereabouts,' Albert told him. 'A lot of wildlife too – and some of it is none too friendly, Davey. If you meet bears, just keep still and do nothing to attract their attention, cougars too, though they're mostly over there,' he said, pointing in the direction of the dark smudge of mountains that were shrouded in mist that day. 'There are a lot of things that might enjoy feasting on a small boy from London, so best stay close to the shack and Pa until you learn what's dangerous and what is more likely to be afraid of you.'

Davey looked at him anxiously, unsure whether he liked the sound of this new life. 'Supposing he doesn't want me?'

'I'll take you back and find someone to look after you until I can sort things out.'

'I'll find a ship going back to England and sneak on board.'

'You'd need a stock of food with you,' Albert told him with a wry smile. 'Otherwise, you'd get caught creeping to the kitchens. Stowaways don't often manage to hide from the crew.'

'What do they do when they find them?' Davey asked curiously. 'Would they throw me overboard?'

Albert looked thoughtful. 'Once upon a time they might have marooned you on a deserted island or made you work your passage, if you were lucky, but it depends if they like you – someone might help you to hide out and give you food. Otherwise, the captain would be informed and he could lock you in the hold and then hand you over to the authorities in the next place they'd dock – and who knows what they would do?'

Albert looked stern and Davey shivered. It would be a desperate measure to be a stowaway. He just had to hope that Albert's pa liked him.

*

Sitting in his corner of the shack, which was surprisingly tidy and clean and smelled of a woody scent, eating a chunk of fresh bread and some cheese, Davey listened to the argument between the two men.

'I'm not a fool!' The old man sounded angry. 'Do you imagine I can't see through you, boy? You want him to keep an eye on me. It's plain daft! What good is a lad like that to me?'

'He's a bright boy. Besides, he has nowhere else to go. He'll be no trouble to you, Pa – and he can help in lots of ways. Davey can light fires, make coffee – if you show him how you do it – and fetch and carry. Teach him what you want him to do and he will.'

'Nowhere to go?' Albert's father turned to where Davey sat wiping his mouth on his sleeve. 'Ain't you got no manners, boy? Where's your handkerchief?'

'I lost it,' Davey said. 'I gave it to Beth on the bus cos she'd got wee on her dress and was cryin' and I never got it back.'

'That was daft,' the old man said. His hair was thin and grey and his face weather-beaten and wrinkled, but Davey noticed now that Bert had a twinkle lurking in his eye and his courage asserted itself. 'Always make sure you keep what belongs to you – and get back what you lend.'

'I was bein' a gentleman like me dad told me,' Davey said cheerfully. 'She cried a lot, see, and I felt sorry for her.'

'Looked after her, did you?'

'Yes, sir.'

'You don't call me sir – my name is Bert, like my son. Only he prefers the name his mother gave him.'

'Yes, Mr Bert,' Davey said respectfully and the old man gave a snort of laughter.

'Determined little monkey, ain't you?' He turned back to his son. 'Well, you've saddled me with him so I suppose I'll keep him for a while – but if he's trouble, I'll send him to the orphanage in Halifax.'

'Yeah, all right, Pa,' Albert said in a relieved tone. 'He won't be any problem, will you, Davey?'

'No, Mr Bert,' Davey said. 'I'll do whatever you ask me to do.'

'How old are you?'

'I'm eleven now. I 'ad me birthday on the voyage out here.'

'You didn't tell me,' Albert said. 'I'd have got you a cake or something.'

Davey shrugged. 'It didn't matter.'

'Birthdays are for girls and women,' Bert grunted. 'Your ma set store by birthdays, but I always thought she was making you soft, boy. Davey here has got it right. They don't matter. It's just another day in another year.'

'Ma liked something nice on her birthday and you always got her something,' Albert objected. 'I remember the clock you brought back one time, and a wireless another year.'

'Like I said, birthdays are for women,' Bert replied gruffly. 'Your ma didn't get as much as she should have, but we did our best for her until she went . . .'

Davey caught sight of tears in the old man's eyes and his fear of him vanished in an instant. Bert wasn't as tough as he made out; there was a soft spot inside him for the wife who had died of a fever some fifteen years earlier. Albert had told him about that on the journey here.

'What do you want me to do?' Davey asked, looking round. He couldn't see that much needed doing. Bert kept the place well – better than he'd expected from what Albert had said.

'I'll find you some chores later,' Bert said. 'Go outside now and have a look round. I want to talk to my son in private – and don't think you'll get away without schooling. You can't get to a school living here, but I'll send word to friends of mine and they'll arrange for a whole chunk of books and lessons to be sent out here. And if I catch you shirking, you'll feel my belt.'

Davey went outside. He could smell the salty tang of the sea even though he couldn't see it. The shack was set down in a hollow where there were trees and a vegetable patch but he knew the sea was just over the bank of tough grasses and wildflowers. He climbed to the top of the bank and looked out, feeling thrilled by the stretch of dark golden sand. The tide was going out, he guessed, and the sea looked calm. Here in the inlet, it was protected from the worst of the sea breezes which, Davey supposed, could be harsh when the winter wind blew in from the Atlantic. On the beach he could see nets laid out in the sun to dry and there was a rowing boat pulled high up the shore and anchored. He wandered over to it and then turned to look around him. Behind him he could see lush vegetation, lots and lots of trees, closely packed together, and smaller bushes with big leaves. It was an isolated place, some considerable distance

136

from the town where Albert had hired his truck for the journey out here.

Davey wandered about the shore, picking up coloured stones and bits of driftwood or seaweed, examining them curiously. The beach seemed to stretch endlessly away into the distance and the sound of the sea was soft and gentle that day as it rippled on the sand. It was a miraculous place, filled with wonders and new things that set his curiosity on fire. Birds flitted in and out of the greenery, their jewel colours seeming to flash at him in the sun, and he wanted to know what they were.

He was looking at a piece of green stone in his hand when Albert came out of the shack and walked towards him. 'Found something interesting?'

Davey showed him and he nodded. 'That looks like what they call sea glass, a bit of glass broken off from a bottle someone's chucked in the sea which has worn it smooth by its movement. Green is the most common sort but you may find blue and yellow glass and other interesting bits and pieces if you look hard enough, lad, maybe even something valuable.'

'Is Bert all right about 'avin' me?' Davey asked anxiously. He didn't want to leave this wonderful place too soon. Yes, he wanted to go back and see his mum, his sister and his dad one day, but not too soon. For the first time Davey felt good about what had happened to him.

'Yeah, he's fine about it – says you seem a likely lad, and that's a compliment coming from him,' Albert told him. 'I've just come to say goodbye. I'll be away about four weeks or so this time, and then I'll be back with provisions. Think you can manage OK?'

'Course I can,' Davey said and grinned at him. 'I like your pa, even if he'll be a bit grouchy sometimes.'

'Good word, describes him well,' Albert said and ruffled his hair. 'You keep your word to me, son, and I'll keep mine to you – is that a bargain?'

'Yes, sir,' Davey said and held his hand out solemnly. 'Take care of yourself, sir. We need yer – so don't go and get yourself killed.'

'That ain't going to happen,' Albert told him easily. 'Don't you worry.'

'Good.' Davey laughed and saluted him and then ran off as he saw that Bert had come to the door of his shack and was looking for him.

'Are you ready for something to eat, lad?' he asked as he reached him, and Davey nodded.

'Yes, please, Bert. I'm hungry.'

'Good. I'm glad I haven't got a fussy one on my hands. We're having stew – and don't ask what's in it, because you might not like the answer – but you'll like the taste.'

Davey followed him into the shack. A big black pot had been brought in and placed on the table and an enticing smell was coming from it. Davey licked his lips, anticipating the meal to come.

A plate of meat, with potatoes and vegetables in it, was placed in front of him and he fell on it hungrily, enjoying every mouthful. Chunks of bread and butter accompanied the stew and Davey ate that too. The air from his exploration of the beach seemed to have made him hungry and he relished every last bit.

'I can see I shall have no trouble feeding you,' Bert

said, a twinkle in his eyes, though he didn't actually smile. 'Did they starve you on the ship, then?'

'No, but the cook wasn't as good as you.'

'You don't say.' Bert stared at him and then suddenly his head went back and a great shout of laughter came out of him. 'Me and you will get on just fine, young'un,' he said. 'Now, the pot wants scouring and you'll find a tin bath out the back. You carry the pot and the dishes out there and wash them. There's hot water in the kettle and cold in the butt out back. Pour the hot water over to scald them and then put some cold in before you put your hands in, lad.'

'Yes, Bert,' Davey replied and grinned and then did exactly as he was told. There was a stool next to the bath and he used it to climb on to take water from the butt, and then he sat on it to wash the pot and the plates thoroughly. He found a wire contraption that looked handy and he placed the washed plates and pot on it to dry. Glancing back at the shack, he saw Bert was watching through the open window, nodding in approval, so he'd guessed right.

'What do I do with the water I've used?' he asked Bert.

'I'll empty it on the vegetable patch.' Bert pointed towards a long stretch of earth, which had things growing in it. Davey saw a bucket standing near the bed of vegetables and ran to pick it up. He had the bath empty of the water he'd used with two refills and enjoyed pouring it over the earth, which looked dry in-between the clumps of green vegetation. 'I'd have done that, lad,' Bert said, coming out to him.

'You don't have to now you have me,' Davey said.

'Albert brought me here to help you and I'd like to do as much as I can.' He was keen to learn everything Bert could teach him. This beat going to school back in London by a mile.

'Well, I shan't hide the fact that I don't always feel like doing as much as I used to, but you must keep up with your schoolwork once we get the books for you. I suppose your can read?'

'Yes, sir,' Davey said and saw his frown. 'Yes, Bert. I can read and do sums. I'm good at measuring and I can repeat all my times tables in my head.'

'What's eleven times ten then?'

'One hundred and ten,' Davey came back swiftly. 'Twelve times is one hundred and twenty – but that's the easy one. The eleven times table is harder, but I know eight times is eighty-eight and nine times is ninety-nine, but what is ten times . . .?'

'A hundred and ten of course . . .' Bert began and then saw the mischief in Davey's face. 'All right, of course you know that one – you were testing me, you little devil. So, you know your tables and you can read, but you need to know much more. What do you know about the world then?'

'Not very much,' Davey admitted. 'Our teachers thought we didn't need to know much more than where we lived, at least in my class it seemed that way.'

'Well, mebbe I'll teach you what I know,' Bert said. 'I'll ask for an atlas and some books on geography and I can teach you about this part of Canada and the people who live near us – but now we have work to do. I have to visit my traps and see if I've caught anything for our supper.'

'What was in that delicious stew?' Davey asked curiously.

'It's called a skunk and if we catch another, I'll show it to you,' Albert promised. 'Come on, I've no time to waste explaining now.'

CHAPTER 12

'Mrs Blake.' The young woman behind the counter looked at Dora uneasily. 'My supervisor isn't in today.'

'I don't need to talk to her, Christine,' Dora said testily. 'You know why I've come. I was here yesterday, and I'll be here every day until you tell me what I want to know. Have you found my son Davey yet? Do you know what happened to him?'

'No, Mrs Blake. I'm very sorry but . . .' The young woman gulped and drew a sheet of paper to her, clearly nervous. 'We did locate the purser from the ship when he docked again a few days ago and . . .'

'And?' Dora asked, her annoyance showing. She had been visiting each day and this was the first time anyone had seemed prepared to tell her anything.

'H-he thinks he recalls Davey being at supper the night before they reached Halifax harbour. He says he didn't see him when all the other children were taken off to meet their new families and the crew searched the ship but couldn't find him.'

'So, he disappeared in one night? That's impossible.'

'Unless he fell overboard and was lost,' Christine

said unhappily. 'It seems the most logical explanation, Mrs Blake. A terrible tragedy, if that's what happened, but we just don't know where Davey got to. I'm so sorry.'

'Rubbish!' Dora's voice was sharp with anxiety. 'My husband won't accept that and nor will I. Since it is obvious you people aren't capable of looking after him, we want our son found and brought back immediately.'

'But we can't do that – we have neither the time nor the resources!'

'I was promised my son would be taken proper care of. If you don't do what I ask I shall go to the newspapers.'

Dora left the girl spluttering and slammed the office door for good measure, but inside her heart was sinking. Supposing Davey had fallen overboard during the night and been lost at sea? It seemed strange that he was there for his supper the previous evening but then nowhere to be found the next morning. A part of her was crying out in protest and yet the other half of her was saying that Davey couldn't be dead because she would feel it if he were. So, why couldn't he be found? Why hadn't he left the ship with the other kids? Unless he didn't want to be found. Dora nodded. That fitted with her son's stubborn character. He might have hidden so he could return to England, or for some other reason. The thought gave her hope, something to cling to – and she needed that, because she was feeling terrible.

Blinking back her tears, Dora headed home. She had to believe that Davey was alive and well or she couldn't cope. Gran's remission had been short-lived, and now

143

she was desperately ill. Every day Dora expected it to be her last and dreaded those final moments. After her mother died, she would be alone and at this moment she wished so much that Davey – dependable, practical Davey – was home with her.

'Anything wrong, Dora, love?' A voice she knew stopped her in her tracks and she looked at Mick. He always seemed to be around these days and suddenly her resistance crumbled.

'They lost Davey on the way out to Canada,' she told him. 'He disappeared the night before they docked. If he's dead, Dave will kill me!'

'Not if I have anything to do wiv it,' Mick said and reached out for her, drawing her into his arms. She just let him, her will to resist seeming to have deserted her. 'Don't you fret about anything, Dora, love. Let me take care of you – please?'

She looked up at him, hesitated and then nodded. What was the point of holding out any longer? Her marriage was over. She'd seen it in Dave's eyes – the disgust when he'd learned what she'd done. She knew that her husband would never forgive her for sending his son to Canada, and even if Davey was found, it would not be the same. Mick had always wanted and loved her, and she needed help.

'I'm so tired, Mick,' she told him as the tears trickled down her cheeks. 'Mum is very ill and I can't cope, and Dave hates me.'

'I love yer,' Mick said gruffly and held her tighter. 'You leave it all to me, Dora. I'll get someone to help with the care of Sally and I'll see if anyone knows what happened to your boy. Trust me, Dora. You won't be alone anymore.'

She looked up at him, eyes shining through the tears. 'Maybe I can go see Alice – perhaps even let her come home again?'

'Yeah, we'll see. Once Sally's ordeal is over, you can move in with me, Dora, and then the girl can come and live with us. Davey too if we can find him.'

'You're so good to me, Mick,' Dora said and shut all thought of Dave out of her mind. It was no use regretting what she'd lost, she had to think of the future. 'If you want to come round for supper one night . . .'

'I'll bring a pie and chips with some mushy peas,' he said and smiled at her. 'You'll be mine now, Dora, and everything will be all right.'

Rose stood watching the tender scene from the end of the street. She'd been on her way to Dora to ask for the address to send Alice a birthday card and postal order. Rose reckoned the little girl would enjoy having a little money to spend as she pleased and postage for parcels was too expensive these days.

She hesitated and then turned away. Seeing her friend embrace that man in public had given her a start. Dave would be furious if he heard – but Rose knew they'd had some terrible rows when he was home. Rose was sorry if their marriage was over, but she didn't want to interfere. If Dora knew she'd witnessed her embracing Mick George she would be angry and embarrassed and Rose didn't want to make her feel bad so she would leave it for the moment. After all, one day wouldn't make much difference. Alice would be just as happy to get her gift a day or so late. It was the thought that counted.

Sighing, Rose walked home. She wished she could get on a bus or the train and go down to visit Alice, but Dora had made her promise she wouldn't.

'If you do that, she'll only get upset and want to come home and I can't have her here yet,' Dora had told her. 'You'll see her when I fetch her home, Rose.'

So, Rose had to be content with that, but she would get the card in the post the next day. She'd walk round in the morning and get the address. She smiled as she thought of Alice's pleasure. It would please the child to know that her Aunt Rose hadn't forgotten her, and Rose would never do that. Her heart ached for the little girl who had been banished from her home. If her parents split up, it would be sad for those kids – and they'd already had too much trouble in their young lives.

So engrossed in her thoughts was she that Rose failed to hear the lorry as it turned the corner just as she chose to cross the road. It caught her in a blow that tossed her up onto the bonnet of the lorry, and as she hit her head on the kerb as she rolled off, everything went black . . .

Alice looked at the cards and the parcels waiting beside her breakfast plate. She'd never had so many in her life. She opened all the cards, which were from Auntie Annie, Mary, her school friends but nothing yet from Gran and Mummy. Perhaps they would arrive later that day with the morning post. She smiled widely and opened her gifts, of which there were many from Auntie Annie,

Mary, Uncle Bill and others from school – but nothing from her mother, nothing with a London postmark.

Alice noticed the omission but with all the pretty clothes, books, puzzles, the lovely necklace Uncle Bill had given her and her new red shoes that Auntie Annie had taken her to Ely to buy, she forgot to feel slighted. Mummy had sent a present, of course she had. It was just delayed in the post. Perhaps it might arrive later in the day – but it didn't matter. Her mother had never given her anything like the things she'd been given today, and Alice knew she was fortunate. Her life had settled into a comfortable routine and apart from getting her hair pulled by the evacuee boys staying at the farm, especially by that horrid Josh Baker, she had been happy. At first, she'd shed tears into her pillow at night, missing her family, but now the farm had become her home. Mary was like a sister to her, and the boys – except Josh – were her friends. Josh was always in trouble with Uncle Bill – for letting the cows out of the shed before they'd been milked and riding on the back of the sows and falling into a cowpat, which smelled awful. He was a proper boy, so Auntie Annie said, and laughed when her husband told her his latest escapade. Uncle Bill had been cross, though.

'Do you think Annie has nothing to do but wash your clothes?' Uncle Bill had asked harshly and given him a clout. He'd run off crying and Alice felt a bit sorry for him, but when she tried to comfort him later, he just scowled at her and went off on his own.

Josh didn't seem interested in the work and wonders of the farm but Alice liked to see the animals. The

147

cows were so big, but they were gentle and their eyes looked at you kindly, especially when they'd been milked and turned out into the fields. Alice loved to watch the milking and sometimes she was given a cup of milk fresh from the cow; it tasted sweeter than the milk from bottles they had at school.

She liked to see things growing in the fields and it seemed to Alice that there was always something new to see.

Alice wished her big brother was there on the farm. Davey would have sorted Josh out and he would have loved the life, she knew he would. Alice had a sort of idea where Canada was now, because her teacher had shown them Canada and America on the big map on the wall, as well as India and Malta and Germany. Some of the children had fathers away fighting and the teacher was helping them to write letters and make gifts to send to them.

'It means the world to our men to get letters and gifts from home,' Miss Smeeton had told her class. 'We can all improve our spelling while sending cheer to fathers and brothers too if they are also away.'

Alice sometimes felt weepy when she wrote letters to her daddy. She didn't know where to send them, but Auntie Annie did so she took them home to the farm. Alice wrote to her mummy too. Simple little letters of perhaps three or four carefully formed lines:

Dear Mummy,
   I am well. I hope you are well and Gran. I long to see you and Davey and Daddy.
   Love from Alice xxx

As yet Mummy hadn't written back, at least not since the first one when she enclosed two shillings for sweets. Alice looked eagerly for letters and one day a letter came from her father. It was short but kind and loving and told her that he was thinking of her and loved her very much.

Alice shed a few tears but then she put her letter in the little tin box with a pretty picture of kittens on that Auntie Annie had given her and kept it beside her bed. All the little treasures she'd collected were in the old biscuit tin; a hair slide and a bead bracelet that Davey had given her for a birthday or Christmas, a little sparkly necklace Daddy had given her for her last birthday before he went away and a handkerchief that Gran had given her once. There were no trinkets from her mother – Alice wasn't sure why, but when Mary asked about it Alice said it was because her mummy bought her things to wear instead. The doll, a little the worse for wear, had been a Christmas present from Mummy and Daddy, but it was several years old. Whatever else she'd had bought her had to be left in London.

'You can't take much in your bag,' Mummy had told her. 'Your other things will be safe here.'

Sometimes, Alice found it hard to remember what was left behind or the home she'd lived in most of her life. Being at the farm and walking the short distance to the small school where there were only around thirty-five children including Alice, Mary and the other evacuees was so different from what she'd known in London. Alice found it easier and pleasanter. She missed her parents and her brother. She thought she missed Davey most of all and she thought about him often, wondering if he was all right. When Alice told her teacher that Davey was coming home at the end of the war, she got a funny look on her face and said, 'Is he, dear? Yes, well, let's hope he does for your sake. But it's a long way and he may like it there better.'

Alice considered the idea. She thought Miss Smeeton might be right, because she liked it better here in the village than she did in London. Perhaps there had been a time when it was nice at home, when Mummy and Daddy were happy and Gran was always waiting with a big hug and a slice of her favourite cake. Yet the memories that stood out now were of Gran crying with pain, Mummy looking tired and shouting at her to get out and that awful smell of sickness and urine that pervaded the house.

Most of the children talked hopefully of the time when war would be over. Many of the evacuees, like Alice, had arrived after Dunkirk, when the British Army had been driven onto the beaches there and had had to be evacuated from them. On a July morning at school, Freddie, one of the London boys, in tears, begged to go home, but Miss Smeeton comforted him and then explained to the whole class just why it was so important they stay in the village. She told them that nearly 400,000 British and French troops had been taken to safety from Dunkirk, thanks to the fishermen and ordinary folk who owned pleasure boats and small yachts and had gone over to help fetch the poor soldiers. They had been queued up on the beaches, being bombed and strafed by German warplanes. Miss

Smeeton said only small boats could go into shallower water and they did, picking men off the beach and from the piers and breakwaters.

'Some boats,' she said, 'took a load and went back to England and then returned to do it all again; and some of those brave men died, sunk by enemy planes or U-boats, just as the bigger navy ships were. A lot of men died to bring the survivors back but if they hadn't, the whole army could have been lost on those beaches and we would have no one to fight for us.

'And the reason so many city children have been sent into the country is because the Government believes German planes will soon bomb British cities,' she said, 'now that France has been conquered. Freddie, you are much safer here and your parents will be able to look after themselves and not have to worry about you. So please be happy to be here – all of us hope that all our London guests will enjoy living in the country for however long it takes to win this awful war.'

'You know my dad is in the Royal Navy, the one that fights?' Alice, worrying about the ships that had been sunk, said to her family at the farm when she got home that lunchtime. 'Do you think he's all right?'

'I expect so. We would soon hear if he wasn't,' Auntie Annie said but she didn't smile as she usually did.

Alice sensed something was wrong and went to her, looking up at her face in concern. 'Is something wrong, Auntie Annie?'

She hesitated and then nodded. 'You're old enough to understand, Alice. I've got a brother named Tom and he was wounded in the fighting before Dunkirk, but it was only a slight wound and no one was worried about it and they thought he was on the mend. But we've just heard that it went bad and he's now in a hospital down in Portsmouth, very ill. We don't know if he'll live . . .'

Alice hid her face in Auntie Annie's skirts, tears streaming down her cheeks. She didn't know this Tom, but she was sad for the woman she had learned to love and wanted to comfort her. Auntie Annie knelt down and held her tightly.

'Don't cry, darling Alice. We have to be brave and believe he will come home again.'

But it was just after the school holidays began that the bad news came in a letter. Tom had died and Auntie Annie collapsed and had to be put to bed. The doctor came and looked at her and said she was suffering from shock and would be better soon. After five days in bed – during which time everyone went round with sad faces and even the evacuee boys were quiet – she got up again and started making dinner just the way she always had.

Alice thought that was the day the cheerful happy lady who had given her such a warm loving home began to change. It was little things at first, like the way she was losing weight and clutched her back sometimes as if she was in pain . . .

CHAPTER 13

Rose looked at the doctor hopefully as he stopped at the end of her bed and studied her chart. Perhaps this would be the day that she could go home at last. For more than a month she'd been lying here with various broken bones and fractures, fretting because she could barely move for the pain.

Dora had visited her the day after she'd had the accident. She'd taken Rose's card which had miraculously arrived at the hospital with her, to post to Alice, saying that she was sorry for Rose's trouble and would visit her again when she could. After that, however, she'd only popped in once. Other friends from the lane and the factory had visited, and Harry Smith had told her not to worry and that he wanted Rose back at work the minute she was fit enough. It felt, however, that the doctors were so busy caring for the wounded men who had been brought home in their thousands that her case had been pushed to one side. She pleaded with the nurses to let her go home, but was told she needed an operation on her leg or she wouldn't walk properly again.

In the end, it had been done successfully and Rose was told she was healing well. Now all she wanted was to get home, even if she couldn't return to work until the plaster came off. Neighbours had been taking care of things for her and Harry Smith had made certain her rent was paid, which was good of him, but made her feel beholden. She would pay it back as soon as she got out of here – whenever that was.

'Well, Mrs Parker – how do you feel this morning?' the doctor asked after replacing her chart. 'That leg seems to have healed well. What about your shoulder, eh? Any pain?'

Rose still felt pain all over but she was determined to leave so she shook her head. 'Can I go home today, Doc?' she asked eagerly. He hesitated for a moment and then inclined his head in assent.

'I think we've done what we can for you. You can visit your own doctor if the pain in your shoulder keeps up – oh yes, I know you're lying to me so that I'll let you go – but I think the pain is something you will have to live with for a while, and, to be honest, we need your bed. Just watch where you're going in future, please. We don't have time to be patching up young women who should know better than to get themselves knocked over. In case you hadn't noticed, Mrs Parker, we do have a war on . . .'

Rose was about to deliver a mouthful when she saw that his eyes were twinkling and realised that she was being teased. 'Right, Doc, thanks,' she said and laughed. 'I just came in 'ere for a rest that's all.'

'Pull the other one,' he quipped. 'I'll see that you get an appointment for a check-up in three months' time, all right?'

'Yeah, whatever you want,' Rose agreed and he nodded and left. A nurse stayed behind.

'I'll bring your clothes when rounds have finished,' she promised. 'One of your friends brought you some clean clothes – yours were covered in blood when you arrived. I doubt you'll wear them again but they're in a bag for you.'

'Thanks.' Rose grinned at her. 'I am really grateful for all you've done – but I need to get back home and to work.'

'Yes, I expect you do,' the nurse replied, smiling. 'Just don't overdo it, Mrs Parker. You'll feel tired for a time, I imagine.'

'Yeah, maybe,' Rose replied. She felt that she had been resting for months and hated it. Her whole life she'd worked and worked hard. Lying around in bed was the last thing she needed. Losing her wages was bad enough, but she couldn't stand the boredom another day. She needed to know what was going on in the world and she would get back down the factory, plaster cast and all.

Dora had shivered as she listened to Prime Minister Churchill's speech about fighting on the beaches on the wireless back in June. During the evacuation of Dunkirk she'd listened avidly to the stories of the hundreds of thousands of British men trapped on the beaches and wept when she saw pictures of the rescues in the newspapers. Even Mick had been gripped by what was going on, though he had no intention of serving in the forces himself.

'Mug's game, I reckon,' he'd said once. 'No offence to Dave, but at least he's in the navy. They'd put me in the army if they could.'

'But what if they make you go?' Dora had asked him fearfully, because she'd come to rely on him, and the extras, he gave her. He'd winked at her.

'I've fixed it,' he'd told her and coughed. 'It's me chest, yer see, and me flat feet.'

Dora looked at him. He never coughed and he didn't have flat feet that she'd noticed. 'How did you get away with that?'

'I sent someone else to take me medical,' Mick said and grinned. 'There's ways round it, love. You just have to use this,' he said and tapped the side of his nose. 'You can get away wiv most things, so don't you worry. I shall be here to look after you.'

Dora had smiled at him back then, but now, in September, she was frightened. The nation was on high alert. Invasion was imminent and the bombs they'd expected months ago had started to drop on London and the RAF and Luftwaffe fighter planes fought an endless battle in the skies overhead. Thus far, most of the bombs had fallen down near the docks and apart from the terrifying noise and the way the fires lit the night sky, Dora hadn't been affected yet. She hadn't been close to an explosion, but Rose had.

'I thought me last bleedin' moment had come,' she told Dora when she came round to see her. 'It was as I was passing that old disused factory down near the East India Docks – well, the buggers got that.' Rose had been too far from the underground to make it there in time, because she still wasn't up to running yet.

'That place weren't much good to anyone,' Dora said, thinking the old factory was best gone. 'The papers said our fly boys are reacting magnificently and winning most of the battles in the air.'

'Well, the papers would, wouldn't they?' Rose sniffed her disbelief. 'Jack Carter – you remember he was disabled in the last war? – well, he says we don't stand a chance. He reckons the bloody Jerries will march right over us within six months and the Home Guard ain't got a hope in hell of stoppin' 'em.'

'What is he, another Lord Haw-Haw? One of them bleedin' propogandists?'

'Nah, he's just a bloke I meet down the pub sometimes. Your Mick would know him. He's got a weak chest and flat feet so he works as a night watchman at the factory and he's in the Home Guard. He's all right, but I hope he's wrong about us being taken over.'

Dora nodded but didn't answer. She knew quite a few people felt the same, that invasion was inevitable and the Home Guard – Dad's Army, as they were nicknamed – wouldn't be much help. Many of the older men who couldn't join the fighting forces had joined and they did a lot of marching and planning, but Mick said they were badly equipped and wouldn't be of much use if the invasion came.

'Mick reckons the fly boys will stop 'em,' Dora said.

'He ought to be in the army,' Rose said, annoyed at Dora's determination not to agree with her.

'Yeah, I know,' Dora said and heard the noise she dreaded from the bedroom. 'I'd better go up . . .'

Rose nodded. 'Sally's hangin' on much longer than you expected, ain't she?'

'It seems like years,' Dora admitted, 'and I didn't think she'd last this long. I tell you, Rose, those bleedin' doctors, they wouldn't let a dog suffer the way she has. I've asked them if they can give her somethin' to finish it and they looked at me as if I'm a murderer – but if she were an animal, they'd put her down.'

'Bloomin' heck, Dora!' Rose looked horrified. 'What yer sayin', girl? Your Sally wouldn't thank yer for it. She ain't the sort to give in. Why do yer think she's lasted so long?'

'I know.' Tears welled in Dora's eyes. 'She's so patient and good and I'm a cow. I'd better go up to her now.' She walked as far as the door. 'It's just I can't bear to see her suffer like this!'

Rose had just looked at her and Dora lifted her head and went up to her mother. Sometimes, she found her suffering unbearable and even though she now had help through the night, because Mick George paid a woman to come in for a few hours, and so she wasn't as tired, Sally's suffering still tore at Dora's heart.

It was months since she'd thought of anything but her mother's sickness. She hadn't even been down to see her daughter. Alice would think she'd been deserted. Mick said the letter she'd had from Annie proved Alice had settled in and was fine, but Dora still felt vaguely guilty about sending her away. She'd also had these recurring nightmares about what had happened to Davey because there was still no news of his whereabouts and the council people were convinced that he'd fallen into the sea and been lost the night before they docked.

'Yes, Davey lad, that's good,' Bert encouraged, as Davey finished scraping the skin off the racoon they'd caught in their trap. He'd told Davey that if he made a good job of skinning and scraping the animal's skin, he could have it made into something. 'That will make you a proper warm hat, it surely will.'

Davey nodded, happy in his task. At first, he'd been squeamish about handling the trapped creatures, especially when they had to kill something to finish it off. He'd wanted to protest that it was cruel and wrong to kill a living thing, but Bert had explained that he couldn't catch enough fish to keep them both alive. He'd told him, 'You'd soon get tired of eating just fish or seafood every day. No, this is how it is meant to be, lad. I use the meat for food and the skins make all kinds of things – bags, clothes, bed covers and the like. Sometimes I sell them at the trading post – it's not called that these days; they have a fancy name I can never recall – ah, yes, Conrod Stores – it's owned by a guy named Corky and there's a schoolhouse, a few homes and a couple of shops built near a ford across a river and they've started calling it Waterford because of that, though it's not even a village. Mostly, though, I use what I trap. The people who used to live on this land used everything – teeth for jewellery, claws, bones, the lot. They didn't have fancy pots of jam or sacks of flour delivered in those days.'

Davey had thought about it and then he realised that they were not the only ones to eat the creatures they caught. The groundhog was plentiful and popular for food, and, as Bert pointed out, 'If we didn't eat them, we'd have to cull them and throw their bodies to the bears, because they'd become a nuisance, way too many of them.'

Bert's nearest neighbour was a Mi'kmaq man called Two Bears who dressed in a mixture of western and native clothes, with a much-worn bowler hat with a feather in it and buckskin breeches with fringing, a worn jacket that might have been worn by an East End docker and soft boots he made from leather he'd cured. He kept himself to himself and troubled no one, often disappearing for weeks at a time. Davey wouldn't even have known he was there if they hadn't met when he was checking the traps with Bert. He'd just appeared from nowhere and stood watching for a moment. The two men had nodded and exchanged greetings before passing on. As Bert said, you just left folk to themselves if that was the way they preferred it, and although he knew Two Bears trapped animals, he would never have touched anything in the other man's traps, nor the other man his.

'I respect him and he respects me. It's a pity so many people can't be like that.' Bert had shaken his head. 'Then maybe we wouldn't have wars like the one goin' on now.'

In the opposite direction from Two Bears' home, but a similar distance away, was another neighbour, a man who called by sometimes to buy skins from Bert for a few coins. He had a foreign-sounding name and Davey didn't much like him, even though Bert always seemed pleased he'd called, because he bought the pelts from the groundhogs they trapped.

The groundhog was a bit like the squirrels Davey had seen in London parks when his father took him on an outing, but it lived in burrows rather than in the trees and its tail wasn't the same. It had a cute face and Davey felt sorry when they caught one, even though they made good eating. Bert often roasted them over an open fire outside and the meat was tasty – he thought it a bit like chicken, only with a stronger flavour.

He continued his work until Bert called him in. 'Davey, it's time for your schoolwork, lad. I shall get into trouble if you don't complete the exercises they gave you.'

'They're too easy,' Davey replied. However, he came in obediently and settled down at the board table Bert had made himself. The assortment of chairs had each been made by a different cabinet maker, and although none of them matched, in a funny sort of way that gave them a charm all of their own.

'This one is genuine George IV, made by an English maker, a good one I was told.' Bert had shown him one of the dark mahogany elbow chairs that stood by the kitchen range and was Bert's favourite place to sit after he lit the fire inside the range of an evening. Nights were very cold in the shack, though the days were sunny and often warm. If you went up into the mountains it would be colder, which suited the animals that ranged there, like the cougars and bears that came down now and then to feed, especially when they had young. The bears would catch fish in the streams and small lakes that threaded the landscape for miles in this area. Bert had told him that in the old days, wolves were sometimes to be seen, though they'd usually stayed clear unless it was a Wolf Winter.

'What's a Wolf Winter?' Davey had wanted to know.

'It's when the weather is so bad that wolves are starving and they come down to human settlements to try and steal food. Mebbe farm animals, or people's babies if they get the chance, so it is said. Wolves'll even attack people if driven to it by extreme hunger.'

'I don't want to be eaten by a wolf!' Davey had looked uneasily behind him, but Bert only laughed.

'Well, I most always have my gun with me in case I see somethin' worth eatin' and they do say one shot over their heads and they're off. But there have been no wolves in Nova Scotia for about a hundred years, I reckon, cos men used to hunt them and eat their hearts to become strong and brave like them.

'What you do get around here are black bears,' Bert said. 'And they're too lazy to attack us, I reckon, unless they're starving or scared or mebbe protecting their young from us. You'll mebbe see a couple of bears wandering through if they're looking for food – they have a real passion for honey, just like that Winnie the Pooh – but unless you do something to startle them, they'll leave you alone. Best thing is to stand absolutely still and stare at them and they'll just go away.'

Davey hoped Bert was right. He knew the woods

around the lake and the little streams that fed into the inlet were teeming with wildlife of all sorts, bright, beautiful birds as well as small animals, and it made sense that predators would be there too. However, he saw little sign of them, because he stuck close to Bert when they visited the traps and spent his free time wandering the shore of the inlet, where he could smell the salty tang of the sea and watch flocks of geese fly over and different kinds of seagulls and he tried to put a name to them. One of the books the schoolmaster had sent for him had pictures of geese and other creatures he might see, and he'd been told to write whatever he saw down in a log each day. He enjoyed doing it and his handwriting was improving, because Bert monitored Davey's work and grumbled if he couldn't read it.

'Why do I have to do so much schoolwork?' Davey asked him one day when he'd been given an essay to write and had no idea what to write down.

'Because one day you will leave here,' Bert said. 'You'll go out into the world, perhaps to a town or city here in Canada – or perhaps you'll return to England – but you'll need a job and for that you need education.'

'Why do I have to go anywhere?' Davey asked. 'I'm fine here with you, Bert.'

The flicker of a smile crossed the old man's face. 'I'm fine with you here too, Davey, but one day I shan't be with you any more and it would be a lonely life for you then. Besides, I thought you wanted to go to sea and see something of the world?'

'I did – I do,' Davey admitted reluctantly. 'One day

– but not yet. I like what we do, how we live here.' It was an idyllic life at times, especially when the sun was warm and his bare arms and legs went brown in its rays, freckling across his face and turning the ends of his hair a dark blond. He was growing up too, into a leggy thin boy with wide, inquiring eyes and a thirst for knowledge that Bert did his best to quench with all his tales of life at sea and here in Canada.

'Yeah, me too.' Bert looked up at the sky. 'I reckon a squall's comin' out there.' He looked towards the inlet and the wider ocean they could just see from here, which was shrouded in a thickening mist.

Davey was happy most of the time, though at night his thoughts would go to Alice and he'd wonder if she was all right. Had she got used to being without him now? Had she forgotten him? Davey hadn't forgotten his promise to look after her, but he was far from anywhere and the only news from England came to them when Albert visited. So he contented himself with learning all he could and helping out the man who was so kind to him. One day he would go home and look for Alice but for now he must stay here.

The long summer had been gorgeous, working and playing in the sun, but now snow fell and winds from the north-east that Bert called nor'easters blew hard and it was cold at night in the shack, despite the furs they piled on their mattresses and the big fire Bert kept burning in his trusty old range. But it was a good life and if he'd Alice with him he might have thought he was better off here than at home.

164

Albert came to visit every three to four weeks with his heavy sack filled with provisions over his shoulder to make certain they were coping and bring the luxuries they both looked forward to, but there was never any definite time when they knew he would come. Why was that? He asked Bert now.

'Because the sea is unpredictable,' Bert said, 'and you can never guarantee when you'll get back to your home port. Come on, lad. I caught some fresh fish for our tea tonight and they're just about smoked. We'll eat and then batten down the hatches just in case the storm comes inland. It can be fierce at times.'

Davey nodded and followed him to their cooking fire where the fish were on a spit over the smoking wood. They tasted amazing that way – salty and smoky – and they pulled the tender flesh off with their fingers. Davey smiled at Bert as he wiped his finger on his shirt. His friend made him take a bath once a week and their clothes were washed then, too, but Bert wasn't all the while fussing over keeping them clean like his mother. He said there was no way they could live like that out here and it suited Davey just fine. Left to himself he would probably not have bothered to wash or cut his hair, but Bert lopped his hair when it got too long and put his head under a jug of cold water if he didn't wash it in his bath so he didn't neglect that too often. Bert didn't fuss but his rules had to be respected or he could heft a heavy clout behind Davey's ear that near fetched him over.

Not that Davey deliberately disobeyed him. Right from the start there had been mutual respect and now he'd come to care for the old man like the grandfather he didn't remember. Dad's father had been dead before he was born, and Mum's father was seldom mentioned. Davey had asked Gran about him once but she'd shaken her head.

'Just as well you never knew him, Davey. He wasn't a nice man to live with, unlike your dad who is a good man. Just be glad you've got him to look up to.'

Davey missed his father. He lay awake at night sometimes, wondering where Dad was and what he was doing. He thought about his mother and Gran but supposed his grandmother had passed on by now. Where was his mother and what was she doing? Had she fetched Alice home? No, she wouldn't have, Davey realised, because the bombs were falling on London. Albert had told them that on one of his visits. He'd brought a newspaper with pictures so that they could see what was going on. People had been killed and injured so it was a good thing Alice was safe in the country. Perhaps Mum had gone down to be with her. Davey hoped so because she'd be safe there. He wanted her to be safe, even though she'd sent him away.

Albert had brought them news each time he came. He'd told both of them, because he said it was best that Davey knew the truth.

'There's no use in you worrying about your family,' he'd told Davey, 'because you can't do anything, and you couldn't even if you were there. If your ma has any sense, she'll get out of London and head to that farm where your sister is living.'

'Yeah. Let's 'ope so,' Davey had replied with a

shrug. He cared what happened to his mother, but it was so far away, and he couldn't picture what it must be like, despite the English newspaper with pictures that Albert had brought. '*Flames lit the night sky*' the headlines proclaimed, but there was no mention of Silver Terrace so it didn't worry Davey too much, because it was surely factories and stuff like that the enemy planes were after. He saw Bert shake his head over it and look sad.

'Why will they do it?' he asked of no one but himself. 'You'd have thought they would learn. Just look at the last time. As if enough didn't die back then!'

Davey had learned about the First World War at school so he knew what Bert meant and asked no questions. Albert had told him that his father had been on merchant ships during the last great war.

'He always says it was better than being in the army, especially back then,' Albert had told him. 'But I think he had a couple of narrow escapes – don't ask him, though, because he won't talk about it.'

After Albert left the last time, Bert said to him, 'I've been thinking, mebbe it's time we tried to get a message to your ma. If you want to write her a letter – and one for your sister too – Albert will see they are sent next time he comes.'

So, Davey had written his letters – one for his father too – and now they waited for Albert.

CHAPTER 14

Rose's leg was nearly back to normal. She'd missed her home more than she'd expected when she was in hospital, missed the peace and quiet and the independence she'd had, and it didn't seem a bit lonely on her own as she'd thought it might after the bustle of the wards. Not that she was on her own that much. Neighbours kept popping round with meals they'd cooked and saved a plate for her and Harry Smith called twice a week to ask how she was and whether she was ready for work, and Dora had popped in for two minutes but couldn't stop, because Sally was worse again.

'So will you fetch your Alice home when it is over?' Rose had asked Dora. 'You must miss her, love? I know I would if she were mine.'

Seeing the flash of annoyance in Dora's eyes, Rose knew that even the mild censure in her voice had upset her friend, but she wasn't sorry. Her opinion of Dora had dipped these past months. Letting those lovely kids be sent away and then taking up with that Mick George. It wasn't right and Rose would

168

have let her have a mouthful if she hadn't been afraid that she'd never see Alice again if she did. Surely, Dora must miss her kids? She hadn't been a bad mother, just a careless one sometimes.

'Why do you have to remind me, Rose?' Dora asked and there were tears in her eyes. 'If you must know, I wish they were both here – especially Davey. I know where Alice is and I can fetch her home when it's safe, but my poor boy is lost, and I think he must be dead.'

'You can't know that.' Rose tried to reassure her, sorry now that she'd upset her. Dora had a lot to cope with these days. 'Your Davey isn't the sort to fall overboard. I reckon he just ran off because he didn't like the look of the folk that came for him.'

A spark of hope appeared in Dora's eyes. 'Do you really think so, Rose? His father said he didn't believe Davey would fall over the side of the ship either, but supposing someone pushed him in?'

'Why would anyone do that to Davey? He's a good lad. They'd be more likely to have taken a fancy to him and carried him off with them,' Rose said and then, seeing the alarm in Dora's eyes, added, 'I didn't mean for any wrong purposes, but because he's a clever, lovely lad. I reckon he's somewhere having the time of his life and one day he'll come back and tell you all about it, love.'

'Oh Rose, you're a good friend,' Dora said and rushed to hug her. 'I'm sorry I haven't been a better friend to you when you needed help.'

'Nah, don't worry, Dora. I 'ad plenty of 'elp.'

'I'll make it up to you,' Dora said eagerly. 'When Ma has gone – and it won't be long – we'll go and

169

visit Alice together. Have a nice day out and then we'll bring her home and she can spend some time at yours. Maybe we could work it so you're home when I'm at work and the other way around?' Dora was arranging things to suit herself but it would suit Rose too.

Rose gave her a warm hug and smiled. 'Dora, you can be a lovely person when yer want and I'd love to 'ave a day in the country wiv you and Alice.'

'That's what we'll do,' Dora promised. 'But I have to go – it can't be long now and I daren't leave Ma for more than a minute or two.'

She tore herself away and stopped at the door to look back and wave. 'We're still friends, aren't we?'

'Course we are, you daft thing,' Rose said and chuckled as Dora looked relieved before she went out. Dora could be both selfish and careless but you couldn't help loving her all the same – and those kids, well, they were a joy, the pair of them, and she just hoped she was right and Davey was having a good life, wherever he was.

So that was it. All over at last. Dora sat on the side of the bed and looked at her mother's peaceful face. Sally had passed away in her sleep and never made a murmur. After all the sleepless nights and the worry, pain and frustration, she'd slipped away without saying goodbye and Dora felt guilty. She hadn't been with her that night because Mick had called round and he'd stayed over.

Sally had been sleeping when Mick arrived and the woman who sat with her for a few hours each day had gone home. Dora had meant to sit with her all night but Mick wanted her to be with him and so she slept beside him until he left in the early hours. She'd gone to Sally's room then and found her, pale and still and out of her misery at last. Had she cried out or opened her eyes and looked for Dora in the night? If she had, Dora hadn't heard her and there was no sign of the sickness that had so often plagued her in these past months.

The sound of an explosion in the distance made Dora start. Was it a daylight raid? They were getting bombing raids most nights now but, so far, she and her neighbours had been lucky. A lot of folk went down the underground at night or took shelter in the dugouts in their back gardens but Dora reckoned she'd be just as safe under the stairs or the kitchen table. Besides, the bombs were not falling near her home. The noise had come from somewhere near the docks and might well have been caused by a fractured gas main. It was the damage done to the gas mains that caused a lot of the destruction and set off the fires that were terrorising people, and they could suddenly go off hours after the raid had ceased.

'I'm sorry,' she said and bent to kiss her mother's cold face. 'I hope you went peacefully. I never heard . . .'

Sighing, Dora returned to her own bedroom and made herself look decent and then went next door to ask her neighbour to pop down and ask the doctor to come. After he'd certified her mother's death, she would ask the woman who did the laying out to call. She'd help Molly Briggs when she came but couldn't face doing it alone. Molly was used to it and would

171

do all that was necessary – and she was so down to earth that it would stop Dora fretting when there was no earthly use in crying and making a fuss now. Sally was gone and it was a mercy to see her peaceful. It might have been better had she gone weeks ago, though, and been saved a lot of suffering.

Her mind started to think of what she had to do now – Sally's funeral, and a bit of a tea for her friends as well as registering the death – and then she might at last have time to visit Alice at the farm. Dora felt guilty over the neglect of her daughter. No wonder Rose had that tone in her voice. But it was good that Alice was safe in the country – thank goodness she had sent her! For months she'd felt bad about it, but now her actions were justified, though she ought to have visited somehow.

Life was worrying these days. People were being killed here in London and others were losing their homes. The sound of sirens in the night were frightening and those people who left their houses and rushed to the underground stations or the nearest air raid shelter were terrified. Dora's neighbour had an Anderson shelter and he'd offered to get one for her, but it cost money and she hadn't bothered. Mick had pointed out that she couldn't get her mother into the shelter anyway.

'You couldn't move her, Dora, love,' he'd told her. 'So you might just as well get under yer kitchen table. That will be as much good as that thing they've got next door, I promise you.' Dora hadn't needed much convincing. She'd been in an Anderson once and found it damp, cold and stuffy.

Sally's condition was the main reason Dora hadn't run to the underground or bothered with a dugout in her garden. There was no way she was going to abandon her mother and run for safety herself, so why bother? If they went up in a puff of smoke, they'd go together.

Mick said if a bomb had your name on it, it would get you wherever you were and Dora thought he was probably right, because people had been killed in the shelters when there was a direct hit. She listened to the wireless and heard the reports about how the battle for Britain was being fought in the air – all them brave young men risking their lives to stop the bombs. Mick said they weren't making much of a job of it if the amount of damage in London was anything to go by, but he was quick to complain, even though he did nothing but make money where he could.

Dora had learned more than she wanted to know about Mick's business and the things he did to make money out of the war. She didn't like a lot of what she heard but she'd learned to hide her feelings. Mick looked after her, but at times, she wished she'd never let him into her home. Yes, he'd taken care of her and Sally these past months, but she'd managed before he took over. Now, she felt he would make a bad enemy.

Dora knew the die was cast. Dave would never take her back now and Mick loved her. He couldn't do enough for her, but at times she looked at herself in the mirror and hated who she saw. How had she come to this – the kept woman of a criminal? Dave had thought Mick was small-time, but he had his fingers in a lot of pies these days and his wallet was bulging. He'd told her that after the war was over, he intended to buy a big house for her and the kids away from the East End.

'We'll have everything,' he'd told her more than once. 'You're mine now, Dora. I'll look after you – but don't you let me down. I wouldn't like that and I wouldn't just walk away like that husband of yours.'

Dora had felt a shiver at her nape when Mick had said that, but he needn't have worried. She was too scared of being on her own to try anything. Now that her mother had gone, she felt suddenly lonely. Tears filled her eyes as she tried to carry on and then, suddenly, she was weeping.

After a while, she pulled herself together. No use in crying over spilled milk. Dora had made her own choices and she just had to live with them.

CHAPTER 15

Annie Greene looked at the letter she'd written and sighed. She'd done something she'd never wanted to do but she didn't have much choice. After what the doctors had told her at the hospital, the evacuee children were going to have to move on. It broke her heart to have to write the letters that would see them taken to new homes or back to their parents – what mother would want her child back in war-torn London?

Annie knew that it would cause her real grief to part with the two little girls, especially Alice. That child had become special to her; she wasn't sure why exactly, but there was just something about her. Add the fact that her mother seemed to have abandoned her, and it tore her heartstrings. No letters since the first and no visits.

'Nearly done, love?' Annie's husband said, entering the kitchen, a worried look in his eyes. 'It's time we left for the hospital.'

'Yes, I know . . .' Annie sealed her final envelope. 'You will see these letters get posted, Bob?'

'Yes, of course I will, Annie, love. You're not to worry about anything. Jack Saunders' wife is coming in to cook and clean while you have the operation and rest in hospital. We'll manage fine for a few weeks.'

'I'm thinking of those poor little children,' Annie said, tears filling her eyes. 'You can't look after them, Bob. It means they will have to go away – back home or to another family that will take them on.'

'Yes,' he agreed, because even if he could manage a few weeks on his own, Annie needed to take things easy when she got home after the operation. 'But some of the boys want to go back to London and the others – well, it isn't our fault. We've done our best for them and we might have them back when you're ready, love.'

'Yes, I suppose we might,' Annie agreed. She wanted to tell him how she felt about Alice, how she'd like to adopt her if her mother didn't want her, but knew he was already too worried. The Government had brought in so many new restrictions for the farm that it took all his time to keep up with them and he was anxious for her too. Her operation wasn't just a routine one and if the disease had gone too far . . . but she refused to think about that until they told her the results. She was expecting to have the hysterectomy and come home in a few weeks' time to complete bed rest for a while. There was no way she could keep her evacuees but if she recovered fully, she could apply to have them – or some of them – back again.

In the kitchen, Alice and Mary were sitting side by side on the mat, playing with the kitten, who was a young cat now but still liked to play. Knowing she might not see either of them again brought tears to her eyes and as they jumped up and came to her, she gathered them into a hug.

'Be good while I'm away,' was all she could trust herself to say.

'You will come back?' Alice asked, looking uncertain and anxious.

'Yes, I'll come back,' Annie promised. The girls would not be there and she felt guilt at not telling them but, surely, they would be fine once their mothers came to fetch them? She whispered to her husband as they left, 'Be certain to send that letter to Alice's mother, love. You mustn't forget.' It was little Alice she worried about – because what kind of a mother would simply ignore a lovely little girl like that?

Sally's funeral was going to be the next day. Dora sat alone in the little front room where they'd set up the coffin on a stand so her neighbours could come in and say goodbye. Mick had stayed away the past few days, out of respect for Sally's passing, so he said, and Dora had been thinking she might take a trip down to the country on Saturday. She could see Alice and spend some time with her, perhaps stop until Monday. They could talk about when Alice was coming home, plan for the future. Surely these raids couldn't keep up much longer? The battle in the air was fierce and the papers claimed Britain's air force was holding its own, if not actually winning.

When she heard the siren, Dora got up and started to look for her coat but then she sat down again.

By the time she reached the shelter it would probably be too late. Besides, if the bomb had her name on it . . . She sat looking into the fire as the noise of the planes grew louder. It sounded as if they were right overhead and Dora stood up uncertainly. All of a sudden she wished she'd gone to the underground earlier and her heart throbbed with fright.

'I'm sorry, Davey,' she whispered and wished her son was with her to tell her what to do. She made a dive for the table and crawled under it just as the bomb hit. 'Davey!' she cried in terror, and that was the last thing she ever said or would. This particular bomb had Dora's name on it.

'It was a direct 'it,' Rose told her fellow workers at the factory two days later. 'The poor little cow didn't know what 'it 'er. I told her to go to the underground whenever the siren sounded but she wouldn't listen; time after time, I said it – now look what's 'appened.' Rose struggled against her tears. She might sound harsh, but she was upset – and angry, too, that Dora had been killed.

'Good thing them kids wasn't 'ere,' Rose's neighbour on the assembly line said. 'They'd 'ave been killed an' all.'

'Yeah.' Rose sniffed into her hanky, her eyes sore with weeping. 'I shall miss her somethin' rotten. I was lookin' forward to seein' her back at work now Sally's gone – poor woman never got her funeral. Leastways, I suppose, they'll bury what they can find but they said there wasn't much left after that fire.'

'Bleedin' 'ell, Rose!' one of the women protested.

'You're givin' me nightmares. It's bad enough she's gone. We don't need all the gory details.'

'I was just sayin',' Rose muttered. 'Whatever 'er 'usband will think if 'e gets back.'

'The way things are goin' I ain't sure any of us will survive,' Rose's neighbour said. 'Does anyone know where the kids are?'

Rose shrugged. 'Alice is in the country on a farm but it's anyone's guess what happened to Davey. He went out to Canada but no one knows what happened to him after that.'

Oh God, she thought. What was Dave Blake going to do when he got back? He'd doted on those kids – and Dora at one time. Now he'd have nothing to come back to and that was terrible.

Everything Dora had possessed was gone in the fire but her neighbours in the lane had had a whip round and there would be a funeral of sorts for the remains – whatever they could find of her and Sally. They would put a wooden cross on a plot of ground and at least Dave could visit that when he got back, if he ever did. Rose knew that Dora hadn't heard from him for months, but was it likely she would after what she'd done?

Rose grieved for her friend and she grieved for those poor, motherless kids. Would someone tell Alice kindly? Rose would have done it herself if only Dora had given her the address but she'd never got around to it and Rose had asked round the council office, only to be told that she wasn't family so she couldn't be told. Bloomin' officials! Rose would boil the lot of them in oil if she had the chance. Alice needed love and kindness, especially now. Rose would have gladly taken her in and given her a home but when they wouldn't let her know where she was, how could she find the child she loved? As for Davey . . . well, Rose could only cling to the hope that he was all right wherever he was.

Alice stared blankly at Uncle Bob, Auntie Annie's husband. He was usually smiling and easy-going but now he looked so stern that he frightened her.

'What do you mean I'm going away?' Alice asked tremulously. 'What have I done wrong? Doesn't Auntie Annie want me any more?'

'Your Auntie Annie isn't coming back,' he said, his face going a strange grey colour. 'She went into the hospital to have an operation and . . . and . . . she didn't make it.' His words were strangled so that she could hardly hear them and he looked as if he were crying. Why was he crying? 'I'm sorry, little one, but you're the last to go and I can't keep you any longer. My Annie wrote to your mother and asked her to come and fetch you but . . .' He shook his head as if he found it impossible to continue. 'I had a letter from the council. It means she isn't coming so there's no other choice. I've arranged for you to go to a place where you'll be looked after.' Uncle Bob didn't look her in the eye, and she sensed he was hiding something. 'Your mother can't take you home.'

Why not? She wanted to ask but knew it was useless. Her mother didn't want her anymore.

'I want Davey,' Alice whimpered, tears welling over. 'I want my dad . . .'

180

'Sorry, I can't do any more.' He sat down at the kitchen table and buried his face in his hands. Alice moved away, sitting down on the mat to cuddle the cat that was no longer a tiny kitten. She was still sitting there half an hour later when she heard the sound of a car outside and then Mrs Saunders, who was helping out, brought a strange woman into the room.

'It's the lady for Alice, Bob,' she said and went to put a hand on his shoulder.

He struggled to his feet but he didn't look at Alice. 'My wife was fond of her,' he said in that strangled voice to the stranger. 'She'll be all right with you?'

'Of course, Mr Greene. We take good care of our children.'

'Is that her bag?' The unknown woman held her hand out to Alice. 'I am Miss Button,' she said. 'Come along, dear. Say goodbye and thank you to Mr Greene – and put the cat down. You can't take it with you where you're going.'

'I'll take good care of it,' Mrs Saunders said and took the cat from Alice's reluctant hands. 'Don't worry, I'll look after it for you.'

Alice didn't answer. She was too scared to speak. Miss Button looked terrifying and Alice was frozen with fear as she was firmly led away. Where was she going and would she ever see her family again?

The orphanage was a forbidding building, dark with small, narrow windows and three storeys high with a big brown door that Miss Button knocked at loudly. It was set back from the road in a garden with tall hedges and trees and everything looked dark and colourless. The door was opened by a girl of about thirteen wearing a grey pleated skirt and a grey blouse with an apron over it. Inside was a hall with a high ceiling and a steep staircase. Rooms led off from the hall but the doors were all firmly shut and it felt cold. The change from Auntie Annie's warm airy kitchen and the open fields around the house was so stark that Alice felt as if she couldn't breathe.

Miss Button didn't speak as she led the way up the stairs. She'd hardly spoken to Alice the whole way and she hadn't dared to ask where they were going but she'd read the name ORPHANAGE over the gate as they drove in and the word sent cold shivers down her spine.

Alice knew that an orphanage was the place where they sent children who had no one to care for them or were considered in moral or physical danger. Mum had labelled them as cold, uncaring places and from what Alice had seen so far, she was right. Miss Button had stopped walking at last and now she opened a door and indicated that Alice should enter. The room was about the size of Alice and Mary's room at the farm but it had five beds in it and she was led to the one at the end, near a window but furthest from the door.

'Last in always has the end bed so that we can keep an eye on you for a while,' Miss Button said, 'but you have a view of the playground so you're lucky. You put your things in that little cupboard by your bed. There's room to hang your spare dress and places for your underwear.'

'Where is this place?' Alice asked. 'I wonder if it is near London so my mum can visit.' She'd grown out of calling her mother Mummy because everyone else at the farm spoke of their mum. 'Can I write to her?'

'The housemistress will see to all that,' Miss Button said and looked annoyed. 'You should have been told the truth but it isn't my place to do it. Miss Weatherspoon will be here shortly. She has taken one of the boys to the dentist this morning, which is why I was asked to collect you.' She looked round the neat room that was painted in two shades of cream with its neat row of beds and cupboards. Nothing that might have made it a home had been provided so there were no pictures, toys, chairs or personal possessions. 'Well, I'll leave you to unpack your things and come to terms with your new situation, Alice. Someone will come for you soon.'

As Miss Button walked away, Alice felt bereft. She hadn't liked the stern woman who had delivered her here like a parcel, but now she was alone and it felt scary. She looked out at the square of concrete below. Miss Button had called it a playground but there were no children, no benches to sit on and nothing to play with. Sitting down on the edge of her bed, Alice felt the warm salty tears trickle down her cheeks. She hated this place and she wanted to return to the farm where Auntie Annie had been so kind and loving towards her. Alice felt so lonely and miserable.

After a few moments she brushed her face and got up to unpack. She had grown up since leaving her mother in London. She knew that she had no control over her fate and that she had to obey the rules or she would be punished. Auntie Annie had never punished her, but Uncle Bob had given one of the boys a hiding for stealing eggs from under the chickens and breaking them. At school, she'd seen boys being given the cane on their hands for naughty behaviour, and the only way to avoid such punishments was to do as she was told and keep silent.

She had just finished putting away her things when the door opened and a girl of around her own age entered. 'You've been crying,' she said in a matter-of-fact way. 'There's no use crying – if you do, they'll pick on you.'

'Who will?' Alice asked tremulously.

'The older girls can be spiteful – and the boys are horrid, though they mostly stop in their half of the building. We only meet when they take us into Cambridge for an educational treat.' She pulled a wry face. 'We go to the museum or to walk round the colleges. I'd like to go on the river in a punt but they don't take us to places like that, though last month we went to a swimming pool for lessons, because it's healthy, but it was cold in the water and I didn't like it.'

Alice just stared at her. She knew that some of the boys from the farm had gone swimming in the river during the summer and they'd loved it. In fact, they'd sneaked off on their own and got told off for going into the water naked and without supervision.

'Anyway, you've got to come. Miss Weatherspoon told me to fetch you and she's in a bad mood. Tim played her up at the dentist. Be careful not to get on the wrong side of her or you'll get your hands caned,' the girl said. 'I just say yes miss and no miss. Some of them aren't so bad but she's tricky.' She led the way up through the dormitory and pointed to the bed near the door. 'That's my bed near the door because I've been here the longest.' She paused to look at Alice. 'I know you're Alice, but my name is Molly and, if you like, I'll look after you until you get used to it.'

Alice hesitated and then a slow smile curled her mouth. 'My gran was called Sally. I loved her – and I like you.'

'Most people do, because I work at it,' Molly replied confidently. 'You need to get the house-mistresses on your side and then it isn't so bad. I'll show you what to do, Alice. You just do as I tell you and you'll be all right.'

Alice nodded, following in silence as Molly led the way down the stairs and further into the huge house. There were lots of doors and halls and it was the third door round the corner in the back of a very dark hall that Molly stopped in front of. She knocked at the door and a sharp voice told her to enter.

She went ahead of Alice and then stopped in front of a woman who was all grey: grey suit, grey hair, grey skin and grey eyes. Her eyes were very cold and her lips were thin. She didn't smile.

'So, you're Alice, are you?' she said, but it wasn't really a question so Alice didn't answer. 'I see, one of the sulky types. Well, we'll soon knock that out of you. Hold out your left hand.' Alice obeyed reluctantly and got a sharp rap from a wicked-looking cane. She held back the whimper of pain and Miss

Weatherspoon's eyes narrowed but she didn't hit Alice again. 'You'll learn to obey and answer when you're spoken to or you'll *really* feel my tickler.'

Alice saw Molly giving her a meaningful look and remembered. 'Yes, miss. Sorry, miss.'

'Very well, go with Molly,' the housemistress commanded. 'You have five minutes' play before you eat lunch. We feed our children well here and you're given all the benefits you wouldn't have had in the slum you came from.' She switched her hard look to Molly. 'Teach her the rules, Molly. It's your job and I'll want to see an improvement or know the reason why there hasn't been one.'

Alice followed the other girl from the room, feeling more scared than ever, but Molly winked at her. 'Old Cross Knickers must like you. You only got one stroke. I had three the first time she saw me, and a lot more until I learned what to do.' She tucked her arm through Alice's. 'You'll be all right. It's horrible here, but you can learn to make the most of it if you try. Sometimes we get free time and then we go exploring. There are fields not far away and horses. I love horses, do you?'

'Yes. I love all animals and there were lots on the farm where I was before I came here. Auntie Annie gave me a kitten but I wasn't allowed to bring it with me.'

'No, we're not allowed them,' Molly said and for a moment there was sadness in her eyes. 'We had a dog before . . .' She shook her head. 'I don't talk about before I came here. I know I'm here until I'm old enough to leave, because I'm an orphan. Are you?'

'I don't know,' Alice said honestly. 'I haven't seen my mother or my father for months, but I think they might still be alive.'

'Then you're lucky,' Molly said. 'You might get to leave here one day. I'll have to wait until I'm fourteen unless I run away.'

Alice looked at her in alarm. 'You won't, will you? Where would you go?'

'I don't know,' Molly replied. 'If I did, I'd go tomorrow – but at least I get fed here and there's a bed to sleep in. It isn't much fun on the streets. I tried it once but it was even worse than being here.'

Alice couldn't imagine anything worse than being here, but she looked at Molly respectfully. She suddenly understood that in Auntie Annie she'd had a loving friend, who had been like a mother to her, perhaps a better mother than her own. Alice had been lucky for a short time and now she just had to accept what had happened and bide her time until someone came for her. She felt sad and wished she was back at the farm or with her mother in London, even though the bombs were still falling.

'Can I come with you when you go to see the horses?' she asked, and Molly nodded.

'Yeah, course you can,' she said. 'Come on, there's time for you to meet some of the others before we eat.'

After the food she'd been given on the farm, the meal served that day was almost inedible. The meat in the stew was gristle and fat and the dumplings were heavy and tasteless rather than light and delicious.

They lay on Alice's stomach and made her feel queasy but Molly seemed to think it had been a good lunch and Alice dreaded to think what was to come. Even at home, when Mum had been short of money, the food she was given was more to her taste than this. Alice would much rather have had a piece of bread, butter and strawberry jam, but she suspected even that might not taste as good here.

She wept silently into her pillows that night before she finally fell asleep. If only Davey had been here, Alice was certain he would have helped her to escape. Molly said it wasn't nice on the streets, but they could all go to her home. Surely Mum wouldn't turn them away if they told her how horrid it was in this place?

Davey had promised to come back for her, but people didn't keep promises – though she thought her brother might if he could. If Davey came for her they would run away together.

CHAPTER 16

Rose knew it wasn't much use but she went round to the council office anyway and asked if she could be given Alice's address. 'I want to visit her, see how she feels about her mum being killed and take her a little present,' she said. 'She's only young and I'm the closest to family she's got now – her Aunt Rose, I am, see.'

Rose crossed her fingers behind her back as the girl behind the counter hesitated and then drew a book towards her. She read the entry and then frowned. 'She isn't at the farm anymore.' Her finger ran down the entry. 'It says here she has been put down on the list for an orphanage, but it doesn't say where.'

'Surely it must?' Rose said sharply. 'I can't allow my Alice to be put in an orphanage. Give me the address and I'll go and sort it.'

'It doesn't say.' The girl looked uncomfortable and then frowned. 'I'll have to ask my superior anyway – and you'll need to bring something in to prove you are her aunt.'

She looked relieved, as if she'd found a get-out for herself. Rose knew she was stumped. She couldn't prove she was Alice's aunt in law, because she wasn't – and that meant they wouldn't give her the name of the orphanage even if they knew it.

'It seems mighty strange to me you don't have her address,' she said accusingly. 'I've a good mind to go to the police about you lot.'

The girl looked alarmed. 'It isn't my fault, we had a fire during a raid last week. It got put out quick and the records in the metal file were safe but some papers that were due to be filed were lost.' She looked guilty. 'I'm sorry I can't help you – but if you bring your identity papers in, I can release the name of the farm to you and they might know.'

Rose nodded and left. She'd known there wasn't much chance of getting the address before she went, but she'd hoped she might get a junior – and juniors sometimes made slip-ups. Damn officialdom and the rules! Rose wished she'd got the address of the farm from Dora. It hadn't seemed important while Dora was alive – especially after her promises to take Rose to visit.

Tears stung Rose's eyes once more. She was glad they'd made their differences up before Dora was killed in that blooming raid, but she wished her friend was still here. Several of the houses had been damaged by the raid, but Rose's home only had a couple of windows broken, which Harry Smith had got patched up for her. Why did it have to be Dora's house that took the direct hit and why hadn't the silly woman gone to the underground for shelter?

Alice in an orphanage! It didn't bear thinking of. How had she taken the news of her mother's death – her gran's, too? Though she would have been expecting that.

Rose's heart ached for her and the lad who had been sent off to Canada. He might never know what had happened to his mother, might never return to his country – though once Dave got home from the war, if he did, he would leave no stone unturned to find his children. Rose wondered if she should write to Dave Blake and tell him what had happened – and yet if she did that, he would surely find it too hard to bear. He was probably at sea and when he docked the news would surely be waiting for him? If he came back to search for his son and daughter, Rose would do all she could to help.

What of Alice in the meantime? The thought of the child's pain and anxiety was tearing Rose apart. She felt frustration and anger at the plight of the little girl she loved. Even the best of orphanages were not nice places to be sent to and some were terrible. She clenched her fists. She could kill that lot round the council who had just sent her off to strangers again. If only they'd asked locally if anyone would take her on.

'No one has told you that your mother was killed in her own home by a bomb last month?' Miss Weatherspoon's hard eyes gleamed with an emotion that was hard to decipher. 'Well, that is quite disgraceful. You should have been told by the people you were with; it was their responsibility. Never mind,

I've told you now. I'm afraid your home was completely destroyed too – so there is nothing left. Anything you didn't take with you when you went to the farm would have burned in the fire. So, you see, you're lucky to have a new home here and the clothes we provide for you.'

Alice felt the coarse material of the grey dress itching around her neck. They'd taken the two pretty dresses Auntie Annie had made for her away and given her this shapeless thing to wear. Her dresses had to be kept for best, if she went visiting with someone. She hated it, but it was the rule that everyone wore the same clothes and her dresses were being stored in case she was called for and taken out for a few hours.

Some of the children did have rare visits from relatives who gave them a lovely tea at a restaurant in Cambridge. They were the lucky ones. Only five or six out of the two hundred children housed in the orphanage had people on the outside, as Molly called it.

'I think of it as being in prison,' Molly told her once when they had escaped to visit the horses in a field a mile or so away from where the orphanage was situated. 'My crime is that all my close family died. Only my Aunt June is left. She's my mother's sister but she isn't married and she can't afford to have me live with her because she says folk might think I was hers and she could lose her job. When she can, she sends me a little money.' She shook her head. 'One day I'll be set free and so will you, Alice. Always remember that. You won't be here forever unless you die, and you don't want to do that. Only the cissies do that. We're tough, aren't we?'

Alice agreed that they were, but she didn't feel that way inside. If it hadn't been for Molly, she thought she might have sat in her corner in the dormitory and died. She was regularly called out by Miss Weatherspoon and given a rap across the hands, but it was only ever one. Some of the girls in her house got three or even four and Alice had seen them run away in tears – but they were the defiant ones. Alice had learned to take her punishment meekly and to answer when she was spoken to but say nothing at any other time except when she was with her Molly. She played with some of the other girls in games like tag and skipping with a rope, but she seldom joined in the chatter.

At school, she wrote busily in her exercise book when given work to do and it was often praised. Her teacher reported that she was a studious, industrious girl, but the truth was she was too cowed to do anything else.

She thought often of her time with Auntie Annie, who had died in the hospital while having an operation to remove something from her tummy. Alice didn't really understand, but Molly had heard Miss Button telling Miss Weatherspoon about it and so she'd told her what it meant. Alice understood then why Uncle Bob had cried and seemed so helpless. Auntie Annie had done everything for him at the farm and he must miss her.

Alice cried for her mother, and for Aunt Annie, but she cried into her pillow when the other girls were asleep, because Molly was right. Some of the older girls were cruel and spiteful and they punished any sign of weakness. They seemed to delight in pulling her hair as they ran past and if she cried or complained they would just bully her more. There was no one she could tell except Molly, and she said it was best just to ignore what the bullies did.

'If you get them into trouble with the house-mistresses, they'll get you back another day and make your life a misery. You have to keep quiet and eventually they'll get fed up and ignore you. There's always another new girl they can torment soon enough.'

For the moment Alice was the new girl, but there was no one she could ask for help anyway. Daddy was at sea fighting the enemy. Did he even know where she was – and what could he do if he did? Alice didn't trust the housemistresses and Molly could do nothing. She tried to think of someone who might help her and suddenly saw Rose's smiling face. Aunt Rose had always been kind to her. Perhaps if she could send her a letter she would come and fetch her away from this horrid place? Alice knew Aunt Rose lived near where she'd lived but she didn't know the number and she couldn't recall her second name. If she sent a letter to Aunt Rose in Silver Terrace, would it reach her? Or would it be best to try and write to her father?

Alice didn't know and she didn't have any paper or envelopes or the money for a stamp. Would the housemistress give her one if she asked? She wasn't sure and was too afraid of having her hand caned to ask.

CHAPTER 17

The mother bear brought her cubs down to drink at the water as it gently rippled over rocks at the edge of the lake. She had suddenly appeared from the wooded slopes of the rise, her cubs following her once she gave the signal that it was safe to come out of hiding. Davey saw her while he was fishing for their supper. There were some wonderful fish here; Bert said they had come up the inlet from the sea and were coming home to spawn, which meant to lay eggs in the shallows here. Then, Bert said, they would likely die after they'd deposited their eggs.

'If we take them before they've spawned it means there won't be any new fish here next year, but if we take them from the shallows after they've spawned, in June it's a good thing, for us and them. They make good eating, those salmon.'

Davey had never eaten fresh salmon before he'd come to Canada, though he'd once had a pink salmon sandwich at someone's birthday party. He hadn't liked that much, to be honest, but the way Bert fried them in the pan with a little fat they'd saved from cooking one of the ducks they'd trapped, they were delicious. So he was quite happy to sit and try to catch a fish as it wallowed in the shallows.

The bear was much better at fishing than he was, Davey soon realised. It watched patiently and then suddenly dived forward and flicked the fish with its paw onto the bank, where it flapped helpless until caught and held in the bear's teeth. Instead of eating it, the bear let her cubs eat the fish and returned to the water to watch for another. At that moment Davey saw his chance as a salmon seemed unable to move out of the shallow water close to him. He jumped in after it and gave a cry of triumph as he managed to seize it, tossing it onto the bank, where he intended to kill it with a wooden club they used for the purpose. He had his back turned towards the bear when he felt icy cold at his nape and, turning quickly, he saw the bear no more than two yards away. She had clearly seen Davey's salmon and decided she wanted it.

For a moment Davey was tempted to stand his ground and try scaring her off, but remembering what Bert had said about the bears only attacking when they were hungry, he stood absolutely still as it approached, stared at him for a moment and then snatched the salmon and lumbered off. Davey breathed again as the mother bear disappeared into the trees with her salmon, which had been a big one, her cubs following obediently.

Davey's legs felt shaky and he sat down abruptly on the ground just as Bert came running towards him. He was carrying his gun and looked anxious.

'Are you all right, lad?' he asked breathlessly. 'I was coming to see what you'd caught and saw the bear heading towards you. I went back for my gun but I thought I might be too late . . .'

'She only wanted the salmon I caught,' Davey said as his breath came back. 'It was amazing, Bert. She caught a salmon and let the cubs eat it – and then I caught a really big one and she sneaked up behind me as I was thinking how best to kill it.'

'Thank God you didn't try to save your salmon,' Bert said, sighing with relief. 'She could have torn you to pieces before I could do anything, lad.'

'She stole our supper,' Davey said ruefully. 'It was the first one I managed to catch all afternoon.'

'Not to worry,' Bert said. 'I caught one with my net down by the inlet. I wasn't sure you would get anything – the June spawn isn't always that good here – and one is enough for us, Davey. We can always try again tomorrow. As long as you were not hurt, that's the important thing.'

Davey grinned at him. 'It would take more than one old bear to get me,' he bragged and saw Bert smile. The old man had clearly been really worried about him and that meant he cared. Davey felt warm inside, because he'd never been sure whether Bert put up with him just because Albert asked him, or whether he liked him being around. Now he knew that Bert had got fond of him, just as he'd learned to love him.

They walked back to the shack together. Davey looked up at Bert. 'What are we going to do if Albert never comes?' he asked, because it was a question that needed to be asked. It was more than three months now since Albert had last visited and that was too long – he'd said he would only be gone for three weeks. Albert had to be ill – or dead. If his ship had been attacked, he might have been drowned and they might never know.

'Not sure I know,' Bert admitted. 'If it was just me, I'd probably make do on what I could take from the water and the traps, but you need more so mebbe we'll have to go into Waterford one of these days.'

'That's where Albert hired the truck to come out here – it's a long way to walk,' Davey observed doubtfully.

'We shan't walk all the way. Just to where the bus passes,' Bert told him. 'It passes twice a week on Mondays and Thursdays as you know and it goes all the way to Halifax, but we don't need to go that far for a pot of jam. We can get all we need from Corky's place.'

'Do you know Corky well?' Davey asked curiously and saw a look of sadness pass across Bert's face.

'Aye, lad. I knew him well once – when my wife was alive. She used to do a bit of school teaching and she was the local seamstress. Lovely woman she was, but after she died, I just wanted to be alone.'

Davey respected his privacy and didn't ask any more questions. Bert would tell him what he wanted him to know, and it was no use asking for more.

'Yep, that's what we'll do when I'm certain Albert ain't coming back,' Bert said as if to himself. 'Corky will buy a trinket from me, give me enough for what we need for a while.'

'You won't sell your chair?' Davey said, feeling sad that Bert must sell his treasures.

'Nay, not the chair, lad,' Bert agreed. 'I've a few bits put by for an emergency. Corky would have bought them years back but I had no need of the money. They'll see us through for a while, and maybe Albert will turn up one of these days. He might have gone on the Atlantic run for some reason.'

Albert had been adamant that he wouldn't make the dangerous journey but perhaps he'd been ordered to. After all, there was a war on and he might not have been able to get the short voyage he'd wanted. It was a faint hope, Davey knew, but if it kept Bert's hopes alive, perhaps it was a good thing.

Alice saw that Molly had a letter that morning and inside it was a postal order. Her friend showed it to her with glee, her eyes shining.

'It's from Aunt June,' she told Alice. 'She must be feeling rich because she's sent me five shillings! I'll buy some sweets this Saturday when we get taken out and I'll share them with you.'

Alice nodded and smiled at Molly's excitement. She didn't grudge her friend the five shillings, not one iota. She just wished there was someone who cared about *her* even a little bit, but it seemed there was no one. Mummy had gone to Heaven and she didn't know where her daddy was. Davey had been sent to Canada and she didn't know how to contact him. She'd hoped and hoped he would write to her, but he hadn't so she supposed he'd forgotten her.

Holding back her tears as the bell for classes set them scurrying to their form room, Alice wished that she had a few pennies, because then she might be able to write to Aunt Rose in London.

Rose stared at the ruins of her house in disbelief. She'd spent the night sheltering in the underground when the raid came, not emerging until this morning when the all-clear sounded. When she'd reached Silver Terrace it had been almost obliterated, only a few houses left standing at one end. Her own home was a smouldering ruin and, by the looks of it, she wouldn't even be able to save her biscuit tin full of photographs.

Most women these days carried their most precious things in a bag of some sort and kept it with them down the underground. Rose was no different; she had all her personal papers, her Post Office Savings book, a few really precious photographs and her few items of jewellery as well as a change of underwear and a new twinset she'd bought the previous day and hadn't remembered to take out. She was also wearing her one good coat.

'This your place, missus?' a kindly voice asked, and she turned to look at the ARP warden with tears in her eyes.

'Yeah. Bloody Jerries have destroyed nearly everything I had – not that that was much, mind you. Blast that Hitler to Hell. What am I supposed to do now?'

'You get down the Mission Hall, missus,' the warden told her. 'They'll give you a cup of tea and a bacon sandwich and see if they can find you clothes to fit and a bed to sleep in until you can make your own arrangements.'

Rose sighed. She didn't know why she'd asked – she knew the drill. Plenty of her friends had already been made homeless and she was aware how difficult it was to find good accommodation.

'Bloody Jerries,' she muttered again and turned away, walking bang into Harry Smith. He was staring at the scene of devastation and shaking his head.

'That's rotten luck, Rose,' he said. 'I heard that Silver Terrace had been hit so I came down to see if you were all right. I'm sorry you lost your home but you can come and stay with me – no strings. I've got a spare room and you can have what you want of my late wife's things. She didn't have your style, but you can use them until you get better. They give you some extra coupons if they know you've been bombed.'

'Yeah, I know, thanks, Harry.' Rose hesitated and then decided it would be better than sleeping on a mattress on the floor in a church hall, which was about all she would be offered. 'I'll come on those terms but it's only until I can get my own place – and I'll be hauntin' the council until they come up with something decent.'

'We can get your letters redirected,' Harry said as he saw the postman looking at the devastation in bewilderment. 'I'll check if he has anything for you, Rose.'

He went up to the man and inquired and was given an envelope, which he brought back to her. 'It looks like it's a bill from the electric, Rose. Don't worry about it, I'll sort it out.'

Rose inclined her head. She would pay him any money he spent out for her, just as she had when she was in hospital. Her aches and pains were much less now though she still walked with a slight limp, but it didn't stop her doing her job at the factory and she would carry on, even though Harry would be happy to take her over. Rose didn't want that – at least, she wasn't ready for it just yet and if Reg ever came back, he would probably knock her head off for going to live with Harry, even if she was in the spare room. Yet what was her alternative? Not one she fancied much, so she would take her chance and when Reg came back, she would leave it to Harry to explain.

As she entered Harry's house, Rose thought she must have died and gone to heaven. He'd got a good job at the factory and she'd expected him to have a nice home, but this was something more. His furniture was good mahogany and he had quality carpets on the floor rather than a bit of cheap lino. It smelled beautifully of lavender polish and there wasn't even a hint of drains or old cabbage.

'This is posh, Harry,' she said. 'I didn't know yer were rich?'

'I ain't,' he said and grinned at her. 'My late wife had a little bit of money left to her. I told her to keep it for herself and spend it how she liked, and so she bought the carpets and furniture. Sadly, she didn't live more than a few months to enjoy it.'

'I'm sorry, Harry. I didn't know.'

'I kept what she went through to myself. She was a private woman, a lady, really, and it's what she would have wanted. I don't know why she took a shine to me. I'm a common bloke and she could've done better.'

'Nah,' Rose said and smiled at him. 'You're a good bloke, Harry. The girls down the factory don't realise you've got a soft heart – and it's a good job they don't. You would never do anything with them.'

'I am having a job sorting some of the younger ones out,' he admitted. 'I've asked the bosses if I can have another supervisor and if they say yes, I shall ask you to take over a certain section, Rose.'

'You said that before.' She gave him a look. 'I ain't heard anything of it.'

'I know. They ain't answered me so I shall have to put in another request.' He sighed. 'I'm glad you've come, Rose, even if it is only for a short time. I get lonely here nights.'

'I know the feeling,' Rose admitted. 'But you know what my Reg is like – if he comes back and hears I've moved in with a bloke he'll think the worst and he can be a violent man.'

'I can box a bit,' Harry said and grinned. 'Don't you worry, Rose, love. I'll sort him out if he comes after you.'

'He'll likely be after you and he won't be usin' his fists,' Rose warned but Harry just grinned. She decided to leave well alone. If Harry realised that Reg might use a knife on him, he would change his mind and she'd be back down the church hall sleeping on a mattress on the floor.

CHAPTER 18

Davey wandered down the inlet beach, a worried expression on his young face, which was now tanned to a deep brown by the sun. It was surprisingly chilly on this sunny June day, but he had a jerkin made of various animal skins to keep him warm and he was used to cold days like this now. Besides, he had more on his mind than the weather. He was certain that Bert was feeling unwell, though he wouldn't admit to it and carried on setting his traps and cooking and tending his vegetable patch just as if everything was all fine. But it wasn't. Apart from anything else Bert was fretting about Albert.

'Something must be very wrong,' he'd said that morning, looking more anxious than Davey had ever seen him. 'Albert always lets me know if he's going to be delayed for some reason, arranges for supplies to be sent out to me. He wouldn't do this if he could help it. A few weeks late and I don't worry too much – but it's too long this time.' No letters, postcards or groceries had been received since Albert's previous visit and they'd eaten the last of the jam and there was hardly any flour left.

'I'll have to go into the store and buy what we need,' Bert said. 'We'll walk to the bus stop and you can meet me when I get back.' Davey knew it took nearly an hour to walk to the bus stop and that Bert would find it hard to carry the sack back home once it was filled.

'Why don't I come with you?' he asked. 'We can take two sacks and it will be easier to carry the stores home if we have half in each.'

Bert considered the idea and nodded. 'Yes, all right, that makes sense,' he acknowledged. 'If I leave you on your own, goodness knows what mischief you'd get up to.'

They decided to visit Waterford the next day because it was one of the days that the bus came by. Bert had an elaborately carved wall clock in the shack and also a silver pocket watch. The watch was very precious to him, a present from his wife, and he was careful how he wound it. Most of the time it stayed in the dresser drawer but he'd taken it out a short time earlier and checked that the time it was showing matched the hour on the wall clock.

'We don't want to miss our bus,' he'd told Davey. 'We'll need to be up early in the morning.'

It would be the first time since he'd arrived that Davey had left their home and wondering about what Waterford would be like to visit after so many months had passed made him think about the voyage out here and how long it was since he'd come to Halifax, to the port and the crowded city. Out here it seemed a world away from all that and he was almost reluctant to leave it even for a day, though they were only going to the settlement and not into Halifax itself. He'd been with Bert almost a year and in all that time, Albert had never let them down, but now he had and Davey had a very bad feeling about it. He thought Bert did too, but of course the old man wouldn't say anything. He kept things like that inside and the only way you could tell he was upset was the missing twinkle from his eyes.

A lot of the buildings in Waterford were made of wood, just like Bert's shack, only bigger and more than one storey high, and they looked as if they were painted regularly. They had outside verandas and staircases up the side to the top floor, and the shop windows were filled with things. It was very different to Davey's home streets in the East End of London, brighter and cleaner and friendlier too. Some of the shopkeepers were outside, sweeping their verandas and talking to their customers, most of whom had arrived in lorries or trucks and were busy filling them with provisions of all kinds, from farming implements to sacks of food. One of the shops sold bits of furniture as well as books, clothes, and China plates and mugs. It was a strange mixture, but all the shops were different to anything he was used to.

'Do you want to have a walk round while I buy what we need?' Bert asked him, but Davey shook his head. He didn't have any money to buy anything from the stores and there was really nothing he wanted. Bert had given him his own knife and Albert had brought him a new pair of stout boots the last time he came. Davey was wearing a pair of breeches that Bert had made him out of the hide of a deer they'd found lamed and in pain. Its leg was broken in two places and it had sore places on its hindquarters. Bert said it looked as if it might have been mauled by a cougar and the kindest thing was to put it out of its misery.

Bert had seen the doubt in Davey's face and said, 'Not sure how it managed to survive this long, but even if we tried to mend its leg, I doubt it would live.' He'd killed it quickly and cleanly and Davey had shut his eyes and whispered a little prayer, because it was a beautiful creature and he'd felt sad they couldn't take it home and make it well again. 'No good being sentimental, lad,' Bert had told him. 'I looked after a young doe once, even though my father told me I was a fool – I nursed it, fed it and thought I'd made it well again, and then one morning I got up and found it dead. My pa said it was the shock to the system and that I'd just prolonged its suffering.'

He'd given Davey the chore of cleaning and curing the hide and then one evening he'd fetched out an ancient sewing machine and fashioned the breeches for Davey. They felt warm and comfortable and covered his legs to just above his ankles; they had no buttons or zips but fastened with laces at the sides, much the same as the ones Two Bears wore.

Davey had asked Bert where he'd learned to make things like that, but he'd just shrugged and said when needs must you did what you had to. However, he understood that Bert had lived amongst the Mi'kmaq for some time and picked up some of their ways. Davey had learned not to ask a question more than once because Bert never answered a second time. He spoke no more than was necessary and they got on fine the way they were.

When they entered the grocery store, the man behind the counter gave a cry of recognition. 'Well, bless my hide,' he shouted. 'Bert! I thought you must be dead. It's more than a year since I saw you, I'm sure.'

'Been busy,' Bert replied. ''Sides, you know Albert fetches my goods as a rule. How are you, Corky – and how is that wife of yours?'

'Rodie!' Corky hollered, going to a door which, when opened, led into a large kitchen. 'Get out here and see what the wind blew in.'

A plump lady with red cheeks and dark hair caught up on top of her head in an untidy bun came bustling in with a rolling pin in her hand. 'What's all the fuss about . . . ? Well, as I live and breathe, if it isn't Bert – and that will be young Davey. Albert told us all about him.' She came round the counter and threw her arms around Bert, hugging him for all she was worth, and then turned to Davey. 'How are you getting on out there by the inlet, young'un?'

'It's good,' Davey told her and was immediately enveloped in a big hug. She smelled of baking and soap like flowers and Davey felt a lump in his throat, because it was so long since he'd been hugged with such warmth. 'Thank you!'

'Bless me, what lovely manners the lad has,' Rodie exclaimed. 'Just you come through with me and try my lemon and honey cake while Bert does his shopping.'

Davey tried to protest that he wanted to help Bert but he was propelled behind the counter to the long, clean kitchen. It had a warm, homely smell and the scrubbed pine table was covered with baking of all kinds, scones and tarts and small cakes and larger ones, all warm and fresh from the oven. Davey realised that she must bake them for her customers as well as her family, because no family could eat all this food.

He sat at the table and a dish of cake slices was offered. 'Go on, take a slice, lad,' Rodie encouraged. 'I know you don't get much in the way of treats living with Bert out there near the shore. Eat up and I'll give you some more to eat on the journey home.'

'You're very kind,' Davey said and Rodie smiled. 'Have you known Bert long?'

'Forever. His wife, Sarah, was like a second mother to me,' Rodie told him. 'She went to school with my mother who introduced them when he was back from the sea once and she thought he looked as if he needed a wife. It worked!' She beamed at Davey, then shook her head sadly. 'He nearly died after she went. Wouldn't eat nor get out of bed until my Corky sorted him out. Don't know what he said to him, but it worked. Best of mates they are.' She nodded to Davey. 'We thought he might come in soon, long as Albert hasn't been for a while and there's been no letters.'

Davey nibbled his cake, savouring it. 'Would you send a letter to my family in England for me, Mrs Rodie?'

She laughed, her chins wobbling. 'Course I would, Davey – but it's just Rodie. Me and Corky never got married. Ain't never needed a bit of paper to say he's my man. You write it and give me the address.'

'I don't have any money,' Davey told her doubtfully. 'But I could make you something from the skins?'

'Can you make me a fur muff?' Rodie asked, a gleam in her eyes. 'I've got a niece wants a fur muff for Sunday church. My brother's girl. Nice girl she is, getting married soon, I dare say.'

'A muff?' Davey thought about it. 'I know what you mean. I've seen one in a book they sent me from the school.'

'Well, you write your letter to your family,' Rodie said, smiling, 'and I'll send it – and see what you can do for me. You know where we are now and mebbe someone will call round to see how you are now and then.'

'I can send it back with my schoolwork at the end of the month,' Davey suggested. 'Unless Bert brings me in before next month.'

'He won't be doing that unless . . .' Rodie shook her head. 'I don't know how he'll manage if Albert doesn't come back.'

'He will come back, won't he?' Davey asked anxiously. 'He promised me . . .' There was no point in saying what Albert had promised because he knew that only one thing would keep his friend away permanently.

'I heard something about a ship,' Rodie said uncertainly. 'Don't know if it was Albert's, but Corky says they're attacking American shipping and ours – any country that supports Britain, and I heard a ship was sunk not long out from Halifax.'

'I'd almost forgotten the war for a while, but that makes it come back,' Davey admitted and she nodded. 'I do hope he isn't dead.'

'It doesn't bear thinking of,' Rodie said and shook her head. 'The pair of you relying on him for everything, too.'

She fetched a piece of muslin from the pantry and wrapped some scones and cakes in it, clearly upset by the idea of their plight if Albert never returned.

'Take these, Davey, and remember, if things are bad and you need help, you send word to us or you come and fetch us. Bert is a friend and we need to look after him.'

Davey promised he would and she nodded to him to return to the shop as she resumed her endless baking. As he went into the shop, the men stopped talking. Bert had two sacks ready for them to carry.

'I'll keep an eye out for Albert and if I hear anything, I'll take a ride out your way.'

'Thanks, Corky,' Bert said. 'Come on, lad. We've been offered a lift most of the way home so we may as well take it.'

Outside was a rusty and dented truck. A man was loading it and he turned and nodded at Bert, grunting but not speaking.

'You get in the back with the sacks,' Bert said. 'Stand on that box there and I'll hand you our stuff over. It may be a bit draughty back here but it will save the fares.'

Davey nodded. He knew the man who had offered

them a lift. His name was Mr Gordon and he'd called at the shack twice in the past months, buying the furs they didn't want for a few coins. Bert said he didn't pay much but he accepted what he was offered without comment. Davey supposed it was all the income Bert had and realised that without Albert's visits and the money he gave his father they would find life much harder.

CHAPTER 19

Rose looked at the letter addressed to Mrs Dora Blake and noticed the postmark was from abroad; it looked like Canada and that could only be young Davey. She felt her heart quicken. If it was from him, it meant he was still alive and that was a miracle. What was she supposed to do with it? She turned it over in her hand, considering whether or not she ought to open it. Dora's neighbour from across the road said it had been delivered to her by mistake. She'd handed it to Rose after they'd bumped into each other when Rose went back to the terrace to see how the clear-up was getting on. Most of the debris had gone and the street was almost unrecognisable from the one she'd known, apart from the few houses still remaining at the far end.

'I thought you might know what to do with this, Rose,' the woman said as she passed her the letter. 'I thought of it when I saw yer on the street and I wasn't certain where yer livin' now.'

Rose didn't enlighten her. She didn't want gossip about her and Harry if she could help it. 'When did it come?'

'Not sure. I reckon they just shove anythin' they don't know what to do with through my bloomin' door,' she'd told Rose. 'I would've put it back in the post box but then I thought of you. Her poor 'usband might want it when he gets 'ome – if he ever does, poor bleeder.' She spoke of Dora's husband with respect, as everyone in Silver Terrace had when he lived there. 'Though it's a blessin' he never knew what his wife was up to behind his back.'

Rose had been doubtful about taking the letter, but in the end she took it, thinking she would leave it untouched for Dave's return. Now she was back in Harry's sitting room and it was on her mind, so she looked at it again. Should she read it? What could she do if the poor kid was pleading to come home? She wasn't family and wouldn't be listened to – and it wasn't her problem. Yet her conscience wouldn't let her throw it out, so she opened it.

Dear Mum,

I just wanted to tell you I'm with my friend Bert. We look after each other and he makes me do my schoolwork. I can spell proper now, because Bert taught me and I'm learning about the world. One day I'm going to be a seaman like Dad, though I'd like the merchant ships more than the cruise liners.

I hope you and Alice are both well and you've been down to see her. I hope Dad has been home again and things are all right. I think about you

214

*all. Please write back and tell me if Alice is happy
at the farm.*
   Your loving son, Davey

'Cor blimey,' Rose exclaimed to herself. 'He writes
a fair hand; I'll say that for 'im.' It was brief but
cheerful and it seemed that Davey was making the
most of things and getting on with it. He hadn't said
a word about wanting to come home so perhaps he
was settled now and happy where he was.

Life moved on and Rose was busy at the factory.
She'd heard nothing from her husband in months or
from either of her sons. She worried if they were all
right. They weren't good at writing letters but she'd
expected to hear something. She'd let her daughter-
in-law know her new address but apart from a short
letter saying how sorry she was, she'd had nothing
more from her. Of course, the Post Office should
redeliver all her mail these days but Rose didn't trust
that they would. She wished she'd had a daughter,
because a girl might have settled near her mother, but
the boys had moved on away as soon as they left
school. They normally sent her cards and gifts at
Christmas and on her birthday but hardly ever visited.
She knew she had a grandson but she'd only seen a
photograph and hadn't been invited to visit and stay
for the christening, although she'd thought her daughter-
in-law might have asked her for that.

Sighing, Rose put the letter away in the big old
handbag she used to keep her important things in. It
was easy to pick up and take with her when the siren
that warned of the air raids that had continued night

after night for months, taking lives and causing terrible destruction, sounded. In some parts of the East End, whole streets had gone, obliterated by explosions and fire. When she'd inquired about a new home with the council, she was told she had no chance of a house.

'Our priorities are families, Mrs Parker. I'm sorry. You wouldn't even get on the list at the moment – perhaps when the rebuilding starts you might stand a chance of a small flat.'

When she told Harry what they'd said, he nodded wisely. 'It's to be expected, Rose. All the old back-to-back houses are being destroyed by Hitler. He's doing what successive British Governments have promised and never done: clearing the slums. They won't be rebuilt. It will be high-rise in future to make more of the land.'

Rose knew he was right, so she would have a big decision to make one day. Living with Harry was fine for the moment. He'd kept his word and she had her own room, though she never slept there at night. There were hundreds like her and a warm camaraderie existed, everyone sharing sandwiches and flasks of tea or cocoa. However, Rose knew it couldn't go on this way forever. Harry wanted her and he wanted her on a permanent basis. One day she would have to find a room somewhere, unless she left London and her work in the factory. Perhaps in the countryside – or near the coast – she might find a decent home for herself.

She'd always had to think for herself. Her father had been hard-working but he'd died young, leaving

Rose's mother to struggle alone until she too died, and then she'd lived with her grandmother for a while before she found work and a room she could afford. Rose had expected marriage to change her life and for the first few years she'd been content with her home and her family, but her husband had let her down too many times to count, teaching her she had only herself to rely on – and she expected it would always be that way. She believed she was too old to find love again, even though she could have had a relationship with Harry if she'd chosen. Rose wasn't bad looking, even if she was getting on for thirty-five, but once bitten . . . And her old man would skin her alive if he came home and found her living with Harry. Reg would never believe it was just friendship and a kind heart. He'd beat her and drag her off somewhere, Rose knew, so there wasn't much choice. She had to find somewhere she could be independent of them both, but not just yet. Something was tying her to the East End and it wasn't just her job. Rose could find work anywhere. She thought about it and nodded to herself as she understood what it was she was waiting for.

If Dave Blake came looking for his family one day, Rose would give him the letter, she promised herself. She would tell him what happened to Dora, too. He was a decent lad and he didn't deserve what had happened to him. Rose just hoped he would get back from the war safe and sound.

The sound of the naval guns boomed to the right of Dave's ship. They were in the middle of a sea battle, being attacked from both the surface and below the waves. His ship was helping to protect a convoy carrying food to Britain from Canada and the attack had begun just one day out from the port.

Dave had been pleased when he learned they were bound for Halifax. He knew that was where Davey's journey had ended, though all his attempts to discover more had ended in failure. On his last leave in London, Dave had haunted the council offices, which had instigated his son's voyage to Canada, badgering them for information. They still had none to give, but the girl behind the desk had let slip that it wasn't the first time their records had been incomplete.

'We put the missing register in a special file,' she said. 'Some of them have turned up safe and sound months after, it was just that someone forgot to put a tick by a name, that's all. It's probably what happened to your son, sir. He's sure to be with a family somewhere.'

'That's not good enough,' Dave had told her, barely holding his anger. 'I did not give my permission for Davey to leave the country and if anything has happened to him, I'll make sure someone carries the can for it. You had no right to send him without my permission. You did not have a court order and he wasn't in any danger, physical or moral.' He'd glared at her and at her supervisor who had come out of her office to see what was going on. 'This war will be over one day and then I'll haunt the life out of you lot.'

Dave had walked out angrily. He'd told the girl that Davey was in no moral danger, but he was no longer sure that was true. Dora had taken up with

Mick and he wouldn't have wanted his children to be contaminated by that crook's influence. Dora had always been a bit flighty but he'd believed she knew when to stop. Yet, he was a fair man and he knew that her behaviour had been partly his fault. He'd been so furious with Dora that he'd threatened her with his fist and then told her he'd kill her if anything happened to Davey. It might have pushed her into an unwise decision. He'd later regretted saying what he had, but it had taken him a few days to calm down, by which time he was mid-ocean once more, heading at that time for many months in the Far East and then he'd been informed that Dora was dead . . .

Now, back in the cold waters of the North Atlantic, he scanned the surface of the sea with his binoculars, watching for signs that they were about to be attacked from below. You didn't get much warning – sometimes, if you were lucky, you spotted a periscope some distance off or your radar expert would pick up soundings from the depths, but large sea creatures could sometimes interfere with readings. Often in the middle of a sea battle, the first warning you had was when your ship had already been hit. Davey hated the unseen enemy below. You could only fight what you could see, as the guns behind him clearly were, booming away at something.

The fighting was fierce, fires and smoke obscuring much of what was going on as he kept his vigil, warning of any new attack. A merchant vessel had been sunk and the crew that had made it to the water were being picked up. Dave frowned as he thought of the probable fate of those that went down on the ship and of the terrible death that was drowning. It made him think again, as he had so often, of what had happened to Davey. Had he met a watery end? No, Dave couldn't believe it. Inside, he was sure the boy was still alive.

It was a long shot, but he'd hoped that he might pick up some news of his son on his brief visit to Halifax. The children had disembarked there but most had been taken off by their adoptive parents and the families that had claimed them. Still, he'd asked around the waterfront bars and the men sitting in the cool sunshine mending nets. One old seaman had sucked his pipe and taken his cap off a couple of times to scratch beneath it.

'I might have heard the name . . .' he said consideringly as Dave had turned to him with the same question that he'd asked fifty times without result. 'Davey, nice name. I reckon I heard Albert mention his name when he stopped by for a drink but I ain't completely sure. I used to know Albert's father years ago and so he always buys me a drink when he's in port. Now I think of it, might have seen them catching the coastal bus a day or so after some evacuees arrived . . .' He nodded thoughtfully. 'I know he said something about a young lad but I can't rightly remember what.'

'Albert who?' Dave had asked eagerly.

'Albert Cox; he usually works the coastal ships carrying cargo from here to the USA and back. It suits him because of his father.' The seaman had scratched his balding pate again. 'Yes . . . I reckon it was something to do with his father and getting a

220

lad to help look after him.' He looked at Dave sadly. 'Sorry – it was a long time ago.'

'Where can I find Albert's father?'

'No idea,' the seaman had said. 'Somewhere in the boonies, don't even have a name. Yeah, that's it! I reckon he said he was taking the boy to his father, and I think the lad's name was Davey.'

'Did you see the boy? How old was he? What colour hair did he have?'

The old man shook his head firmly. 'Now that I do not know cos I never saw him.'

'Thanks.' Dave gave him a packet of cigarettes. 'I have English money – would you send word if you hear more, please?'

'I reckon I might.' He'd held out his hand for the English pound note. 'Where do I send word if I hear?'

Dave had thought for a moment. His mind moved over the people he knew and settled on Rose Parker. Rose was all right; he could trust her. He'd smiled and written down Rose's name and address for the old salt, who told him his name was Jacob Riley. 'Come and see me if you're back this way, and I'll send a letter if I hear anything.'

'Thanks, Jacob, I shall, but I doubt we'll be here again any time soon.' Dave knew he could be sent anywhere in the world. When you were in the navy you went where you were sent and did what you were told.

It had been so little to go on, but Dave's spirits had lifted as he'd returned to his ship and they'd prepared to sail, his thoughts busy with a boy who might be his Davey. Not much, but something – the first time anyone had told him anything positive and it had given him hope. He had the name Albert Cox and next time he returned to Halifax he would search for his son.

Davey sat up and shivered and then got out of bed. It felt very cold, as if the range had gone out, but he padded across to Bert's bed on bare feet and looked at him. The old man was breathing easily and seemed to be sleeping, but he did sometimes cry out in his sleep and Davey touched his hand gently. He was warm enough, not icy cold. It was a fear he had that one morning he would find him dead.

Bert hadn't been well these past few months, had got slowly worse after their trip to the store. When Davey thought about it, Bert seemed to have been failing since Albert stopped coming. So far, they'd managed to buy a few luxuries: a pot of Rodie's homemade strawberry jam and another of honey, the flour to make their own bread, some sugar, salt and coffee, but there was none of the tinned meat or fish Albert had always brought, nor yet rice or milk, fresh or canned. They drank their coffee black with a half a spoon of sugar. Bert liked his sugar – it was one of the few luxuries he'd been loath to give up.

'I've got a sweet tooth, my Sarah always said so,' he'd reminisced. 'I can drink my coffee without but it ain't the same.'

Davey had found the thick black drink almost undrinkable when he'd first arrived, even with the sugar. He'd preferred water, but coffee was hot and it kept you going and now he drank it without sugar, leaving that for Bert and his sweet tooth. He didn't enjoy it, but it was warm and helped when there wasn't much food to fill your stomach. Most days they either trapped or caught something but there were days, particularly when it got colder, when there was nothing. Bert didn't like to shoot big animals. He kept what little ammunition he possessed in case they were attacked by a hungry bear. Besides, he said, they were better off keeping their food supply adequate and fresh, though sometimes it wasn't quite enough for the two of them. Bert would probably have had more than enough for just him, but Davey was growing, shooting up in leaps and bounds and he got hungry. The only time Bert willingly used his gun was when they found a wounded bear. It was old, its leg was torn so badly that it couldn't hunt, and Bert said it was a kindness to put it out of its misery. Just like the deer, Bert didn't like to see any animal suffer.

Its flesh was all right to eat roasted, though Davey didn't relish it, and its skin made a few coins for Bert which they would spend on more supplies when they went in to Corky's place.

Davey worried about his friend. He seemed disinclined to do much these days and it was Davey who visited the traps every morning and evening, Davey who skinned and prepared the catch for their meal. He'd got over his squeamishness, because the meat and fish they caught was their means of survival. Without the extra supplies they'd relied on, it was the only way they could live now.

Davey's days were too busy to feel sorry for himself.

His hair was long and tied back with a piece of string and his skin was golden and freckled. Life was hard but he'd never had an easy life and he enjoyed being with Bert and didn't mind doing most of the work. He reckoned there wasn't that much to do, really, and he had plenty of time for the books he was studying in the evenings. The books often had pictures and showed him maps of where they were and of the rest of the world. Davey learned that Canada was so much bigger and so different in other places to their home; there were big cities and towns, also wild open spaces where the bears and cougars roamed amongst the snow in the mountains. Here by the inlet it was beautiful, with a lake a little further inland, streams that tumbled over boulders, and all the wonderful trees that Davey had learned the names of, like the Northern White Cedar and the balsam fir, the spruce and the red oak. Davey hadn't seen many trees before he left the East End of London, and certainly not these magnificent specimens. There were lots of flowers too, like Nova Scotia's official flower, the trailing arbutus, which was also called the mayflower and spilled over the ground with its ever-green leaves and small scented pale pink, white, and deep pink flowers. Bert had shown Davey the samphire greens, also known as sea asparagus, that he used in cooking and various other herbs and plants that were good to eat, also some that were poisonous.

Davey didn't want to lose his friend and mentor and it wasn't just for selfish reasons. He'd come to respect, like and perhaps even love the old man who had taken him in, and his thoughts of returning home were now few and far between. His letter to England had been sent months ago now but he'd had no reply, perhaps he hadn't expected one; he suspected his mother had given him up because he was too much trouble for her and she hadn't replied so it must be she didn't want him. That hurt, but not as much as it would have once. His new life was too busy for him to dwell on such things, although he would have liked to hear from his mother about Alice. Davey missed his sister and worried for her. He'd given Corky's address, because there were no deliveries here except those Corky occasionally made and Bert's old friend drove out to see them once every few weeks now, not at a regular time but when Rodie sent him.

'She's worried about the pair of you,' Corky had told him during one of the visits, handing over a piece of linen packed with Rodie's cooking. 'What will you do, Davey, if Bert becomes too ill for you to manage alone?'

'I don't know, sir,' Davey admitted, feeling anxious. 'I don't know how I could let you know. It's a long way to Mr Gordon's house or the bus, even if I could find the money for the fare, and if Bert is very ill, I can't just leave him.'

'No, that's what we thought, so we've arranged for you to signal for help. Can you climb that tree over there, the tall one?'

'Yes.' Davey nodded. 'But I don't see . . .' His face brightened as Corky took out a big red flag.

'Siggy Gordon will see it with his binoculars,' Corky said. 'He'll drive in to me and I'll come.'

Davey nodded. It wasn't ideal but at least it was something. 'Yes, sir,' he said. 'I promise I'll do that, but only if he seems worse, else he'd have my guts for garters if I got you out here for nothing.'

'Aye, he would,' Corky agreed and laughed. 'He'd have mine too if he knew what I'd just done, so make it our little secret, yeah?'

'Yeah, all right,' Davey agreed and grinned. He counted Corky and Rodie as friends, but wished they lived nearer. Mr Gordon was their nearest neighbour apart from the Mi'kmaq man, Two Bears, who didn't relish visitors, and Davey didn't truly trust him to help in an emergency, but it was the best they had for the moment. If only Albert would turn up . . . But that was like wishing for the moon. In his heart, Davey knew that Albert must be dead. After all, ships were attacked all the time and Davey wondered if his father's ship was all right. If anything happened to his dad, he might never know.

Davey felt a strange ache inside his chest, an over-whelming feeling of loneliness. He didn't even know if his father was alive or dead and wasn't sure whether he would see any of his family ever again. It hadn't felt so bad while he knew he had Bert and Albert, but if the old man died, would Corky and Rodie help him get back to London? He had to return one day to keep his promise to Alice. Sometimes, he lay awake thinking of her and wondering if she remembered him and his promise that he would return for her . . .

CHAPTER 20

It was Alice's birthday. She was eleven now, but no one wished her happy birthday or mentioned it, not even one card or present. Today didn't feel like a birthday, with no cards or presents or even a cake for her tea. It was semolina pudding, which Alice hated, bread and butter or stewed plums with a lumpy custard. Alice chose the plums. At least they tasted nice, though she left most of the custard. It had been made with powdered egg and had a peculiar taste, but then most things made with that sort of egg did. It was what people had to use because of the war and some food was in short supply. On the farm there had always been plenty of lovely fresh eggs. She often longed to be back there with the kind woman she'd called Auntie Annie and thought about it more than her home in London.

Thinking about her home made her sad. Her mother had sent her away and she hadn't written to her while she was alive. Now she was dead and Alice had cried many tears over her. She'd been happy when Mum and Daddy and Davey had loved her. Aunt Rose had made a fuss of her and given her cakes to eat but that seemed so long ago; it was almost as if it was a dream and only Daddy and Davey seemed real, but they were far away and she wasn't sure they even knew where she was now.

Alice went to bed that evening in the dormitory as usual. She was feeling weepy and was crying into her pillow when she felt a hand on her head and then Molly crept into bed with her.

'You're sad,' Molly whispered. 'Why are you crying?'

'Tis nuthin',' Alice said but Molly pushed a paper bag at her.

'It's pear drops,' she whispered. 'You know my auntie sends me pocket money every now and then and Miss Button gives me threepence a week because I'm a monitor now. I bought these when we were taken to the park yesterday and I went into the little shop near the gate that Miss Button lets those of us with pocket money go into and buy sweets.'

'I wasn't allowed to come because Miss Weatherspoon said I wasn't paying attention in history class.'

'I know,' Molly sympathised. She was still Alice's only real friend at the orphanage, though the older girls had got tired of tormenting her and no longer pulled her hair, having found new victims. 'But you never get pocket money, do you?'

Alice shook her head. 'Not even on my birthday. Daddy used to give me tuppence to spend sometimes, and Auntie Annie gave me a whole sixpence once and a penny most weeks.'

'Is it your birthday soon?' Molly asked.

'It's today but I didn't get a card from anyone.'

'Not even one?' Molly's eyes widened. 'I thought you might get things when you first came, because you've got a father and brother so you're not an orphan like me – but my aunt sends me presents on my birthday and Christmas. If she can afford it, she takes me out to tea, as near to my birthday as she can . . .'

'I know. You had a birthday last month . . .' Alice said and swiped a hand over her face. 'Mum sent me sweets once after I went to the farm but nothing else. She promised she would and so did Daddy – and Davey said he would if he could, but they all forgot . . .'

'Perhaps they just couldn't,' Molly murmured sadly. 'Things are very hard now because of the war. My auntie said so. Have another pear drop, Alice. Next time I get my pocket money I'll buy you a sherbet dip.'

Alice took a sweet and popped it into her mouth. It felt nice with Molly in bed beside her, the way it used to be at home when Davey would sit with her if she was frightened and upset.

'You're nice to me but I have nothing to give *you*, Molly.'

'You can help me with my sums,' her friend said. 'You're better at sums than I am and we have sums in the morning. Show me your answers and I'll give you a penny of my money each time I get pocket money.'

'All right,' Alice agreed, glad that she could help Molly. 'Auntie Annie helped me learn my times tables and showed me how to divide, but sometimes I get the complicated sums wrong.'

'I get them wrong all the time and get the cane,' Molly said ruefully. 'I'm never going to do sums when I'm old enough to choose what I want.'

'How are you going to cook, or measure a new dress if you can't add up?' Alice said. 'It's a good thing to learn your sums for those things, Molly.'

'I'll get someone to help me measure the dress,' Molly replied serenely. 'And most people just use a cup of this or a cup of that, that's what Miss Button says in cookery class.'

Alice had discovered that Miss Button wasn't the ogress she'd thought when she escorted her to the orphanage. She was stern but her classes – cookery, sewing and knitting – were some of the best lessons they were offered at the orphanage school they all attended. She taught the girls in the afternoons, and lived in a room at the orphanage and oversaw the evening meal, just like Miss Weatherspoon, who did morning lessons and lunch, but she was nice once you got to know her. Other housemistresses were there for breakfast, which was always lumpy porridge, and at lunch it was just a sandwich with jam, chicken paste or, on rare occasions, grated cheese. Alice liked the jam or chicken paste days, though the strawberry jam wasn't full of berries like they'd had on the farm.

She'd been so lucky to have that time with Auntie Annie but then she'd had to come to this hateful place. Alice wondered why she was forced to stay here but supposed it was because of the bombing, although Miss Button had told her class that the terrible bombing in London had eased off considerably.

'The blitz of London is over, at least for the time being. It may start again, of course, but it seems Hitler has turned his attentions elsewhere for the moment and we may thank God for that.'

All the children had said Amen. Miss Button often told them to thank God for something. Especially when they'd had one of the rare cooking classes and were allowed to eat what they made. Things like jam tarts or rock cakes were all tasty and often nicer than anything they were served at mealtimes – though occasionally they had Spam with mashed potato and cabbage. Alice didn't like the soggy cabbage much, but she loved the Spam, which was a treat all the children enjoyed.

Now that she'd settled down and learned to accept the way things were, her life at the orphanage was bearable but not happy. It was a grey place, with dull paintwork, dark and dreary furnishings and the atmosphere was just heavy. Alice felt sad inside most of the time, but she'd been told to hide it by Molly and she'd found it was best just to be meek and quick to obey. That way she didn't often get punished but she was still unhappy and longed for her father to come and fetch her home as he'd promised.

'If you ever get pocket money you can save it and send a postcard to your dad or your auntie,' Molly suggested and Alice turned to her, suddenly alert.

'Could I?'

Molly squeezed her hand. 'Yes, save it for a week or two and then buy a card and a stamp. You can get them from the sweet shop near the park – and there's a post box on our way back. You can bring it back, write it and send it next time – or ask someone to post it for you.'

'I'd only ask you,' Alice said. Molly was the only one who cared enough to creep into her bed and give her a sweet. She was the only real friend Alice had and she clung to her hand. 'I'm glad you're here – if you weren't I think I'd die.'

'No, you wouldn't, you'd just put up with it, because we can't do anything else,' the practical Molly said. 'But I like being with you, Alice. One day, when we leave here, we'll still be friends, won't we?'

'Yes,' Alice sighed, 'if we ever do.'

'My aunt says that when I'm old enough I can live with her, but I have to be able to work because she can't afford to keep me. I expect when the war is over, one of your family will come to fetch you, but don't forget me, will you?'

'No, I won't,' Alice promised. 'And when I'm old enough to work and earn money we could have a house and live there together.'

'We might get married and have children,' Molly said, looking thoughtful. 'If I do, I'll make sure they never have to come to a place like this.'

Molly sounded fierce, unlike her normal placid self and Alice knew how deeply she hated being here. She pretended not to care and she would never let anyone see her cry, but inside she was vulnerable. Just like Alice. She squeezed her friend's hand.

'One day we'll have people who love us again,' she whispered.

Molly snuggled up to her. 'I love you, Alice. You're the sister I never had.'

Alice put an arm around her and was comforted. It didn't matter that all her family had forgotten her birthday, because she had Molly.

It was a week since her birthday and Alice had forgotten it, almost. Molly had kept her word and given her half her pocket money on their outing to the park that Saturday.

'Aunt June sent me sixpence this week and I was allowed to keep it,' she said. 'I got all my sums right because of you, so you can have half of it. You can buy a postcard with a stamp for that and write to your auntie . . .'

Tears stung Alice's eyes but she didn't cry. 'One day I'll do something nice for you,' she promised.

'You already did,' Molly replied and smiled. 'We really are like sisters, Alice, and I'll share with you whenever I get pocket money.'

Alice smiled at her. She bought her postcard and the nice lady in the shop gave her and Molly a Black Jack chew each. They were six for a penny but she didn't charge them anything.

'You two are nice little girls,' she said. 'Some of the lads from the orphanage try to steal from me, but you don't. Take these and come to see me again.'

They thanked her, giggling as they looked at each other after they left the shop. It wasn't often anyone was so kind to them, and so they accepted the small treat with as much joy as if it had been a whole bagful.

The next week, when they went on their outing to the park, Alice posted the card to her Aunt Rose in London. It had taken her ages to write it and she'd been careful with her letters and her spelling – but her message had been clear: *Please, Aunt Rose, can I come home soon for a visit*? She had asked the question with hope in her heart and Molly was sure her auntie would come down as soon as she could and take her back to London.

'Of course she will,' Molly said. 'It's what people do if they love you.'

However, as the weeks passed with no reply and no visit from Rose, Alice felt the sadness in her heart once more. No one loved her anymore. It was the only explanation.

'Perhaps she didn't get it,' Molly suggested when she saw Alice's disappointment. She had received a letter from her aunt and she was waiting until the evening to read it. 'I like to save it until I go to bed,' she explained.

'I wish I had a letter from someone,' Alice said with a sigh. 'Your aunt seems nice, Molly.'

'She is, and it's such a pity that I can't live with her because she doesn't have the money.' Molly looked rueful. 'She works in a factory and lives in a room at the back of a grocer's shop. It's nice. I stayed with her once for a few days, before she found this place for me.' A big sigh escaped her. 'She couldn't afford to keep me then and I don't think she ever will. But when I can work, then we can live together.'

However, when they were in bed that night, Molly climbed in beside Alice, excited and bursting to tell her news.

'Has your aunt sent you sixpence again?'

'Better than that!' Molly said, barely managing to keep her voice to a whisper. 'She's getting married and her husband has a house with two bedrooms. He says that I can go and live with them!'

'Molly!' Alice started to tingle all over. 'Will you leave here for ever?' Her chest felt tight and her throat hurt as she asked the question. What would she do here alone?

'Yes – she says they're looking forward to having me, because they're too old to have children of their own but I shall be their daughter and Aunt June says they love the idea of having me.'

'That's wonderful,' Alice said and tried not to let a sob out. She was going to miss her friend terribly. 'I'm glad for you, Molly. It's what you always wanted.'

Molly sensed her fear and hugged her. 'I won't forget you,' she said. 'I'll see what Aunt June's husband is like and if he is nice, I'll ask if you can come and live with us too.'

Alice snuggled into her warm body, holding back the tears that threatened. She couldn't make a fuss and spoil this wonderful news for her friend, but it hurt so much to know she would lose Molly too. Once Molly had gone, there would be no one to climb into bed with her to share confidences – and pocket money. She would be completely alone again and the ache inside her was so bad that she wanted to die so she didn't feel anything any more. If only there was someone who cared for her.

Rose looked at the postcard that had just been handed to her. It was grubby and the postmark was from weeks ago. It had obviously been hanging around in

235

someone's house for a long time before being passed to her.

'Old Mr Johnson had it for ages, I reckon,' the woman from the house at the end of Silver Terrace had told her. 'He didn't know what to do with it and then I saw it on his mantel when I took him half an apple pie I'd made. I thought of you and I've been meaning to pop round, but there's always somethin' to do, ain't there?'

'Yes, there is,' Rose agreed and slipped the card into her apron pocket. She'd read it several times since she got home and the sadness in the few words wrung her heart. Had Alice thought to write the address of the orphanage on the card, she might have got on a train and gone down to see her straight away.

Rose wasn't sure if she could afford to take the child in, much as she felt for her, but she would have visited now and then if she knew where to go and if she ever got that promotion at the factory that Harry kept promising her, she would find a place to live somehow. The date on the postmark was legible but the ink had run and she couldn't make out what the area was. Rose squinted and squinted at it but she just couldn't make it out.

She placed it on the mantel with the letter from Davey. If Dave Blake ever came looking, she would hand them both over. Maybe his eyes were better and could make out the postmark more clearly than she could . . . Her thoughts were suspended as someone rapped on the door.

'All right, all right,' she muttered as she went to open it and then her breath died in her throat because it was the telegraph boy and he had a little buff envelope for her. She'd thought the Post Office couldn't find her, because she'd had so few letters, but here was one she didn't want. 'Oh, my gawd, what's that?' she asked, shaking too much to reach for it.

'Sorry, missus, it's one of 'em,' the lad said, and she gasped and placed a shaking hand to her breast. 'It ain't my fault I 'ave ter bring 'em.'

'Not blamin' you,' Rose said faintly. 'It's that bloody Hitler!'

'Yeah, that's what they all say.'

The boy cycled off, no doubt on his way to deliver more bad news to someone else. Rose opened the envelope and read the few lines, before sitting down with a shudder of relief and sadness all in one. It wasn't either of her sons, but her husband had gone down with his ship. She blinked hard. Reg hadn't been a good husband, but he was what she had, the father of her sons and she supposed she'd been fond of him once. The shock had taken her breath and made her go numb all over, her knees giving way as she tried to stand, so she sat down again quickly.

'Poor bleeder,' Rose managed at last and shoved the telegram into her apron pocket. Well, that was it then. She was a widow like so many others, robbed of years of married life by this terrible war.

A great emptiness swept over her. They hadn't always got on and Reg had given her a backhander too many times, but he was the man she'd married and there was still something there, just a small spark that made it hurtful to have lost him that way. It hadn't been a great love affair but sometimes, on a visit to the pub, they'd had a laugh and he'd been affectionate for a while, before he had too much and turned nasty. It was the drink that had given him a nasty temper, but she'd known how to handle it, she just kept out of the way until he sobered up and gave him a mouthful until he looked abashed and apologised the following morning. Now he was gone and there was nothing.

She would spend a lonely old age working until she couldn't work any longer and then what the hell would she do? Rose sighed. It was a bleak prospect but she wasn't sure she wanted to end her days living with Harry Smith, even though he'd been good to her. Besides, he could get fed up and ask her to leave at any time. Rose vowed she would never marry again; all most men were after was a quick visit to the bedroom or, if they weren't interested in that side of things, their feet under the table so they could be fed a good meal.

What the heck did she have to look forward to now? Her thoughts went to little Alice Blake. If only she could make out that flamin' postmark she could go right down there and fetch her back to live with her. Rose had seen a decent room advertised recently and she'd a good mind to go after it. She would manage somehow, even if she had to badger Harry for that job. At least she wouldn't have to be alone if she had Alice. And she would think about taking Davey on as well if he ever came back this way.

CHAPTER 21

'Come on, try a little of this broth,' Davey pleaded and held the spoon to the old man's lips again. It had been warm and delicious when he'd first made the stew, which had a little meat in it and was more of a thick soup made from potatoes, greens and the small amount of meat left over from their stew two days ago. Davey had visited the traps that morning but the weather was bitterly cold and nothing had been in his snares. He'd felt guilty that he had so little to offer his friend, but Bert lay with his eyes closed, his hand clenched and his breathing slow.

Davey had placed the red flag on the highest part of the tree two days ago when Bert had started coughing up a dark phlegm that looked as if it might have little traces of blood in it. Since then, he'd hardly been out of the shack other than to fetch wood for the fire and water to make a hot drink or to check the traps. He was afraid to leave his friend in case he took a turn for the worse. Bert had sat hunched by the fire all yesterday, drinking every drop of the coffee Davey made and swallowing the food he'd prepared, but in the night the coughing had got worse and when Davey had got up to investigate, he'd discovered Bert had vomited a lot of dark fluid. He'd fetched a bucket of water and a cloth and wiped it up and the water turned a murky red. A cold feeling spread through him and he'd realised it must be blood Bert was bringing up.

Davey felt very afraid then, apprehensive of what would happen to the friend he'd relied on for almost two years now. Davey wasn't exactly sure how long he'd been here now because Bert had taken the tally board he'd made to keep track of the days and used it for their fire when they'd run out of wood and the snow was thick on the ground. After that his counting became a bit uncertain but he'd found another piece of wood and started again, and he thought it might be a year and ten months so that was nearly two years.

In that time, Davey had shot up and looked much taller than when he'd first come to the place he now thought of as home. The pictures of London's grimy streets had faded in the mists of time in his memory, though he remembered his dad and Alice and his mum too, but he couldn't picture her face any more. He thought about Alice the most, wondering how she had settled with her life on the farm.

'Davey, are you there?' Bert's voice startled Davey, because he'd thought he was too sick to talk.

'Yes, Bert,' he said and went to the side of his bed, kneeling down by the mattress and bending over him. 'What can I do to help you?'

'There's nothing I need now, lad,' Bert said in a

clear strong voice. 'We have to think about you, lad. I've been wrong letting you stay here with me. At first, I thought I was helping you, teaching you things and letting you live here in this fresh clean place – better than the slums of London, like Albert said, and I liked having you here – but it wasn't fair to you, you should have been with a family.'

'I'm all right,' Davey told him and took his hand, which was clammy. 'I've loved living here with you, enjoyed learning the things you taught me. I know lots about the world now, all the places you've been, and I'm going to see them one day, too.'

'Good. I'm glad I've given you some ambition,' Bert said and Davey knew he was smiling inside, even though he couldn't on the outside. 'It's all I could do. I should never have agreed to you staying here. I should have told Albert to take you back and hand you over to the proper authorities at the start, but I was too weak and let him persuade me and then I came to like you being around too much and when he – he stopped coming, I couldn't do the right thing. Corky and Rodie will see you get help, lad. There's enough money in the pot to pay your bus fare into town. Get to Corky's place and tell him what you need . . . sell anything I've got if it helps you to get home, lad.'

'I'll go back to London one day,' Davey told him. 'I can hide on a ship and jump off when we get there. I can swim now so I can just slip over the side.'

'Aye, I know you can swim,' Bert said. 'I taught you myself, but you might still drown. The sea is a powerful and cruel force. Ask Corky to give you a job and save

241

enough for the fare home, Davey. It might take you a while but by then the war might be over and hopefully you'll find everything safe and sound back home.'

Davey didn't answer. He wasn't sure what he wanted to do yet – that was in the future. For the moment he had to look after Bert the way he'd cared for him, pay him back for all the hours he'd spent teaching him how to make things, like a new handle for a hunting knife or how to skin and cook, to swim. Davey had been afraid of water and some of the things that lived in it, but Bert had shown him the little pool that was protected by rocks and the tumbling water that kept it clear and shallow. It was just deep enough to reach Davey's chest and the bottom was sandy to the touch. A few fish darted in and out of the pool, their scales silver in the sunlight, and Davey had learned to swim with Bert's help and to enjoy dipping his head under where the water cascaded down from a rocky hillside above.

He recalled the day they'd seen the cougar sitting on the rocks above. It had been coming down to drink, scattering birds and small animals that fled in terror of its sharp teeth and claws. Bert had fetched his gun and fired one shot. The big cat had run off and the two of them had laughed. 'I could've killed it,' Bert told him. 'Gordon would have paid me a couple of dollars for the skin but we didn't need the meat so I let it live. Take what you need from nature but don't be greedy, Davey. Live and let live where you can.' Davey reckoned that was the most important thing his friend had told him – and yet there was so much else he'd learned here, too.

'You taught me so much,' Davey said as Bert lay back against his pillows. 'I don't want you to die, Bert!' Tears were streaming down his cheeks though he made no sound and Bert didn't answer. He'd used up all the strength he had telling Davey what to do for the best, but he wasn't dead. His breathing was still steady, though slow and shallow.

Davey had no experience of death, but he knew in his heart that Bert was dying, and he also understood that nothing he did would stop that – perhaps even a doctor couldn't but he wished Corky would come.

Corky finally arrived late that afternoon. Davey heard the sound of his old truck and ran outside to greet him.

'I think Bert is dying,' he said, rubbing at his eyes. His face was steaked with dirt, though he had no idea what he looked like. Bert didn't have a mirror in the place. 'He took real sick two days ago – coughing and I think he brings up blood.'

'Rodie sent you some food,' Corky said. 'It's in the basket, lad. Eat while I take a look at him.'

Davey retrieved the basket from the back of the trunk. Rodie had packed ham and egg pie cut into slices, fresh bread and some cinnamon buns. Davey was starving and ate two slices of the pie and a hunk of bread, was about to start on a bun when Corky came out to him.

'He's too ill to move,' he said, 'and there's no use in trying to get him to hospital. I told Rodie I might stay for a day or so if he was bad. You OK with that?'

'Yeah, sure,' Davey replied calmly. Inside, he was thanking God and crying all at the same time. He'd known Bert was dying but hearing it from Corky somehow made it worse and there was nothing he could do about it, except grieve for the man he'd learned to love like the grandfather he'd never had.

Bert died during the night. Corky had sent Davey to bed after they'd eaten supper and he'd fallen asleep, worn out by the worry and work he'd done the past few days and weeks looking out for his friend.

Corky asked him to help him get Bert's body into the back of the truck. 'Just help me drag him on the blanket, lad,' he said. 'He can't feel the bumps now and it's the only way we'll get him there. We'll take him back and give him a proper burial near his wife.'

Davey did as he was bid and, between them, they managed to get Bert into the truck without too much rough handling. Corky was surprised at how strong Davey was for a boy his age but said it must be living wild. Davey looked about fifteen now, but in fact he wouldn't be twelve until this summer if he wasn't too far out in his calculations. He wasn't; Corky told him it was actually March 1942.

'Get your things together,' he told him when he was covering Bert in the back of the truck for decency. 'You won't be coming back here, Davey. Rodie has made a space for you in the shed, made it warm and cosy – you'll like it there.'

'What about Bert's stuff?'

Corky considered. 'We'll leave it for the time being. If Albert returns one day it belongs to him, but otherwise I suppose it is yours. Bert said you were to have what you want, so if there's anything . . .'

He made it sound unlikely, but for Davey a lot of the things were precious, and he whipped round the shack, picking up books, knives Bert had made and various other small treasures, and Bert's favourite chair that he'd said was genuine Georgian – everything he knew Bert had treasured. If Albert turned up and wanted them, Davey would give them up, but he wasn't leaving Bert's treasures for Siggy Gordon to just walk in and take if he fancied them.

Corky's shack was out in the backyard and made of slatted wood very like the one Davey had lived in with Bert but Rodie had used a whitewash inside to brighten it up and put net curtains at the small windows, which had glass in them.

'We used it to store stuff in here,' she told him, 'but I put a curtain up and the sacks of dried beans are out there.' She pointed to the heavy curtain dividing off an alcove cubbyhole. 'They shouldn't bother you there, Davey, and we don't have anywhere else for you.'

'It's fine,' Davey told her. 'When I was a kid, I shared a room smaller than this with my sister Alice. She used to climb into my bed when she was frightened or felt unwell.'

'You must have missed her when you were sent out here,' Rodie said, looking at him with sympathy. 'I reckon you've had a rough ride, young Davey.'

'Nah, I was all right,' Davey said and grinned at her. 'Bert was good to me, Rodie. He taught me lots of things and – and I loved him.'

'Of course you did, and I know he loved you in his way,' Rodie said and smiled at him. 'Come here, lad, and let me hug you.' She put strong arms around him and gave him a bear hug that almost stifled him. 'You'll be all right with us, lad. We'll see you have a decent life.'

'I'm going to find a job and work hard,' Davey said. 'One of these days I'll have enough money to go back to London and find my family.'

'You know things are hard over there?' Rodie asked him. 'They still have bombs dropping on them, even though the Blitz ended. Your air force stopped Hitler from invading, but the people don't have much to eat and things are difficult. You'll have to stay until the end of the war anyways – no one is taking passengers while the war is on – and then perhaps you can decide if you really want to go back there.'

Davey nodded. He could tell that Rodie didn't want him to go. She was a kind, friendly woman and she didn't have any children of her own – Bert said she couldn't and it was a sorrow to her. Perhaps she was looking forward to having him around and he was grateful to her, because he had nowhere else to go and he didn't think he could manage on his own back at Bert's shack.

'Yes, that's best,' he said. 'Because I haven't any money I was thinking I might stow away on a ship going back home but Bert said they would be bound to find me and send me back. But if I earn enough money, I can buy a passage home, can't I?'

'Yes, you could,' Rodie said, nodding. 'Well, what are you thinking of doing, Davey?'

'I don't know,' he admitted. 'Do you know of anyone needing a boy to help with chores? I'll do anything.'

'How old are you, Davey?' Rodie asked suddenly. 'Now you're here in town you should probably go to regular school. Take your time to decide what you need to do in the future.'

'That's easy. I'm going to sea as soon as I'm old enough.'

Rodie smiled, inclining her head. 'Then you really do need to go to school for a while. But you can help Corky and me at weekends and in the evenings with deliveries and unpacking goods when they come on the lorry and earn some pocket money that way. By the time you're ready, hopefully the war will be over and you'll have enough to go home.'

Davey looked at her doubtfully. Would she believe him if he told her that he was fourteen and old enough to leave school and get a job? He decided against the lie. She would know and then she wouldn't trust him.

'I'm twelve, Rodie.' And then: 'I could carve things you could sell in your shop,' Davey said suddenly, making Rodie look at him with interest. 'Bert showed me how.'

'What sort of things?' she asked.

'Spoon handles, knife handles, animals out of wood . . .'

'Mebbe they might sell – if they're good enough,' she said cautiously. 'Could you make me a nice box to put things in with carving on the lid?'

'That's easy,' Davey said. 'I just need a good piece of wood.'

'We've got lots of wood in the shed,' Rodie told him. 'You wash up and come and eat your supper, Davey. We'll talk about what you can do in your spare time tomorrow – and on Monday morning you're going to school. No excuses and no running off. Bert would haunt me if I didn't look after you right.'

'Yes, Rodie,' Davey said meekly but inside his head there was lots going on. 'I can write to my mother – and perhaps my father, too. Would Corky send letters on for me?'

'Yes.' Rodie nodded an affirmative. 'Where is your father serving?'

'In the Royal Navy,' Davey said proudly. 'He signed up as soon as the war started. We were all right for a start but then my gran got ill, and Mum sent us kids away.'

'I suppose she had to because she couldn't manage and the Government were telling her to,' Rodie said. 'It was hard luck for you, Davey – but life isn't too bad here, is it?'

'I like it,' he told her. 'I want to go back and see everyone and then one day, when I can, I'd like to bring my sister back to live here. Find a nice home for her where she can live while I'm at sea.'

'That's a good lad to think of your sister. You bring her back here and we'll take care of her for you.'

Davey thanked her and smiled. He wondered how long it would take him to earn his passage home. If he could earn enough, he would go as soon as he got the chance, find his sister and, if his mother still didn't want them, he would bring her back here. But for that he would need to earn more than his fare home.

Davey realised that it was a huge task and well beyond what he was able to do yet. Perhaps he should still try to get home by hiding on board a ship, and here he was much closer to the huge port where all the ships docked. Still, there would probably be a lot of security at the docks and, even if he succeeded, when he got to England there would still be a mountain of problems to solve.

For a moment his heart sank as he realised what a huge task it was – but Bert had taught him it was possible to do almost anything. 'You can do what you want to do, Davey,' he'd said as he showed him how to carve the wood and then polish it with sand and beeswax until it shone like gloss. 'Just never give up trying.'

Anything had seemed possible for the future as they'd sat outside by their campfire at night and talked of Davey's future as a sailor, but now it was all different. Bert had wanted him to learn and plan for his future, but he had a feeling that Rodie just wanted him to stay here with her and Corky.

'*Don't worry, Alice,*' he said to his sister in his thoughts. '*I haven't forgotten you and I won't. I'll come looking for you just as soon as I can . . .*'

Davey could hear Rodie calling him in to supper. He finished washing his hands and face and ran. The food was tasty and plentiful and Davey understood that life here would be much easier than the life he'd shared with Bert, but Rodie's kindness made him feel a little suffocated as he had in her ample embrace – as if she was trying to tie him to her, to hold him here for always . . .

CHAPTER 22

The man stirred and opened his eyes, looking up at the sweet face that seemed to hover above him. He was still finding it difficult to focus and blinked, wondering if he was in heaven and the face belonged to an angel, but then a stern voice asked, 'Is he awake, Nurse Lynn?'

'Yes, Sister Chapman, but I'm not sure he is properly conscious yet.'

Another face swam into his vision and he was aware of the strident tones that had chivvied him and bullied him back to life when it had seemed so much easier to just let go. He was in hospital and, when he'd just wanted to let go, Sister had dragged him back to life by her care and her bullying. He smiled at her.

'Well, then, young man, have you had enough of just lying there in bed then? Are you ready to sit up and take some nourishment?'

'I could murder a cup of tea,' he said and then, quite suddenly, his eyes focused and all the memories came rushing back at him.

'Look out!' The shout had come from behind Dave

at almost the same moment as he'd felt the judder from below and knew they'd been hit by a torpedo. He'd glanced up, seen a piece of heavy metal falling towards him and jerked sideways but it caught him on the side of the head, knocking him to the deck. As the blackness had folded around him, his last thought had been of his son and he'd tried to mouth the words 'I love you . . .' but the effort had been lost, and Dave had known no more . . .

'I was wounded, wasn't I? I remember seeing the trail of the torpedo in the water . . . how long have I been here, Sister?'

'For nearly three months,' Sister Chapman replied and smiled. 'About time you came back to us, Lieutenant Blake. I was beginning to think you disliked my company.'

Dave laughed and tried to sit up. His head spun for a moment as the room went round and round and then came into focus once more. 'That must have been some bang on the head!'

He reached up and touched his head, half remembering bandages, but they'd gone now. He was obviously getting better at last.

'It wasn't just the bang on the head, though; you had multiple cuts to your face, arms, chest – and damage to your ribs and a punctured lung. If someone hadn't dragged you out of the water and transferred you to a hospital ship, you would most certainly have died.'

'Where am I?' Dave asked. 'Am I back in Britain?'

'Not yet, though you will be soon,' she replied. 'As soon as the doctors here release you, you'll be transferred to a hospital ship and taken back – you're in Gibraltar at the moment.'

'How in Hades did I get here?' Dave exclaimed. 'We were in the North Atlantic!'

'You needed surgery and the nearest ship available to help was bound for Gibraltar, so you were brought here, having been operated on while aboard the ship. Had the ship not been available to help, you would probably have died. The damage to your lung was quite extensive.'

'What does that mean?' Dave asked, feeling icy at his nape. 'Is my career in the navy over?'

'Quite probably. I haven't been given that kind of information. I've been too busy saving your life.'

'Yes, I know, thank you,' Dave said. 'It's just that I need to make a living for my kids.'

'Yes, of course you do, and you will in time. I dare say it won't be on fighting ships but you'll find work. A man like you always can.' She sounded so practical and sure that he found himself believing her.

Dave stared at her and then lay back against the pillows. It was no use fretting. He felt exhausted and knew it would be a while before he could leave his hospital bed. When he was discharged he would find a way to earn money, even if he couldn't have the fishing boat of his dreams. The most important thing now was to get well enough to go home and find his kids. At least he knew where to find Alice at that farm with that nice woman he'd met.

Molly had been gone for a long time now and life at the orphanage was hard and cold without the support of her one real friend. Alice missed her terribly. Molly had written twice to say she was having a good time at her aunt's home and promising to ask if Alice could join them, but then the letters stopped and she had nothing left to look forward to. No one wrote to her, no one sent her cards and presents, and no one took her out to tea. Several of the other children received gifts now and then, and some had relatives that came to take them out occasionally. Some found new homes and left the orphanage, but Alice had nothing.

The only solace she had found in this soulless place was books. She had discovered that there were marvellous stories on the shelves of the library if you sat down and read them. Now, instead of joining the other children after supper for games in the playground, she usually took a book up to the dormitory and read before the others came to bed. Some of them asked why she didn't join them, but when Alice just shrugged, she was left alone and became even more solitary than she had been when she first came.

She sent Molly a postcard when she was given tuppence a week pocket money by the housemistress. 'Since you have no one to send you pocket money it has been decided that we will give you something. If you have no experience of handling money you will not know what to do when you leave here,' Miss Weatherspoon told her. 'Do not waste it – you may be asked what you did with it, but it is yours to do with as you wish,' she added grudgingly and Alice knew it wasn't her who had decided she should have the money.

Alice had thanked her for the unexpected windfall and, as soon as she could, she sent a postcard to the address in Molly's two letters. She crossed her fingers and hoped that she would get a reply but none came. It did no good to cry. Alice had learned that much the hard way. The other children laughed and taunted the cry-babies. You had to be tough and stand up for yourself, so when one of the older girls pulled her hair, which she now wore in plaits, Alice scratched her face. She screamed and Miss Weatherspoon appeared out of nowhere and caned Alice three times on each hand but she didn't cry and no one pulled her hair after that, they just left her alone.

Gradually, Alice came to like it that way. She escaped into the world of the French Revolution with Baroness Orczy's *The Scarlet Pimpernel*, into the adventures of Bilbo Baggins with The Hobbit by J.R.R. Tolkien and many, many other places with all the books she found on the shelves of the library, which was just down the road from the school she now attended each day. The younger girls received lessons at the orphanage but the older girls went to school. Alice was sent there two months after her housemistress discovered she was ten and she was glad. It was more like the school she'd gone to in Ely and she enjoyed learning. She felt that she was alive when she was at school, but when she returned to the orphanage, she became trapped in a dark world that had no light or hope in it. So she escaped into her books and dreamed of the day when she would find her family and go home.

Sometimes, she thought she heard Davey talking

to her but perhaps that was her imagination. The stories she read were make-believe and Alice thought the pictures in her head of Davey must be too. She didn't even know if he was alive, just that he'd gone a long, long, way across the sea.

Once, she'd dared to ask Miss Weatherspoon if the children sent to Canada would ever come back and the answer had felt like the lash of the cane. 'Don't talk nonsense, Alice. How could he? It costs a great deal of money to send a child to Canada and he will owe the people who took care of him. He can't come home unless they release him after the war and he can afford to buy a passage home – and how will he do that? Then there is the question of papers. He will have to apply for all kinds of things to get back home, to prove he is a British citizen and I doubt most of those children have papers to show they came from England in the first place.'

Alice was confused and frightened by that answer. Davey wasn't much older than she was and she had no idea what her housemistress was talking about. What sort of papers would Davey need? And why did he need them? He'd been born in London so, surely, he was entitled to return here whenever he chose?

Rose looked at the postmark on the letter. It was from Canada again and from Davey. She shook her head. Why did everyone give her the letters and cards that came for Dora? She had no idea what to do with them. Supposing Dave didn't get back? A lot of ships had gone down and hundreds – thousands –

of men had been killed in this war and it wasn't done yet.

Rose sighed. She still didn't know what that postmark was on Alice's card. She'd hoped another would come but it hadn't – or it hadn't come to her hand. Turning Davey's letter over, she decided against opening it. She'd read his first one but they weren't her letters – they were Dora's, poor woman. Rose missed her. She'd been a friend and Rose liked her, even if she didn't approve of what she'd done with her kids.

This damned war had a lot to answer for. Rose passed a hand over her forehead. Sometimes the prospect of a lonely future was more than she could bear, and she'd wondered if she should just stop here with Harry. She looked at the bottle of beer on the kitchen table and considered opening it, though she'd got it for Harry. A drop of pale ale might help lift her mood, but she'd seen others go that way and didn't want to end up on the slippery slope.

Rose needed to have a clear head in the mornings to hold her job down on the production line because there were plenty eager to take her place. Most women who could pack their kids off to school worked these days; the extra money was a godsend and there was no shame in it the way there had been in the past. Women had been told it wasn't decent to have a life of their own for years; they'd had to stay at home and do as their fathers and then their husbands told them. Well, two world wars had put paid to that idea. Of course, some women had always had to work, scrubbing or skivvying for others – but there was a lot more choice now.

When the men came home a lot of women would be pushed out of the better jobs just as they'd been in the first world war, and they'd have to go back to being stay-at-home wives and mothers, but some would decide that they were going to go on working – and there were better and more interesting jobs for women these days. Bosses had discovered that in some cases women were more reliable and less trouble, though not always. Rose grinned as she thought of the way she'd put Mrs Winters in her place at work.

She'd been shouting at some of the girls but it was a machine's fault, something Mrs Winters should have fetched Harry Smith to sort out, not the girls' fault. Rose had waded in and given her a mouthful, something she might not have done once upon a time, but the woman didn't know her job as she should and ought to be sent back for further training. Rose was no longer scared of anyone. If Hitler's bombs hadn't managed to get her, she could handle a mere supervisor. Mrs Winters been shocked into silence by the time Rose had finished and the girls had crowded round Rose after their shift, begging her to be their shop union leader.

'We're women and we should have a woman looking out for us. You told old Icy Drawers where to go, Rose.'

Rose thought their manager might very well tell her where to go and she would be looking for a new job come the weekend. So when Harry Smith stopped her as she was leaving the factory and asked for a word, she'd thought that was it, that he'd been ordered to let her go, but she'd been surprised at what he'd had to say.

'I wanted to thank you for spotting the problem,' he told her. 'Truth is, Rose, I've got more to do than I can manage – and some of these girls don't know their heads from their backsides if you ask me. I've had a strong word with the boss and he agrees – I've been told to make you a supervisor for the women under thirty. I want you to lick them into shape, Rose. I know it was my fault this morning for not spotting that fault; Mrs Winters isn't up to the responsibility she has, but those youngsters drive me round the bend. Talking, smoking and standing around when they should be working; you never did that.'

'And they won't by the time I've finished,' Rose had told him with a feeling of satisfaction. 'So, what do I get out of it then?' It hadn't been his fault, because Mrs Winters was the line supervisor and should have reported it, but Rose wasn't going to contradict him if there was a promotion going.

'An extra ten bob a week?'

'Done!' Rose offered him her hand. She knew it was still less than the male supervisors were getting but it was a start. She wouldn't just lick the girls into shape – she'd sort out the management too and see what she could do to bring the women's pay a little closer to what those men who were still considered essential and therefore excused military service were paid. It wasn't right or fair, but it had gone on for years. 'That will do for now . . . but I'll be wantin' more once the work rate has gone up.'

Smiling now at the memory of Harry's wry look, Rose placed Davey's letter on the shelf. She might feel a bit lonely at times, but she wasn't going to sit down and cry about it. She had work to do and one day the war would be over. Reggie wouldn't be coming home but hopefully her sons would and perhaps Dave Blake too. If he did, she would make sure he got the letters and Alice's card. And if Alice were to send another with a legible postmark, she would do what she could to bring the child back to London now the bombing seemed to be over.

CHAPTER 23

'Alice Blake, come here this instant.' Miss Weatherspoon looked at her angrily as she reluctantly went to meet the housemistress. 'Hold out your hand.'

'Why?' Alice asked, suddenly feeling rebellious as she eyed the cane in the mistress's hand. 'I haven't done anything wrong.'

'Indeed? I shall be the judge of that.' She brought the cane down sharply on Alice's hand four times in rapid succession, bringing tears to her eyes. 'Two are for being caught reading in class at your school – oh, yes, I know what goes on! – and two are for answering back. I shall always punish rudeness severely and that means no pocket money for a month.'

Alice looked at her, blinking back the tears. She'd given Miss Weatherspoon a reason to punish her in a way that hurt her equally as much as the cane, because without her pocket money she had no way of buying postcards – or of saving for the day she left here.

It was something she'd decided to do when Molly stopped writing to her. She didn't want to stay here in this awful place any longer than she had to, and she realised that there was only one person she could ask for help, and that was Aunt Rose in London. She'd sent one postcard ages ago and got no reply, but she'd realised that she'd put no address on because she hadn't known it. Now that she went to school, she knew the names of the roads nearby, so she could write an address on the card.

Of course, Alice knew that Rose Parker wasn't her real aunt, but she'd always been kind to her and if she knew how unhappy she was, she would surely help her. Even if she didn't want to have her to live with her, she might know where Alice's father was and he would surely help her if he knew how miserable she was here? He wouldn't want her to be caned for nothing.

Dismissed with a look that Alice could only think was gleeful, she held back the tears and walked slowly up to her dormitory. She had nothing to read because her teacher at school had taken away the book she was reading and banned her from using the library for a week.

'If you cannot be trusted to attend to your school-work, Alice, we may have to stop all your library privileges. Reading is good for you and I am pleased that you enjoy it – but you will not read *Little Women* during my history lessons. I need your full attention, do you hear?'

Alice had apologised but the book was not returned and the ban remained. She had not been caned at school – Mrs Morris never caned anyone. She just removed privileges and she always knew which ones would hurt the most. Without her books, Alice's loneliness returned and she was forced to sit on her bed and just look out of the window. Her view was of the janitor's shed and a small, dull courtyard where nothing much ever happened.

After thinking about her situation and the various options open to her, Alice decided she must write to Rose Parker again. Running away would be difficult, because she didn't have enough money to pay for her train fare to London and she wasn't as brave to do what Davey had done. The time they'd run back home to Mum, they'd hidden in the toilets, but there was no Mum to go to now and Alice wasn't sure if Aunt Rose would take her in. So she would send her a postcard from her small store of money and see what happened. If Aunt Rose replied, then she would tell her how much she hated living here and ask if she would let her live with her until her father came home – if he did. Alice hadn't had a letter from him since she'd left the farm and she sometimes wondered if he knew where she was living now. She didn't think he would just desert her if he knew – and she'd already sent two postcards addressed to:

Mr Dave Blake. The Royal Navy. England.

And had written on both:

Dear Daddy, I am very unhappy in the orphanage. It is horrid here without Molly. She was my friend but she went away. I miss you and Davey so much. Please take me home soon. Love from Alice

There was no room to put anything more on the card and, besides, Alice hadn't known the address of the orphanage until recently. She did know it was near Cambridge, somewhere on the outskirts of the city, so Molly had said. She thought her friend had told her the horses they went to look at and pet in the field were at Trumpington but she wasn't sure because she'd only been listening to Molly's talk of the big horses and marvelling at how gentle they were when her friend scrambled on their backs and they walked about the field with Molly clinging onto their mane.

Alice had heard nothing back from her cards to her father. She wasn't sure that she'd put the right address on them, but her father was in the navy so surely they would get to him when he returned to England? If only she knew where Davey was she could write to him. He had promised to come back for her but Alice thought it must be too difficult – at least until he was much older.

In the meantime, her only hope was either to run away or ask for help – so she would begin by writing to Aunt Rose. And this time she would let her know where she was . . .

Davey counted his money. He had twenty dollars and fifteen cents that he'd earned doing chores and errands for Corky and Rodie. In the evenings, when the work was done, Davey made the carvings and Corky put them in the shop for sale. Thus far, they had sold one of a mother bear with two cubs following her. Corky got five dollars for it but it had taken weeks and weeks of work and it hardly seemed worth the effort because he earned as much from doing chores as he did for the intricate carving he'd put so much love into. The box he'd made for Rodie he'd refused to be paid for, because she was always giving him cakes and he was living in her home.

He seldom spent anything from his store of money on himself, because it took lots of work to add to it and he knew he would need quite a big amount to buy his passage home and then he would need to travel on to London – and he would need food. Davey wasn't sure what kind of reception he would get when he got home. His mother had never replied to his letter and he'd given her Corky's address in his second letter, telling her his situation, so it seemed she didn't want him back. Once, that would have hurt him and he might have given up all hope of returning to London, but he was stronger now and he knew that he wanted to see his sister, his father – and his mother. His mother might not want to see him, but his sister and father surely would, wouldn't they? If Alice was happy at that farm perhaps he could find work near it so they could be together sometimes.

Davey worried that something might have happened to his father. Corky had made a lot of inquiries about Albert and they knew now that his ship had hit a mine. Albert had broken his rule and taken a job on the Atlantic run and his luck had gone just like that.

'It was a bit of bad luck, son,' Corky had told him. 'I've asked a lot of questions, Davey, and it seems that most of the crew were lost. A few were picked up later by a fishing boat but Albert wasn't one of them.'

Davey nodded, feeling sad that he'd lost a friend, but he'd known in his heart that Albert wouldn't have let them down. He would never have stayed away so long if he'd been able to return.

'Does that mean I can keep Bert's things then?' he asked after he'd thought it over for a few days.

'Yes, I reckon you can,' Corky said. 'If you want to sell them, give me the offer first. There are a couple of things I might like if you don't keep them.'

Davey nodded, but didn't say anything. He knew that Corky had actually got ten dollars for the carving of the bear and kept half for himself. Davey couldn't complain because Corky had sold it and he'd given him a home, but he didn't intend to let Bert's treasures go cheap. A lot of them would probably only fetch a few cents, but Davey was shrewd enough to guess that Corky would want the two or three items that might be worth more – Bert's chair, a silver-backed mirror that had been hidden at the bottom of his sea chest and a beautiful brass compass in a wooden case.

Davey wanted to keep the compass for himself for the future, but he might sell the mirror and the chair. He would inquire about the price of a similar chair he'd seen in the shop that sold all sorts and then ask Corky what he thought – but he wouldn't sell unless he got a fair price. His savings were his only means of escape, of a return to the home he'd been forced to leave. Something inside him reckoned that wasn't fair – if folk sent lads like him out here, they should be prepared to help them get home if they wanted.

Although he enjoyed his life in Canada, Davey's desire to return home was increasing as time passed. At the back of his mind he had an uneasy feeling about Alice. He wasn't sure why, but she kept coming into his head and he was anxious about her. She was in his thoughts far more than she had been when he was living with Bert. It was as if she was calling out to him, just like she had when they were at home and she was frightened. Davey knew he had to go home and find her as soon as he could.

If it hadn't been for his feeling about Alice, Davey might have settled to living at the store. It wasn't a bad life, though he worked hard. Rodie was good to him and Corky was cheerful and easy-going, though careful with his money. So, he kept his thoughts to himself and waited. He thought that perhaps when he had sixty dollars saved, he might venture into Halifax on the bus that passed through once a week and ask how much it would cost for a passage to England.

Once, he'd asked Corky that question, but he'd just shaken his head and said he didn't know. 'I've never thought of going, Davey,' he'd told him. 'I reckon it's a lot more than you've earned just yet, lad. 'Sides, you don't want to think about leaving us so soon. You couldn't get passage on a ship while the war's on and even then Rodie was kinda hoping you'd stay here with us . . .'

Davey hadn't answered. It wasn't that he was unhappy or that his friends were unkind, they were good to him and he counted himself lucky to have found such a comfortable home and people to help him – but he missed his family. He worried about Alice and his father – his mother too in a way, though he supposed that Mick was still looking out for her. Was Alice still living on that farm? Was she all right or was she miserable? And what about his father? Davey thought about him all the time. He knew that the war wasn't going all that well for Britain and too many ships were being sunk. Was his dad still alive? If he returned to England, would he find any of his family? The doubts assailed him when he was in bed and he wondered if he would be better off staying where he was, but then he would picture Alice looking up at him, sweet and vulnerable, pleading with him to help her and he knew he had to go. Whatever he might find when he got there.

Dave Blake opened his eyes. He'd been ill again with fever on the ship taking him home to Britain from Gibraltar and recalled little of the journey. Now he was in an English hospital and the fever was waning, though he still ached in every limb and his head felt as if there were a hundred drums beating inside it.

'Hello,' a voice said as Dave opened his eyes. 'So you've decided to come back to us again, have you?'

'I've seen you before,' Dave said wonderingly as his vision cleared and he saw the lovely face he'd seen once before. 'You were in the hospital in Gib.'

'Yes, I was,' the nurse agreed with a smile. 'My name is Judy Lynn and I volunteered to bring you and some others back to this military hospital in Portsmouth.'

Dave nodded, closing his eyes again for a moment. 'Good,' he said and then, without thought, added, 'You're very pretty, Judy . . .'

'Thank you,' she said and laughed. 'And you've been very sick, Lieutenant Blake.'

'Don't you mean Ensign?' Dave remembered that

the sister had also called him Lieutenant and said, puzzled, 'I was just an Ensign last time I looked.'

'Well, it says Lieutenant on my sheet so perhaps you've been promoted,' Judy replied with a smile that seemed to him to light up the room. 'Now, I'm going to leave you to rest for a little while and then I'll bring you a cup of tea and perhaps a ham sandwich, if you could eat it?'

'I'd rather have a tot of rum and a good beef stew,' Dave said hopefully, and she burst out laughing.

'Not today I'm afraid,' she said, 'but if you continue to improve, who knows? I might manage the rum and the kitchens do a decent stew sometimes. All we want is for you to get better.'

Dave smiled and relaxed. It was only as his eyes closed that he began to think. Now he was home, he was going to take custody of his children – Alice as soon as he could find a woman to take proper care of her, and Davey as soon as he could find him. He frowned as he became aware of the pounding in his head. He'd recovered from the fever it seemed, but he wondered briefly if these blinding headaches were something he would have to learn to live with in future. He'd been told his lungs had been damaged and it would lead to the end of his naval career, though if he'd been promoted, perhaps he wasn't completely redundant yet?

It was still too difficult to think things through properly. Dave wasn't sure what sort of a future lay in store but he did know he would never rest until he had recovered his children, wherever they were.

CHAPTER 24

Rose decided to take a walk down Silver Terrace. She'd heard there was a house for rent just off it in Cobble Lane and although it wasn't a place she would have chosen to live, being a narrow alley off the ruined street that had been her home, it was worth investigating and she would call on Mavis Carter and take her a small bag of the fudge she'd always been partial to.

Mavis was delighted to see her and accepted the small offering with as much gratitude as if it had been a banquet at the Savoy. 'You're a real friend – and that's why I'm telling you, Rose. I haven't let on to anyone else, but I'm off to live with a cousin on the South Coast next month. If you put in for my house, I reckon you might get it.'

'The council said I'd be last on any list cos I've got no kids,' Rose reminded her.

'Yes, but no one wants to live 'ere. They'll pull these old places down and mine ain't council anyway. It's a private landlord, always has been, and if I put in a word for you, you'll get it – anyway, you've got two sons. We don't 'ave ter tell 'em that they're grown up and moved away.'

Rose nodded and grinned. 'You're a wise old bird, Mavis,' she said. 'I'll miss yer when you've gone.'

'I'll miss you too, Rose.' Mavis turned as she suddenly remembered. 'Oh, I've got something for you – a postcard. The postman was going to take it back, said it ought ter 'ave been redirected or something. I told him I should be seein' yer soon so he left it with me.'

'A postcard?' Rose looked at it casually and then her heart quickened. 'It's from Alice Blake! Oh Mavis, they've only gone and put her in an orphanage and she's very unhappy.' Then Rose's smile came from deep inside as she saw Alice had written down the name of the orphanage and told her that it was somewhere near Cambridge. Turning the postcard, she saw that the stamp was clear and easy to read as Cambridgeshire.

'Poor little mite,' Mavis said and sniffed. 'She had a rough deal with that mother of hers. I know Dora was good to her mother and I give her credit for that – but she never ought to have sent them kids off the way she did.'

'No, she didn't,' Rose agreed. 'I've been wanting to find Alice for a while, Mavis. You don't know what this means to me. I shall go down this weekend and fetch her back to live with me.' She looked at Mavis as a thought occurred. 'Would you let me bring her here – and if you're moving to stay with your cousin, could I buy your furniture? I'd pay you the same as the second-hand shop.'

'Gawd love yer, Rose. It ain't worth more than a couple of quid. I've already had the skinflint round and he wanted to charge me to take it away – it ain't much but I'd reckoned on two quid.'

'It's yours,' Rose said quickly. 'Thanks, Mavis. We'll move in when I get back and I'll give you your money.'

'Do you reckon they'll let you have her?' Mavis asked doubtfully. 'Those places ask for identity and stuff, don't they?'

'Yeah, they do as a rule,' Rose replied, 'but if I just take her and disappear, they won't know where she's gone. I'll register her as Alice Parker for rations, say that I'm 'er aunt and that her mother's place was bombed and she's lost all her papers.'

'You're a game one,' Mavis said admiringly. 'Well, my lips are sealed. All I can say is good luck, Rose. I just hope yer don't get locked up.'

'You tell your landlord that I've got my niece staying because her mother was killed in a bombing raid and that's why I need the house and I'll tell the same story,' Rose said, a determined look in her eyes. 'I know what the council lot are, Mavis. If I try to do it proper, they won't let me – so I'll just bring her home and chance my luck.'

'It would almost be worth stayin' around just ter see it,' Mavis said and chuckled so much that she started coughing. 'Don't worry, Rose. I can't look after meself much longer; that's why I'm off to the coast. The doc reckons I might 'ave a bit longer with some good sea air.'

'I wish you luck too then,' Rose said and felt sympathy for the plucky woman who had lived alone for the past thirty years since her husband was killed on the docks. She'd ignored the Blitz same as the rest of the residents but even though Hitler's bombs hadn't managed to get her, it seemed that life had caught up and she didn't have much of it left.

'I don't care,' Mavis said stoutly. 'My Derek has had long enough to wait fer me and I know he'll be waitin' tellin' me to hurry up and get on with it – same as he did when we lost the babies, three of them, one after the other. That's why we adopted Keith, but the war took him . . .'

'You've had too much sorrow,' Rose said and wanted to hug her but Mavis was too independent for that and would shrug her off. 'Enjoy what you've got left to you then.'

'I'll have a good laugh whenever I think about you,' Mavis replied with a grin.

'Moving out?' Harry looked at her and Rose saw the look of hurt in his eyes. 'Why? I've stuck to my word and never laid a finger on yer – even though I've wanted to many a time.'

'I know that, Harry, and you're a good friend,' Rose told him with a smile. 'I'm going to have my niece live with me in Mavis Carter's house – she's moving to the coast.'

'That place is falling apart,' Harry said scornfully. 'You're better off here, Rose. Now your Reg has gone I thought we might get hitched one of these days.'

Rose stared at him in astonishment. 'I didn't think

you were the marryin' kind, Harry, not since your Nell went?'

'Well, I ain't been – but you were taken,' Harry said and looked embarrassed at speaking so plainly. 'It was always you I wanted, Rose. I only asked Nell after you married. I would have asked you years before, but you never looked at me. Why would you? You could have had anyone back then and I always wondered why you chose Reg. He wasn't a good husband, Rose, but I would be.'

'Yes, I know you would, Harry . . .' His words had given Rose pause. She'd believed he just wanted someone to have a quick flirtation with and one day she'd be out on her ear with her reputation and her self-respect in tatters. 'Well, this is a surprise, Harry. I'm goin' to 'ave ter think about this one.'

His face lit up as if a dozen candles had been lit inside him. 'You mean you'll think about it seriously?'

'Yes, yes, I will,' Rose promised. 'I'm fetching my – my niece at the weekend and I'll stay at Mavis's for a while – it is a big decision, one for life, cos if I married you, Harry, it would be for as long as we live.'

'I'd want that.' He moved towards her. 'I shan't rush you, Rose. You're still a good-looking woman and I know I'm not much of a catch, but I'll be good to you.'

'I know that,' she said and smiled. A part of her almost agreed then and there but something inside held back. She needed to think about the future because she wasn't one to run out on someone if she gave her word – even when they turned out the way Reg had. 'I'll let you know in three weeks.'

'Right. I know if you say something you'll do it,' Harry said, smiling. 'Do you want me to come with you to fetch your niece?'

'Not this time,' Rose said. 'But I'll bring her round one day and we'll have tea together, see how you get on.'

'I always wanted a family,' Harry said wistfully.

'Well, if you behave yourself, you might get one.' Rose winked, because her mind was rushing ahead. Married to Harry Smith she would have a new identity and no one would ever know that she'd run off with Dave Blake's daughter. Of course, she would have to give Alice back if Dave came looking, but no one had heard from him in over a year, so it was hardly likely. For all she knew he was at the bottom of the sea.

Alice looked at the card in its white envelope and tingled with excitement. No one had ever sent her anything like this – so was it from her father or Rose? She couldn't remember what their handwriting looked like.

Opening the envelope, she saw it contained a pretty card. Enclosed was a postal order for two shillings and sixpence and the words written inside were from Aunt Rose.

My dear Alice,
I am coming down on Sunday this week and I'll take you back to London with me to live if

274

*you'd like that. You must find an excuse to get
out of that horrid place and I'll be waiting nearby
at a point where I can see you come out. I'll be
there after two o'clock in the afternoon. Don't
tell anyone, Alice, love. I've been trying to find
you for ages!*

All my love,
Aunt Rose

Tears filled Alice's eyes, because she couldn't believe
that someone still cared about her. She knuckled the
tears away but not before one of the bullies had
noticed it. Alice slipped her card and postal order
inside her blouse quickly and turned to face her, but
she didn't respond to the taunts. She didn't want to
be punished now, because this was her chance at last.
She was going to escape.

'Did you want something, Hilda?' she asked
politely and took a wrapped lemon drop from her
pocket. 'It's my last sweet but you can have it.'

The surprised Hilda snatched the sweet and ran
off with it and Alice smiled. She didn't mind giving
her sweet to her. Hilda had been here forever, and
Alice was going to leave on Sunday; the thought made
her heart sing with joy.

Her mind was busy as she filed in to have supper
with the others, eating her slice of cold apple pie and
drinking her cocoa with a smile on her face. She had
decided that she would take nothing with her but the
clothes she wore. The dresses Aunt Annie had made
no longer fitted her and had been given to another
child. So she wasn't stealing anything. She would

meet Aunt Rose and they would sneak away – as long as no one suspected anything.

'What are you looking so pleased about, Alice Blake?'

Alice looked up, startled, as she was singled out by Miss Weatherspoon. 'I was just enjoying my apple pie, Miss Weatherspoon.'

'Really? I thought it remarkably insipid without cinnamon,' the housemistress said. 'No accounting for taste, I suppose. Go upstairs and study your homework, Alice.'

'Yes, Miss Weatherspoon.'

Alice hid her smile. Her reading privileges had just been restored and she had a book she wanted to read.

Rose could hardly wait for the weekend. She was terrified something would go wrong and she would be prevented from leaving London by some calamity, so when she heard the siren, she bolted for the underground, determined not to be caught out, but it was a false alarm. They got them all the time now, but it was better than if they didn't warn you and a bomb really dropped.

She emerged when the all-clear sounded and left the shelter. It was dark and Rose walked hurriedly through dim streets to where she was staying with Harry. Almost there, she became aware of footsteps behind her and looked uneasily over her shoulder. Normally, Rose didn't bother much about walking alone at night, but something made the back of her neck prickle. Determined not to let anyone take her by surprise, she turned to confront whoever was following her and then the shape of a man loomed out of the darkness and she gulped, because she knew who it was even though she couldn't see his face.

'Reg! They told me you were dead!' she gasped.

'And you couldn't wait to move in with that bastard from the factory,' Reg snarled in fury. 'I always knew what a slut you were, Rose.'

'I'm not living with Harry,' Rose protested as he moved closer. 'I'm just a lodger in his house – besides, how was I to know that telegram was wrong? It was official you were dead.'

'Most women don't shack up with another man five minutes after their husbands kick the bucket,' Reg said and raised his fist. 'I'll teach you a lesson you won't forget in a hurry.'

'You touch me and I'll have the law on yer,' Rose said defiantly. 'I've done nothing wrong – and you don't own me, Reg Parker. If I wanted to leave yer I'd have done it years ago. Our house is gone, burned down after an incendiary hit it. I just needed somewhere to stay.'

'There's plenty of rooms goin' cheap,' Reg muttered as he brought his fist down and caught Rose full in the face. 'You slut! Did yer think yer could get away wiv it?'

Rose looked him straight in the eyes after the first blow landed. 'Yeah, go on then, knock me about, Reg. It's all you ever did and I've had enough of it. You can beat me senseless if you like but I'm finished with you. I wouldn't live with you again if you won a fortune on the pools!'

His fist came in hard and Rose collapsed to the ground as he punched her three times in succession and then, as she lay on the ground, screaming, kicked her in the stomach. She cried out in pain but then the blackness descended and she knew no more.

'Rose is badly hurt?' Mavis looked at Harry Smith in shock. 'How did that happen, then? Everyone round here likes our Rose. She's always cheerful and she'd do anything for yer – why would anyone hurt her?'

'Jack Hunter used to live round here, couple of streets away. He's an air raid warden now and he was on his rounds when he heard the screams and went to investigate. He challenged the bloke, who ran off, and he says he's sure it was Reg Parker.' Harry shook his head over it. 'I always knew he was a bully, but Rose thought he was dead. If I catch the so-and-so round here again, I'll have him behind bars for what he's done to her. The nurse told me they're not sure if she'll live. He broke ribs but it was the damage to her head as he knocked her to the ground that they're worried about . . .' A little sob of despair broke from him. 'She was looking forward to fetching her niece here too.'

'I know . . .' Mavis looked at him for a moment. 'You ought to know the truth, Harry, just in case Rose don't make it.'

Harry nodded. 'I guessed there might be more to it. Fire away then, Mavis. I shan't tell anyone else, I promise you.'

CHAPTER 25

'You're talking about that genuine Chippendale elbow chair of Bert's?' Jim Sutton nodded thoughtfully. 'Yes, I know it well. Bert was fond of that chair and he showed it to me one time. I think it's worth a bit of money.' Jim scratched behind his ear and then nodded. 'Well, I shan't cheat you, lad. A set of six chairs and two elbows would be worth a considerable sum, but I'd be willing to give you ten – no, twelve dollars – for it. I shan't look to make a profit, because my wife would enjoy using that in the parlour. So I'll be fair with you. That's a right good chair if I'm any judge.'

Davey looked at him in suppressed excitement. He'd already sold the silver hand mirror for three dollars and with the twelve dollars and his earnings he now had over thirty-five saved. Would it be enough to bribe a seaman to hide him on a ship going to England? Davey wasn't sure but thought it might be.

He had no hesitation as he told Mr Sutton that he was happy to sell the chair for twelve dollars. Corky had said he thought about five, but Davey had reckoned it had to be worth more, because he'd seen others in the shop that were not as nice priced much higher. He told Mr Sutton he would bring it in later that day and, after he'd finished all his chores for Corky and Rodie, he carried it round and accepted the twelve dollars, feeling excited as he returned to his room. Next weekend he would spend a few cents to get the bus into the busy port and search out a suitable ship and a sailor to bribe.

'Where have you been?' Corky asked cheerfully as he entered the room a few moments after Davey got back. 'I wanted you to help with unpacking some stock that came in this morning but when I looked for you, you'd gone.' His eyes went round the room. 'And where's Bert's chair?'

'I sold it to Mr Sutton at the shop. He said it was genuine Chippendale and gave me twelve dollars for it,' Davey replied easily.

Corky's smile vanished and Davey sensed he was angry. 'That was a sneaky thing to do, selling the chair behind my back,' he said. 'You knew I wanted it.'

'Bert said I could have his things,' Davey said, 'and I wanted as much money as I could get for it, so I sold it for twelve dollars. I'm sorry if you really wanted it, Corky. You said it wasn't worth much . . .'

'I didn't know it was genuine Chippendale,' Corky said. 'Rodie liked it and I wanted it as a present for her birthday.' He looked at Davey, seeming both annoyed and disappointed. 'I thought you were happy with us, Davey? We've done all we can for you, lad.'

'I *am* happy,' Davey said, 'and one day I'll come back and visit you – but I need to get back to see my family and I can't wait until the war ends. I need to find out what's happened to my sister so I'm going to bribe a sailor to get me aboard a ship as soon as I can.'

'Well, I'm disappointed you sold the chair. If it's genuine, it's probably worth a lot more than Jim Sutton gave you – but I'm more upset that you went behind my back and Rodie will be hurt that you want to leave us so badly after all she's done for you.'

Davey felt dreadful. 'Maybe he'll let me have it back if I ask,' he said lamely but Corky laughed.

'Not unless you've got another twelve dollars to pay his profit,' he said. 'You wait, he'll have that in his shop for double the price at least.'

'He said it was for his wife.'

'And if it's true, that makes it worse. Rodie will be right mad when she visits and sees it in Lizzie Sutton's parlour instead of hers.' He sighed. 'Well, it's gone now, so no point in fussing. Just make sure you tell me before you sell anything else to that shark.'

Davey didn't answer. He'd felt bad over what he'd done and that wasn't really fair. The chair was his and he had a right to sell it where he wanted. But now his pleasure in the money had evaporated and it made him wish he could leave right now and go home. Mum might not be pleased to see him but Davey had thought it through and he reckoned Aunt Rose might let him stay with her. He was big for his age and could work well. He would do lots of chores for her until he could find a job and pay his way – after all, in another year or so he could leave school for good and then he could work on the docks or in a factory until he was old enough to get a job at sea.

'I've been thinking,' Corky told him after a few moments of silence. 'I ain't seen your travelling papers. There must have been some when Albert brought you off the ship, have you got them?'

'Travelling papers?' It was the first Davey had heard of such a thing and he wasn't sure what it meant. 'Albert didn't give me anything. Maybe the purser had them in his office?'

Corky shook his head but there was a gleam in his eyes. 'You can't travel without papers, Davey, because you'll need them when you get to England. It ain't no good having the money to bribe yourself a passage if you can't prove who you are when you get to England.'

Davey stared at him in dismay. 'There has to be some way to get some!' he said, feeling sick in the pit of his stomach. 'I came from London – surely I can just go back when I like?'

'Not without papers,' Corky said, dashing his hopes. 'Write to your mother again and ask her to send a letter confirming your date of birth and enclosing a copy of your birth certificate. Then we can get papers from somewhere.'

Davey's heart was sinking. He'd written to his mother twice and she hadn't replied. If he had to wait for her to send his birth certificate, he would never get home. Inside he was close to despair as he knew he might never see any of his family again. Where was his father? Was he still alive – and what had happened to Alice? The desperate thoughts went round and round in his head. How could he get home and find his sister if no one would help him?

Alice's heart was beating with excitement all morning because it was Sunday and Rose was coming and her nervousness grew as she waited for the appointed time. When Miss Weatherspoon came up behind her and tapped her on the shoulder, she nearly jumped out of her skin.

'Come with me, Alice Blake,' she said in a voice of command that brooked no disobedience. 'I have a job for you this afternoon. You can help me sort through some clothes that have been donated to us.'

Alice groaned inwardly. She had been picked for this unpleasant duty more than once in the past and hated it. Why must it happen today when she wanted to be certain of meeting Aunt Rose? However, there was no getting out of it.

'Yes, Miss Weatherspoon,' she said meekly and followed the mistress into the room where several bags of old clothes were waiting to be sorted. Some of the donations were still wearable and these would be washed, mended and given to the children to wear outside the orphanage for a trip to the park or to tea with a relative. Occasionally, people came to adopt a child, but it was usually one of the very young children who were offered, dressed up for the occasion.

As Miss Weatherspoon tipped out the first bag the smell made Alice want to wretch. A lot of the stuff they were given was no better than rags and dirty; they had to be put to one side and were sold to the rag-and-bone man for pennies. Some of the better things would be sold to a market stall and only a few actually went to the children at the orphanage.

Alice took a deep breath and started to sort the things. As she'd suspected, she was directed to put almost everything in the bag on the pile for rags. Only one pair of boy's leather boots were selected to keep. It took only a few minutes to sort that pile but the next sack took much longer and the minutes ticked by, making Alice restless. It would soon be time to meet Rose and she'd wanted to be early, because she would hate to miss her only friend.

'May I be excused, miss?' she asked at last. 'I need to go to the toilet.'

'Can you not wait another half an hour?'

'No, miss.' Alice jigged about as if dying to pass water and with a snort of disgust the housemistress sent her off.

'Come straight back,' she ordered. 'We haven't finished yet.'

'Yes, miss,' Alice replied and rushed off. She went straight down the stairs and out of the side door, which was always left unlocked, glancing back once to see if she was observed, but for once it seemed her luck was in. The afternoon was cool though it was only September and the sky threatened showers but Alice didn't bother to go back for a coat. She was so afraid she might have missed Aunt Rose.

She went out of the gates, keeping close to the high wall that surrounded the building, pressed against the wall so she couldn't be seen from the windows of the orphanage.

What time was it – and when would Rose come to meet her?

It must have been nearly eight o'clock when Alice accepted that Rose wasn't coming; that rotten Miss Weatherspoon had made her miss her and it wasn't fair. She'd got cold and wet and hungry after the first three hours or so and now she felt wretched. Or maybe Rose had changed her mind. She didn't want Alice after all, so she hadn't come looking for her and that hurt – it hurt even more than when she'd been brought here the first time. Yet no, Alice had been late. Perhaps she would come another day?

Alice knew she had to go back inside. She was shivering, partly with disappointment and cold and partly with fear – because Miss Weatherspoon would be so angry with her for not returning to finish the sorting. She'd been so sure Rose would come that she hadn't given a thought to any punishment, but she knew it would be severe. Having missed supper *and* disobeyed her housemistress, she would lose all privileges and also be physically punished. Fear gnawed at her insides and she considered running away, but where could she go? If Rose had broken her promise, it meant that her last hope had gone . . .

Walking back into the orphanage with a heavy heart, Alice's head was spinning. She felt that she would be here for the rest of her life and she didn't want to go on. There was nothing to look forward to, no one to care for her.

Tears hovered in her eyes but she tried to hold them back and then she heard the voice behind her and turned to face the irate mistress as Miss Weatherspoon demanded to know where she had been. Alice couldn't think straight because she was so distressed and the lie came out easily.

'I've been outside, miss, because I was sick and I feel ill.'

'Don't tell lies, Alice Blake. I always know when a girl is lying. Hold out your hand immediately.'

Alice obeyed but received only one lash of the cane, because the next moment the room started spinning and she gave a little sigh and collapsed at the feet of the angry housemistress.

CHAPTER 26

'Alice,' Rose moaned as she opened her eyes. 'I told her I was coming and she'll be so disappointed . . .'

'Nay, lass, you're goin' nowhere for the moment,' a voice filled with concern and care said, and it warmed Rose inside. She struggled to focus and saw Harry Smith sitting by her bed. He was leaning forward, tired and anxious. 'Thank God you've come back to us. I thought you weren't going to make it, Rose.'

The little sob in his voice told Rose how much he cared, and she gave him a weak smile. 'It's good of you to come, Harry, but shouldn't you be at work?'

'It's a Sunday,' he told her. 'But I've been here a lot of the time anyway.'

'It was good of you, Harry.' Rose frowned as she tried to recall what had happened. 'Did I get hit by a bus or something?'

'Can't yer remember? It was that bastard Reg who done this to yer, love. He'd better stay well clear because if I see him, I'll beat the living daylights out of him. I'll swing for him, Rose, afore I let him touch yer again!'

'Oh, Harry!' Rose choked back the tears. 'I wish he was dead. I've told him I'm done with him – but he's the sort that never gives up.'

'He's been reported to the police but he's vanished. If he shows up again, I've got a few mates owe me a favour. He'll be the one in hospital next time, believe me.'

Looking at his determined face, Rose did believe him. She knew she would be safe with Harry around and that she would move back in with him when she was well enough. Harry really cared for her and she'd be a fool not to let him. She was finished with Reg and there was no way she would give him the opportunity to move in with her – and yet it wasn't her most pressing worry.

'How long have I been sick?' she asked, giving a little groan as she felt the throb at the back of her head.

'It's two weeks since they brought you in and you developed a fever. They thought you might not survive the first few days,' Harry told her and gave her hand a gentle squeeze. 'I love you, Rose – and if there's anything worrying yer I'll do whatever I can to help.'

'Thanks, Harry.' Rose knew she could trust him now so she told him the truth – told him what she'd been planning. He listened carefully, making no comment until she'd done and then he nodded.

'I reckon that would work,' he agreed. 'We certainly can't leave the poor lass there, Rose. Not if they're mistreating her. Well, I reckon I can do something.' He grinned. 'I happen to know a man who can fix papers,' he said and then held his hand out to her.

'Meet Dave Blake, just back from the war. I don't reckon them folk would have a leg to stand on if I made out I was Alice's father – they ain't to know what he looks like.'

'No, but Alice does and she doesn't know you. They would be sure to ask her if you were her father.'

Harry's smile dimmed. 'Never thought of that.'

'Never mind, it was a good idea,' Rose comforted and then smiled. 'How about you get papers for me as Miss Rose Blake? I can be Alice's aunt and they'll have to let me take her out for the day and I just shan't take her back.'

Harry nodded, pleased he could do something to help her. 'Well, we can try it – otherwise we'll just whisk her off from under their noses.'

'Can you get me a pretty card for her? I'll write and tell her I'm going to visit. I'll explain why I didn't turn up and tell her I'll come as soon as I'm better.'

'That's right, love, you do that,' Harry encouraged. 'We'll get her away from there somehow, don't you fret.'

Rose lay back with a little sigh and closed her eyes. She felt exhausted and was soon sleeping again, unaware that Harry bent to kiss her before leaving her to rest.

'When am I going to get out of here?' Dave asked, looking up at the pretty nurse. 'I can walk with a stick now and most of the pain has gone – why can't I go?'

'Are you fed up with my company?' Nurse Judy Lynn teased with a smile. 'I was hoping you might want to stay around for a bit longer.'

'If I wasn't already married, I wouldn't mind staying around you for the rest of my life,' Dave said and grinned at her, 'but I'd still want to get out of this place.'

She laughed and shook her head at him. 'I'll ask the doctor what he thinks after his rounds, but why the hurry?'

'I'm worried about my children,' Dave said, and his teasing smile vanished. 'I need to find out where they are and contact them both – my boy Davey is lost in Canada and I don't know where my daughter Alice is.'

'I see. Now I understand why you've been fretting,' she said and looked at him with compassion. 'I'll explain to the doctor and we'll see what we can do for you, Lieutenant Blake.'

Dave sighed and nodded. It still felt odd being called that and he wasn't sure where his life was heading. He couldn't be sure he would have a way of making a living when he left hospital but that made it all the more important that he should leave and start the search for Alice and Davey. Once he had the kids safe, he could think about what to do next.

Where were they? He hoped Alice was still with that nice lady at the farm but Davey? He shuddered to think what might have become of his young son. His one hope was that Davey was like him. At his age, Dave had started to shoot up and he'd become stronger and very independent. If Davey took after him, he had a fair chance of surviving whatever kind of life he'd had, but how was he faring?

CHAPTER 27

Davey wasn't sure whether he believed what Corky said about him needing papers, so after thinking about it, when they spoke again the next Saturday, Davey held his head high and looked him in the eyes and said, 'I don't reckon I need papers – I'm too young to have had any.'

'You would have had something to travel out here with – clearance from your parents, a letter or form giving permission, your birth certificate, or some sort of document to prove who you are.'

'Well, if I did, no one gave them to me,' Davey said. 'So where do I apply to get them?'

Corky considered for a moment. 'I reckon that would be the passport office . . .' He frowned. 'So, you've made up your mind to go?'

Davey nodded. 'Yes, I have, sir. I'm sorry if you feel hurt. You and Rodie have been kind to me, and so was Bert, but I don't belong here.' He set his face stubbornly. 'What does it cost to get papers?'

'Not very much,' Corky replied. 'You leave that to me, Davey. I'll write and explain the situation, say you want to be ready to go home when the war's over, and I'll let you know what it costs when they reply.'

Davey nodded and grinned. 'Thanks, sir. I'm sorry if you think I've let you down – but I'll work all day for you now and you don't have to pay me.'

'No, I'll give you your due and you'll keep going to school,' Corky said and looked at him sadly. 'Rodie will be proper upset when I tell her – but you've a right to go home if you want, that's what I reckon.'

Davey thanked him and then asked what he needed him to do. He spent the remainder of the day catching up on his chores and most of Sunday too. That didn't bother Davey. He liked to be busy and even when there was nothing asked of him, carved his little figures for Corky to sell in the shop for a few dollars. He thought that must be the sailor in him. Bert had told him that most sailors knitted or carved to while away the time on long journeys.

'You have to have something to do when you're off duty and reading is all very well, but a man likes to be using his hands.'

Davey was glad that Corky was arranging to get his papers for him. It wouldn't have been easy to do it himself. Corky had said he would pay but Davey wanted to make things right and so he started making gifts for both of them, which he would give them when he left. Rodie liked boxes to put her bits and pieces in so he would make her another, but this time he would find a way to incorporate some of the treasures he'd collected when he was living with Bert, pretty bits of sea glass and a beautiful rich yellow stone that Bert had said might be amber.

'If it is, it might be worth a couple of dollars,' he'd said with a smile, pleased to see Davey's treasures, of which he'd collected quite a few.

Davey decided he would make something of the 'might be amber' for Rodie before he left. He'd found three pieces of the same stone and he would take the other two with him when he went home. His mother might like it – and he could have it made into a piece of jewellery when he earned some more money. Davey wasn't sure how he would earn money when he got back to London, though he knew he'd shot up in height over the nearly three years he'd been away. He'd been eleven on the ship coming out so he was almost thirteen now and, tall for his age, looked more like fifteen; soon it would be legal for him to work somewhere – perhaps in a factory, though that held no appeal. Davey loved being outside and near or on the sea. Maybe he would be able to find work as a cabin boy. Bert had told them they used to have cabin boys for running errands in the old days – did they still do that? Would it be possible to work a passage home that way too if they didn't know his age?

Davey shook his head. He knew it was unlikely that anyone would take him on. The war was still raging and a lot of ships were still getting sunk, though the well-armed convoys were helping to get essential supplies through to England – and that meant food from a country that had plenty could be sent to one that at the moment had very little.

Davey hadn't given much thought to what life would be like back home now. He'd been told that the people couldn't get lots of food he had become used to in Corky's house. Here there was meat, cheese, eggs, butter and bread and in the spawning season in June and the autumn, fresh-caught salmon that tasted wonderful the way Rodie did it in a pan, roasted with little onions and fried with butter and a drop of white wine.

He knew in his heart that he'd been lucky to find a home with good people here in Canada and didn't want to hurt anyone. When Rodie looked at him with reproachful eyes, he went to her and touched her hand.

'I just have to go home to see my folks,' he told her. 'But I'll come back one day and visit you when I'm on the ships.'

Rodie's eyes filled with tears. 'I wish you'd stay with us, Davey. Make this your home. You can visit your old home when you're a bit older, it's too dangerous for you to travel yet, honey. There are still bomb attacks over there, you know.'

'You've been very kind to me,' Davey said and gave her an impulsive hug. 'I'm definitely coming back one day – but if I don't go back now it might be too late to find my family.'

Rodie nodded her head in unhappy agreement and didn't say that it might already be too late. It made Davey sad to think he was causing Rodie and Corky grief. However, nothing was going to stop him getting home to his sister and his mum and dad.

Davey went to the loose floorboard and lifted it, looking into the empty hole beneath. Where was the little bag of leather that he'd made to keep his coins in? He'd thought it would be safe there, with a chair standing over it. He put his hand into the hole and felt around, but the bag had gone. All his savings – all the months of working for nothing! Someone had taken it!

How could he buy anything without his money? Even if he managed to stow away for free, he would need money once he got to England. He just had to reach London and his mother. He'd pushed away his doubts about whether she would welcome him home or not and he refused to think about the possibility that she'd moved or something had happened to her.

'Why hasn't she answered your letters?' Corky had asked him reasonably. 'It makes me wonder if something happened to her, Davey.'

Though Davey had known there might be some truth in Corky's words, he'd still been determined to leave the moment he could – but now his money had gone. Who could have taken it? Why would anyone want to steal from him? Despair washed over him as he realised it would take him months, most likely a year or more to get back what he'd lost. He'd been so close to getting home and now it was as far away as ever. What was he going to do? How could he let Alice know he was thinking of her and wanted to be with her? She must believe he'd abandoned her and the thought made his eyes fill with tears that he dashed away. He set his face determinedly. Somehow he would get home and in future he'd put his money somewhere safer.

CHAPTER 28

Alice's head ached as she opened her eyes and finally found she was able to focus again. Something in white swam into view and she gave a little moan as she tried to sit up.

'Lie back, young lady. I'm Dr James and I've been looking after you for the past two weeks. You're in hospital and you gave us all a fright but there's nothing to worry about. You're on the mend now.'

'Th-thank you.' Alice let her gaze travel round the ward, which looked clean and nice, and saw there were vases of flowers on the windowsill and a table with books and toys. 'Is this a ward for children?'

'Yes. You were in intensive care until yesterday evening when we moved you here. This is a nicer place to recover in, Alice.'

'You are kind,' Alice said and then remembered. She had stood outside in the cold and drizzle. 'I got cold and wet . . .'

'Yes, and contracted a chill that turned to pneumonia.' He frowned. 'You ought to have been brought in sooner. It was lucky you didn't die of neglect in that place. I am going to recommend that you be moved to a new home, young lady, perhaps fostered if we can find someone nice to take you.'

Alice smiled at him uncertainly. She didn't like the orphanage but she remembered the place where she'd gone with Davey and thought that was even worse.

'M-my auntie might,' she said, deciding to confide in this man with the nice smile. 'She lives in London on our street – Silver Terrace but I don't know the number.'

'What's her name and perhaps I can find out?' the doctor said. 'Nurse is going to bring you a glass of warm milk and something to eat. Just rest and relax, Alice. I'm going to do what I can to make you safe.'

Alice smiled up at him. She felt safe and warm and he reminded her of her father, so she told him Rose Parker's name and how kind she had been to her.

'I was waiting for her to come and she didn't,' she said. 'So perhaps she doesn't want me after all.'

'If she told you she was coming, I really think she meant to,' Dr James said with a smile that made Alice believe him, 'and something happened to prevent her. You wait and see – once I contact her, she will tell me why she didn't turn up and then we'll see if we can't arrange for you to go to her.'

Rose looked at Harry as he helped her down the hospital steps and into the taxi he had waiting. 'This is a bit of all right,' she said with a smile. 'Bein' fetched home in style.'

'That's what you'll get from me, Rose, love,' he replied with a grin that she thought made him look almost handsome. Harry was no film star, but he was kind and generous and he cared for her – and Rose had realised, when she was lying in that hospital bed and seeing him smiling at her over the biggest bunch of red roses she'd ever seen, that she cared for him too. 'And if that bugger ever comes so much as in the same street as you, he won't breathe no more. The word is out, Rose. I'm tellin' yer, my mates would as soon stick a knife in his ribs as let him near you.'

'Harry! You can't take the law in your own hands,' Rose reprimanded but she was smiling because she felt loved and cared for and that was a nice feeling after so many years. She'd finally realised that she'd go a long way before she found a better man than Harry Smith and she knew she was going to settle with him, even though she would be living in sin. What did it matter in a war like this? 'Still, I don't mind if they put him in the hospital. Serves him right!'

'Well, he wouldn't be comin' out as soon as you, love,' Harry said with a smile. 'We'll be hiring a car to visit Alice the minute you're able and then we'll see if we can't get her home here as quick as yer like.'

Rose smiled at him. 'That's grand, Harry. I hope you know how much I appreciate what you've done for me?'

'I'd have done it even if yer told me to clear orf,' he said and grinned. 'I care about you, Rose – and don't yer forget it.'

'I shan't, Harry,' she replied, and he could hear the sincerity that was in her voice. 'And I'll be there for you when the time comes that you need me. I ain't goin' anywhere.'

'Good.' He looked at her with satisfaction. 'That's my Rose.'

'Could we just take a detour to say goodbye to Mavis in Silver Terrace? She's off tomorrow and I'd like to wish her well.'

'Good thing you went to wave Mavis off, else you'd never have got that,' Harry said as he finished reading the letter from the Cambridge hospital doctor. He shook his head. 'I never heard such wickedness, Rose. Leaving a little girl to just lie there and suffer in her room until it was almost too late.'

'She told me she wasn't happy there,' Rose said, tears trickling down her cheeks. 'To think that all the time I was in hospital and couldn't get to her, she was sick and thinking no one cared for her.'

'We'll go down and get her right away; tomorrow if you feel up to it,' Harry said and Rose nodded. 'I'll nip up the corner to the phone box and ring this Dr James.'

'Yes, you do that,' Rose agreed. 'Don't wait until the weekend, Harry. Take a day off work for once.'

'I will. And if they complain I'll tell them what they can do with their job – and walk into another one tomorrow.'

Rose smiled and nodded. She was getting to know Harry better every day and he meant what he said. Her feeling of loneliness, which had hung over her for so long, had vanished and she felt loved and cared for. He might not have the looks of Dave Blake, but he was,

Rose realised, hers right down to the tips of his toes and you couldn't ask for more than that.

'I am so glad you came,' Dr James said and nodded approvingly. 'She was due to leave any day now and we didn't want to place her with another institution. Alice has suffered enough and we need to be certain that she will be loved and cared for.'

'You needn't worry about that, Doctor,' Harry said. 'My Rose is the most caring woman I know, and she loves that little girl.' They both looked across the ward to where Rose and Alice were sitting together talking and their faces needed no explanation. It had been obvious the moment Alice saw Rose that she was happy and now she was laughing and chattering excitedly.

'We've spoken to the adoption people and agreed that you should foster Alice for a period of three years, giving her father time to return from the war – should he still be alive – and claim her. If he doesn't, well, after that time, and if all parties are agreeable, an adoption order will be made.'

'That sounds fine,' Harry told him. 'Rose will be happy to take her for as long as she's needed. She told me that if Dave Blake does turn up, she'll hand Alice over when he's ready to take her – but if he can't manage that for any reason, we'll keep her.'

Dr James nodded. 'Normally, they'd insist on a married couple . . .'

'We shall be as soon as it can be arranged. I've told Rose to go for a divorce after what that bugger – beggin' your pardon, Doc, but if you'd seen what he did to Rose, and for no reason . . . She hadn't moved in with me then, not proper. It was just a roof over her head, after hers went up in smoke.'

'And now you really are together?'

'Yes,' Harry said firmly. 'She's given me the right to look after her and the child and that's just what I'll do.'

Dr James offered his hand. 'We'll shake on it, Mr Smith, because I can see you're a man to be trusted. What do you do for a living, may I ask?'

'I'm foreman at a munition factory. That place wouldn't run without me and they know it. Got a job for as long as the war lasts and then we'll go back to making parts for farm machinery. Job for life, I've got. Never been out of work since I was fifteen.'

Dr James nodded. 'I guessed as much. You can always tell – good man.'

They shook hands and then Rose signed the papers placing Alice in her custody for three years or until her father returned.

'It was a bit of luck that nice Dr James was concerned with children's welfare, wasn't it?' Rose said as they sat on the train going home, Alice looking a little frail, asleep between them. 'And that he's on the board for adoptions and fostering. He got it all sorted and arranged. Otherwise, it could have dragged on months.'

'When we were talking earlier, he told me they were glad to find responsible parents for the children. There are a lot of orphans now, Rose, and most of them don't have someone like you to take them home.'

'I didn't think the authorities would let me have her.' Rose was still a little bemused by the speed at which Dr James had arranged it all. 'It seems he was so angry with the way she'd been treated, he'd made up his mind she wasn't goin' back there. Apparently, she told him a lot of things that go on in that place and there is now goin' to be an investigation.'

'So there should be,' Harry said and looked grim. 'He was tellin' me that some of those places actually physically . . . well, abuse the kids in their care. Can you believe that?'

'It didn't happen to Alice, not that kind of abuse,' Rose said. 'He said they looked for signs but she wasn't hurt, not in that way.'

'No, they just neglected her health so much that she might have died had one of the mistresses not decided to take a look for herself. The mistress in charge of her hadn't bothered to ring a doctor but this Miss Button summoned an ambulance and they got her there just in time.'

A little shiver ran through Rose. 'Just think if she hadn't, Harry!'

He looked across at her. 'Don't torture yourself, love. We've got her now and she's ours until her father comes to claim her – if he ever does.'

'For his sake I hope he does,' Rose said. 'I love her and I should be sorry to let her go, but I've got you now, Harry.' Her smile said it all and he grinned at her.

'I reckon there are more than a few war orphans looking for a new home, Rose. It might be that the foreman of an important factory and his wife would be thought suitable foster parents for other children – especially as they've already been approved by Dr James.'

Rose's eyes brimmed but she smiled and didn't let the tears fall. 'Do you really think I can get that divorce, Harry?'

'I know you can, love,' he replied firmly. 'I've got all the evidence lined up. That so-an-so hasn't got a hope of preventing it, and if he ends up in prison, as he deserves, it wouldn't surprise me.'

'Oh, Harry, I don't know what to say . . .' Rose made a little sobbing sound in her throat. 'You're so good to me.'

'All you have to say is, "I do," when the time comes. I'll sort everything else. And don't think you owe me, because you don't. I want you to wed me, Rose, but, if you prefer to be free, I'd let you go – even after we were wed, if it made you happier.'

Rose looked at him. 'You mean every word, don't you?' she said in wonder. 'When you first started to show an interest, I thought you had only one thing in mind, but you *really* care.'

'Yes, I do. I'm not a man for flowery compliments, Rose, but I've always had an eye for you, and you were the woman I should have married years ago. I denied my feelings while my wife was alive, but I'll not deny them now.'

'Oh, I shan't be straying,' Rose said, and her face lit with mischief, making Harry want to kiss her. 'I know a good thing when I've found it, Harry Smith.'

He nodded and reached out for her, drawing her close and kissing her hard on the lips right there on the train. 'Just because I'd put your happiness first, it doesn't mean I don't fancy yer, girl.'

Rose giggled and sounded like a young girl. 'Well, maybe I quite fancy you too, now I think about it, Harry – but not in front of Alice. Look, she's waking up, poor love.'

Alice looked up at them, her face a picture of smiling innocence.

'Aunt Rose, could I have a kitten, please? I had one on the farm but when they took me away, I had to leave it behind.'

'Yes, of course you can,' Harry told her. 'You're coming home with us, Alice, and whatever you want you can have it – as long as it ain't the crown jewels.'

Alice laughed and hugged his arm. 'You're a nice man,' she said. 'I'm glad Aunt Rose has you now!'

Alice sat on the edge of the bed and looked around her. It was another strange bedroom but this time it didn't scare her. Aunt Rose had asked her what kind of things she liked and had promised to take her to the library the next day so that she could choose some books to borrow, but in the meantime, she'd given her a big teddy bear – she knew she was a bit old for a teddy bear but somehow it made her feel even safer and happier – and some pretty things for the dressing table.

'They ain't new. You can't buy a new teddy bear for love nor money at the moment,' Rose told her. 'I bought them in a second-hand shop but they'll be something until we find what you like, love. I'll be buying yer some new clothes tomorrow an' all.'

'You're very kind to me, Aunt Rose,' Alice had said, feeling her throat tighten with emotion.

'I never wanted yer mum to send yer away,' Rose had told her sadly. 'She was worried sick over yer or she would never 'ave done it, love. It was a bad business, sending yer both off like that.'

'I wish I could find Davey,' Alice had said wistfully.

'Well, there's an address you could write to,' Rose informed her. 'I don't know whether he's still there – it's in Canada. We can try, love. I'll give yer some paper and a pen and we'll post it tomorrow.'

Alice smiled as she saw the paper and envelopes waiting for her. She would write to Davey and tell him how nice it was here and ask if he could come home to be with her.

CHAPTER 29

Davey told Corky and Rodie about his lost savings that evening. He asked them if they'd seen anyone in the store and they both shook their heads, looking at one another, their expressions a little odd and hard to read. Davey felt the knot of suspicion harden inside him. He'd suspected it almost immediately, because there was no one else. To get to the store you had to come through the shop itself and there was a fence all around the backyard. In London that might not have stopped a thief but here anyone climbing it would be noticed and questioned, because it just didn't happen.

'Must have been a rat,' Rodie said after a moment's silence. 'We've had them in the store shed before. It must have run off with your bag of savings, Davey. Must have chewed the leather and thought it was food inside.'

Davey knew then who the culprit was. Otherwise, she couldn't have known what he'd stored his money in. Besides, a rat might chew the leather, but it wouldn't run off with his money, because it couldn't eat metal and Davey's savings were all in coins. It would surely just have made a hole in the bag and then run off.

He didn't say anything, because he couldn't accuse her of taking his money. He had no proof and it would just make things worse for everyone but he was certain she'd taken his little bag and it made him angry but it also hurt that she would do it. How could she? After all his hard work! Davey shook his head and looked away. He left them eating their tea and went out to the store, shutting the door with a bang after him.

What was he going to do now? If he simply stowed away on the ship – providing he could get on it! – without money or food, he would die of starvation, if not on the ship, then once he got to England. On board he might be able to steal scraps. Perhaps he could do that in England, too. Truth was, he was anxious and worried about how he would manage on his own. Even a few shillings would have helped him, and he could have changed his Canadian money for English when he got home; at least, he thought the bank would do that.

The disappointment was strong and Davey sat on the edge of his mattress cross-legged and thought about what he should do next. He could earn some more money, but it would take ages to get enough together. Davey glanced up as the door opened and Corky entered. He stood looking at him for a moment in silence.

'How much is missing, Davey?'

'Around forty dollars.' Davey didn't look at him.

'That's a lot of money – sure it was that much?'

'Yes, I sold a few of Bert's things, remember?'

'So you did.' Corky reached into his back pocket and took out a wallet. He counted out four ten-dollar bills. 'Take this then, lad, and keep it with you in future.'

Davey shook his head. 'That's your money. I can't take all that from you.'

'I don't hold with theft,' Corky said, 'and I know you wouldn't lie to me. If your money disappeared, someone took it, and they'd have to come through my store to do that.' Corky nodded. 'I ain't sayin' any more but we both know . . .' He bent and thrust the money in Davey's hand. 'Don't let it out of your sight, lad. And I'll do my best to get those papers without a birth certificate somehow.'

'Thanks . . .'

Davey stared at the door as it closed behind Corky. He obviously knew Rodie had taken the money but rather than accuse her, he'd just given Davey his savings back. Davey picked the paper money up and tucked it inside his shirt. He would do as Corky advised and not leave it lying around in future.

Corky didn't want him to leave any more than Rodie did but he wouldn't see him cheated of the money he'd earned and Davey was grateful. Bert had said he was decent and he was – a hard man in business but honest.

Davey's eyes stung with tears. Once again, he was torn with emotion and uncertain what to do. Was he foolish to want to leave these good people for a future that might be lonely and difficult? Even if he could get to England safely, it wouldn't be easy to make his way home and then make a living, because he wouldn't be able to go back to school. For all he knew the schools were still closed – and if he had no way of bringing in money his mother might send him straight back to Canada.

Yet Davey knew he couldn't stay here and the longer he dithered the harder it would be to leave. He had to go now, or he might find it easier to forget where he came from and never return.

It was Rodie who decided him in the end. She was talking to Corky in the shop that evening and didn't realise that Davey was home from school.

'After all this time, why now?' she said. 'This woman isn't his mother – she says Dora Blake was killed in the Blitz. She's got the girl now and is thinking of adopting her, so why should she have our Davey too?'

'Who is she?' Corky asked. 'And why did you open this letter addressed to Davey? That ain't right, Rodie, and you know it, prying into the lad's things – and you took his money, didn't you?'

'I'll give it back when he's got over this nonsense,' Rodie said sullenly. 'I ain't a thief and you know it. But I don't want to lose him, Corky – can't you tell him there's no way he can travel without his birth certificate?'

'I haven't heard a thing from the authorities,' Corky said, 'because to tell the truth I ain't tried yet. I'm worried about what they'll say. We should have reported it months ago, Rodie. We may be in trouble, and they might say we should have told them years ago, when Albert first told us about him.'

'You didn't know then that Albert had just taken him off that ship without consent.'

'I did, because he told me. He knew he might get into trouble one day over it, but he was going to let it run for as long as he could. It was kidnap in the eyes of the law, Rodie. Taking an underage boy like that is against the law. If I admit to knowing the truth, I could be accused of condoning it, which I did.'

'There you are then, you can't get them papers and that's an end to it,' Rodie said with a note of triumph. 'He won't be able to leave us – and when he's older we'll make out he's our lad and apply for a passport as if he's your son, Corky.'

'I don't know, Rodie, the lad wants to go home and find his family.'

'But there's only his sister!'

'We don't know about his father; he may be looking for the lad.'

'He's got the girl, hasn't he? I want Davey to stay.'

Davey crept away because what he'd overheard was a lot to take in. His mother had been killed in the Blitz. Davey's chest hurt but he didn't cry. Life had taught him that crying didn't change anything. His mother was dead – so that was why she hadn't answered his letters. Davey was ready to forgive her the rest. She would've let him come home if she'd been alive; she'd promised he could one day.

And now some woman – who was she? – was going to adopt Alice. Did Davey's father know? Did he approve?

Davey knew he had to find out who this woman was and he had to get home. He would ask Corky for the letter, because he knew he would give it to him.

*

Corky handed him the letter without a word. He didn't ask how he knew it had come, just looked at him and gave his head a little shake.

'I'll go down to the docks, Davey,' he told him. 'I've got a few friends in Halifax and I'll ask around, see if someone will take you on board and keep you under their wing on the journey home.'

'That's very kind of you,' Davey said and hung his head. 'I don't like to upset Rodie.'

'I know that, lad, but maybe you will come back and visit us one day?'

'Oh yes,' Davey said eagerly. 'I owe you so much.'

'I reckon you've paid your way,' Corky told him. 'Bert was a good friend of mine and he couldn't have managed the last months without you. You could have run off anytime you liked with whatever you fancied but you didn't.'

'I ain't a thief, sir.'

'I know that,' Corky sighed, 'and nor is someone else we both know – even if she *has* behaved badly. But it was only because she didn't want to part with you, Davey.'

'I know and I'm not angry with her, really I'm not. I promise I'll write and send her cards and I really will come to visit one day.'

'Then there's no more to be said,' Corky agreed with a nod.

'I wish I'd let you have Bert's chair,' Davey said wistfully. 'I should have . . .'

'Nah. I only wanted to buy it to help you out,' Corky said but they both knew that wasn't true.

'I tried to buy it back, but he wouldn't let me,' Davey admitted.

'Well, learn a lesson from that,' Corky told him. 'More isn't always the best, Davey. If that teaches you something it was a good experience.'

'Yes.' Davey looked at him feeling a little sad. He'd been wrong to distrust Corky. If he had thought to make a few dollars – or give the chair to Rodie as a gift – there was no sin in it. Nor was Rodie guilty of real harm. She'd only wanted to look after him for a bit longer. When he reached England and found it difficult to make a living, he might look back and wonder why he was so anxious to return to London, but he had to go. He had to see his sister, because he'd promised he would, and even though the letter said she was safe with Rose now, he'd still like to make sure – and hopefully one day they would be reunited with his father.

Now that his immediate future was settled, Davey's thoughts were centring more and more on his father. Something told him that all was not well, but he'd heard nothing from him for months – years! – and it was natural to be anxious. Once he was back in London, someone would help him to discover the truth. Perhaps Rose Parker, who seemed to have parted from her husband and was now with someone she called Harry. He glanced at the few lines Alice had penned.

Dear Davey,
  I hope you're well. I've been ill with pneumonia and nearly died. I don't mind because I'm better

now and they let me go and live with Aunt Rose.
It was horrid where I was but lovely now. Please
come home and live with us. Harry says you can
and I'm having a kitten.

Love, your sister Alice

PS: This is Aunt Rose. Harry and me would love
to have you live with us, Davey. If you need
money for the fare – if there's any way you can
get a passage home – let us know and Harry will
pay it for you.

Davey frowned over the letter. It sounded as if Alice
was happy now but had been badly treated. That made
it all the more urgent that he should get home to her.

'I've managed to get you papers but they're under my
surname. Are you OK with that, Davey?'

'Course I am,' Davey said. 'I don't know your name,
though.'

'It's Raymond Cork,' Corky said. 'Never could stand
the name Raymond so told people to call me Corky
and it stuck. So you'll be David Cork – don't forget
that. I'm your uncle and you're travelling to stay with
your grandmother, Mrs Blake. Can you remember all
that?'

'Yeah, easy,' Davey said with a grin. It wasn't his
lie, it was Corky's and if it saved him having to explain
where he'd come from and perhaps getting into trouble
it was fine. 'But didn't you have to produce a birth
certificate for your brother's son?'

'That was easy. My nephew died a few years back

313

of a fever. His name was David, and my brother died of the same fever, as did his wife.'

Davey was shocked into silence. 'Does that mean you haven't got anyone at all?' he asked after a few moments.

'Just Rodie and me,' Corky said heavily. He didn't cry or show much emotion but his eyes looked full of unshed tears. 'I reckon that's why we were so happy to take you in. Rodie doted on that lad, just as if he were her own. Just a year older than you, so you'll pass for nearly fifteen.'

'Thanks, Corky.' Davey took the papers, including the birth certificate, and put them in his pocket. 'I know how much this must mean to you, so I'll bring them back when I visit. I'll have my own papers then.'

'Yes, you will,' Corky agreed and smiled. 'Well, you're in luck. I found a guy I know at the docks, the First Mate of a small merchant vessel leaving for England next week. They don't take passengers these days, of course, but he's willing to take you as a favour to me and to keep an eye on you – so don't you give Joel any trouble, right?'

'I won't,' Davey said and grinned. 'I'll do exactly what he tells me – well, within reason.'

'Just take care of yourself and don't go falling over the side of the ship in a storm.'

'I won't,' Davey promised. 'Thanks, Corky. You won't get into trouble, will you?'

'Nah, we never registered David's death. He went into a family plot with his folks and just his parents were registered. We didn't realise that for some time and then I didn't think it was worth bothering over, but his birth certificate came in handy and I'm sure he wouldn't mind.'

'Thanks.' Davey sniffed but didn't let himself cry. Corky didn't always stick to the letter of the law but he was a decent man and what he'd done made it easier for Davey to get home. 'I'll write and tell you how I get on.'

'Just don't forget us . . .'

'I couldn't do that,' Davey said. 'You and Rodie were good to me and one day I'll repay you.'

His mind was busy with all he wanted to do in life. Going home to England to see Alice – and his dad, if he could – was only the beginning.

Joel was older than Albert had been and a little on the morose side. He had no idea that Davey wasn't Corky's nephew, so the boy said nothing to enlighten him, even when he asked if his grandmother was meeting him off the ship.

'I know where she lives,' Davey said. 'I've got my fare to London and she's expecting me so it will be easy.'

'Yeah, likely so,' Joel said and spat a lump of chewed tobacco into the sea. 'Well, you just behave and stay below decks. The captain only allowed you to travel because I told him I'd look after you – and I will, but I don't want any trouble, boy.'

'You won't get any,' Davey promised and went below as the mate gestured with his head.

The cabin was Joel's and he'd been given a hammock strung across one corner. Fortunately, he'd used a hammock on sunny days at Bert's home, because his friend told him it was the sailor's friend.

'If you can use that you've a bed wherever you are in the world,' he'd told him and Davey had been determined to master it, even though he'd tumbled out a few times.

They'd been good days with Bert. As Davey looked back on his adventures in Canada he did so with a smile. He'd been really lucky and Corky had told him of a few others who hadn't been as fortunate.

'Some folk took the kids and expected them to work all the time, and without pay,' he'd told Davey. 'I don't pay you much, but you get a little, more than most in your shoes.'

Davey had believed him, because he still remembered the shopkeepers in England. They had expected both him and Alice to work, and it sounded as if she'd had a bad experience at the last place she went to as well. He chewed his lip over that, because his sister had been young and innocent when she'd gone to that farm and he wondered what she'd been made to do. Dad would be furious if she'd been treated badly.

If his dad was still alive. Davey wondered why no one had heard from his father in a long time. Even if he'd fallen out with Mum he would surely still keep in touch with his friends.

If it meant that his father had been killed, it would be hard for both Alice and Davey. They would be orphans and would Rose really want to look after them until they could go to work and support themselves?

CHAPTER 30

Dave opened his eyes, groaning as the wave of nausea struck, and leaned over the side of the bed to vomit, narrowly missing the shoes of the nurse he'd privately called his angel.

'Sorry,' he muttered and wiped his mouth on the handkerchief she handed him. 'I'm such a nuisance . . .'

'Don't be foolish,' Judy said and smiled at him. 'You're a patient and these things happen. You've been very sick. Just as we thought you were getting better, you developed a fever and you've been delirious and vomiting for a few days now.' She took his pulse and nodded. 'That seems a little better. Perhaps we'll be able to send you home in another week or so after all.'

'I've been too long now, cluttering up the place,' Dave retorted. 'I'm sure you want me out of the way, Nurse.'

'I do not,' she assured him. 'I want you better – but I know you have a home to go to. Did you want to send a letter to your family?'

317

'I'd like to write to a Mrs Rose Parker,' Dave said, 'if you could supply a pen and paper. She is a friend, and my wife and I are . . . well, we're not together any more. It all has to be sorted, but it's over. I want to make sure my children are all right and at the moment I know they aren't. The only person I trust to care for them is Rose.'

'Are you fond of her?' Judy asked in an odd voice.

'Good grief no,' Dave said and laughed. 'Rose is a mate – known her for years. She was three years ahead of me in school and she looked out for me. I know I can trust her. She'll tell me the truth if nothing else.'

Judy was smiling again and Dave's heart fluttered. Was it possible she liked him enough to be a little jealous when she'd thought he might have a girlfriend?

He shook his head mentally. He must be ten or twelve years her senior. It was madness to even think of anything more than gratitude for the way she'd nursed him – and yet he found her fascinating. Maybe that was the patient/nurse relationship he'd heard about from others and when he was out of here, he would laugh at the very idea of a romance with Nurse Judy. Besides, for the moment all he had time for was the search for Alice and Davey.

Dave stood looking at the remainder of the rubble with grass growing through where Silver Terrace had once stood and felt sick to his stomach. For a moment his head spun like a top and he thought he might fall but it steadied itself as he took a few deep breaths.

Why had no one told him that Dora was dead? He'd certainly not had an official notification and only when he'd met an old friend emerging from the underground as he arrived in London had he discovered that his home and his wife had gone.

Dave felt upset inside. He'd admitted that his marriage was over a long time ago. Dora had preferred Mick George and that had rankled and festered inside for ages, leaving him, if not bitter, empty of feeling. He blamed himself in part for their quarrel but if she'd waited, he might have found a way to forgive her for what she'd done to their kids, now he knew the danger they'd been in in London – but never the rest of it.

As he recovered his balance and his thoughts, he saw that Rose's house had gone too. Dora had been killed in a direct hit, he'd been told that, but had Rose been killed too? Was there anyone left who could tell him where his children were? He felt chilled all over. Supposing they had just disappeared? Supposing he could never find them? The prospect filled him with dread and grief. Maybe if he had come home sooner? But he'd been so angry over Dora's infidelity and afraid of what he might do to her and that little crook if he caught them together.

Poor Dora, he thought, and his anger and fear turned to sadness for a life lost too soon. For a few minutes all he could think of was the early days when they'd been very much in love – or he had. To give Dora her due, he thought she'd cared once, but perhaps it wasn't in her nature to be faithful forever. Whatever she'd done, she didn't deserve this. As he turned to leave, he saw someone walking towards him and, recognising him, the fury surged once more and he stood stock still until Mick George came up to him.

'What are you doing here, you bastard?' Dave demanded. 'I wonder you dare to come in the same street as me. I could bloody kill you.'

Mick stared at him. 'Do me a favour, mate. I don't care if you do beat me to a pulp. I deserve it. It was me that told her she'd be all right 'ere – told her if a bomb 'ad 'er name on it that was it. I wish I'd told her to get out and down the flamin' underground as soon as she heard the siren.'

Dave glared at him and then, gradually, the anger drained away as he saw the grief and regret in the other man's eyes. He'd really cared for Dora and Dave couldn't grudge her that. He'd realised long ago that they weren't truly suited but he would never have left her had she remained faithful.

'You'll live with that then,' he said, not without a feeling of satisfaction. 'Don't worry, I shan't knock your head off, you ain't worth it.'

Dave walked away with his shoulders straight. It was only as he reached the end of the street that he realised Mick George could probably have told him where to find Rose. He wouldn't go back and look for him. Instead, he would go to the council and make a few inquiries.

A week later, Dave was still looking and wondering. The council hadn't supplied accommodation to Mrs Rose Parker and no one he'd asked seemed to know where Rose had gone.

'Someone told me Reg attacked her and put her

in the hospital, because she'd been playing around,' a man Dave knew casually said. 'Can't tell yer where she is now – might have left London to get away from it all.'

Dave nodded. It didn't sound right to him. Rose wasn't the sort to play around. She'd never been like Dora, never been flighty. He'd asked at each of the three houses left standing in Silver Terrace but no one seemed to know anything. He had no idea where to start next and a phone call to the farm where he'd last seen Alice had delivered worrying news. His daughter had been placed in a home – an orphanage. His little girl!

Dave didn't know who he was most worried about, Davey or Alice. He'd found a bed at the seaman's mission for now, and when he'd rung his cousin Marie to find out how she and her family were, she had invited him to go and live with her in her cottage in Norfolk.

'You're welcome to stay until you and the kids are back on their feet, Dave,' she'd told him. 'Nick was killed over a year ago and with both my sons in the merchant navy I've plenty of room for you and the kids, and I'll keep an eye on them while you work, when you're ready.'

'Not sure what I can do yet,' Dave confessed. 'I want a life at sea on my own boat when the war is over.'

Marie gave a harsh laugh. 'When! You've got time enough to think about it. Might be deep-sea fishing is too hard if you're not 100 per cent physically, but the lobsters and crab pots are easier and I always had my own little stall selling what Nick caught – still got it and his boat. It ain't a trawler but it earned us a living, especially with his other job.'

'And what was that?'

'Relief lighthouse duties. He did two nights a week to give our local man some time off. I warned him he was too old for the merchant navy, but he would go back when the war started.'

'A lot of men did that, Marie.'

'Aye, poor devils – well, the offer is there and I'm sorry for your loss.'

'Thanks.' Dave had shaken his head as he replaced the receiver. Lobsters and crabs weren't what he'd had in mind when he'd planned his new life, but it might be that he could find something similar and still be on the sea. But he couldn't think about that until he found Alice and then started the search for his son. Yet where to start? He'd been to the council, but they claimed they still didn't know where his son was and were evasive about Alice's whereabouts. All the girl behind the desk would tell him was that she'd been placed in an orphanage somewhere but she couldn't reveal details without the permission of her supervisor. Dave's temper had almost erupted as he'd replied, 'I'm her father! I never gave my permission for her to be placed in an orphanage.'

'Her family couldn't keep her,' the girl said vaguely. 'You were known to be away, Mr Blake, and—'

'It's Lieutenant Blake and if I don't get my daughter back safe and sound, there will be serious trouble.'

Dave had left before he said too much, but he was angry. He'd given his health and strength to help protect this damned country and they had just let his little girl be taken off to an orphanage. Surely one of his neighbours would have taken her in if they'd been asked? It was the way of the East End and Dave thought one or two of the good-hearted women who had lived in Silver Terrace might have done so given a chance.

Yet, as he cooled down, he realised that had Alice and Davey been in London they could have been killed by the Blitz, just like their mother. Still, they ought to have been able to tell him where the kids were, he thought, his anger and regret rising to choke him again.

It was plain daft to keep dithering, Dave told himself as he strode towards a pub that he'd some-times stopped for a drink in. There was bound to be someone he knew there and they might know what had happened to Rose Parker. He must find Rose and ask her what she knew. She'd been Dora's closest friend so she must know something.

It was a relief to see the shores of England. Davey reckoned that the white cliffs of Dover looked green on the morning they first sighted them. He felt like jumping for joy as he saw that the sun was shining as if to welcome him home. He knew they would be docking later that day and he'd been told to prepare to leave the ship with the captain.

'I ain't got shore leave yet,' Joel told him, 'but Cap'n will see yer right, Davey lad.' Joel smiled at him. The gruff sailor had become more friendly over the period of the voyage, just a little over three weeks.

'I reckon he's taken to you. He says you can join the crew in a couple of years if you're still after a life at sea.'

'I shall be,' Davey said and thanked him for being there during the voyage, which had not been without its perils. The convoy of merchant ships and escorts had been attacked from the air and two ships had been hit, one of them quite badly, but it had managed to limp home with the rest of the convoy. 'As soon as I've settled things back home and I'm old enough, I'll sign on.'

'That's right,' Joel said and put his hand in his pocket, coming out with something that glittered. He handed it to Davey. 'This is a half sovereign and its gold, Davey. I kept it for luck for years, but I want you to have it to bring you the same luck.'

Davey looked at the coin in his hand. 'This is beautiful, sir, but it must be valuable and I can't accept such a gift.'

'No, I want you to have it,' Joel said. 'Don't sell it or lose it and it will bring you luck. One day, if you like someone and wish them well, you can pass the luck on.'

Davey hesitated and then his fingers closed over the coin that he knew to be valuable. His throat felt a bit tight and he smiled shyly.

'Thank you for looking out for me, sir. It was a bit scary when those planes were attacking, but I wasn't frightened because you told me they weren't after us.'

'It was the bigger ships they were going for,' Joel said. 'Our luck seems to hold, don't know why –

maybe because they think we ain't carrying much of importance.'

They had been carrying food and cotton to boost the supplies of a nation that Corky reckoned was almost on its knees. Rodie had begged Davey not to go back but when she saw he was adamant and would do so with or without her blessing, she'd told him to come back if he couldn't find his family. She also returned his savings to him.

'I shouldn't have taken the money,' she said. 'I'm sorry, Davey. I just wanted to keep you safe until the war is over.'

'I know.' Davey hugged her. 'I love you, Rodie, and I shan't forget you. I promise I'll be back one day.'

'I love you, boy,' she said and hugged him so tight he had to wriggle free because he couldn't breathe. 'Don't you forget you've got a home here if you ever need it.'

Davey had tried to return Corky's money, but he wouldn't take it. On the ship the captain had changed Davey's Canadian money into English, looking up what it had been worth last time he'd been able to check.

'I reckon it's worth about thirty-five pounds,' he told Davey. 'Is that acceptable to you, lad?'

'Yes, thank you.' Davey smiled. He'd seen from the captain's calculations that he'd rounded it up to the nearest pound, giving the extra to Davey. It was such an honest thing to do. Davey had found most of the men on board tough but fair and friendly. Some of them could be surly but the majority were all right, and they'd let him wander around wherever he liked on board – except during the attack, when they'd ordered him below.

He'd watched what he could from the little porthole and thought it looked exciting until he'd seen what happened to the ships that were hit and then the reality of pain and death hit home and he was sad for those who had suffered and glad they had escaped on the *Seagull*, which had been right in the centre of the convoy. The ships hit had been nearer to the escort ships, which had returned fire and saved the convoy from even worse damage. Davey thought they were very brave men and when he'd gone back on deck later, he'd waved at them to thank them, though they probably didn't know why he was waving. Some of them waved back.

Now they were docked in England and Davey was almost sorry that the voyage was over. He'd said his goodbyes to Joel and the rest of the crew who had all wished him well, some giving him small gifts to take with him.

The captain approached Davey after his ship was safely docked and those with shore leave were about to disembark, smiling at him. 'I'll get you on your way, lad,' he told him and handed him the papers Corky had acquired for him. 'These have all been checked and approved, David, and you're free to stay here until your permit runs out.'

'Thank you, sir,' Davey said, not quite comfortable with the lie. Yet it had been his best way of getting home. 'If I could just get on a train or a bus to London, I'll be fine.'

'I'm going on the train myself, so I'll take you,'

the captain said. 'It's no trouble to me – and we have to take care of you.' He smiled down at Davey. 'My crew all thought you were very brave when we were attacked, David, and they wouldn't think much of me if I let you get lost now.' The captain called him David as it said on his papers but the crew had called him Davey, because he'd asked them to.

'Can I really sign on with you when I'm ready?' Davey asked, looking at him in awe. 'If I find out when you'll be in port, and then just come and ask?'

'That's right. There are several ways of finding out where we are, young man,' the captain told him. 'You can ask the port authorities in that office over there, but there are lists and you'll find them at shipping offices all over, in peacetime, anyway. For the time being we keep the date of a convoy's departure secret in case of spies, but this war should be over in another year or so.'

Davey looked up at him. 'Do you really think so, sir?'

'Yes, David, I do. We are winning. What happened on the way here was nowhere near as bad as it's been in the past. The heavy escorts are protecting us so that we can get on and deliver our cargoes in safety. At the start of the war the losses were terrible but it isn't happening as often now and we got away lightly this time – just one ship hit badly and another with minor damage.'

It was on the tip of Davey's tongue to tell the captain that his father was in the Royal Navy, but he remembered Corky's story just in time and held it back. What he'd witnessed through the porthole had made him proud of what his father was doing, and he longed for the day when he would be able to tell him so.

So Davey's thoughts were mixed when he finally parted from his companion at Liverpool Street Station, after assuring him that he knew London well and could find his own way now.

'Well, you're fifteen and capable,' the captain said and smiled, offering his hand. 'Don't forget me when you're ready for your first job at sea, David. Have a good life.'

Davey thanked him for everything and left the station. For a moment the noise of the traffic hit him like a blow. He had forgotten how rushed everything was here and how loud. After years of living in the wilderness, London seemed gigantic, dirty and loud. However, his natural confidence reasserted itself and he soon found a bus that would take him to Commercial Road; from there he could find his own way home. Davey tingled all over as the thrill of excitement finally caught hold.

He was back in London. He was home! Now all he had to do was to find his family; he knew that Alice was with Rose, because her letter had said so. Neither she nor Alice had given him the address, but he knew where Silver Terrace was and someone would be sure to know where Rose Parker lived.

CHAPTER 31

'Don't tell me you still haven't found this Rose Parker?'
Dave's cousin looked at him and clucked her tongue
sympathetically. He'd gone to Norfolk to stay with
her and discuss perhaps living with her for a time.
'Surely someone must know?'

'I've asked quite a few but none of them seemed
to know more than that she'd gone to live with
someone called Harry Smith.'

'You don't know who he is?'

Dave shook his head. 'There are a lot of men called
Smith in London, Marie, and he wasn't from our
area. They seemed to think he was a foreman at a
local munition factory, though, and that's where I'm
going next – but I can't take Alice to the seaman's
mission so I'll need to find a place to stay before I
can take her back.'

'Have you given my offer any thought? Do you
think – could you settle here with me?'

'Are you sure you want that?' Dave asked. The
house was large enough, not smart but comfortable
and built to withstand the winter winds that blew

in from the Norfolk coast. It was only a couple of miles from the beach and down a lane where only a few other cottages had been built. 'It's a nice home, Marie, and has some history I should say.'

'Three hundred years they reckon,' she replied. 'It's a family home – and there's no one left but me to live in it now. You'll need someone to care for the children when you get them back and I'm happy to do that for you.'

'It is a big thing to ask – to share your home and land you with two children, both of whom may be damaged. I don't know what they've been through, Marie – or if I'll ever find them.'

'You keep looking and you'll find them,' Marie said and smiled. Her face was lined and weather-beaten from the sun and rain and the chill winds that whipped around her home in winter. In her eyes there was both sadness and wisdom and Dave knew that he'd been lucky to find a welcome like this in his cousin's home. 'Bring them to me, at least until you know what you want and can find whatever it is you're looking for.' Her eyes narrowed. 'Is there a young lady somewhere?'

'Perhaps, a nurse . . .' Dave smiled shyly. 'I don't know. She was kind, gentle and lovely, Marie – but I don't really know her. I don't know what she wants, and I couldn't hang around to find out, because I had to find the kids.'

'Then do just that, bring them here to me, and then go and sort out your life,' Marie said. 'I've got friends and I'm not lonely, Dave, but I'd like to have your children stay with me for as long as it suits you.'

'Bless you, Marie,' Dave said and hugged her. 'I'm glad we've always stayed in touch.'

'Well, we didn't do much except exchange a card at Christmas for years, but as soon as you wrote, I had a few tears. Family means the world to me, Dave.'

'Yes, I know.' He smiled at her. 'I can't wait for you to meet mine, Marie. I swear I'll find them if it takes me the rest of my life.'

Marie placed her workworn hand over his and patted it. 'You're a good man, Dave, and I can't believe the Lord won't be there for you, looking out for you and the children. You wait and see, it will all come right. Let me know and I'll have everything ready for you when you've found your Alice.'

'Alice is in this country somewhere. I'm pretty sure of that,' Dave told her. 'I'm heading back to London this evening and in the morning I'll be talking to Harry Smith at the munition factory. I just pray he's the right one and knows where Rose is. She might be able to help me find Alice, at least.'

Davey stood looking at the place where his home had been and felt as if the whole world had crumbled. This was where his mum had died and the tears welled up inside, spilling down his cheeks as he understood just what had happened and how frightened she must have been for a short time in this house all alone.

'I should've been with you, Mum,' he said aloud. 'I'd have made sure we went down the underground until the all clear went!'

'I'm sorry, Davey. Sorry for sending you away . . .'

For a moment it was as if his mum stood there smiling at him, but in the merest fraction of a second the illusion had gone and, as he wiped the tears from his cheeks, Davey knew he was on his own. In Canada he'd had friends, even on the ship coming home, but now there was no one and it frightened him. He'd thought Aunt Rose would be just down the road where she'd always been, but she wasn't; her house was gone, just like most of the terrace houses he'd known. Most of the rubble had been cleared away, but some lingered and there were weeds growing through it.

Turning his head, Davey glanced at the houses at the bottom of the street, which were the only ones left. Perhaps someone there knew where Rose lived now. She'd said she was with Harry Smith in her letter, but she hadn't been clear about where that was and Davey had no idea where to start. He didn't think there was much point in going down the council offices, because he didn't trust that lot. He would find Rose and then his sister if it was the last thing he did.

'Is it really Davey?' a voice he vaguely recognised said behind him. 'What are you doin' 'ere, lad?'

Davey turned slowly and then saw a man he recognised but didn't much like. 'I might ask the same of you, sir,' he said. 'You don't live here, do you?'

'No, but I come to bring these,' Mick said and brought a small posy of flowers out from behind his back. He moved forward and placed them in the rubble. 'Your ma liked flowers and she never got many from any of us while she was alive.'

Davey looked at him curiously. 'Did you truly love her?' he asked.

'Dora was the love of my life. If she'd married me when I asked her, you'd be my son,' Mick replied sadly. 'She thought I wasn't good enough – thought your dad would suit her better, but he never understood my Dora. You couldn't cage 'er. She needed to be able to fly. If he'd given her space, she would have come back. Bloody Hitler took my Dora, but he can't take the memories. Only one woman I ever cared about.'

'I'm sorry,' Davey said. 'I didn't know.'

'Nor did most, they all thought I was a complete wrong 'un,' Mick said. 'Maybe I ain't always honest but I was straight with Dora and I would've looked after her – better than he did for all his upright ways.'

'You're talking about my dad.' Davey's eyes narrowed. 'He loved her too.'

'Did he?' Mick's eyes flashed with anger. 'She was always a bit scared of not livin' up to 'is standards – she deserved better than he ever gave her, and you can tell him that from me when you see him.'

'I don't know where he is,' Davey said sorrowfully. 'He may be dead for all I know.'

'Nah,' Mick said. 'The so-and-so is 'ere in London somewhere. He threatened to knock my block orf about two weeks ago now.'

Davey stared at him in amazement, his heart lifting. 'You spoke to him – he's alive?'

'Yeah, course he is,' Mick said. 'I've been told he's looking for Rose Parker – her that has shacked up with Harry Smith from down the munition factory.'

'You know where Rose lives?' Davey stared at him in wonder.

'Nah, don't know where they live, but I know the factory. She worked there too – the same place as yer mum did.'

'Thank you!' Davey cried, overjoyed. 'I'll go there and ask. Someone will know where they are.'

He ran off leaving Mick George standing on the pavement.

'Bloody kids,' Davey heard Mick mutter but didn't turn his head. He knew that the factory was only a few blocks away and it felt as if his quest was almost at an end.

'You wanted to see me?' Harry asked as the tall, handsome man knocked and then walked into his office. 'Not lookin' for a job by any chance? We could do with a strong man about the place.'

'I'm looking for Rose Parker and my daughter Alice,' Dave said, and Harry's heart dropped like a stone. For one moment he was tempted to deny all knowledge, because Rose was going to miss the child, but his honesty and compassion stopped him. 'I was told you might know something.'

'You've come to the right place,' Harry said and grinned. He paused and then started to strip off his brown working coat. 'I'll put me jacket on and take you to see them now. It won't take more than a few minutes on the bus.'

'Rose *and* Alice?' Dave Blake was looking thunderstruck, and Harry laughed. 'You've actually got my

Alice? They said she was in an orphanage but didn't seem to want to tell me where.'

'That lot down the council?' Harry nodded in dismissal. 'Fat lot of use they are to anyone, if you ask me. They send people's kids off without a by your leave and then don't know where they are – had a fire down there last year and probably lost all the records.'

'That would explain it,' Dave said, sounding relieved. 'But how did you and Rose come to have Alice?

'I'll explain it as we go,' Harry said. 'Just need to get someone to tell my deputy I'm going out.' He signalled to one of the women supervisors. 'Let Mike know I have to leave the premises for a bit. I'll be no longer than twenty minutes so you can give everyone their break early and then I'll be back, save you panicking if a machine breaks down.'

She gave him an indignant look and Harry winked at Dave. 'Have to keep them in their place,' he said as they left the factory together. His smile disappeared as he glanced at Dave. 'Have you heard about what happened to your wife?'

'Yes, I did – a bomb hit and she was inside with her mother.'

'Your mother-in-law was in her coffin. Dora should have left her and gone down the underground, but Rose says she never would because a friend of hers had told her she was just as safe under the stairs.'

Dave nodded. 'That sounds about right – though I know it's stupid. Dora always wanted to believe things if they suited her and she wouldn't have wanted to leave the coffin alone.'

'As if it could have affected her mum!' Harry shook his head over it. 'Sad waste of a young life, but she wasn't the only one. Quite a few refused to run when the siren went. They used tables and homemade contraptions in the kitchen to keep themselves safe and a lot of 'em caught it – not that you want to know that.'

Dave shivered in the cool wind that had blown up. Harry saw the way his face creased with pain, though he fought it. Autumn was unpredictable and could change from sunshine to bitterly cold in an instant sometimes.

'Been ill 'ave yer?' he asked sympathetically.

'Yeah, only out of hospital a few weeks.'

Harry nodded. He wasn't one to pry and Dave would tell them what he wanted them to know. 'Well, your Alice will be pleased to see you.'

'I hope so,' Dave said. 'But you haven't told me how she came to be with you and Rose.'

Harry frowned and took a deep breath. Dave Blake wasn't going to like the way his daughter had been treated, but he had to know the truth and as he told him Alice's story, he saw the anger in his eyes start to grow.

'Can I see Mr Harry Smith?' Davey asked a woman at the factory. She was sitting on a wall just outside, her hair in a turban and smoking a cigarette. 'Please, it's important.'

'It ain't up ter me,' she said, glaring at him. 'Stopping

work for a break an hour too bleedin' early. Whatever next?'

'I need to see Mr Smith now,' Davey persisted.

'Well, yer can't cos he ain't 'ere,' the woman snapped, clearly angry about something that had nothing to do with Davey. 'I hope this don't mean we'll 'ave ter work late,' she hissed at another woman sitting next to her, also smoking.

'Nah, it just means old Smithy wanted to get 'ome and give her one.'

The first woman gave a cackle of laughter and ground the last little bit of her cigarette out. She glanced at Davey. 'Still 'ere? Wash yer ears out, lad. Dot forgot 'erself. Smithy will be back shortly but yer can't 'ang around 'ere because it's dangerous. Clear orf and wait over there until you see him come. Thin bloke with hair what recedes a bit at the sides.'

The two women got up and went back inside the factory, leaving Davey to wander outside the open gates and wait. He was still there when he heard the explosion and suddenly all hell broke loose.

Women and a couple of older men came rushing out and Davey saw smoke billowing from inside the factory and flames beginning to shoot into the air. Not really knowing why he did it, Davey sprinted to the phone box and dialled 999.

'Fire and ambulance service,' he gasped when the operator answered. And when he was put through he said, 'There was an explosion in the munition factory in Redditch Street. There's a lot of smoke, flames and people screaming.'

'We're on our way.'

As Davey emerged from the phone box, he saw a man resembling the description he'd been given of Harry Smith, but instead of running away from the fire he was running to it and, as Davey watched, he disappeared inside.

Davey wanted to shout at him, to call him back, but no one had time for him now. An anxious crowd was gathering as Davey watched for a moment, uncertain what to do next, but then, as the fire engines and ambulances arrived, he walked away.

He couldn't chase after Mr Smith when he'd got trouble like this – but until he could, he had no way of finding Rose or his sister.

CHAPTER 32

Alice was sitting on Dave's lap, being held and cuddled when they heard the explosion. They looked at each other, wondering what had happened.

'That wasn't a bomb,' Dave said. 'At least, there was no siren.'

'Either gas or the factory.' Rose started to her feet. 'Harry may be in there, I have to go.'

'I'll come with you,' Dave offered but Rose shook her head. 'No, stop with Alice. She hasn't seen you in years and you can't do anything, Dave. The professionals will be there in minutes. We had a minor explosion on one of the shop floors when I was there, and the fire engine was there before you could turn round.'

'Good thing you weren't there this morning.'

Rose nodded but didn't answer. She was too worried about Harry. Had he already been inside when the explosion went off? And even if he wasn't, she knew that he would have gone into the building to see what he could do to help those hurt in the blast – if it was the factory. She had a sick feeling inside her and couldn't shake the idea that it must be. Gas mains did make a noise and caused fires too, but that stink in the air was chemical – the kind she knew only too well from working on the production line at the factory.

Harry had only been gone a few minutes, twenty at most. What the hell could have gone wrong in that time? Whatever it was, it would mean loss of life, property and production of vital supplies and that could mean trouble for Harry. He might be blamed for deserting his post in the middle of a shift – that's if he got out alive.

'Please God, let him be alive,' Rose prayed for all she was worth. They could deal with anything else when they came to it. 'Don't let him die, not now, just when we've got together.'

Tears trickled down Rose's cheeks but she barely noticed them. She was tense as she turned the corner and saw the smoke and flames. It was bad – much worse than when she'd been working there and a small explosion had been quickly contained. What could have happened?

She saw one of the women she'd worked with and went up to her. She was streaked with soot and looked pale and shocked.

'What happened, Queenie?'

'It was in the nitrates storeroom,' Queenie said and then coughed, holding a dirty rag to her mouth. 'Someone shouted there was a fire in the storeroom and that Mrs Winters went barging in there; as soon as she opened the door it just blew.'

'She should've got you all out and left it to the

professionals,' Rose said with a frown. 'I always suspected she didn't know her job properly.' She looked at Queenie. 'Are you all right, love?'

'Yeah, I'm all right,' Queenie said. 'I stopped work as soon as I heard the word fire and told my lot to get out. Just made it as it went up. It's the poor buggers still in there I'm worried about.'

'Mrs Winters must have caught the full blast . . .' Rose said. She'd never liked the supervisor but felt sorry for what had happened to her, something that would not have happened had Harry not left the factory. He would have warned everyone not to enter the store where the explosive materials were kept and got them all out. If that door hadn't been opened some of the damage might have been contained. At the moment it looked as if the factory would be out of action for months, despite the prompt action of the firefighters, who seemed to be winning the battle to stop it spreading to nearby buildings. 'Poor woman.'

'Stupid woman, more like,' Queenie said bitterly. 'She's the one responsible for this, and we'll all be out of work – not to mention them poor devils what have caught it in there.'

Several stretchers were being brought out now. Rose counted six and on two of them the faces were covered. She left Queenie and approached one of the stretcher bearers. 'Men or women?' she asked anxiously.

'Two women, one hardly recognisable. She caught the blast – the other's much younger and was standing too close when the explosion happened.' He hesitated. 'If you want to identify her . . . ?'

Rose nodded and pulled the blanket back. The young woman's face had been burned and damaged by flying glass, but she knew her. She stood very close to the storeroom and always wore a blue turban. 'Her name is Jean – Jean Marsh – just nineteen years old.'

'Poor little devil,' the stretcher bearer said. 'Hardly lived at that age. Well, someone is going to be in trouble for this little lot.'

Rose nodded as he passed on by to the waiting ambulance. None of the others on stretchers were Harry and Rose stood looking at the smouldering ruins until she was ushered back by a policeman.

'It could still be dangerous,' he told her. 'There may be more inflammatory materials the fire didn't reach that could be in an unstable condition.'

Rose knew that was true. When the women were working on the line, they all took the utmost care, but it was only when it reached its final stage, and the explosives were added, that there was any real danger and only the most trusted employees were allowed near that area, but in the rush to get out after the explosion something could have been left that might cause another explosion unless it was made safe. In that instant, Rose knew where Harry was and her eyes went to the far end of the factory, as yet untouched by fire. He would have helped anyone he could and then he would have gone to try and prevent more damage.

Her heart raced as she looked towards the smoke-damaged window. He was there somewhere, she knew it, and she wanted to call out, to tell him to be careful, but she couldn't because her throat was choked with emotion and the smoke.

'Harry,' she whispered as the minutes ticked by and she waited, terrified that there would be another terrible explosion.

'Clear away, all of you,' a policeman was saying. 'We've been warned there could be more explosions so move back.'

'Harry is still in there,' Rose gasped as he motioned to her impatiently. 'He ought to come out and leave it to the professionals.'

'The people still in there know what they're doing, madam. Leave now or I'll have to arrest you.'

Rose turned away, her heart heavy. She moved back, out of the factory yard, watching tensely from the pavement as the activity continued. There were no further explosions and still Harry didn't appear – but then she heard someone cheering and glimpsed another stretcher being brought out and saw Harry emerging from the factory. His face was smeared with soot and it looked as if his clothes and hair had been singed, but he seemed otherwise unhurt. One of the ambulancemen draped a blanket round his shoulders and gestured for him to get in.

Rose saw him hesitate and then apparently give into persuasion and she slumped back against the wall, feeling drained. Thank God he was alive! And then, as she glanced round at the devastation, she knew that Harry would carry the burden of this for life.

'Harry always said they would blow the place up if he wasn't there,' Rose said as she sat drinking the cup of strong tea that Dave had made for her. 'I used to laugh and say there were plenty that could take his place, but that daft woman . . .' She shook her head. 'It's one of the first rules you learn when you start. Never open a door on a fire. Keep it closed and alert others, get your nearest colleagues out and call the fire brigade.'

'Well, someone did that immediately,' Dave said. 'For them to be there by the time you got there, someone acted promptly. It isn't easy to keep a cool head when something like that happens.'

'Yes.' Rose nodded. 'I think the whole place would've gone if it had got any worse. It's bad enough now. Two dead, several injured, and the factory out of action until they can clear the mess up.'

Dave shook his head. 'It was a terrible accident, Rose, but I don't see that Harry is to blame just because he left for a bit. He has a second in command, after all, so how can he be blamed?'

She shook her head. 'They always look for someone to carry the can, Dave, so he may lose his job, but I don't care about that, as long as he's all right.' She looked at the telephone that Harry's employers had recently had installed so that he could be called if necessary. 'I wish that thing would ring.'

'Shall I ring the hospital for you?' Dave offered. 'Just ask how Harry is – or you can. Tell them you're his wife, or they won't tell you anything.'

'I don't want to trouble them just now,' Rose said uncertainly. 'They'll be busy with all the casualties.'

But her hand strayed towards the receiver just as it rang, making her jump. She picked it up. 'Hello,

Rose speaking. Yes, Harry Smith's wife,' she said, telling the small lie and nodding at Dave. 'How is he? Oh, thank God! You're keeping him in overnight for observation because of smoke inhalation? Does that mean he's OK?' Rose's eyes widened as she listened. 'I knew he could make anything safe! My Harry is brilliant with stuff like that – and you say he enabled the firemen to save someone's life? That's wonderful.'

Rose replaced the receiver and looked at Dave. 'One of the women was trapped by a heavy girder. The firemen couldn't move it because there were explosives right next to her. Harry had to crawl under the girder to defuse them so they could lift the weight and get her out.'

'Brave man. They could have gone off at any moment,' Dave said and smiled at her. 'Sounds as if you've found a good man for yourself this time, Rose.'

'I know I have,' Rose said and smiled at him. 'I wasted a lot of time with one that wasn't, but I intend to make the most of what I've got now.'

'I'm glad. And thank you for taking care of Alice.' He gave her a rueful look. 'All I have to do now is find Davey.'

'Well, we might be able to help a little,' Rose said. 'Davey wrote two letters to his mother and Alice wrote to the address a few weeks back. We haven't heard back but it takes a while for the post to go abroad these days.'

'Months, in some cases,' Dave replied and took the letters from Rose. 'That's wonderful, means I can make inquiries and if it weren't for this damned war, perhaps go and fetch him home once they discharge me.'

'Will they do that?' Rose asked doubtfully.

'If anything, I'll be given a desk or training job.' Dave touched his chest. 'There's a few problems, nothing life-threatening, but I'm not sure what work I'll be fit for yet.'

'I'm sorry. Is there anything I can do?'

'I've been offered a home, a job with the crab and lobster pots and someone to watch over Alice. My cousin lost her husband a while back and I could take over his pre-war business. It's up to me, really.'

'You were after a boat of your own, I know.'

He shook his head. 'It's a hard life, Rose. Frankly, I doubt I'm up to it now, but I may be able to manage the cruise ships once the war is finished and they can safely sail again.'

'Well, you know best,' Rose said and then swore. 'This bloody war – all the lives lost and for what?'

'Lives on both sides,' Dave said. 'I wish I could say I knew what it was all about, but I only knew that I had to fight.'

'It made a mess of your life and all,' Rose said bluntly. 'Ruined yer marriage, you lost yer kids and now yer health. It ain't right, Dave. It just ain't right.' She shook her head. 'That poor young girl at the factory, nineteen she was . . .'

'I'm still alive, Rose, and I'll make a future for the kids and myself somehow. At least I've got Alice back and all I need now is to find Davey.'

'You can leave Alice with me until you're settled,' Rose offered. 'I'm not sure how long it will take to arrange a passage back home for Davey – in fact, I doubt if you'll be able to until the end of the war.'

Dave nodded. 'Well, I'll take Alice to meet my cousin Marie this weekend and see how they get on. If she's happy, she can stay there while I try to find my son and if she doesn't like it, she can come back to you until I'm sorted.'

CHAPTER 33

Davey stood outside the factory. The smell of smoke lingered in the air, its acrid odour catching in his throat. The gates were chained and everywhere looked black and forlorn. He sighed; after discovering that Silver Terrace had all but disappeared, Davey had centred all his hopes on finding Rose Parker. He'd been excited yesterday, believing he would be sure to find Rose or Harry when he'd visited and he had no idea where to start looking now that there was no one to ask. His heart plummeted, because he had no idea where to go or who to ask next. He'd asked the folk who still lived at the end of Silver Terrace, but no one knew where Rose had gone. London was such a big place and with many of the familiar streets he'd known gone, it was an impossible task. Standing outside the pub and asking if anyone knew Rose just brought him curses or an impatient shove.

It seemed as if he was on his own. Davey had spent the night down the underground. Although no sirens had sounded, quite a few people had gathered there. It must be a habit they'd got into and kept to – just in case. As he wandered away from the factory, Davey wondered what he ought to do next.

He was afraid to visit the council offices. He doubted that he'd be sent back to Canada because of the war but they might send him to people like the shopkeeper and his wife, but who else could he ask? He still had money so buying something to eat wasn't a problem now but in time it might be. Perhaps he should look for a job and then start to make inquiries? He toyed with various ideas. If he advertised in the local paper perhaps Rose would see it, but for that he would need a home address. Would one of the hostels he'd seen as he wandered about the streets take him in if he could pay, or would they ask too many questions and get him taken off to an orphanage or somewhere else he didn't want to be?

Davey had seen other children wandering the streets. Some of them looked hungry and dirty but he reckoned he was better equipped to survive than most. His years with Bert had taught him to be self-sufficient and if he went to the country, he could live off the land, or at the seaside he could fish and find driftwood and trap rabbits.

He smiled to himself as he remembered the good times that he'd shared with Bert; that mother bear and her cubs had been something that would live in his mind forever. Yes, he could live at the seaside or in country better than in town but he could go nowhere until he'd done something about Alice. Dad had a cousin in Norfolk somewhere, Davey seemed to remember, but he had no idea whereabouts she lived. He squared his shoulders. No, he had to find Rose and through her perhaps Alice and his father too if what Mick had said was true. Was his dad really here in London and searching for his family? Well, why would Mick lie about it? He'd seemed angry at the way Davey's father had spoken to him.

Would his father be looking for him as well as Alice? Davey felt sure in his heart that he would, and the thought gave him renewed hope. Perhaps his dad would have more luck in finding Rose and Alice, but how could Davey let him know that he was here in England and not still in Canada?

The house had gone during a bombing raid so where would his father stay? Davey thought about it and remembered the seaman's mission he'd lingered outside a few times, considering whether he dare ask for a room. It had cheap rooms so, as a seaman, his dad would have known about the place, and he thought his dad might be careful with his money for his own accommodation, saving what he had for when he found Alice.

With a new spring in his step, Davey set out for the seaman's mission. He had a good reason to ask about rooms now and perhaps his luck would turn – he'd find his dad and then they could look for Alice together.

'Oh, Harry,' Rose exclaimed as she saw him sitting by the hospital bed. He'd suffered a few burns to his face and hands and inhaled a lot of smoke, but they said he was ready to return home now, and she'd come to collect him. 'How are you, love?'

'Better for seein' you, Rose,' Harry said cheerfully. 'I shall be glad to get 'ome, they make such a fuss in 'ere.'

'They wouldn't let me visit yesterday,' Rose said, frowning as a nurse looked at them. 'Said you weren't up to it, and then this mornin' they said you can come home.'

'Yeah, cos I told 'em I would discharge myself if they didn't let me go. I need to get back to the factory and help them sort it out.'

'They're leavin' it closed for a couple of weeks,' Rose told him. 'Out of respect for those that were killed and injured. You've been given two weeks' leave but they want you back on the next weekend. They said they'll have it back running within a month.' She shook her head. 'It looks like a ruin to me, Harry. Made me shudder to see it, you might have died in there.'

'Wouldn't 'ave 'appened if I'd been there,' Harry said with a deep sigh. 'I shall regret that to me dyin' day, though I've been told it wasn't my fault. I'm allowed a break and my deputy should have seen to it that that silly cow didn't do something daft.'

Rose nodded. The very fact that he was being rude told her the depth of his distress that Mrs Winters had done something stupid that caused the accident and her own death plus that of a young woman. He would normally never say such a thing.

'She knew the rules, Harry.'

'She should have called Mike's attention to it and spent her time getting her girls out to the yard and safety.' Harry swore. Another sign of his distress. 'How many times have we practiced that, Rose? I ask you, how many times?'

'Hundreds,' Rose told him. 'It's up on the wall for everyone to see and it should've been in her head, but she wasn't much good at her job, Harry. We all knew that.'

'Only got the job because she knew the boss's wife.' Harry shook his head. 'I suppose I should've reported her a long time ago, but I felt sorry for her, she only had the job, no 'ome life at all . . .'

'I never knew that,' Rose said and shook her head. 'You never know what happens behind closed doors. Speakin' of which, Dave took Alice up to Norfolk to stay with his cousin for a while. I gave him those letters from Davey and that made him smile, I can tell you. He says he'll be seeing the medics tomorrow an' he'll send a telegram to Davey in the meantime, tellin' him he's alive and that he's got Alice.'

'Well, that's lovely,' Harry said and looked at his silver pocket watch. 'I wish that doctor would hurry up and give me my discharge. I want ter get 'ome, love.' He looked up at her, eyes searching. 'You'll be missing Alice, I know.'

Rose hesitated and then inclined her head. 'Yes, I'm fond of her, Harry. Love her, I suppose, but she belongs with Dave and he'll decide what's best for them. Besides, I've got you now and I hope I'll have a job again to go to shortly.'

'We'll be up and running before long. If the old factory is too badly damaged, they'll find us another building.' He looked at her, slightly shy. 'You're enough for me, Rose, but, like I said afore, if you wanted – and only if it's what you'd like – we could foster another child. More than one if the chance arose. From what I've been told there's loads of the poor little mites looking for a home.'

'Oh, Harry, what a lovely idea,' Rose said and smiled at him. 'We'll see how things go when I'm back at work but a child of school age would be no trouble at all, because they would go to classes while we worked, and I could finish on the early shift.'

Harry nodded. 'I thought you might like the idea, but I didn't want to push you – you'll make up your mind.'

'I've said we would keep Alice for a while if she doesn't settle with Dave's cousin, but I like your idea for the future, Harry. It's a good thing to do an' all.'

Dave looked towards the sea and felt the familiar lurch of his heart. The sea had always called to him. She was in his blood and she never let go, but he had to think of his health and his family now. Alice was clinging to his hand as if she would never let go, though she'd taken to his cousin and Marie had taken to her. Alice loved baking, it seemed, and she enjoyed standing at the long pine table in Marie's kitchen, helping with the cooking. She had a lovely room of her own, which Marie had cleaned thoroughly. Nothing was new but the curtains were blue and pink paisley pattern and matched the pink satin bedcover. There was a dolls' house and an old wooden cot on rockers with a much-loved and worn doll in it, as well as books and games – and a cat that had made a bed on hers and kept her company at night. Marie claimed there was always one about and said they kept the mice down.

'Some of the books belonged to my sons when they were your age,' Marie had told Alice, 'but the other things were mine. I brought them here when I married and thought I might have a daughter, but I never did.'

Alice had looked so happy and Dave's heart had caught as he watched the motherly lady and the young girl together. It was clear they knew they were family and had felt affection for each other almost immediately, yet whenever they left the house Alice clung to Dave's hand.

'Will you be happy here with Marie while I go to London?' he asked her now.

'Cousin Marie won't send me away, will she?' Alice asked, her eyes wide and dark with fear. 'I don't want to go back to the orphanage, or anywhere else.'

'Of course not. And if anything happened to Cousin Marie, she's made arrangements for a neighbour to let Rose know and she'll come and fetch you and look after you until I'm home. I'm not sure what the navy wants of me yet, Alice love, but I shall be with you as much as I can, and if they retire me, I'll be living here with you.'

Alice nodded. 'Cousin Marie is nice and I like her lots, but sometimes people die . . .'

Dave squatted down so that he was on a level with his daughter. 'You're thinking about your mum?'

'Yes, and Gran and Auntie Annie,' Alice said, tears in her eyes.

'I know you missed your mum,' Dave said. 'I expect she wanted to keep you safe when she sent you away.'

'Why did they die?' Alice asked, her bottom lip trembling.

'Your mum ought to have gone down the underground and your gran was old and sick, but Auntie Annie, the lady you lived with on the farm, that was very sad, Alice, because she wasn't very old, but she had an operation and something went wrong. Her husband just wasn't able to cope without her, so that's why they took you away to that place. I know what happened next was hard for you. They weren't kind to you there . . .'

'I didn't care while Molly was with me,' Alice told him, 'but she went to live with her auntie and promised to write to me, but after two letters she stopped. I wrote to her, but she didn't answer.'

'Maybe she didn't get the letter, love. Things go astray in wartime. Ask Cousin Marie to help you write to Molly again and perhaps she might come and visit you.'

Alice nodded silently but didn't smile and she still clung to his hand.

Dave bit his lip. Alice had been through a lot and the experience would scar her, perhaps for the rest of her life. He wasn't sure what to do or say and then it came to him.

'If Davey was here too, you'd be all right, wouldn't you?'

'Yes!' Alice's face lit up like a beacon. 'Davey always looked after me. We walked to school together and he would stop the older boys pulling my hair, only it was girls who did it at the orphanage.'

'Then if you stay here and get to know Cousin Marie, you can make a room nice for Davey and I'll try and arrange to have him home as soon as I can.'

'Yes, please, Daddy.' Alice suddenly let go of his hand and skipped along the beach that was more stones than sand. The surf was rough, spraying several feet into the air as a chill wind blew in. Dave smiled as he watched her. Once her brother was home his little girl would be fine.

'Come on, love. It's time we got back for tea. Cousin Marie said it's crumpets and jam today, and in the morning I'll catch the train to London and then we'll see where your brother is.'

CHAPTER 34

'Hello, can I help you?' The voice made Davey turn sharply. He recognised it as a voice from his past and knew it was his old headmistress. Davey didn't know what had brought him to the school he and Alice had once attended, perhaps a forlorn hope that it would be open again and he'd find his sister there, but the playground was empty. 'I know you, don't I? Is it Davey Blake?' Miss Bristow said, staring at him in a fixed manner. 'Good gracious – it *is* Davey Blake! You've really shot up. '

'Yes, miss,' Davey said, poised to run if she suggested he must go with her to the council.

'Well, I never. I thought you went away to Canada?'

'I did, but they sent me back,' Davey said and hesitated. 'My mother was killed by a bomb and I'm looking for my aunt, Mrs Rose Parker. Do you know her?'

'Mrs Parker? No, but I know *of* her – she's a friend of Mr Harry Smith who runs the munition factory, poor brave man.'

'Do you know Mr Smith?' Davey seized the chance. 'Could you tell me where he lives, please?'

357

'Well, yes, as it happens, I do know,' Miss Bristow said. 'I visited the factory a while back for information and he told me where he lives, said to go there if I needed to know anything more.' She smiled a little. 'I've been writing some articles for the local paper, you see – I had to find something to do while the school was closed, though there is talk of opening it up again next year.'

'You'll be pleased if they do, miss,' Davey said. 'Can you recall the address, please?'

'Naturally. It is number 20 Benson Lane and that is about three streets away from the mun—' Before she could finish Davey was sprinting away and Miss Bristow made a tutting sound. Really! These children had no manners at all. Goodness knows, the schools did their best, but it all began in the home. Several yards down the road, Davey suddenly turned and lifted his hand in salute.

'Thanks, miss!' he called and then was off again like a hare. Miss Bristow found herself smiling. Well, there was always the exception and she'd always liked the Blake children and their father. Someone had told her Dave Blake was home. He'd been in hospital for quite some time, badly injured, but no doubt he was here to see his children.

Davey found the house easily. It hadn't taken long, and he'd asked a woman he saw coming out of her house in the street. She'd directed him and he'd gone straight to Mr Smith's house, but it was empty. A neighbour came out as Davey was knocking enthusiastically at the door.

'Harry's in hospital, lad, but Rose has just gone to fetch him home. Wait there and they'll be back before long.'

Davey thanked the woman and leaned against the wall next to the door. He wondered how long he might have to wait. He was hungry and the chippie he'd passed two streets away was frying. He could smell the delicious odour as it wafted through the air and he was tempted to go in search of something to eat as the smell seemed to be getting stronger, calling to him. Then, just about to nip round and buy a bag of chips, he saw a man and woman walking arm-in-arm towards him and the woman had a string bag with a parcel wrapped in newspaper – fish and chips by the smell of it. He stared for a moment and then gave a yelp of joy and set off at a run.

'Aunt Rose!' he cried excitedly. 'Aunt Rose, it's me – Davey!'

Rose stopped dead and then screamed and opened her arms wide, throwing them around him as he rushed at her and hugging him. It wasn't smothering like when Rodie hugged him, it was warm and nice and Rose smelled lovely, of talcum powder and soap.

'Davey, lad!' she said, and she was crying. 'Your dad is looking for you, love. He's gone to take Alice to his cousin in Norfolk, but he'll be back in London later today or tomorrow. Come on in and share our meal – we've got fish and chips with mushy peas.'

'I know, I can smell them,' Davey said and grinned at her following her inside. 'I've been looking all over for you, Rose. No one knew where you'd gone but they said you were living with Harry Smith. I went to the factory the other day but there was an explosion . . .' He looked at Harry. 'Are you all right, sir? I saw you dash into the fire and I thought you might die but someone told me you were in hospital, and this morning I discovered where you lived.'

'You're a bright lad,' Harry said, 'the sort I could do with at work! But come in, Davey, and tell us how you got here. We thought you were in Canada?'

'I was until a few weeks ago but I wanted to come home, especially after I got the letter from Alice. She didn't put her address on it else I'd have been straight round here.'

'There, and after I told her three times to be sure and do it!' Rose said, shaking her head as she started getting the plates out. 'Can you put the kettle on, Davey? We could all do with a cuppa and I don't want Harry lifting a finger just yet.'

'Course I can,' Davey said and laughed. 'I can skin a groundhog and cook a stew and wash up in a tin bath. Boiling a kettle on the gas is easy.'

'Well, fancy that!' Rose said. 'It sounds as if you've had some adventures, Davey Blake, and you've got quite a Canadian accent. You'd best sit down, eat your meal and tell us all about them. Did they treat you right?'

'I had a wonderful time and I'll visit Canada again one day,' Davey said and smiled at her. 'But I'm glad to be home, Aunt Rose. Can I stay with you until Dad comes?'

'Of course you can, love. You can stay with us whenever you want, for as long as you want, come and go as you please. We're just glad to see you home safe and sound.'

'Well, Blake, I'm glad to say that your recovery has been as good as we could expect, considering your injuries,' the doctor said, smiling at him. 'You won't be returning to a ship again – you might not be able to stand up to the life at sea – but I've been told they want you for training purposes and you'll be transferred to Portsmouth in due course.' He flicked through his notes. 'This address in Norfolk – that will find you?'

'Yes. I'm staying with friends overnight and then I shall return to Norfolk in the morning. How long do I have, sir, before I need to return to duty?'

'Perhaps a month. But why? Is there something you need to do?'

'I have to find my son. My wife sent him out to Canada because she couldn't cope and the authorities lost sight of him so I want to make sure he doesn't get lost again. I just wish there was some way of getting him home now.'

The doctor shook his head. 'Even if you could it would probably be best to leave him where he is until the war is over. You don't want to fetch him home only to hear that he's been killed by a U-boat on the way.'

'No, sir.' Dave saluted and accepted the envelope he was given.

He left the hospital a few minutes later, pleased that his recovery was better than expected. Dave had felt really well in himself these last few days, since the trip to Norfolk, and he smiled and started to whistle as he made his way to the underground. Rose had insisted he stay with them overnight and he wanted to tell her the news was better than had been expected.

Rose flung open the door as Dave approached, beaming all over her face. She rushed out and grabbed his hand, propelling him into the house and almost pushed him over in her eagerness to get him into the big kitchen.

'There!' she cried. 'Look who's here, Dave – would you believe it? He came all this way alone.'

'Not quite alone – I had a ship's crew keeping an eye on me! They were very kind . . .' The tall young man with the bronzed skin smiled at Dave. 'Hello, Dad, are you pleased to see me?'

'*Davey?*' He stared in shock and disbelief and then he was across the room as his son threw himself into his arms. Hugging him tightly, Dave could feel the tears running down his cheeks. He never cried but he was crying now, sobbing helplessly. 'My God, Davey, you've grown! You're nearly as tall as me now.'

'I shall be soon,' Davey said and hugged him back. 'It was living the way we did in Canada, and because I'm like you.'

'I'm so glad to see you – are you all right? Were you wretched out there?' Dave held him at arms' length just to look at him properly. 'That's a daft question. Just look at you! A picture of health.'

'I'm fine now I've found you, and Aunt Rose found Alice for us,' Davey said and smiled at her. 'I was worried if she was all right, especially when I discovered what they'd done to her.' He looked at his father. '*Is* she all right?'

'She really will be when she sees you,' Dave said and hugged him again. 'I want you to look after her until I can come home for good. I won't be sent to a combat zone – that part of the war is over for me, son, but I'm going to be training new recruits down in Portsmouth until they discharge me.'

'As long as you're safe,' Davey said, looking like the sensible young lad he now was. 'I'll look after Alice and I'll go to school and do everything I should, but when I'm old enough I'm going to sea. I want to see the world, Dad. My friend Bert told me so much about other countries and I want to see them for myself.'

'And I want to hear about this Bert.'

'Tell him about the bear and her cubs,' Rose said. 'Come to the table, Dave. I've got a cottage pie for tea tonight and we can all listen to Davey as we eat.'

Alice knew Davey the moment she saw him, a scream of joy building up inside her. Davey saw her and yelled her name. She shrieked and then they just ran to greet each other, not hugging as Davey had with his father and Rose, but just looking into one another's eyes the way they often had in the past. It was a moment of tense emotion as they studied one another, each seeing the other's love and the shared grief of their forced parting.

'I promised I'd come,' he said thickly, 'but it took a while . . .'

'I've missed you, Davey,' Alice said, tears trickling down her cheeks. 'It's been horrible without you – but it's lovely here. Cousin Marie is nice, and she cooks gorgeous things. I like helping her.'

'Good,' he said and took her hands, holding them firmly. 'I missed you so much, Alice. It's why I came home. I could have stayed in Canada. It's a great place and I'll take you there one day. I'm going to travel all over the world and when I get rich, I'll take you travelling too.'

'Will you ever be rich?' Alice said, her eyes wide with wonder at this new, confident brother with his attractive drawl who was just the same to her but so different in other ways. 'I'd like to travel with you.'

'We shall – and that's a promise,' Davey said. 'I'm going to be the captain of my own ship one day, but first I have to work for others and save money. Then I'll come back and fetch you and we'll go to Canada together.'

'You won't go away yet?'

'No, not until I'm old enough,' Davey said. 'I need to study at school if I'm going to be a ship's captain. I learned lots about it on my way home. I know what I want, Alice, and I'm going to get it.'

Alice nodded as she looked up into his eyes. 'I'm glad you're home, Davey, but I'm happy you know what you want. I do too – I'm going to be a librarian one day.'

'Well, they have them in Canada too, Alice, so you can still be one when we live there.' He smiled at her as a woman came to the door of the house and looked towards them. 'I guess you'd better introduce me to Cousin Marie . . .'

'So it's back to Portsmouth for you soon,' Marie said as they sat before the fire long after the children were both upstairs, though they guessed the two of them were still talking, still planning their adventures for the future, and not asleep. 'I suspect you've got more than one reason for going back there . . .'

Dave smiled and nodded. 'I don't know for sure, Marie. Judy is younger than I am by several years and I'm better than I expected to be but still not A1 fit. Why should a beautiful young woman be interested in me? And I've two children to think of . . .'

'Look in the mirror if you don't know why she might say yes,' Marie advised. 'You are a good-looking man, Dave Blake, and always have been – you could get any woman you set out to charm.'

'She was the first thing I saw when I opened my eyes in a hospital bed and discovered I wasn't dead,' Dave said with a grin. 'I thought she was an angel – and that's how I'll treat her if she takes me.'

'Just make sure you ask her,' Marie said and laughed. 'I can see you're head-over-heels for her, Dave. She'd be crazy not to take you, and those children are an asset. No woman could fail to love them, and I'll willingly have them until they're ready to fly the nest. They're both of them full of ideas – he's going to be captain of his own ship and she wants to be a librarian.' Marie shook her head. 'These young things! We never dreamed of such a life, did we?'

'I always knew I wanted to go to sea,' Dave admitted. 'When I was taken to live in London, I hated it, and I was off on the ships as soon as I was old enough. I dreamed of my own fishing boat.'

'Save your money and perhaps when your son is old enough . . .'

Dave inclined his head. 'I was thinking the same thing myself. I reckon I might take you up on your offer of working the lobster pots, Marie, just for a start after the war.'

'And you could do tourist trips round the coast if you bought a pleasure boat,' she suggested. 'You'd be here for your family and yet you could still answer the call of the sea.'

Dave smiled at her. 'Dora never understood that but you do, don't you?'

'My grandfather, father and husband all followed the sea as did my brother and my sons. If it's in the blood there's nought you can do, lad. Don't fight it, adapt and grow, that's my advice.'

'Just the way Davey has – and Alice in her own fashion.'

'Alice took solace in books,' Marie agreed. 'But that lad, well, by the tales he tells, he could do anything – write a book about his adventures, I shouldn't wonder.'

'Aye, mebbe,' Dave agreed and chuckled. 'Mebbe that's how he's going to get rich.'

CHAPTER 35

'I wondered if you'd like to go somewhere with me?'
Dave said when he met Judy from work the following
Sunday evening. 'We could go to the pictures one
night or have a nice meal at a posh hotel?'

Judy looked at him for a moment and then smiled.
'Yes,' she said in her gentle voice that had captured
his heart from the first time he'd heard it. 'Yes,
Lieutenant Blake, I should like that.'

'My name is Dave,' he said and felt himself grinning
like a Cheshire cat. 'I'd love to take you for a nice
meal so that we can talk and get to know one another.'

'I'd like that too,' she replied and her smile was a
little uncertain. 'Thank you for telling me about your
wife, and thank you for being honest about your situation, but I knew that side of it anyway. I'm glad the
outcome is better than the doctors first thought. I
couldn't bear the thought of anything happening to
you . . . Dave.'

She looked so shy when she spoke his name that
Dave's heart caught with love for her. It was early
days yet and he understood that he would have to

take his time courting her. Judy wasn't the kind of girl who would be rushed into anything – and he had to consider what *she* wanted of life. He knew that she was an excellent nurse, a career she would likely want to continue, perhaps even after the war ended and she was married. Dave wanted to make her happy, and the children were now safe and settled in Norfolk with his cousin, so he would take his time, give their relationship a chance to grow and see where it led, though if he'd had his choice, he would have swept her up and run off with her now.

He'd married Dora when she was very young and had seen little of the world and that, he knew, had been a mistake – although he wouldn't be without his children for the world. Yet Dora and he had not truly been suited. It was young love and had burned itself out. Dave suspected that had he just returned from the war and found her still living, they would not have gone on in the old way for long. Dora had needed to spread her wings and find what she wanted for herself. Any anger he'd felt for her had gone and he hoped she'd been happy with Mick in her last days.

Smiling, he offered his arm to Judy. 'I'll be working here for the next year at least and then they'll review the situation,' he told her. 'We've plenty of time to get to know each other, and when you have a few days off, I'd like to take you to meet Davey and Alice.'

'I'd love that,' she replied. 'I have a small sister at home, and I do miss her. Yes, Dave. I want to meet your children. I just hope they'll like me.'

'Bound to,' he assured her. 'No one could help

loving you, Judy, and my children need all the love they can get. I believe you will love them in time.'

She looked up at him swiftly and then away, her eyes wide, wondering and yet nervous. Dave smiled to himself. Judy was a very efficient nurse, but he suspected that she was a novice in affairs of the heart. It warmed him inside and made him protective of her, even more determined to make certain that she felt secure every step of the way.

'I'm glad you said that,' she replied, keeping her head down. 'It shows you have a kind nature and I think kindness is the most important quality of all. I like my friends to be lively, happy and confident, and I think you're most of those things, but kindness is a basic need in us all. When we are sad or ill, we need someone to be kind and loving, it makes us want to live again.'

'You've very wise for someone so young.'

'I'm twenty-two,' Judy replied and laughed. Her laughter had a joyous, tinkling sound like water over stones and made him want to laugh too.

'I'm thirty-five,' he said and saw her eyes widen. 'Is that too old, Judy?'

She looked up into his face for a long moment and then smiled. 'No, it's just right,' she said. 'Absolutely perfect . . .'

'Well, what do you think of her, Davey?' his father asked as they walked along the beach together. A dog had decided to tag along, and Davey had been enjoying himself throwing sticks for it. 'Do you like her?'

'She's a smasher, Dad,' Davey replied and grinned. 'Very pretty, kind and, well, nice. She smells lovely and when she smiles you can see she means it.' He gave his father a straight look. 'Are you going to marry her?'

His father laughed. 'You don't pull your punches, do you? The answer is yes, if she'll have me. I haven't dared to kiss her yet – well, only on the cheek!'

'You should,' Davey said. 'You should tell her how you feel. Anyway, she thinks the world of you. It's in her eyes when she looks at you, and she watches you all the time.'

'Does she?' Davey's father looked over his shoulder and saw what Davey had already seen, that Alice was clinging to Judy's hand. There was no doubt they'd taken to one another from the start. He smiled and lifted his hand. Davey chuckled to himself. He reckoned the future looked bright for his dad and his sister, and that meant he could go off on his travels when he was ready. Already they were like a family with Judy and Davey felt warm inside as he watched Alice giggle at something Judy was saying to her. 'I'd like to ask but I don't want to rush her, Davey.' His father's words brought his head round sharply.

'That's daft,' Davey told him straight. 'You tell her you love her and ask if she wants to get married – I would in your shoes. If you don't, she'll start to think you don't care.'

'You're very grown up for your age, young man,' his father said, looking at him seriously. 'I'm sorry you were sent off like that, Davey. I wouldn't have allowed it if I'd known what your mother was planning.'

'Don't be sorry,' Davey said. 'I was a bit scared at

the start – but then I realised it was an adventure and I had a great time with Bert. He taught me so much and it's because of him that I know what I want to do, Dad. I always thought I'd go to sea one day, but now I want so much more. There's a whole big world out there to explore and I want to see as much of it as I can.'

'Yes, I agree. Seize the chance while you're young, Davey. So many people don't follow their dreams and I'm glad you're going to, but don't forget you need to go to school for a while longer yet.'

'I know. But I like school and I'm going to learn all I can so that I can be as good as I can be.' Davey smiled at his father. 'Why don't you ask her now?' he said and, without waiting for an answer, ran off and grabbed his sister by the hand. As they careered madly up the beach, the dog rushed after them, barking wildly with joy at having found friends.

Davey glanced back and saw that his dad was walking with his nice girlfriend and smiled to himself. Dad had always been one to take his time, but anyone could see Judy was aching with love for him. It was a good thing he'd spoken up. It would save them all a lot of time.

The small church was overflowing with guests and curious villagers, the ones who attended all weddings and funerals if there was room inside, although this time Judy's family and friends had taken most of the pews. She looked radiant in white. Alice and Judy's sister were standing just behind dressed in pale pink and holding little posies as well as the bride's roses.

Davey had refused the offer of being a page but said he would be his father's best man and was dressed in a smart navy-blue suit and shoes that shone so much you could see your face in them.

Rose had come up with Harry and looked happy and Davey reckoned that had turned out well. He didn't know what had happened to her husband, but hoped for her sake that Reg Parker kept well away from her in future. He was fond of Rose, whom he no longer called aunt, but not as much as he was of Judy and Cousin Marie. They were special, like his dad and Alice – he loved his sister, and she was his number one for the moment. He'd had to stand up for her a few times at the school they were now at, which meant he was sporting the remains of a black eye for the wedding, but, as he'd said to his father, his opponent had *two* black eyes so he reckoned that was all right.

Harry was winking at him and looked as proud as punch. Something was going on there, but Davey wasn't sure what, though he thought Rose might be in the family way. And she was older than his dad! Still a lot of women had babies in later life, it was just that he hadn't expected it to happen to Rose – and he thought she was as surprised as he was. Davey chuckled to himself.

Bert had taught him so much and some of the books he'd given him to read had made Davey wiser about life, love and everything else, more than anyone realised. He wouldn't need his dad to explain the facts of life to him when the time came, though he reckoned there was probably more to it than he'd read in the books.

Following the happy couple from the church, Davey wondered how long it would be before he had a baby brother or sister to care for. His father and Judy were going back to Portsmouth to continue their work, and he and Alice would live here with Cousin Marie until the end of the war. It suited them all for the moment. His father and Judy would visit often, and occasionally Alice and he might be taken to Portsmouth for a visit. Davey was looking forward to that – it would be a chance to see the ships and perhaps to mix with sailors. His father had asked if he wanted to join the Royal Navy when he left school, but Davey's heart was with the merchant ships. He knew just what he wanted from life and, as the months passed and he grew taller, fitter, stronger and learned all he could, he knew that his exciting future was waiting just around the corner . . .

Read more about Cathy Sharp's orphans whose compelling stories will tug at your heartstrings.

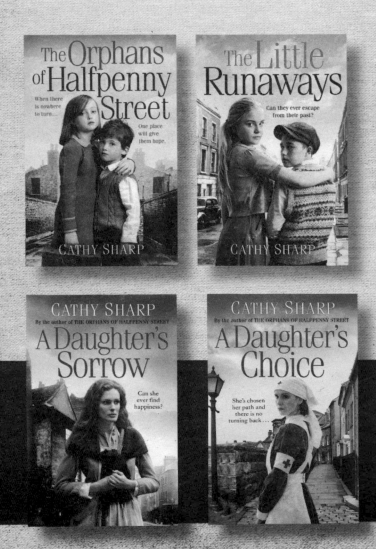